EVA GARCÍA SÁENZ

THE WATER RITUALS

Eva García Sáenz de Urturi was born in Vitoria and has been living in Alicante since she was fifteen years old. She published her first novel, *La saga de los longevos* (*The Immortal Collection*), in 2012, and it became a sales phenomenon in Spain, Latin America, the United States, and the United Kingdom. She is also the author of *Los hijos de Adán* (*The Sons of Adam*) and the historical novel *Pasaje a Tahití* (*Passage to Tahiti*). In 2016 she published the first installment of the White City Trilogy, titled *El silencio de la ciudad blanca* (*The Silence of the White City*), followed by *Los ritos del agua* (*The Water Rituals*) and *Los señores del tiempo* (*The Lords of Time*).

THE WATER RITUALS

THE
WATER
RITUALS

EVA GARCÍA SÁENZ

Translated from the Spanish
by Nick Caistor

VINTAGE CRIME/BLACK LIZARD
VINTAGE BOOKS
A Division of Penguin Random House LLC
New York

A VINTAGE CRIME/BLACK LIZARD ORIGINAL,
MARCH 2021

Library of Congress Cataloging-in-Publication Data
Name: García Saénz, Eva, author.
Title: The water rituals / Eva García Saénz ;
translated from the Spanish by Nick Caistor.
Description: New York : Vintage Crime/Black Lizard, 2021.
Identifiers: LCCN 2020032844 (print) | LCCN 2020032845 (ebook)
Classification: LCC PQ6707.A7325 R5813 2021 (print) |
LCC PQ6707.A7325 (ebook) | DDC 863/.7—dc23
LC record available at https://lccn.loc.gov/2020032844

Vintage Crime/Black Lizard Trade Paperback ISBN: 978-1-9848-9861-6
eBook ISBN: 978-1-9848-9862-3

Map illustrations © Gradual Maps
Book design by Elizabeth A. D. Eno

www.vintagebooks.com

Printed in the United States of America
10 9 8 7 6 5 4 3 2 1

To my children,
because you will never live where forgetting resides

The greatest trick the Devil ever pulled
was convincing the world he didn't exist.
—Verbal in *The Usual Suspects*,
quoting Charles Baudelaire

Arnía Beach
Portío Beach
(Liencres)
Somocuevas

University of Cantabria
●SANTANDER

Santillana del Mar ●

Cabezón de la Sal ●   ■ Monte Dobra
                          (Puente Viesgo)

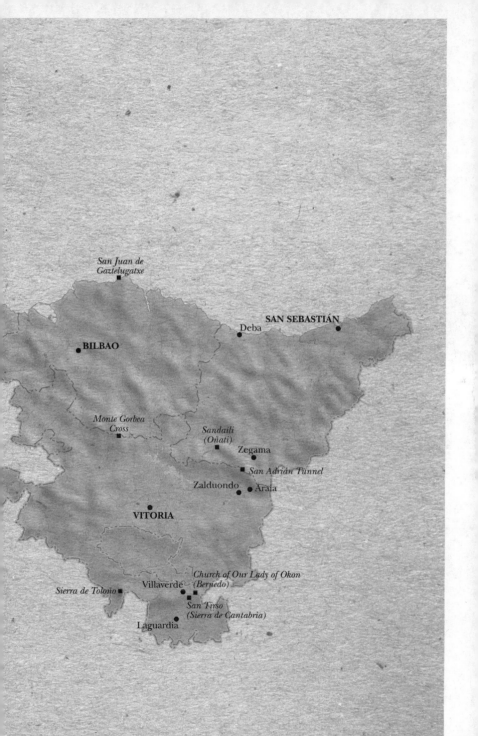

Santa Isabel Cemetery

Calle Fray Zacarías Martínez, 110, la Torre de los Anda (Milan's Home)

Restaurant El Portalón

Calle Fray Zacarías Martínez, in front of la Plaza de Santa María (Golden Girl's home); Cantón de las Pulmonías (old seminary)

Atxa Park (avenida del Zadorra, 24) 2,500 m

Plaza de los Fueros ■

coriaza-Esquivel Palace

Medieval wall garden,
calle Fray Zacarías Martínez, 3 ■

Plaza de la Virgen Blanca, 2 ■
(Unai's home)

Canton de
la Soledad ■

Calle del Prado, 22 ■
(Alba's home)

Pando-Argüelles building
■ (calle San Antonio, 42, on the
corner of calle Manuel Iradier)

Cantón de
San Roque

Florida Park ■

Paseo de la Senda

New Cathedral ■

Calle Portal de Castilla, 1 ■
(Estíbaliz's home)

Sequoia garden,
calle Magdalena, 12 ■

Palace of Justice,
avenida Gasteiz, 18 ■

THE WATER RITUALS

PROLOGUE

THE SAN ADRIÁN TUNNEL
THURSDAY, NOVEMBER 17, 2016

I've been pregnant since August," Alba whispered, anxiously judging my reaction. "Since las Fiestas de la Virgen Blanca, Unai."

I can still remember the intense joy I felt hearing her news. An involuntary smile lit up my face for the entire month of November. A pregnant Alba. I did a mental calculation: fourteen weeks. The baby had already lived longer than my twins. Fourteen weeks. We were past the dangerous first trimester. A son, a daughter. Alba and I were going to be parents.

I closed my eyes, rejoicing in the happiest moment I'd experienced in years. I turned to look out over the balcony where a blurry Vitoria lay drenched by the driving rain. The white balconies on the far side of the Plaza de la Virgen Blanca were almost invisible. It didn't matter; the warmth coursing through my veins could have heated the universe.

But when I studied Alba's face, her eyes were warning me—bad news was on the way.

What? I typed, not understanding. *What's wrong? I know it's not the best way to start a relationship, but—*

Alba clutched at my fingers on the phone.

"I don't know whether the baby is yours or Nancho's."

Her husband's name brought me crashing back to reality, as if I'd been shot. So he was dead, but his seed was alive in Alba's belly?

For those who don't know my history, I'll give you a brief summary: I am Unai López de Ayala, a profiler in the Criminal Investigation Unit of Vitoria's police department. Everyone calls me Kraken. I developed Broca's aphasia after a serial killer shot me, leaving a bullet lodged in my brain. I still can't speak. Sometimes I manage a squawk when I'm really agitated, but generally I communicate through an editing app on my cell phone.

And that's what I was doing with my boss, Deputy Superintendent Alba Díaz de Salvatierra, the woman who was also . . . well, her.

At that moment, the worst possible time, I got a WhatsApp from Estíbaliz, my partner at the Criminal Investigation Unit. I cursed her for the interruption.

> **Kraken, I'm sorry to bother you, but the forensic team is at a crime scene in the San Adrián Tunnel. DSU Salvatierra's cell phone is switched off. You better come with me: it's important.**

I motioned for Alba to read the text. We glanced anxiously at each other, and she quickly removed her cell phone from her pocket and switched it on.

> **Estí, I'm sorry you've been called out, but I'm on leave. The DSU is calling you now. What happened?**

> **A possible drowning. The victim is a young female with a rope tied around her ankles.**

I replied without thinking.

Drowning at the top of a mountain?

The profiler in me emerged as soon as I spotted the inconsistency.

That's right. She was immersed in water up to her shoulders inside a bronze cauldron. The cauldron is a museum piece. We'll have to consult an expert, but it might date back to the Celts. This is no routine murder. It's a strange death in an elaborate setting. I'd like the DSU to ask Judge Olano to authorize you to assist with the investigation as an expert. I hope I'm wrong and that we're not looking at another serial killer, but you're one of the best profilers I know, and if I'm given the case, I want you there to advise me.

I couldn't help speculating, imagining myself at the crime scene, seeing it with my own eyes. But I stopped myself. I was still on medical leave and I couldn't speak. I wasn't part of the team. There was no way I could help her.

It certainly sounds strange, but you can handle it. I can't go, and even if I could, I shouldn't.

I hoped she wouldn't insist.

Kraken, I'm giving you the opportunity to inspect the murder scene and the victim . . .

The press will be all over it soon, and I'd
rather tell you than have you find out from
them. I think you'd hold it against me for the
rest of your life.

                          You've lost me, Estí.

The girl had her ID in her purse, on the ground.

                          Well, who the hell is it?

It's Ana Belén Liaño, your first girlfriend.
The girl you went out with before that
thing happened at that summer camp in
Cantabria . . .

I interrupted her, badly shaken.

                  Okay, Estí. What do you know about that?

Lutxo told my brother the whole story.

Annabel Lee. I couldn't imagine her dead, even though she'd
liked to play games that were all about death and its rituals.
Annabel Lee is dead.

And there's something else you need to
know.

                          What else could there be?

She was pregnant.

1

MONTE DOBRA

Sunday, September 4, 2016

Today I went back to the pool, Father.

My godmother forbade me to look for you. It was the only rule I could break that would really hurt her. We both knew what Bluebeard would do if he knew someone was sniffing around.

I was horrified to read the headline in *El Periódico Cántabro* today. Horrified.

TWENTY-THREE-YEAR-OLD WOMAN
FOUND DEAD ON MONTE DOBRA SUMMIT
The Mysterious Suicides
of Young People Continue

The body of G. T., aged 23, from Santander, has been discovered on the summit of Monte Dobra. She is the third young person who has been found dead on a mountain along the Cantabrian coast. According to the police, all three died from hypothermia, after they removed their clothing and spent the night in the open. None of the bodies showed signs of violence. Could this be a trend, or a copycat phenomenon? No link has been found between the victims.

Yet again, investigators are at a loss. All three deaths
have the same strange characteristics: the victims are
young, barely out of their teens; they climb to the top
of a mountain in Cantabria and take off their clothing;
and they are found dead from exposure the next morning. Investigators have been unable to discover any clues
or motives, despite close scrutiny of the victims' lives.

No surprise there.

How could someone who doesn't want to see what's in front of
their face notice anything?

After a tortuous search, I managed to find a photo of the young
girl. She looks like me. You said she had died. You looked me in
the eye, Bluebeard, and told me she was dead, damn you. But you
kept her.

I swore to my godmother that I wouldn't go near you, that I
wouldn't search for you, but today I'm going to break those promises, because you have no idea the anger that's spewing out of me,
choking the guts you putrefied.

And yet, I still miss you, Father. I miss how attentive you could
be, how you convinced everyone that I mattered to you—before
that last summer and everything that happened between the village
and the cliffs where I lost my first life.

I used to close my eyes and try to become part of your audience,
to pretend that I believed in your public persona, as if there were
a parallel universe in which you were a good father who loved me
the way a father should, rather than the way you did.

But it was pointless. I could never make myself believe it.

I'm smoking and drinking more than usual now, Father. Yesterday I got into a fight. I have to reinvent myself all over again.
I have to put my life in order. I have to become another person,
anyone at all—anyone who isn't me.

I'm back, Father.

2

THE SIERRA OF AIZKORRI-ARATZ

Thursday, November 17, 2016

So who exactly was Annabel Lee? I must have been almost sixteen when Ana Belén Liaño appeared in Cabezón de la Sal, a small town near the Cantabrian coast. It was the first day of the summer camp where Lutxo, Asier, Jota, and I—the core of the San Viator *cuadrilla*—had decided to spend what would become the best July of our short and still-uncertain lives.

She had long, straight black hair that hung to her waist and bangs that covered her eyes, keeping her from seeing the world clearly, although her ideas were so well defined that not even adults questioned them.

At first her attitude annoyed me, then it intrigued me, and by the third night, I couldn't get to sleep because I was obsessed with the mixture of groans and whispers coming from her sleeping bag a few bunks away. I was already, you might say, devoted to her cause.

At an age when most of us weren't sure what we were going to major in, much less what we wanted to be in life, Ana Belén Liaño was already an expert graphic novelist. Known as Annabel Lee, after the character in the Edgar Allan Poe poem, she had already acquired a following in a certain world: erotic, gothic, postapocalyptic . . .

Really, she could have turned her hand to any genre, but her creative influences were Gustavo Adolfo Bécquer, Lord Byron, and William Blake. She was tied to her black Staedtler felt-tip pen, her forearms often covered with sketches—improvised scenarios that could occur to her at any moment. While we were washing the tin mugs we used for breakfast, for instance, or when Saúl Tovar, the summer camp director, spoke to us of rituals and ancient remains as he drove along the northern coast to magical places like San Juan de Gaztelugatxe in Vizcaya or Deba beach in Guipúzcoa.

Annabel Lee stood out in other ways. She seemed to be in a fog, her answers always vague, and we could never quite figure out her mood. She was very protective of her solitude, caring for it as old widows care for their cats: all day, at the exclusion of all else. We knew she was more fascinated by her savage interior world than by the transition to adult life. She seemed almost ageless, neither child nor adult.

After four days and three nights, I was hopeless. I didn't know much about heartache then. Annabel took my poor heart and let it grow accustomed to her silent, disturbing company, and then she spat it out. I still have no idea how it happened.

I don't know what made her dismiss my love with such . . . I was about to say *indifference*, but it wasn't that. Annabel could be warm; she just seemed to function on a different plane. She and her phantasmagorical creations moved through a parallel universe that occasionally coincided with ours but often didn't. That's why her death didn't seem real; it felt more like an alternate ending to one of her stories.

You tend to think that people who live in that kind of fantasy world won't ever disappear or grow old. I always thought she would live forever. I just hadn't wanted to know anything about her—not after the way that summer had ended.

As soon as we reached flat ground where we could park, I got out of the squad car. A freezing wind whipped my face, bringing me back to reality. Estíbaliz's five-foot frame was almost blown up the mountain. She removed strands of red hair from her mouth and led the way. After all the rain over the past few days, the path leading to the tunnel was muddy. The weather forecasts were calling for hail, and the thick heavy clouds that the north wind was sweeping toward us made that seem a definite possibility.

"Are you ready for this, Kraken?" asked Estíbaliz, concerned. "The DSU authorized you to come along as an expert, but she doesn't know you knew the victim."

And I'd prefer to keep it that way for now, I typed.

She gave me a knowing wink.

That's me, keeper of conjugal peace.

"I think that's best for now," she agreed. "Let's go, it'll be dark in a couple of hours. Is there anything I should know about the victim? Anything about her that could be important, given the way she died?"

Not that I can think of, I said with a shrug.

What I didn't say was *I'm not going to tell you everything that happened that summer, Estíbaliz. I'm just not ready.*

We were in the Aizkorri-Aratz reserve, and we had just reached the tunnel by the Zegama highway that led to the parking lot closest to the summit. Two of the forensic team's vehicles were already there, so we started up the hill.

A narrow gravel path led us to the mouth of the tunnel. Estí and I had both climbed this trail a dozen times. We passed through the arched entrance and crossed the sixty-meter cave. On our right were the restored chapel and the small excavation area where a group of archaeologists worked every summer.

Daylight was already fading. An increasingly strong wind tossed the green and gold leaves in the beechwoods behind us.

I used to enjoy listening to the wind in the beech and oak trees when I slept at my grandfather's house in Villaverde. It was like a concert, where the instruments played themselves. But the rustling didn't relax me now—far from it.

The tunnel ended in a wide hole that bored through the rock. Travelers had passed through this natural opening since prehistoric times, and for centuries it had been a landmark for northern pilgrims on their way to Santiago.

According to the legend, even Charles V had to bow to pass through the mouth of the cave. I have no idea how tall the monarch was, but I too had to lower my head to cross to the Álava side, the site of the murder.

Andoni Cuesta, a forensic colleague of ours, was climbing a few yards ahead on the narrow path, and he pointed out the site. The perimeter had been taped off, and we could only enter through one section.

"How are things?" Estíbaliz asked him with a wink. Estí and Cuesta got along very well and often had coffee together when they were on duty. "Tell me you're the one who won the three million euros in the Primitiva lottery, because then you can buy drinks tomorrow."

For weeks, everyone in Vitoria had been talking about the winning lottery ticket and who the lucky owner might be. Was it the fifth-floor neighbor no one had seen for days and who hadn't been at the Club Alavés soccer match on Sunday, or maybe it was the brother-in-law who wasn't answering the phone and had inexplicably quit his job at the Mercedes factory?

"I wish it were me, that's for sure. But it's not. As for the inspection, we just started. There's still a lot we need to process, and I'd like to get home to give my kids a good-night kiss. The eldest has a game this weekend, and he's already climbing the walls. Actually, if I had won the lottery, I'd buy him the entire Baskonia team, board and manager included, so he wouldn't always be on the sidelines," Cuesta said with a mixture of amusement and concern.

He crouched next to his bag to get some protective gear for us. A plump, friendly guy in his fifties with short arms, he was easy to pick out at a crime scene despite the fact that he wore the same white suit as the other forensic techs. Cuesta was methodical; you could count on him to stay at a scene until everything was finished, and I'd never heard him complain. "Put your booties on and be careful where you step. This place is full of footprints. Trying to identify them all is going to be hell."

We did as we were told, and then put on the gloves he handed us.

Judge Olano had authorized the inspection, but I would have bet my life (and won) that he hadn't bothered to come out to this windswept mountain to supervise the removal of the body. I knew he would send the court clerk to complete all the necessary formalities instead.

Following Cuesta's advice, we walked carefully toward a wooded area where we found Doctor Guevara, the forensic pathologist, next to a tree taking notes. A woman's body hung from one of the branches. A few yards away the clerk and Inspector Goyo Muguruza, the head of forensics, were speaking quietly, pointing to a skull-print hoodie that had apparently belonged to the deceased.

The clerk, a left-handed man with white hair and a long nose, nodded as he wrote down what Goyo was saying.

At the clerk's feet, an open briefcase held everything necessary to preserve the chain of custody for the physical evidence the technicians were collecting.

Seeing Annabel like that after all those years, coupled with my aversion to dead bodies, was too much, and I had to turn away to stop myself from retching. Estí covered for me, stepping forward and extending her hand to the forensic expert.

"Inspector Gauna, I'm pleased to see you. I see that Inspector

Ayala is back with us," said Doctor Guevara, pretending not to have noticed the state I was in.

A small woman in her fifties, with smooth cheeks pink from rosacea, Doctor Guevara was like a machine—quiet and efficient. In all the years we'd worked together, she had never complained when I asked her to prioritize an autopsy. She also possessed the rare ability to interact well with all the examining magistrates, regardless of how difficult they could be.

"Today he's just here as a profiling expert. He'll be back on the force again soon." Estíbaliz lied as though she had been doing it all her life. "Do you have anything for us yet, Doctor?"

I stared at the dead woman. She had been my girlfriend, my first love; she had given me my first night of . . . She was tied up at the ankles, head down. Her thick, extraordinarily long black hair swept the stony ground. Some of the strands were still wet, and her bangs left her forehead uncovered for once. Her eyes were open. She hadn't closed them, despite dying with her head submerged in a bronze cauldron full of water.

How brave you were, Annabel.

Her hands were tied behind her back with a zip tie. No wedding ring, and she was wearing hiking pants and a fleece that gravity had pulled down to expose a swollen belly . . . four, five months along? Her linea alba showed some pigmentation. Her ankles were tied to a bough about three yards above the ground.

You had to be a real bastard to do that to her, despite all the games she played, despite the fact that she'd spent her life repelling everyone who was attracted to her.

What did you get mixed up in this time? I whispered to her inside my head.

While Estíbaliz and the pathologist walked over to examine the bronze cauldron, I knelt in front of Annabel and, without realizing it, thought: *This is where your hunt ends and mine begins.*

For a few seconds I felt like myself again, rather than a shadow of the man I used to be. I had an absorbing job and a fresh obsession that I could concentrate on so I wouldn't have to face my short-comings and the trouble that was building in my life. I could, for example, try to ignore the fact that my boss was pregnant and that she didn't know if the baby was mine or a serial killer's.

3

THE MALHECHORES FRONTIER

THURSDAY, NOVEMBER 17, 2016

I forced my thoughts back to the scene in front of me, in order to avoid thinking about something that still stung badly.

For the moment, I ignored the piece of metal that Estí seemed to think was so important. Instead, I waited for her to return with Doctor Guevara, who shared her impressions: "The deceased is a young pregnant female. I will be able to date the pregnancy once I complete the autopsy. Two eyewitnesses found her suspended upside down, submerged up to her neck and shoulders in water, legs bound with an ordinary esparto rope. The zip ties look common and could have been bought at any hardware store, but the forensic team will be able to confirm that."

"Who are the two eyewitnesses?" Estíbaliz asked, interrupting her.

"She was discovered by two climbers coming up from the Álava side. They are from Araia and reached the trail by following the Zalduondo highway. Their car is parked at Petroleras. They both say they ran to pull her head out of the water in case she was still alive, but when they saw the pallor of her face, they could tell that she had been dead for a while. They didn't want to disturb anything, so they just felt her neck for a pulse and confirmed that she was no longer breathing. That's their story.

"She was definitely dead by the time the Mountain Rescue Team arrived. They've already left."

"Yes, they're the ones who called us this afternoon," said Estíbaliz.

Just then Inspector Muguruza came over. He wore a pair of transition lenses on his square head, but somehow his glasses were always darker than they needed to be, making him look like a relic from the 1970s. Always expressing himself with energetic gestures, Muguruza greeted us with rapidly raised eyebrows and then picked up where the pathologist had left off.

"There are fingerprints everywhere, especially on the outside of the cauldron, as Doctor Guevara indicated. Unfortunately, I suspect they belong to the two eyewitnesses. We'll have to take their fingerprints to confirm. For now, all the evidence we've found supports their version of events."

Doctor Guevara added, "The victim's body shows no signs of struggle, although the postmortem will include a more thorough search for defensive wounds and possible skin trace evidence under the fingernails. She was alive when she was strung up, which means the cause of death was drowning. We found evidence of blows and lesions to the head, but this was likely caused by the victim herself as she thrashed against the inside of the cauldron, trying to get her head out."

"Where's the water?" asked Estí, anticipating my question.

"I'm afraid the climbers dumped it while they were trying to save her."

"Where do you think the killer got it?"

"There are springs and small waterfalls all the way up the mountainside. Or he could have hidden the cauldron or some other receptacle nearby for the recent rain to fill. Speaking of which, we need to get a move on," said Doctor Guevara anxiously as a distant roll of thunder rumbled. "We need to get the body into a bag."

"All rather elaborate, don't you think?" whispered Estíbaliz.

She was right. All this staging felt too complicated for a routine murder. It was a very strange way to kill someone. It was as if we had entered the tunnel in the present and come out of it in a different time, when ritual was as important as death itself.

There was something anachronistic, almost timeless, about the setting.

The profiler in me took over and began to catalog my first impressions of the scene: the modus operandi, the killer's signature, the geography of the site. I didn't think about the victimology. Estíbaliz would take care of that.

This was the work of an organized murderer. The scene was staged, and the fact that the murderer used a rope and a cauldron, and felt the need to fill the cauldron with water, meant that we were most likely looking for a psychopath rather than a person suffering from psychosis. The murderer, or murderers—I hadn't ruled out the possibility we were looking for more than one person—had planned the ritual down to the smallest detail. The cauldron was a fetish weapon—that is, an object not intended for use as a weapon, but this murderer had turned it into one. Control also seemed to be important to the killer: the fact that the killer tied the victim's hands behind her back could indicate a fear that the victim might defend herself and ruin the careful staging.

In addition, covering the victim's face postmortem with the cauldron could indicate that the murderer felt guilty and possibly even knew Annabel Lee. It could also mean that the eyewitnesses had interrupted him before he could complete the ritual. It was too soon to know. However, the whole archaeological aspect of the crime—the tree, the historic location, and, of course, the bronze cauldron, an actual artifact—made me think that this was meant to be a re-creation of something.

But I still wasn't convinced that this was the work of a true psychopath. There were certain aspects that seemed to point to a mixed killer. There was something messianic about the murder, as if the killer were fulfilling a mission by killing Annabel Lee in this ritualistic way. And there were also several psychotic elements, which could indicate a pathological mind that had lost touch with reality. In short: madness.

Madness was my greatest fear because psychotic killers are unpredictable and because I like the world to be well ordered and classifiable. I like to be able to control things.

"Any fluids, Doctor?" asked Estíbaliz, turning toward her.

"It doesn't look like there are any traces of blood or sperm," Doctor Guevara replied. "And unfortunately, it will be dark soon, so I won't be able to go over the scene with luminol and UV light. Though I will take a print of her right index finger, even though we have her ID card. I'd like to make absolutely sure."

"What can you tell us about the time of death?"

"Rigor mortis has set in, so she must have died more than three or four hours ago. However, the cold and some of the other environmental factors here can alter algor mortis and body temperature, which makes it harder to determine the exact time of death. I'd say she died early this morning. The Aranzadi company's archaeologists only excavate during the summer, so this is a lonely spot midweek during the winter. Whoever did this had time to tie her up, put the cauldron in position, watch her die, and leave—"

"So if the climbers arrived early in the afternoon, they would have found her dead," Estíbaliz interrupted.

"Yes, if they're telling the truth about when they got here, I'm sure she was already dead."

"Many thanks, Doctor. That's all we need," said Estíbaliz, going over to one of the crime-scene technicians to ask for their report.

Estí and I looked over the sketches of the nearby trees, the entrance to the tunnel from the Álava side, the position of the body and the cauldron. Forensics had also numbered all the evidence so that it could be bagged. One technician was still photographing and measuring tissues and cigarettes. A lot of careless people passed through the area around the tunnel, so there was lots of trash: chip bags, tinfoil, crushed cans . . .

The team had collected soil samples from the soles of Annabel's boots to compare with the Petroleras parking lot in Álava and the parking lot on the Guipúzcoan side to determine which trail Annabel had climbed to the tunnel and where she had taken her last steps. They would also have to process the treads on all the vehicles parked in both lots.

As for the footprints . . . they were a real mess. There were dozens, probably all from hikers who had come to climb Aizkorri over the weekend. Good old Andoni Cuesta was right: it was going to be hell running them all through our database.

I left Estíbaliz studying the report and went over to the mysterious bronze cauldron that was lying in the grass near Annabel. It was about sixty centimeters across at its widest, with bolts and a couple of rings on the sides. The cauldron hadn't been made recently, that was for sure, and I knew exactly who could help me identify its origin.

I took a couple of photographs, one from above and another from the side, and WhatsApped both to an old acquaintance. I wrote:

> I'm looking for the archaeologist. Did you
> already land in Los Angeles?

Tasio responded:

> We're still on the ground in Álava. What
> did you just send me? Are you working on
> heritage crimes now?

Tasio Ortiz de Zárate had been wrongly convicted of eight murders, known as the double crimes of the dolmen, and sentenced to twenty years behind bars. Now exonerated, he was beginning a new life as a screenwriter for an American TV series based on the crimes. We had maintained our friendship of sorts, or whatever relationship we had.

I wrote back:

> I'll explain in return for your discretion and
> your expertise on historical artifacts,
> agreed?

> How could you doubt me? I am a bit rusty
> after two decades. But what you sent me is
> first-year stuff—it's the Cabárceno Cauldron.

> Cabárceno . . . in Cantabria?

> That's right. This is a special piece. Very few
> have been discovered in northern Spain. It's
> an Irish cauldron, made in typical Celtic style.
> This one was unearthed in 1912 on the massif
> of Peña Cabarga, if I remember right. It dates
> back to the Late Bronze Age, which means it's
> between 2,900 and 2,600 years old.

> Where is it supposed to be?

> In a showcase at the Cantabrian Prehistory
> Museum, I think, but give me a few minutes
> to check.

> A pleasure doing business with you . . .
> One more thing, and this is confidential. As

someone who has studied both archaeology and criminology, if you found out it was used in the San Adrián Tunnel, would that mean anything to you?

Shit.

Exactly.

How was it used?

I've told you everything I can, Tasio. Think it over and send me an answer, okay?

Ignacio says hello. How come you're back at work so soon?

I'm not back.

Whatever. I'll dust off my knowledge of the Celts. And . . . Kraken: Thanks for thinking of me. You know I like to be useful to Álava.

You're hard to forget. I'm glad you're on the right side now.

I always was.

I know. I helped bring you there. Send me everything you can find.

And with that, I ended the conversation. I was pleased at how smoothly it had gone. Maybe I didn't need my voice as much as I'd imagined.

I peered into the water left in the cauldron, and then I saw it: a reflection of the man I once was, a Kraken who could be beaten but not broken. Just like the Kraken, I had no exoskeleton. I was flexible, strong, even fearsome. I was a profiler who was more stubborn than brilliant, who never gave up on a case until it was solved and the suspect brought to justice. I saw the man I had been in another life—a life that ended on August 18, when Nancho shot me, infecting everything I did with fear.

I had cut myself off. Although I might have been fine living in my bubble in Villaverde, getting along quite nicely, thank you, at the end of the day I was just making blackberry jelly. Delicious jelly, it has to be said, but that's it.

I turned to look for Estíbaliz, and when I realized she had already left the crime scene, I walked down the slope leading to the mouth of the tunnel. I found her inside the cavern, almost hidden behind the wall of the small chapel inside. I walked up to her, trying not to make a sound or interrupt the phone conversation she was having.

"I'd like to make him our profiler," she whispered. "I know about his injury, I know there are weaknesses, but Inspector Ayala can be an asset even without his tongue. Excuse me," she corrected herself, "without speech. Deputy Superintendent Salvatierra, you know that even if we strengthen our team, we're not the same without him—and this way we can also encourage him to return to active duty. All I'm asking you is to allow him to be an adviser until he's completely recovered and officially rejoins the force."

Estíbaliz listened to the response in silence, but I was too far away to hear what our boss said. I would have given a golden cauldron and plenty more to know.

"Alba," Estí said, more confidently, "you told me the neurologist said he needed to be placed in challenging situations. And that the more progress he makes in the short term, the better it will be for him in the long term. Unai is fine, I promise you. He can do his job."

I was surprised at her friendly tone. I knew Estí admired our boss. You just had to see them together to know they were compatible, but this was the first time I realized that, during my absence, their relationship had progressed beyond the professional. They had become close friends. I was happy for them. They were good for each other. Estí helped Alba feel less isolated in Vitoria, and Alba helped Estí forget her addictions and stay centered. Or maybe they had grown close because they were both recovering from loss: one was mourning her husband, the other her brother.

I was touched that my boss and my coworker were plotting to get me to come back, official leave be damned. And I was especially flattered that my best friend and the woman-who-didn't-know-if-the-child-she-was-expecting-was-mine were taking care of me behind my back and pushing me out of my comfort zone.

And it was there, in the middle of the Sierra del Aizkorri, in a place that was known in ancient times as the Frontera de los Malhechores, that I decided to do everything I could to become Kraken again. I would do it for me, for Annabel Lee, for Alba, and for that unborn child.

I waited for Estíbaliz to finish her conversation and couldn't help noticing her triumphant smile as she hung up.

I showed her my phone.

Are you sure about what you just asked for, Estí? I had written.

There was a mischievous glint in her eye. She wasn't surprised to see me there, but I don't know whether she sensed me behind her or whether she could distinguish my footsteps from everyone else's. Estíbaliz had almost supernatural instincts where I was concerned. The fact that I had grown used to it didn't mean it didn't still freak me out.

"Let's get back to the crime scene. I hope they hurry up. I

really don't like the sound of that thunder, and the way the wind is picking up is worrying me even more," she said as we climbed back to the tunnel's southern entrance. "I know you don't want to come back. I know you don't want to complicate your life, but you're a good profiler, just like I'm a good victimologist. I don't know if this murder is the first in a series or if the murderer has killed before—that's your job to figure out—but this is obviously a distinct way to kill someone. You can help establish what kind of monster did this to Ana Belén Liaño. The fact that she was pregnant concerns me. If there are more murders, I hope that not all the victims are expecting. Just thinking about it makes me want to throw up."

No, Estíbaliz. No one is going to kill Álava's pregnant women. No way. Don't even imagine it, I thought.

But as I gazed at the black sky and the threatening clouds massing above our heads, it seemed as if the forces of nature were going to have their way again, no matter what I wanted.

4

THE SAN ADRIÁN CHAPEL

Do it for her and for her child," Estí insisted. We both peered at the mountaintop as heavy, freezing drops of rain started to fall. Not a good sign.

For her and for her child, I thought, watching them examine Annabel's body. But I wasn't thinking of *her* and her unborn child at all—I was thinking of the *her* who had just hung up the phone with my colleague.

"Let's get back to the crime scene," said Estíbaliz. "We should see if we can help collect evidence. If it rains, it'll be a disaster. We're going to have to keep everything in the tunnel. I don't think we'll make it back to the cars without getting soaked."

I nodded and followed her.

Honestly, after seeing this, I couldn't have stayed out of the case in Villaverde. I'd have spent the entire day calling you to ask about developments, I typed as we drew nearer.

The rain was no longer a few icy drops—now it was coming down hard. What worried me most, though, was the wind, which was picking up speed as it blasted down the bare mountain crest.

"Yes, and you'd have come charging into our offices like a lunatic whenever you thought the investigation wasn't going the way it should. We know you too well, Kraken." Estí laughed. She sounded almost content, and there was a glimmer of hope in her eyes. "Come back home?"

I'm terrified, I wrote. *This morning I woke up in a panic because I had to face a crowd of people and local politicians who want to sing my praises. It feels like this fuss will never end. My big worry today was whether the scar from the bullet wound would show.* I stopped writing to cover the mark with a lock of hair, in a gesture that had become almost automatic.

Not to mention my meeting with Alba, I thought, clenching my teeth to contain my anger.

But you're right, Estí. This isn't an ordinary murder. You're going to need a profiler.

She smiled, and I smiled. It was a tacit yes, and we both knew it.

But I wasn't telling her the whole truth—that inspecting the crime scene had allowed me to forget something I didn't know how to confront: Alba's pregnancy and the possibility that I was going to be a father. I needed to be immersed in a complex investigation, because making bramble jelly and roasted chestnuts wasn't going to be enough to stop me from obsessing about that pregnancy.

"You know something?" Estí asked, interrupting my thoughts. "When my brother and I used to come up here with our friends, Eneko would tell me stories about this place. He had hundreds of them. For centuries, pilgrims on their way to Santiago, medieval knights, horse-drawn carriages, noblewomen, and merchants have all passed through here. But my favorite was the story of a hermit. He lived near the pilgrims' hospital a little farther down, the one built in the Middle Ages that is now the Sancti Spiritus chapel. They say he dedicated himself to helping children who had problems learning to speak."

As she was telling me the story, she unconsciously fingered the silver *eguzkilore* that she wore on a leather strap. So the memory of

Eneko, the Eguzkilore, still haunted her. Estí hadn't completely recovered, either.

That was when Cuesta interrupted us. He held up what looked like a purse in a plastic bag.

"I think you should see this," he said, water streaming down his white suit.

"What is it?" asked Estíbaliz, who was clearly more concerned with what still had to be done at the crime scene than with what Cuesta had to show us.

Just then, the storm unleashed marble-size balls of hail.

"The cauldron! And the hoodie!" shouted Inspector Muguruza. "Come on! Help us!"

"Can you handle the body?" Estíbaliz asked Doctor Guevara.

"Yes, I can get it inside the tunnel, although I'm not sure we'll be safe in there, either. If there's a rush of water after the hailstorm, we'll be trapped and swept away. But I don't see what choice we have. Bring the cauldron and the hoodie if you can. Quickly."

We still had our gloves on, so I picked up the hoodie off the ground, marveling that it wasn't completely soaked, while Cuesta and Estíbaliz rushed to rescue the cauldron.

I could tell that Doctor Guevara and Inspector Muguruza were not going to be able to handle the weight of the corpse by themselves, so I stuffed the hoodie under my arm and went over to help them with the body bag.

Estí and Andoni seemed to have the same thought. They left the cauldron on the ground, and the five of us struggled down the rocky path, already a slippery white slope.

"We won't be able to make it to the cars," said an exhausted Inspector Muguruza. "And if there's a surge of water . . . We'll have to shelter inside the chapel."

"It's closed," said the court clerk, as if we didn't know.

"Then we'll have to force it open. I don't see another option," Doctor Guevara insisted.

We looked at one another, knowing that time was running out. Since we didn't have a battering ram, Estíbaliz, Cuesta, and I took turns trying to kick the wooden door in. It occurred to me that we were desecrating a holy space protected by the conch shell, an iconic symbol used to guide pilgrims heading to Santiago de Campostela. And yet I was relieved when I could feel the door slowly giving way. As soon as we had forced it open, the three technicians, the pathologist, the court clerk, Inspector Muguruza, Estí, and I climbed the two steps at the entrance and piled into the chapel, carrying Annabel's body.

I handed the dead woman's hoodie to the inspector to prevent further contamination. The chapel was only a small room with an altar, the image of the saint protected behind black iron bars, and a window with a grille.

We could hear the hailstorm outside. It seemed to be suffering from arrhythmia: sometimes it struck furiously, other times it slackened off. The technicians' cases and the Cabárceno Cauldron had been abandoned on the hillside. Fortunately the photographic equipment had been rescued.

Shortly afterward, the storm seemed to lessen. Cuesta took advantage of it, sprinting out of the chapel.

"Where do you think you're going?" Muguruza shouted at him.

"I'm going to get the cauldron, sir. We can't leave it up there." Estíbaliz ran after him.

"I'll go with him!" she said. She slipped away to join Andoni's suicidal expedition before anyone could stop them.

I wanted to yell after her, tell her she should stay in the chapel with me, with us, but I couldn't produce a single syllable. As I started to go after her, both the inspector and the pathologist held me back, preventing me from entering that white hell.

"Two is enough, Ayala," said Muguruza, holding me tight. "We can't risk everyone."

"If you know how to pray, do it now. There's the altar," Doctor Guevara whispered.

I waited in the doorway, powerless. Now, in addition to the hailstones bouncing off the tunnel, I could hear the crash of an electrical storm.

Then the avalanche hit.

For the first time, I was afraid.

This wasn't my first mountain storm, but now we had a real problem, because the tunnel was no longer a refuge. Its mouth, which so many pilgrims had passed through, had become a trap. A gushing white river of hail poured in.

Then the unimaginable happened.

I saw the Cabárceno Cauldron hurtling down the slope. I grunted, and the others jostled behind me in the chapel entrance. The cauldron bounced off the tunnel walls and disappeared through the arch on the northern side.

We were horror-struck, fearing the worst. And indeed, the worst happened: Andoni Cuesta's body flew past, his white suit almost invisible on the river of hailstones that carried him down the mountain.

It was like a hallucination. It only took a few seconds, and then he disappeared.

It was impossible to leave the chapel. The wind, storm, and cascading rocks would kill us. Nevertheless, I took the chance.

Where was Estíbaliz? I had to get to her. In less than ten seconds, her body came sweeping past.

The sight of her at the mercy of the storm was enough to breach the dike my brain had built months before.

"Not you!" I shouted. For the first time since August, I spoke. *Not you.*

The clarity of my statement and what it meant left me stunned.

I leaped out of the tunnel, even though I knew I would be flung down the hellish slope after her. At the last second, a strong hand clasped my arm.

A human chain.

This time there was one. I remembered what happened twenty-four years earlier: the hands that didn't reach out, those who chose not to risk their lives . . . and I realized I had never forgiven them. And, of course, I had never forgiven Annabel Lee, either.

I remembered the lifeless body I'd held in my arms for what seemed like hours on a sea stack in Cantabria.

5

THE CANTABRIAN SETTLEMENT

MONDAY, JUNE 29, 1992

A girl with dark brown hair jumped off the train at the same time as the four young men from the San Viator *cuadrilla*. The five teenagers spread out across the bare station at Cabezón de la Sal, a town in Cantabria famous for its salt flats. Their backpacks were full of supplies, and their hearts were full of expectations for the summer.

Waiting for them was the project director, Saúl Tovar, a young professor dressed informally in a checkered shirt. He welcomed them and introduced several student assistants who had already attended summer camp there.

There weren't many: a few second- and third-year girls studying history who swarmed around Saúl, and an older student who was chatting with the tall girl who had driven them from Santander in a used Ford Fiesta. Marian Martínez knew the only reason she had been invited was to be their taxi driver and to visit Saúl, the almighty Saúl. Marian did not share the devotion the entire University of Cantabria seemed to feel for its professor of cultural anthropology. She had heard rumors . . .

A dark-haired girl was watching the group eagerly from a distance, seated on a public bench where her father had told her to wait. These were the first people she had seen since she had been released, other than her aunt and her father. He was affectionate now, as though repenting for what he had done to her.

She knew her brain was still not fully functioning. She wasn't yet cleansed of the medication they had forced on her. She had convinced herself that water would flush out the remaining effects, so she was constantly drinking from her little plastic water bottle and then running to the bathroom.

It was a real pain, but it was necessary. She didn't want to keep feeling hazy. She knew this camp might be her only chance, because when she went back to school in September . . . it would be impossible. Everyone there knew her father; he was a god to them. Plus, she would have to repeat her final year, and he wasn't going to forgive her for that. How embarrassing!

So she couldn't waste this opportunity. She needed to watch these people and choose the one who could help her.

She joined the group as her father led them along the streets to the Conde de San Diego palace, an imposing mansion with steep roofs that had been donated to the municipality by the owners. It could've used a coat of paint, but for the students it was more than adequate.

Two hours later, introductions were over and lunch had been served, but she still hadn't decided. Maybe the tall, dark-haired boy with arms like an orangutan? He seemed to be the oldest in the group from Vitoria. Maybe she would talk to him. She couldn't make up her mind.

She decided to concentrate on the most serious and responsible one in the group, the one with the hooked nose, Asier. He didn't fool around like the others or laugh at dirty jokes, and, most importantly, she hadn't seen him talk to her father at all.

That was key.

She watched the new students go through the welcome ritual. This was the third time she'd seen it—the third summer of the

program. She had been part of it from the beginning, their project
to re-create an ancient Cantabrian settlement. She knew all about
the Celts. Just like her father, who had taught her everything. And
just like him, she had always known that she was going to be an
archaeologist.

For three weeks, Saúl Tovar poured his energy into taking care
of the small group of volunteers who had signed up to finish construction on four Iron Age huts.

They were all high school students, responsible, highly motivated. Clay ready to be molded. It was Saúl's job to instill in
them his passion for history, to sell them on the idea of attending
the University of Cantabria, where he was an associate professor.
He needed to impress the dean, become his right-hand man, in
order to get tenure. He needed to provide stability for Rebeca,
his shrunken family. It was all for his daughter: everything he did
was for her.

This summer he had rented a minibus so that he wouldn't have
to worry about public transportation in July. From his experiences
over the past two years, he'd learned that the students would work
like crazy for the first few days, and then on the weekend, they
would try to walk to Torrelavega or to las Fiestas del Carmen in San
Vicente de la Barquera. He knew their enthusiasm would wane as
the weeks went by. They would start paying less attention to the
history and culture of the Celtic-Iberians and thinking more about
members of the opposite sex. He needed some way to reenergize
them, to get them out of the camp for a few days, so he could remo-
tivate them with his stories.

By midafternoon, after piling all the work equipment into
the minibus, Saúl shepherded the students from Vitoria on
board, and finally they set off for the Picu de la Torre, the hillside where the wooden skeletons of the Iron Age huts awaited
them.

He turned the radio down. He hated Clapton's "Tears in Heaven." It was too unsettling.

The minibus had to avoid a couple of sixty-year-old cyclists who were straining to get up the hills. There were bicycles everywhere now, as thousands of fans had taken to the roads after Miguel Induráin's triumph in the Giro d'Italia and his likely second victory in the Tour de France.

Saúl concentrated on driving. Rebeca was sitting next to him. Both of them were pretending their thoughts were elsewhere, but in fact they were paying close attention to the four boys and their conversation.

"I hope there's a pay phone nearby. I have to call the hospital every night," said the youngest, the good-looking one. He sounded concerned.

He had already caught Rebeca's attention. He was wearing brand-name sneakers and red-label Levi's 501s. This kid Jota was not only handsome, he had money.

A *hospital?* Saúl and Rebeca both thought, but neither asked for an explanation.

Be patient, they told themselves.

I'll find out soon enough, they each decided.

"Of course there'll be a phone," said the dark-haired boy, the one the others called Unai. "Don't worry, I bet there'll be a booth there."

"Yeah, man. And you know, if he gets worse, I'll call my dad and we'll be in Txagorritxu in two hours," said the chubby one. He had a mop of greasy hair and was wearing a black Pearl Jam T-shirt. The others called him Lutxo. He spoke quickly and seemed very sure of himself.

Rebeca found him repulsive.

It was obvious they were all looking out for the handsome one, the baby of the group: José Javier, also known as Jota.

"How are you feeling, Rebeca?" her father suddenly asked quietly, his eyes still fixed on the road as he drove calmly along. He didn't speed; she couldn't hold that against him.

"Fine, Papa."

"Listen, I want you to know that . . . that these three months without you have been hard for me. I missed you so much . . ."

How tempting it was to believe him.

"Me too, Papa."

"You haven't had any more headaches?"

"No, I haven't, Papa. I'm fine."

That's enough. I don't want to talk about it, she thought.

"And did you have time to read the books I sent you? Cunliffe's *Atlas of World Archaeology* and the others?"

Yes, I read them when I wasn't groggy. They were the only thing that kept me . . . sane? she thought.

"Yes, Papa. Thanks for sending them."

"I was thinking that tomorrow, when we run the building workshop for the new volunteers, maybe you could teach them how to make adobe and explain the heather roofs. It'll be good practice for when you're a professor. You know I'll keep my job open for you when I retire," he said, smiling with those magnificent teeth. His lantern jaw really did make him the handsomest father in the world. He looked nothing like her classmates' fathers. They were all bald and paunchy, respectable patresfamilias.

Her father was devilishly attractive, and Rebeca had always known it. The looks her friends gave him when he picked her up from school were a daily reminder.

A large part of Saúl's attraction was his blue-black hair, but he also dressed to look younger, wearing cool jeans, white T-shirts, and flannel button-downs. Rebeca had inherited his hair, but not his green almond eyes, which made him look like he was half sorcerer, half angel.

Her face lit up thinking about what he was promising her, and she realized that her face muscles were taut. She hadn't smiled in months.

Maybe he does love me, maybe he's really concerned about me, she thought, yet she couldn't believe it completely. This kind of uncertainty distracted her from her plan. She couldn't afford it. She wouldn't get a second chance.

6

EL CANTÓN DE LA SOLEDAD

Thursday, November 17, 2016

The human chain we formed saved Estíbaliz from being swept down the mountain. We pulled her inside and then slammed the chapel door shut on the storm of the century. Estí was stunned and almost hypothermic.

"Check your cell phones. I don't think we have any service up here," Inspector Muguruza shouted over the noise outside. The hailstones still crashed against the walls of the chapel. The reverberations turned the inside into an echo chamber.

None of our cell phones worked. We were cut off. There was no way we could call for help.

"We need to stay calm. The Mountain Rescue Team knows we're still up here working the crime scene. They'll figure out that the hailstorm caught us by surprise in the tunnel, and that we couldn't get back down. As soon as the weather improves, they'll find us. We just have to hold on."

We all silently agreed.

I reached into the pocket of my down jacket to feel the outline of my own hills. For my birthday, Grandfather had given me a small piece of carved wood that I always carried on my key ring. It was a perpetual reminder of my home, of the place to which I always wanted to return.

As I felt the silhouette of the San Tirso mountain range, my fingers grazed the small plastic bag of caramelized almonds that Grandfather had given my brother, Germán, and me that morning after breakfast, before we set off for my tribute at the mural in Cantón de la Soledad. It seemed like another lifetime.

There were only a dozen left. Nuts and sugar: just what we needed. I shared them with the group, and they tasted as good as a death row inmate's last meal.

The seven of us—the court clerk, Doctor Guevara, Muguruza, the two forensic technicians, Estíbaliz, and I—slumped against the back wall of the chapel, huddled together for warmth, waiting for the deadly storm to return to the hell it had escaped from.

I tried hard not to look at Annabel Lee's body bag, which was lying in the corner near the door. Who would have thought that this would be the last night I spent with her? And yet, in a way, it made sense. She was always surrounded by death and destruction. I had never imagined her as a mother, a creator of life.

I don't know why.

Annabel used to say that she preferred to live inside her stories, because in the real world she destroyed everything she touched. In other words, her creative impulse kept her occupied; it kept the destructive force inside her in check. Like a dam. At least she was aware of it, even though she'd never apologized for the harm she'd done to us.

As the night drew on, the damp permeated my clothes and hair. My face, neck, and hands, all my unprotected skin, were suffering from exposure to the stormy November night at five thousand feet. The huge hailstones piling up outside the chapel didn't help—it felt as if we were in a refrigerator.

I was obsessed with Estíbaliz's frozen feet for some reason. I rubbed them and held her tight inside my feather-lined coat; she curled up against me in the fetal position. Our intertwined bodies looked like a huge pregnant stomach.

What about her head? I thought anxiously.

I knew that newborn babies lost heat through their heads, which explained all those blue and pink beanies. I cradled my exhausted colleague's head, and she let herself be engulfed, numb from shock, in my improvised nest.

I kissed her all over her forehead and cheeks, to see if my lips could lend a little warmth to her frozen, freckled skin.

Not you. Not you. Don't even think about dying, because that would leave me crippled for the rest of my life, and I'd never forgive you.

I realized that for once I was telling myself the truth. Estíbaliz was my bodyguard, despite her size. She was my wall, my barricade, the moat around my castle. She was my guardian. When she was next to me, I felt as though I was being protected by a force of nature. That revelation, that night, made me rethink my priorities.

You're asking for help, and I'll do it. Broca's aphasia be damned. My relationship with Alba be damned. You are calling me, and I'll be there. That's all there is to it. I'm going to get better, or I'm not my grandfather's boy.

But Alba's name brought back the conversation we'd had that afternoon, when she'd appeared in Cantón de la Soledad and asked me to take her to my apartment because she had something important to tell me. A feeble euphemism. What she really meant to say was that today my life was going to change.

Now are you going to tell me why you came? I had typed on my cell phone, once we were sitting on the soft sofa in my living room.

I suppose I was gazing at her expectantly, but I noticed no response on her face, and I knew something was wrong. She took off her thick white coat and hung it on the coatrack in the entrance. She was wearing a loose-fitting wool sweater to protect her from the Vitorian autumn chill.

"I went back to work a month ago. Even though you're on leave, I'm still your superior."

Believe me, I'm well aware of that.

"I had a worrying talk with your neurologist."

At that point I gritted my teeth. I didn't like the direction this . . . interview? was headed.

"It's been three months since you were shot, and you haven't been to see her yet, or asked her to recommend a speech therapist. Doctor Aldecoa is seriously concerned, Unai. She says that the longer you wait, the more difficult it will be for you to speak normally again. Neuronal plasticity has its limits. Your chances were relatively good in August, but every month that goes by without working on that part of your brain . . ."

So you've said, I indicated, raising my hand.

At first, I had gone to Dr. Diana Aldecoa's checkups with an almost religious fervor. My neurologist was an expert in her field, a capable woman with dark curly hair, a small head, and wide-set eyes that were closer to her temples than her nose. She was so full of energy and spoke so quickly that during the initial weeks of my recovery I found it hard to follow her. She demanded a lot from me, so much that eventually I ended up missing her sessions. I wasn't ready for them.

Is that why you're here? I wrote.

"Partly, yes, but it's not just that. There's something I have to tell you, no matter the cost. Once I do, I'm not sure if we'll still have whatever we used to."

What on earth are you talking about? I typed, bemused.

Alba stood to confront me. She let me get a good look at her, waiting silently for me to say something, but I was at a loss.

"Don't you notice anything?" she asked, as if it were obvious.

I was baffled. I didn't understand anything. Not a thing.

Lifting her sweater, she showed me her belly. Smooth, white skin that still filled me with desire.

"I've been pregnant since August, since las Fiestas de la Virgen Blanca, Unai."

I couldn't help my reaction.

A huge smile.

But not for long. Because then I found out that she wasn't sure who the father was: me, or Nancho.

Nancho. Of course. The ever-present Nancho.

"I slept with him a few days before I slept with you. I didn't want to—I couldn't get you out of my mind—but it was part of our routine, and I couldn't avoid it. I hated it because he wasn't you. And then, after what we did in the entrance to your building on the eighth of August, I couldn't do it with him anymore. It felt like I was being unfaithful to you. I want you to know that I've never been unfaithful to you. But that was the week I became pregnant, and to judge by the size of the fetus, I must now be . . ."

Fourteen weeks, I calculated, staring down at the floor. My head hurt terribly. The bone around the scar began to ache, the way it did when a storm was threatening in Villaverde.

"Fourteen weeks," she ended her sentence.

Is the baby all right? You told me that your first child suffered from a rare illness, I managed to write. I don't know why that was my first concern.

It has to be all right. You can't go through that again.

"Level-two brittle bone syndrome . . . I don't know yet. They can detect it after fourteen weeks, or maybe sixteen. I'm being monitored closely because it's a high-risk pregnancy, in part because of what happened with my first child, and in part because of my age. Primipara of advanced age, as my doctor calls it. I couldn't keep it from you, Unai, but I'm not telling you to make you feel as though you have an obligation to my baby."

It could be mine, too.

She sat down next to me on the sofa, staring at my hand but hesitating to hold it.

"If only, Unai. If only it is yours. When I found out I was pregnant, I was in shock for a week or two. I was still trying to come to terms with the fact that Nancho had killed twenty-one people, that he'd only married me because I could give him access to the investigation, that I lived with a psychopath. I decided to start again from scratch. My mother came to the hospital when I was under observation for the effects of the Rohypnol and the beestings. She took me back to Laguardia, and I asked her to deal with the apartment I shared with Nancho in Vitoria. She gave away all his clothes, and mine, too. I didn't want to wear anything Nancho had touched ever again. I threw away all the photos from our time together. All the furniture, everything in the apartment went to a flea market. She put the place up for rent. I bought a new cell phone. It's like I have a hole in my memory. When anything about our life tries to get in, I block it. I negate his manipulation by forgetting."

But you may be having his child, I wrote, and my fingers shook with fury as I typed those last two words.

Damn you, Nancho. Curse you. Your last act is your worst crime—destroying my future with Alba.

I stood up, suddenly chilled. I walked over and leaned my head against the windowpane, which was moist from the rain. Outside, half an inch away, Vitoria was crying. All I felt was cold.

"You saved my child's life. You should know that," Alba said behind me.

What do you mean? I asked by spreading my palms.

"Do you remember that phone call you made from San Tirso?"

I remember, I typed, turning around to show her the phone.

"I was in Laguardia, on the top floor of our house, staring at the outline of the hills you were calling me from. That week I had made an appointment at a Burgos clinic. I wanted privacy and anonymity, so I knew I couldn't go to Vitoria or Logroño."

The thought that I could have lost the child stung me, even

though I didn't know if it was mine. Acid ran through my veins. Without realizing it, I clung to the window frame.

"I was horrified that the baby might be Nancho's. I thought that my morning sickness was my body's refusal to give birth to that monster's child. I hadn't been sick at all during my first pregnancy. Now I hope this pregnancy will be different because the child is yours. When you called me, I realized I couldn't get rid of the child if there was a possibility it was yours."

So what are you going to do, Alba? Give up the baby for adoption if it turns out to be a redhead like him?

"That would be doing the same thing Nancho's parents did to him. I would be no better than them. No matter who the father is, the baby is mine, too. I made my decision. I thought I would have to learn to love this baby, but the fact is, love just hit me. I don't know how to explain it, but I love him or her as much as I did my first child. There's a direct link between us. This baby means everything to me."

And what do I mean to you, Alba? What role do I play in all this?

"Whatever role you want: I told you because you deserve to know the truth. But if you don't want it, you don't have to have any responsibilities. The only thing I won't do is get a paternity test."

I looked at her in horror.

"Don't do this to me," she protested.

Why not? It would clear everything up.

"Because the child doesn't deserve that, Unai. Whether its father is a murderer or the man I love, this baby doesn't deserve to be judged for something that is not its fault. And anyway, I'm the one who will have to face the consequences."

She said "the man I love," I thought, and the phrase enchanted me. They were words I would have killed to hear only a few hours earlier, but now they were of secondary importance.

Now there was a new life to think about, and a decision that required the judgment of Solomon.

I leaned my head against the windowpane again. The chill did me good.

I don't like anyone to see me cry. I'm very reticent about showing my emotions in public, but now I had to ignore the prickling sensation behind my eyelids.

This wasn't the reunion I had been dreaming about for months. Throughout the end of that summer and the warm start to autumn, while I was holed up in Villaverde with my bramble jelly, refusing to recover, Alba had had to get over the death of her husband and the fact that he had tried to kill her, accept that she had lived with a psychopath who killed twenty-one people, many of them children, and deal with a pregnancy and the decision to keep the child even though it would be a permanent reminder of the worst time in her life.

It wasn't easy for me, either. If only Alba had been certain that the child was mine . . . Her word would have been enough to convince me. A son or a daughter with Alba: I would have been the happiest man in the world, and I couldn't have cared less that we were starting everything backward, beginning a life with Alba while she had a baby in her arms, becoming a family before we were even a couple.

It might still be possible.

But the doubt . . . the wretched doubt.

No, I couldn't do it. I knew I couldn't live with it.

My profiler's brain could only think of the statistical likelihood that the child of a psychopath would inherit his tendencies. What kind of person was I willing to call "my child"?

Yet again I cursed Nancho, his doctor father, and his abused mother. I cursed my great-aunt Felisa for handing Nancho to the monsters who had raised him, who'd turned him into a demon.

Alba, I wrote, *I can't give you an answer now. I need to process . . .*

She came over and read what I was typing: the death knell for our future as a couple, or whatever we might have been.

I think that was the worst part of the day, which I will always remember as one of the toughest in my life. Watching Alba swallow her immense disappointment and react with dignity, even though I was making her suffer. But she was ready for it, and that also wounded my pride. She had come to my apartment prepared for the worst, and that's what I was giving her.

And at that moment Estíbaliz's WhatsApp arrived, informing us of Annabel Lee's death.

It had been a long day, and now the restless night in the elements summoned all my demons: those from my past, with Annabel's dead body laid out in front of me, and those in my present, with Alba and her pregnancy.

As day dawned, we were on the verge of mental exhaustion. There had been periods when all of us were awake, and others when we managed to sleep.

The sun finally peeped though the chapel's tiny window. With first light, our colleagues from the Mountain Rescue Team arrived to save us. They wrapped us in foil blankets, gave us water, and made sure we had no injuries and were out of danger. It was a clear, calm morning, but after the way we had been punished the night before, none of us trusted the silent mountain.

Goyo Muguruza looked sorrowfully at one of our rescuers.

"What about Andoni Cuesta? Were you able to save him?"

"We found his body two hundred yards farther down. I'm sorry."

It was too much for us. No one was able to say a word. We were devastated.

Finally, Estíbaliz reacted. She slipped out of her blanket and rushed out of the chapel. I followed and stopped her from kicking wildly at the tunnel wall.

I couldn't say anything to console her, although I wanted to whisper, *That's enough, Estí, that's enough. Let's go home. There's nothing left for us here.*

7

NUMBER 2 PLAZA DE LA VIRGEN BLANCA

FRIDAY, NOVEMBER 18, 2016

Safe and sound in Vitoria three hours later, I crawled back to my apartment from the Santiago hospital where we had been taken for observation to make sure we had no injuries other than slight hypothermia and exhaustion. All I wanted to do was sleep on a dry mattress under my familiar, welcoming comforter. I couldn't wait to sink into the darkness of a bedroom I could trust not to collapse around me in a storm. In other words, I wanted to go home.

It must have been midafternoon when I heard someone open my front door. I leaped out of bed. I hadn't managed to get much sleep or rest. I was too worried—I hadn't been able to close my eyes. Panicking slightly, I wanted to call, *Germán, is that you?* but all that came out was a strange guttural noise. Frustrated and still uneasy, I left my bedroom, only to find Grandfather coming into the kitchen with a couple of bags of food.

"Your brother tells me you spent the night on the mountain in the storm, my boy."

I nodded. I felt like I was still waking up.

"You must be beat. Sit down, I brought you some meat to build your strength."

Thanks, Grandpa, I said with a smile.

There was no way I could stop him from taking care of me. It wasn't that he spoiled me—he would rather have cut off his own hand than pamper my brother and me. It was just that he knew when I really needed his help.

I sat down on the living-room sofa and stared blankly at the white balconies on the eastern side of the Plaza de la Virgen Blanca.

I switched on my cell phone. I had a million WhatsApp messages waiting.

Before looking at them I logged onto my e-mail and sent a long-overdue message to my neurologist. I asked her for the contact information of the speech therapist she had recommended, so that I could start my recovery as quickly as possible. She replied almost instantaneously. I asked for an appointment and promised myself that I wouldn't cancel or postpone it.

After that I went straight to Tasio's WhatsApp. Apparently, he had found more information about the damned cauldron that was now responsible for the deaths of two people. A colleague and my first love, no less.

> **Hi, Tasio, I'm back at work. I couldn't respond yesterday; we were caught in the tunnel by a hailstorm.**

> **Everything all right?**

> **Not for everyone, unfortunately.**

> **Wow . . . I'm so sorry.**

> **I know. It was terrible. But I can't deal with that now, we can talk about it later. You said you found something. Go ahead, shoot.**

Shoot! That's a good one, Kraken! I see
you've made a full recovery. If you can laugh
at it, you can cope with it.

I was not in the mood for jokes.

Tasio, please don't tease me. You have no
idea what kind of day I have ahead of me.
What did you find?

The image you sent me is the Cabárceno
Cauldron, which was found in a mine on
Peña Cabarga in Cantabria a century ago. It
dates from the Bronze Age, between 900 and
650 years BC. It's similar to the Irish or British
cauldrons found in Dublin or Battersea. It was
likely used in religious ceremonies or during
other important events.

Celtic rituals?

Yes, exactly. The cauldron is usually on
display in the Cantabrian Prehistory Museum
in Santander. Until a few weeks ago, it was
in a temporary exhibition at the Cantabrian
Archaeological Museum on the Costa
Quebrada. The museum reported the theft,
but it didn't make the news other than a short
article in *El Periódico Cántabro*.

I knew the people who ran the museum: the Del Castillo brothers, a historian and an archaeologist. We had met a few years earlier, when I was training in criminal profiling at Santander police

headquarters. I had gotten involved in an investigation into some unusual murders. The brothers had helped. A lot. This was good news; they would be very useful contacts.

Is there any link with the San Adrián Tunnel?

I searched for a Celtic connection between
the cauldron and the tunnel. As you probably
know, Celtic mythology features stories about
underground passageways that link distant
locations. There's always been speculation
that there's a gallery leading to a well in
the San Adrián Tunnel. Rumor has it that a
woman from Zagama went to wash clothes
there and disappeared. Sometime later, an
arm was found in the spring at a village near
Zalduondo called Iturrutzaran de Araia.

I follow you so far. What else?

In that same spring, they found a stone
submerged in the water. Although the
inscription was almost illegible, it was
eventually deciphered. It turns out the stone
was a Roman altar dedicated to nymphs.
It was no more than a hundred yards from
the Araia metallurgy factory, on the River
Ziraunza.

Roman nymphs.

Yes, but nymphs were the divinities that
ruled over fountains, ponds, and rivers long

before the Romans who adapted and then
adopted the religious beliefs of the lands
they conquered. These particular nymphs
are of pan-Celtic, Indo-European origin.
They are *las tres Matres*, the triad of mother
deities. Las Matres was a popular cult that
spread through the center of Europe, to
Gaul, Britannia, and beyond more than two
thousand years ago.

> But what does the cauldron
> have to do with las Matres?

Let me finish, Kraken. Do you realize how
much more impatient you are now that you
can't speak? This triad is associated with
female fertility, both natural and human.
Las Matres are linked to *los Genii Cucullati*,
three hooded figures also related to fertility,
who are their guardians. I'll send you some
images.

I soon received several photos of reliefs showing three hooded
figures. The phallic shape of the hood made the symbolism of these
guardians quite clear.

> You say they protect fertility.
> Are you talking about pregnant women?

You're getting ahead of yourself. Why
would they be pregnant? Does that mean
something?

I hadn't told Tasio that a murder victim was discovered with the cauldron, and that the dead woman was pregnant. Nor had I told him that we'd found her hooded shirt a few yards away. And the notion of a triad stuck in my mind, too: Annabel and two climbers—a father and a son. Were those two hooded as well?

Thanks. That's helpful. Is there anything else?

Tasio couldn't resist prodding me.

That's all unless you can give me any clues
as to what direction I should look . . .

I think I have more than enough for now,
Tasio. It goes without saying that I really
appreciate your help and your discretion.

You said it: it goes without saying. Let me
know if you need any more help, whatever
that might entail.

Same to you. I'll leave you for now.

All I ask is that if your investigation succeeds,
you tell the press in Vitoria that I helped you.

Too good to be true, I thought. I had almost forgotten Tasio's obsession with restoring his image.

After that, I answered Germán's WhatsApp. I had reached out to him right away to tell him that we had been rescued, but my younger brother spent the morning sending me messages asking if I was okay.

I'm fine, Germán. Grandad is here, cooking
potatoes with chorizo and txitxikis. He's
going to clog my arteries.

I know. I was the one who sent him. Can I see
you later tonight when I leave the office?

I have a meeting at work. Will I see you in
Villaverde this weekend? I need to get away.

Germán agreed. Ever since I'd gotten shot, he'd become over-
protective. Then again he hadn't come out of the recent drama
unscathed, and it was my fault. His fiancée, Martina, had been
killed because I hadn't caught Nancho in time. And so I felt like
his insistence on keeping an eye on me was the price I had to pay,
no matter how much I hated explaining my comings and goings
to anyone.

I helped Grandfather set the table and let myself be distracted
by his talk about the damage the previous night's storm had done
to his vegetable patch. Villaverde hadn't been spared, although
what they had suffered was nothing compared to the hailstorm we
experienced in the tunnel.

After that, glancing with concern at a sky that still held the
threat of rain, I wrote a short report about the Cabárceno Cauldron
and its potential link to the tunnel. I didn't include my initial
thoughts on the murderer's profile. I still needed to hear what the
forensic team and the pathologist had to say before I drew up my
official initial report, but I was puzzled by the scene in San Adrián.

I said good-bye to Grandfather, who promised me he would
take the bus back to Villaverde, then headed for my former office
at police headquarters in Portal de Foronda. After our conversation,
I had no idea how Alba and I would cope with seeing each other

every day, but I was now committed to returning to the force. I had a new obsession, and I didn't want to be left out of the hunt. Even though I was physically and mentally exhausted, I was ready to move on from Nancho and his crimes. I was also ready to commit to the speech therapy that was finally going to end my aphasia.

8

LA SENDA PRESCHOOL

MONDAY, JUNE 29, 1992

Jota, Asier, Lutxo, and Unai took their sleeping bags out of their backpacks and spread them out on the narrow mattresses that covered the metal bunk beds. They had chosen one of the empty rooms on the second floor of the ancient mansion, which they named "the Boys' Room," without considering where anyone else would sleep.

So they couldn't believe it when one of the girls—the one who had hair down to her waist and wore yellow imitation Doc Martens—walked into the room and silently began taking clothes out of her backpack.

"What do you think you're doing?" Asier protested, his voice as rough as sandpaper.

"What Asier means is . . . it's great that you're sleeping in here," Jota said hastily, clearing his throat and staring daggers at his friend.

Jota had already told Unai, his best friend among the four, what he thought of her. He had been attracted to this dark-haired girl right away. For Jota, these first ten hours had been an eternity, and this immediate affinity raised a red flag for Unai, especially considering the instability in Jota's life. His father, diagnosed with pancreatic cancer, had only a few months to live. Having lost both

parents, Unai knew what it was like to attend the funeral of someone you loved, and he was determined to ensure that Jota had a
good time. That meant that right now, Jota's taste in girls was
sacred, untouchable.

"No, that's not what I said. Look, there's a room for girls, isn't
there?"

"Yes, but it's a lot dirtier than this one, and I have asthma," lied
Annabel. No way was she going to share a room with a girl. Her
cool, confident, confrontational manner beguiled the boys.

"You think your bad temper's going to scare me away? I collect rejections. If you think I'm staying anywhere else, you've
got another thing coming. And by the way, Saúl wants you all
downstairs."

And with that she calmly continued unpacking her things.

"Of course we get the crazy one," muttered Asier as he passed
her. "Come on, let's get some air."

Asier left the room angry, Lutxo was expectant, and Jota
bewitched. Unai hung back, unpacking his backpack.

"I'll be down in a minute," he called after the others. He was
making sure he hadn't left any T-shirts behind.

"I find it hard to believe you collect rejections," he said to
Annabel once the other boys had left. He continued hanging his
clothes without looking in her direction.

"Look, I have dozens," she said. She took a bundle of letters
from her black backpack. Some of the letters were opened; others
were still sealed in their envelopes. "Come on, don't just stand
there staring. Help me open the recent ones. The sooner we start,
the sooner we'll finish."

Unai cautiously sat down next to her on the rough mattress.

"How do you know they're rejections?"

She shrugged and handed him envelopes with postage from
all over the world.

"From the weight. You can tell they only have one sheet of paper. It's always like that. If they're interested in publishing you, the letter is longer. They want to butter you up."

"What are they rejecting?" asked Unai, hesitantly opening the first envelope.

"I illustrate comics, and I send samples of them to publishers everywhere. There's not much of a market in Spain, but in other European countries and in the States, there's a whole comics culture. And in Asia, it's phenomenal. The bigger the publishing house, the better. I don't have a shot."

"So you do it out of masochism?"

"Yes, rejection makes me stronger. It motivates me. I'm afraid of losing motivation because it's so hard to get started. I need them to reject me. I need the anger to be able to draw. I haven't found any other way, and I've been studying my creative process for years, Unai, since we last met."

They stared at each other for several seconds. She could see he clearly didn't understand. Unai looked down first.

Yeah, I got the crazy one all right, he thought, getting up from the bed.

"You don't remember me, do you?" she said with a gentle smile, addressing his confusion. "What preschool did you go to?"

"La Senda, the one that had a train on the playground . . ." He trailed off. It started coming back to him.

"You still don't recognize me, do you? We've known each other since we were tiny. We were inseparable. I'm Ana Belén Liaño, though I sign my drawings Annabel Lee, from Edgar Allan Poe. You know the poem."

Unai had not read any more Poe than his classes required, but everyone had heard the Radio Futura song in the bars in Vitoria's Cuesta area. He knew it was about a young man's love for a woman who dies and is buried in a sepulchre beside the sounding sea.

"Ana Belén?" Unai said. It was hard to recall those dim and distant days. "I think I remember, your name rings a bell. Did something happen with us?"

"You were my boyfriend. Our love was so great that the angels were jealous of us. Just like in the poem."

Unai started to remember playing and holding hands with someone who occasionally stole a wet kiss from him.

"I used to draw pictures for you. So you helped put me on my career path."

Oh, right, the drawing. Who knows what that was . . . , thought Unai.

He looked at her. Sometimes she did sound crazy, but she drew attention like a lighthouse on a dark night.

"Life has brought us together again," Annabel Lee said emphatically. She quickly reached out to take his hand.

Unai would not have minded if she took his hand, his mouth, anything she wanted, really, but her move was so sudden that he jerked away like he'd been electrocuted. She took his gesture badly.

"What's wrong? Did something change between us?"

"Er . . . Ana Belén—"

"Annabel Lee," she corrected him. "I'm Annabel Lee."

"Annabel Lee, you have to understand that this is practically the first time we've met. It's not that I don't like you, that's not the case at all," he said, clearing his throat. He broke into a sweat. He couldn't believe what he'd just said. He'd just given her a clear view into his brain.

"Well then, I've been mistaken for eleven years," she replied, as if she were already a hundred years old, and eleven years (which was 70 percent of their lives at that point) was for her no more than an instant.

She was a strange girl, too imaginative for Unai's practical mindset. But still, it was impossible not to get caught up in her.

"Jota really likes you," Unai blurted out without thinking. He inched away from her. "I can't do this to him. He's my best friend, and his father is dying of cancer. He hasn't been himself since he got into a fight at the fiesta of San Prudencio. Luckily, Lutxo, Asier, and I dragged him away before he could get too badly hurt, but we're really worried about him. He binge drinks every weekend. It's not normal, Annabel. His uncle is very strict and his mother doesn't even notice it. We've covered for him as much as we could, and we decided to come to Cantabria to see if maybe we could steady him. He's liked you ever since he saw you on the train. I can't put my feelings ahead of his well-being."

Unai immediately regretted his speech. He'd really made a mess of things. It was disloyal to Jota, who had more than enough to deal with at home. Unai had his grandfather to help him when his own father . . . But Jota didn't have someone like Unai's grandfather. He had an uncle who only cared about his academic success, and a mother who didn't seem to notice anything.

"So, Jota . . . ," she replied, after pausing to take in what he said. "Okay, Unai, I get it."

"Do you really?"

"Yes, really. I get it. I've waited eleven years, so I'm not in any hurry. After all, I have my comics. Go downstairs, they'll start to wonder where you are."

Unai bounded down the creaking stairs. He was still flustered by the time he joined his friends. They were already eating Spanish omelets at one end of the long wooden table.

"Jota, can you help me with the garbage?" Saúl asked after they had cleaned up.

It was a warm night. Jota followed him with the bags through the bushes to the trash cans outside the garden.

"Look, I don't want to pry, but I heard you say on the bus that you have to make an important phone call every day. Can I help at all?"

Jota nervously shifted his weight. People always saw him as
weak and wanted to protect him, to sort out his life for him. He
was thankful, but . . . And yet it was true, this time he did need
some support.

"My father is at Txagorritxu hospital. He has pancreatic cancer.
I want to talk to my family every day in case he gets worse and
I have to go back. I don't know if there are any phone booths in
Cabezón de la Sal."

"There are, don't worry. I'll show you."

"No, it's okay, Saúl. You don't have to."

"I know, you're grown-up. It's not that," said Saúl, laying his
hand on Jota's scrawny shoulder. It was hard not to view him as a
chick still in its nest. "The thing is, my father died of cancer, leaving my older sister and me on our own when we were still young,
and—"

"My father doesn't understand that I don't want to be an architect," Jota interrupted, unable to contain himself. "He has cancer,
but all I can think about is that I don't want the future he's set out
for me. I don't want to spend five years studying structural analysis
and cavalier perspectives. He's so self-absorbed that even on his
deathbed he wants me to promise him I'm going to be an architect.
And when he dies, my uncle Julian is going to take the reins and
force me to study architecture. They've already talked about it. I
heard them one day in the hospital. They talk about me like I'm
another project for their studio."

Saúl listened. The story sounded like his own.

"Listen, José Javier . . ."

"Jota. My father is José Javier, and I'm just the first letter, *J*.
I have to earn the rest by myself, okay?"

"Of course, Jota," said Saúl. He had once been in Jota's shoes:
an overbearing father, a future traced by other hands, and an impatient eagerness to make a mark of his own. "I understand, and I'll
do anything to help you, or your father. My sister is head of Endo-

crinology at the Valdecilla hospital in Santander. She's well connected with oncologists in Spain and abroad. If your father needs a second opinion, she could help make sure he's seen by the best. And if money is an issue—"

"It's not about money," Jota objected. He never liked talking about money. His family was well-off, but it was a privilege he hadn't earned yet. Still, he could see the kindness in Saúl's protective instincts. "I'll mention it to my mother and uncle. Thank you for supporting me even though we've just met."

"I have to look after you all for three weeks. So whatever you need, Jota. If you feel down and out, if you don't feel like working on the huts . . . Remember, you're not contracted to do this job. It's much more relaxed, okay?"

"Okay," Jota said. A breeze chilled him, and he realized how late it was getting. "Can you tell me where the pay phone is?"

"I have a better idea. Get in the minibus." Saúl threw him the keys. "Do you know how to drive?"

"Yes, but my license—"

"There's nobody on the road at this time of night. Let's go to Santillana del Mar and clear your head. You can drive me," said Saúl. His smile never failed with his students. He didn't even need to wink; he saved that for more difficult situations.

Jota loved to drive. It made him feel in control of a tiny part of his life. On the way to Santillana del Mar, he had a big smile on his face. Being away from home, meeting Ana Belén, and hearing Saúl's support had lifted his spirits. When his mother told him over the phone how badly his father's last treatment session had gone, the news didn't hit him as hard as it had before. He welcomed the twenty-one days away from the reality of his father's illness and the pressure to study.

Back in the mansion, Rebeca had taken advantage of her father's absence to pull Asier aside, into the kitchen.

She told him everything.

Even what she was most ashamed of. But he stopped her.

"Seriously, enough," he said. "I don't care about your life story. I'm not your therapist. I don't know what gave you that impression. And don't draw me into your drama. I don't want to be a part of it. I have my own life to worry about."

She's crazy, he thought, escaping from the kitchen like it was contaminated.

A few minutes later, Rebeca emerged as well. She hadn't cried in front of anyone yet, but her chin was trembling.

He had hurt her.

Yet again.

She was certain they would send her back. This would be her last summer of freedom.

9

LAKUA

I was seated in the big conference room at police headquarters half an hour later. Estíbaliz was beside me. Then there were two people at the meeting I didn't know, as well as Doctor Guevara and Inspector Muguruza. My tablet sat ready on the table.

We survivors from the tunnel looked haggard and exhausted. Clearly none of us wanted to be there.

Our boss came into the room. Superintendent Medina was a man in his sixties with bushy eyebrows and a beard like one of the Magi. He extended his hand and solemnly offered each of us his condolences.

Alba entered behind him. She was wearing a black coat that hid her bump, and had her hair pulled back. She looked more somber than usual, but I noticed relief in her quick glance at me, as if she was glad to see me in one piece. Balm for my damaged self-esteem. After everything we'd gone through in the last twenty-four hours, I was grateful that her concern seemed genuine.

"First of all," the superintendent began, "I'd like to thank you all for the professionalism, bravery, and compassion you demonstrated under the extreme duress of yesterday's events. We're proud that you belong to our force. We're shocked at the loss of our colleague Andoni Cuesta. His widow has requested a family burial tomorrow in El Salvador cemetery, and we will respect her wishes. I know you are all tired and that this meeting was called last-minute, so I am not going to keep you long. For now, I'll hand things over to Deputy Superintendent Salvatierra."

"Thank you for coming in despite what you've been through," said Alba. "I had a restless night as well, worrying about you, but I know it was nothing compared to what you've gone through.

"The loss of the forensic team's work means we all need to be at the top of our game to make up for lost ground. Discretion will be key. Judge Olano has issued a gag order for one month. If the investigation is still ongoing at that time—and I hope it won't be—we can ask him for an extension. We don't want the press to play the same decisive role it assumed in the recent case of the double murders. We will do everything in our power to prevent Vitoria from suffering that kind of trauma again. I'm sure you can guess what kind of pressure the Interior Ministry is putting on us to find the guilty person or persons. Should this murder be the first in a series, every second the perpetrator is on the streets is another opportunity he could strike. We're working against the clock."

Alba paused. No one said a word.

"The press office will be careful with the details we offer the media. All we are saying is that a climber was found dead on the Álava side of the Aizkorri-Aratz Mountain Range, and that a colleague died in the line of duty. We're not providing names or initials, nor are we divulging the fact that he was part of our forensic team. We are treating it as a climbing accident. Though Andoni Cuesta deserves more recognition for his record as a police officer, his family agrees confidentiality is of the utmost importance at this time. Inspector Gauna will now bring us up to date on the case."

"Thank you, Deputy Superintendent," said Estíbaliz, pushing her red bangs out of her face. I'd never seen such dark lines under her eyes. "Good afternoon, everyone. Our victim is Ana Belén

Liaño, thirty-nine years old, born in Vitoria. She was single and, at time of death, about five months pregnant. To those in the industry, she was a relatively well-known graphic novelist. Her mother is her only immediate relation, and she has been informed of her daughter's death. Perhaps the most important fact for our investigation is that the victim won the BonoLoto, worth three million euros."

"Oh, my goodness," Doctor Guevara let slip, then cleared her throat.

"That's right," said Estíbaliz. "That's what Andoni was going to tell us after he examined the contents of the bag found at the site. We know from a receipt in her bag, which luckily was preserved, that the victim deposited the winning ticket in a bank." Estí placed the piece of paper on the table.

We all stared at the receipt, thunderstruck. It was hard to imagine that Annabel had won three million euros.

What was someone who was as ambivalent about material goods as she was planning to do with all that money?

"Well, that's a strong motive for killing somebody, isn't it?" said Alba, voicing what we all were thinking. "I want you to investigate whether her friends and family had debts, or whether someone near her was in financial trouble. You know what to look for."

"Do we know anything about the cauldron, Inspector Muguruza?" asked Estíbaliz.

"The rescue team found it some distance from the tunnel," he said, readjusting his dark glasses. "It's in a deplorable state: the hailstones left dents that the restorers at the museum are going to have to assess. As you can imagine, the prints we were hoping to collect have been destroyed, meaning we are unable to determine if they belonged only to the two climbers or whether the murderer's prints were on the cauldron as well. The same is true of the footprints and tire tracks we were hoping to process: the storm obliterated them all. I think we're dealing with the luckiest murderer in the world, if you'll pardon the expression."

"Is there anything else?" Alba asked.

I handed her the report with the archaeological details Tasio had provided. She seemed surprised, but I was pleased to see admiration as well. I was still unsure how she would interact with me professionally.

She read the report aloud while the others listened. In another context all this talk of Celtic rituals would have raised eyebrows, but having just solved a case involving *eguzkilores*, yew tree poison, and dolmens, a woman hanging from a tree with her head immersed in a bronze Celtic cauldron didn't seem so outlandish.

"It's possible that Inspector Ayala here, whom we all wish a speedy recovery from his injury, will be working with us on this investigation as a profiler. Inspector Gauna will begin looking for similar deaths possessing elements of Celtic or Celtic-Iberian culture."

Did she say, "It's possible"? I thought with frustration. *Am I still not part of the team?*

I searched Alba's face for an explanation but saw nothing.

"Since this investigation is being prioritized, the superintendent and I have decided to reinforce the Criminal Investigation Unit. I'd like to officially welcome Deputy Inspector Manu Peña and Officer Milán Martínez. Deputy Inspector Peña is from headquarters in San Sebastián, where he also has experience as a detective. Until now, Milán worked in the Central Office on Computer Crimes. She asked specifically to collaborate with our unit, which seemed like a good idea since so much of our job takes place online. I hope this will give our team more agility."

Peña greeted everyone with a nod. He was in his thirties, but I noticed a slight tremor in his right hand. He had an air of experience, so nerves seemed an unlikely cause; perhaps he was covering up a diagnosis that would have been terrible for anyone his age. He was fair-haired and clean-shaven apart from sideburns down his jaw.

I was willing to bet Estíbaliz found his light-colored eyes attractive. He was wearing a black denim jacket and a striped sailor's shirt, and he gave off a faint smell of tobacco. I liked him at once. He looked competent, and we could use the reinforcements.

As for Milán, she reminded me of someone, but I didn't know who. It was hard not to be struck by her height. She was tall—well over six feet—solidly built and slightly masculine, and a bit awkward. Her brown hair was tousled in such a way that it was unclear whether it was straight or curly. Her hunched shoulders threatened to turn into a widow's hump in a decade or two. Her height was probably a sore spot growing up, so I could understand her tendency to slouch, to withdraw into her body. Fortunately, rather than responding to her bullies in kind, she had followed a career apprehending them.

She cleared her throat.

"How are you all?" she said, shrinking into her chair. I smiled at her in encouragement. First meetings in a new unit are enough to unsettle even the most experienced cop.

We were going to be a team of four, counting me, if the deputy superintendent decided to include me. It was a good start: more people, more funds, more time to free us from bureaucratic paperwork so that Estíbaliz and I could concentrate on the case.

"Milán, Peña . . . good to have you with us. You're going to be a great help. Peña, I want you to talk to Ana Belén Liaño's mother, friends, extended family, and work colleagues. We want to find out who the father of her child was. We want to know if she had a stable boyfriend or partner, if she lived with someone . . . Ultimately, we want to know if this pregnancy was planned, or if there was any kind of conflict surrounding it. Look for details that don't fit. Milán, since we haven't found her cell phone, check her social media. She shared her work with her followers, but she also uploaded photos of her personal life. See if she had any persistent trolls or critics, or obsessive admirers. Find her cell-phone number and ask the service provider to give us access to her network. Then draw up a list of her final calls, where she made them from . . . Dig as deep as you can."

Estí paused when she realized Milán was writing in tiny print on a pink Post-it note.

"Milán, are you going to be able to fit everything on there?"

"I'm trying to," she replied, her face flushing until it was almost the same color as the Post-it.

"Next time bring a notebook. It's more practical," Estí advised.

"I can put Post-its in my pockets, though," she murmured. "They don't take up any room. Don't worry, boss, I never lose them."

"Fine," said Estíbaliz, unconvinced. "Let's move on. Hopefully the judge will grant us permission to ask the bank where she deposited the winning lottery ticket for her account details. This is our best concrete evidence for a possible motive. If it wasn't the money, I see two other possibilities. First, some sort of conflict over her pregnancy. Second, God forbid, some monster might be reenacting a Celtic ritual, as suggested by the elaborate way in which she was killed—hung upside down in an ancient cauldron. Note that the crime's location would pose challenges for the killer. A path that's been traversed since prehistoric times on a mountaintop between two provinces is difficult to access and suspiciously specific for a premeditated murder."

I stole one of Milán's garish Post-its and wrote a quick note to Estíbaliz. She read it and nodded.

"As Inspector Ayala is recommending, I also want you to track down the victim's illustrations, which she signed Annabel Lee. She may have kept copies of her published work at home. Her mother might be able to help, or her partner if she had one. If you can't find all of them, check out who her publisher was, and get in touch with her editor. Once you have all her work, I want you to see if any of the elements we found at the crime scene appear in them. Anything related to the Celts, cauldrons, hanged men, pregnant women . . ."

"What about the climbers who discovered her body?" asked Alba.

I had been about to write the same question. The trio of hooded figures Tasio had told me about weighed on my mind.

"We took witness statements from them," said Estíbaliz. She passed around some papers. "Jose Mari Garmendia Sr. and Jose Mari Garmendia Jr., fifty and eighteen years old, respectively, live in Araia, a town on the Álava side where people normally start the climb up to the San Adrián Tunnel. The father runs a small metal workshop. His grandparents worked in the now-abandoned steel factory at Ajuria. But the shop must have fallen on hard times, because there have been layoffs. The younger Garmendia is unemployed and can't claim benefits. Since there was no work to do in the shop, the father says they went climbing on Thursday to cheer up his son. He states that before they entered the tunnel, they saw a body hanging from a tree. It was swaying, possibly due to the strong wind at the time, and he claims they ran toward it when they realized the head was submerged in a cauldron."

"Did he use the word *cauldron*?" Peña wanted to know.

"Yes, from the outset he says 'cauldron,'" Estíbaliz replied with a shrug. "He doesn't say cooking pot or dish or anything like that. But that checks out to me: the father works with iron, so he would be able to distinguish between a cauldron and something else."

"Could we see the photographs of the cauldron at the crime scene?" Peña asked. He extended a trembling hand to the center of the table.

"Yes, we were able to save the cameras during the storm. You can also ask me any questions you may have," said Muguruza. "The cauldron has a rounded bottom, so it doesn't stand upright. Someone must have held it up while they put the victim's head into it.

Since forensics determined that the cause of death was drowning, the victim would have been struggling."

"Yes, she was," Doctor Guevara confirmed. "Her bruises show she hit her head on all sides while she was still alive. Pending the results of the autopsy, I would say the injuries appear in keeping with the size of the cauldron."

"Here's what the report says," Estíbaliz added, jumping in. "'The witness states that the cauldron was surrounded by a small pile of stones apparently placed there in order to stabilize it on the ground.'"

"So where is that pile of stones in these photos?" asked Peña, handing us the panoramic views and those taken closer to the scene. "I can't see it. Can anyone else?"

"By the time we arrived, the cauldron had been moved several yards. The two eyewitnesses stated they had pulled it out of the way to try to help the woman. The movement tipped the water out. After that, they left it on its side untouched. I imagine that trying to rescue the victim might have moved some of the stones. They must have walked all over the pile if there was one."

"So what do we have, Inspector Gauna?"

"Our victim is a pregnant graphic novelist who had just won three million euros. We have a physically active father and son hard on their luck who say they found the victim after she was already dead. We have the cauldron used in the murder covered in unrecoverable fingerprints, and we have a father of the deceased fetus somewhere out there."

"I think that's more than enough to go on."

"Could the father and son have been messing around with Ana Belén Liaño, and things got out of hand?" asked Peña.

"I think that's a question for our profiler," Estíbaliz said, nodding in my direction.

The others didn't know that I knew Annabel Lee yet, but Estí had my back.

"Inspector Ayala, does that seem like a possibility to you?" Alba prompted me.

It might be possible, I wrote on my tablet. I periodically showed the others so they could read. *But nothing about the scene implied anything sexual happened. This isn't like an orgy where a plastic bag accidentally leads to suffocation. Submerging her head in an ancient cauldron and hanging her upside down doesn't seem like a sexual game. It's not a common act, and it's hard to do. I don't think the evidence points in that direction. Also, she was clothed, and she had her hiking boots on, so we can assume she wasn't abducted from Vitoria. At the very least, she must have already been in the mountains or somewhere in the vicinity. What do you think, Deputy Superintendent Salvatierra?*

"I don't have an opinion yet, Inspector," she replied.

I passed another question to Estíbaliz.

"Just one more thing," my colleague said to the head of the forensic team. "Muguruza, do you remember if the two climbers were wearing hoods?"

Peña looked puzzled and glanced at Estí and me in surprise.

"Yes, they were, theirs look just like the hoodie we found a few yards from the body. We still have to confirm that one belonged to the victim. Is it significant that all of them were hooded?"

It could be important if it turns out this was a Celtic rite. In those stories, three hooded figures carried out las Matres's water rituals, I wrote, and showed everyone.

Estíbaliz and I exchanged glances. She looked worried.

"I think I'll go to Araia immediately and interview those two climbers. They might not have told us the whole story about their encounter with Ana Belén Liaño and the Cabárceno Cauldron."

10

THE MEDIEVAL WALL GARDEN

Friday, November 18, 2016

The meeting ended when Estíbaliz left for Araia to interview the climbers. It was too soon to bring them in, but some preliminary questions were necessary. Something about their unlikely rescue attempt didn't sound right.

Though I would have liked to, I didn't accompany her because my aphasia was no help in extracting information. My colleagues gradually left the meeting room, until DSU Salvatierra and I were the only ones left.

Alba closed the door once Peña and Milán had filed out and asked me to stay in my seat.

As you wish, I indicated with a gesture.

"My superiors will expect explanations if I decide to accept Inspector Gauna's request. You're not going to be able to carry out your previous tasks in the same way. You won't be able to question people or take witness statements the way you used to. Your aphasia will attract attention wherever you go, and I'm worried about that given the gag order. You should see it as a vote of confidence that I'm not sending you home today with best wishes for a speedy recovery."

I want to be part of the case. I know I can be useful, I wrote on my screen.

"I wish you had started speech therapy months ago. That was the condition you agreed to in order to come back to work, and if you had you might have been back with us already."

I gritted my teeth. Alba was annoyed at me, and I could understand why. I was asking her to go out on a limb with Superintendent Medina, and so far, I had offered her nothing.

But the Annabel Lee case was too personal. I couldn't stay on the sidelines. That possibility simply didn't occur to me.

I knew the victim, I knew how she thought, and I knew I could be useful in hunting down whoever did this to her and her child.

Alba stared out the window at the cars speeding along Portal de Foronda. I had little daylight left, and even less patience.

I couldn't shout, so I had to write on my tablet.

You're angry because of what happened between us yesterday. I understand that. But this case has nothing to do with our situation. I don't want what we talked about to affect our working relationship as well.

I held the tablet out for her to read.

"'Affect our working relationship'? Sweet Unai, are you really that clueless? Don't you understand how *our* situation is going to affect me at work? In a month or two I won't be able to hide my pregnancy. My superiors, colleagues, and subordinates will do the math and, best-case scenario, will think that my child's father is a serial killer. Worst case, they will suspect that I had a relationship with one of my inspectors while I was married to somebody else. Do you have any idea what I'm going to have to put up with during this pregnancy? And you say you don't want it to affect our working relationship!"

She sighed, seemingly weighed down by a sense of helplessness.

"I don't know what bubble you're living in, Unai. I've accepted that this pregnancy is going to have consequences for me forever, but I decided to come back here despite that, whatever the future holds. As I said yesterday, I wanted to tell you the truth, but I am not expecting an answer from you. As far as this investigation goes,

I'll back you up; in return, you're going to start speech therapy. The neurologist recommended one-hour sessions, five times a week. I want you to stick to that, and there will be no excuses. Professionally speaking, you're a good profiler and it would be a pity to lose you."

I swallowed hard. Alba was still concerned about me. She had accepted her responsibilities, whereas I was selfishly immersed in my own drama. I admired her stoic approach to the storm of gossip that would engulf her in the next few months. She would have to endure the sly looks and the continual suspicion that her child's father was either a psychopath . . . or me.

As it happens, my first session with the speech therapist is on Monday. I made the appointment today. And you should know, Alba, that I'm doing this for the baby, whether it's mine or Nancho's. This is for the baby . . . , I wrote.

I wanted to express my gratitude, but I left the room ashamed for not having responded adequately to the situation.

An hour later, Estíbaliz called. I was lying on my sofa, trying to catch up on lost sleep, but my brain just wouldn't stop.

"Kraken, I'm still in Araia. I just spoke to both Jose Maris. I still have a couple of things to check, but there's not much more for me to do here," she mused.

She sounded disappointed.

I grunted in an effort to encourage her to continue.

"They have an alibi—and it's a good one. There is a closed-circuit camera in their workshop in case of theft, which is apparently common in the area. The father came in to work at seven that morning, and the son brought in breakfast a half hour later. Unless the autopsy proves otherwise, we believe that Ana Belén Liaño was murdered between seven and seven thirty. It couldn't have been them. They cooperated fully with the investigation, and I checked the video footage for the whole morning. They were in the work-shop until they went to climb the mountain."

I made no attempt to reply. I didn't need to, because Estí antic-ipated my questions.

"I have to check a few details, but the recording settles things pretty definitively. You can tell that the street outside is dark, and that the streetlamps are still lit. It couldn't have been them, Unai. We can't ask the judge to issue an arrest warrant. We don't have a thing unless the autopsy reveals something new."

I managed an "aha" instead of a good-bye, and Estíbaliz hung up.

So we had to rule the father and son out for now, unless they could somehow be in two places at once. This was the first wall the investigation had run into: we had to take a step back and look elsewhere.

But something else, something more intimate, more personal—more shameful as well—was pushing itself forward. It couldn't wait.

I had to deal with them. I had to tell them the news, despite the case's confidentiality. I sent a WhatsApp to all three.

Our *cuadrilla* had agreed to meet at ten o'clock that night in El Aldapa, in Cuesta, for some coffee with a shot of rum. I had no intention of going at first because I was exhausted and knew the weekend would be busy.

But once Estíbaliz shared the news with me, I knew they deserved to know. Maybe some of them knew already—maybe they were still in contact after all these years.

I couldn't ask, though, because she was taboo in the *cuadrilla*. And since she was never mentioned, I'd convinced myself that she hadn't walked Vitoria's streets in the last twenty-four years.

I would see her occasionally, but I always avoided her. That was the promise I had made, and I kept it.

So I asked them to meet me a little earlier. We agreed to gather at seven in a small garden in the old part of the city not far from the medieval wall. The garden had few visitors, and the trees would give us some privacy. I sat on a bench and waited for them to arrive.

Vitoria was already dark. A few cats were chasing shadows up the spiral staircase of the illuminated tower that stood beside the restored nineteenth-century icehouse.

Asier was the first to appear. He looked upset. Maybe I'd forced him to come before the pharmacy closed. He had been worried about his business recently. After the previous owner had retired, Asier became the owner of one of the oldest pharmacies in Vitoria in the central Calle San Francisco. He had opened a second one in the new Salburua neighborhood, but it wasn't doing very well. The pharmacy assistants quit regularly. But more seriously, according to the rumor mill, he and his wife, Araceli, were going through a rough patch. It was upsetting because she was a wonderful woman who had quickly become part of the *cuadrilla*.

Jota turned up the way he always did: a little late and a little drunk. His Friday nights always started earlier than ours, and by this time he usually had a couple of liters of alcohol in him.

"Hi!" was all he said.

He might have been embarrassed about the way he looked. He tried to tuck his shirttail into his poorly chosen sweater and smooth down what was left of his fair hair. He might have been thinking it was time to visit the barber.

Lutxo was the last to arrive, his hood up to protect him from the chilly weather. He looked gaunter than ever. Maybe he was exploring more challenging rock-climbing routes or maybe the stress at work was taking a toll. His new job as deputy editor of *El Diario Alavés* was driving him crazy. His coverage of the recent dou-

ble crimes had earned him the promotion, but since then my friend
had learned what managing a newspaper takes, and we hardly ever
saw him or his ridiculous soul patch.

Lutxo took one last drag on his cigarette. "What's going on,
Kraken? Why all the mystery?"

I patted the bench to invite him to sit next to me. This wasn't
going to be an easy conversation, and I wasn't sure how to begin.

"Yeah, over to you, Unai," said Jota, also sitting beside me.

I gestured for Asier to read what I was writing on my tablet.

This new way of communicating meant I had to be concise and
on point. People didn't want to read paragraphs, and I didn't have
the patience to write them. I came straight to the point.

Have any of you seen Ana Belén Liaño recently? I wrote.

All three of them read it, and each of them looked horrified, as
if they had eaten a nettle.

"Come on, Kraken!" Lutxo said. "You're still going on about
her? You have to get over it at some point, don't you?"

It's not what you think, I wrote quickly. *Have any of you been in
touch with Annabel Lee in the past few months? Have you heard anything
about her?*

"No way," Jota said, scratching his stubble. "She moved on
from me quickly, and once we were back in Vitoria, she barely even
said hello after the . . . well, afterward. I lost track of her centuries
ago. Has she done something?"

I ignored his question.

Asier? I wrote. *Anything to say?*

"We weren't part of her circle, Unai. She's been dead to me
for a long time. I'm not interested in having this conversation,"
he concluded.

It was hard to get any emotion out of Asier. His hooked nose,
mousy brown hair, and tough, angular physique reinforced the
impression of a cold and distant man. Even the blue suit he wore

like a uniform sent the same message. I had always been curious about why he became a pharmacist. Alleviating suffering seemed completely at odds with his emotionally detached manner.

Lutxo, you didn't answer my question, I pointed out.

"Yes, I saw her at the start of the week. What's going on, Kraken?" he protested, raising his voice.

Did she say anything that caught your attention? Did she say she was seeing anyone?

"She told me she was about to publish a new graphic novel. She was happy, which was unusual for her—" He cleared his throat. "I mean, I remembered her being reserved, not ever saying much."

She didn't tell you she was pregnant. You didn't notice?

"No, she didn't, and I didn't," he replied with a shrug. "She was wearing a black down jacket, so I couldn't tell."

"Is that what all this is about?" Asier interjected. "I agree with Lutxo, Unai. It's time you turn the page. It's been so long . . ."

This is confidential, I wrote before he could really get going, *so what I'm telling you doesn't leave this bench. Lutxo, there are witnesses to what I write, and it's here on my cell phone. Your newspaper can't leak any of this, do you understand?*

"What the hell, Unai! You're giving me goose bumps. What on earth has happened?" Jota said.

Annabel Lee was murdered. I can't give you any more details. I'm not back on the force officially, but I'm going to be consulting on the investigation. I know she was the first for each of us. Her funeral is on Sunday; I don't know if you want to go, but I think you have a right to know. Don't say a word to the rest of the cuadrilla. I wrote as quickly as I could, then waited patiently for them to finish reading.

The color drained from their faces.

I watched each of them shift nervously and put on their best poker face.

11

SANTA ISABEL CEMETERY

SUNDAY, NOVEMBER 20, 2016

That Sunday began miserably. The air was completely still, like it was holding its breath. Temperatures had dropped almost fifteen degrees overnight, and the morning chill caught me by surprise in my bed in Villaverde.

I put on the funeral suit I always kept at my grandfather's, chiefly because my family had always been buried in the tiny cemetery that lay some two hundred yards from where I slept. That was the advantage of living in such a small village: the López de Ayala family stayed close even in the next life.

I climbed the stairs to the attic, trying to avoid the creaks in the old wooden steps. I didn't want to wake my grandfather.

I hadn't been back there since we'd solved the double crimes. While I was in a coma, Grandfather must have cleared away all the old photographs and press clippings that I had spread out on the battered Ping-Pong table. All that was left were boxes of scraps from my past.

I approached the boxes carefully, making sure not to brush against the fox skins hanging from hooks in the wooden ceiling beams. I sighed as I looked for one in particular: *Cantabrian town of Cabezón de la Sal, 1992*. Opening it made Annabel Lee's death seem more real. Inside were the souvenirs from a summer that was unforgettable for reasons that were darker and more painful than they should have been.

Underneath photos of our young gang—Lutxo with hair on his head; Jota, still a spoiled boy but not yet a habitual drinker; and Asier, already serious and stiff—I found a sheet of paper signed *Annabel Lee*. A drawing of two sweethearts on a tomb opposite the cliffs of La Arnía. A girl, drawn in China ink, embraced by a man whose muscular arm had a tattoo of a Kraken on it.

When she gave me that drawing, she assumed I would get the tattoo. I still hadn't accepted the nickname. I was upset that Lutxo, who dreamed it up to make fun of the unusual length of my arms, had said it in front of her. But Annabel adopted the moniker enthusiastically—mythical origins were one of the only things that could penetrate her disdain for the outside world—and she insisted on doing the tattoo herself.

I refused.

That didn't end well.

"Grandad will give me hell if I come back with a cuttlefish drawn on my arm."

"Do you still worry about what your grandfather thinks?" she asked with contempt.

"Believe me, you'd worry, too, if you knew him," I protested.

I don't know why I kept that drawing. It was time to give it back to her.

I arrived in Vitoria a few minutes before eleven. Ana Belén was being buried in Santa Isabel Cemetery. I was surprised, since that was where wealthy, aristocratic families were buried. I recalled the Edgar Allan Poe poem she adored that spoke of the young girl's noble ancestry. Maybe she had more in common with Annabel Lee than I knew.

I put on my nicest trench coat with a hood, in case the weather god unleashed his fury. The police team was posted at the entrance to the traditional burial ground. Estíbaliz, Peña, and Milán were dressed for the occasion and looked as cold as I was. They kept glancing at the white sky that was threatening an early snow.

Milán looked uncomfortable wearing something other than her usual jeans. She was the first to speak. She took a bright orange Post-it from her huge down jacket.

"I looked into Ana Belén's social media. Two months ago, she announced her pregnancy with a drawing of a woman with long hair and a prominent belly sitting on a tomb facing a cliff. I couldn't find any negative comments," she said.

I thanked her with a smile and wrote to Estí: *Anything else?*

"I'll tell you later," she answered briefly.

"I spent the weekend going through all of Annabel Lee's illustrations," said Peña. "There are some references to Celts and hanged men in her first published works, but only small details. I didn't come across any plotlines that had the slightest connection to what happened to her. Nor were there any pregnancies or fertility rites. Her editor"—he pointed to an overweight man in his sixties who seemed very upset—"has been hit hard by her death. He was apparently very fond of her. When I interviewed him, he was still in shock. He's about to retire and only works on the projects he's particularly interested in. Malatrama is a small publishing house, and it may not survive without her strong sales. But I don't think we should include him on our list of suspects. He's clearly a good-natured guy, and he has an alibi for that Thursday morning. His wife, who's also a saint, corroborated his story with airline tickets. They were at a convention in Barcelona."

Thank you, Peña. That's good information, I wrote.

I could tell from the dark circles under his eyes and the heightened trembling of his hand that he had spent a couple of sleepless nights on Annabel Lee's work.

We followed the procession at a distance through avenues of cypress and arbutus. Annabel's only relative appeared to be her mother, who looked like a carbon copy of her daughter, but twenty years older. She had long dark hair with bangs that covered her eyes, black leather pants, and a denim jacket that featured a Dryades MC design. *The female druids,* I translated. As far as I could tell, she was now the leader of an exclusively female motorcycle club.

How strange. Annabel Lee had always insisted she was the opposite of her mother, but I saw a clone. Annabel's superpower was self-deception: if there was some part of reality she didn't like, she turned and twisted it until she believed it, and then she sold it to the world with astonishing conviction.

It struck me that there were no other women at the funeral. I saw several men around my age respectfully keeping their distance. Who were they? Friends, former boyfriends?

It wasn't clear. Of course, there was no mention of her identity in the press, and nobody had posted about it on social media. How long would it take her followers to miss her?

I stayed in the background and watched as the earth swallowed up Annabel Lee's coffin. Directly opposite the site, a pair of winged sphinxes seemed to be staring straight at her.

At that moment, a kind of poetic miracle occurred: it began to snow, and Vitoria became the white city once more.

The first snowflakes of winter settled on the dark wood of her coffin as gently as feathers. They fell on my shoulders and on the surprised heads of everyone there. It wasn't a heavy snowfall, but it caused a strange shift in the atmosphere—as though in her final journey Annabel Lee was sharing her gothic view of life and death with us.

I didn't realize Jota and Lutxo were standing on either side of me. Jota seemed to have come straight from a night on the town. He'd gone home to change into a suit, but he must have forgotten to shower, because he smelled of enough *kalimotxo* to raise the dead.

Lutxo had no more dressed for a funeral than for Thursday *pintxo-pote*. I wondered if he was there as a journalist or as one of Annabel's exes.

We stood there, three hooded figures facing her body.

In the end, you didn't have your sepulchre by the sounding sea, I reminded her.

Twenty-four years earlier I had promised her: "You and I will never speak again."

It was a promise I kept, but knowing that just made bile rise in my throat.

Don't you see? I wanted to say to my friends. *We'll never feel like we did when we were sixteen. We thought all love affairs would be as epic, with sleepless nights, unbridled lust, and aching tongues. But it didn't turn out like that for any of us. At least not like it was with her, not like the first time for the four of us.*

Speaking of the fourth horseman of the Apocalypse, Asier hadn't shown up.

I was most surprised to see Alba, elegant as ever in her white down jacket. Estíbaliz whispered that she had come as our official representative. Superintendent Medina didn't want to be seen at the funeral and arouse suspicion that Annabel Lee's death was the subject of an investigation. Alba offered her condolences to Annabel's mother and started walking in our direction.

I left my friends and went up to her. I didn't know what to say. That cemetery made me nervous. I wondered whether the angel carved on the Unzueta family vault had anything to do with my uneasiness. Its gaze, according to legend, was fatal.

"Have you visited Nancho's grave?" she whispered, staring dead ahead.

I shook my head. I hadn't even wondered what happened to his body. I missed the postmortem during my coma, and afterward I didn't want to know anything about him.

"His brother Ignacio came to see me in the hospital the day after his death," she sighed. "Tasio was extremely ill for the first few days, so his twin took care of everything. Ignacio asked me if I wanted to handle arrangements with the funeral directors, and when I said no, he asked for permission to bury Nancho with his maternal family, Díaz de Antoñana. He told me they were going to remove their mother's remains from the Unzueta vault and transfer them to her family's crypt. I know he was buried with the name Venancio Urbina, but I haven't been to see him. I haven't been back to Manuel Iradier, either."

I frowned. I didn't understand.

"My husband and I lived on Calle Manuel Iradier, but I haven't even been able to walk past the doorway. I have a new wardrobe, new books, an apartment on Calle Prado . . . I have a new future. But I still avoid Manuel Iradier, and I almost can't believe I found the strength to come here this morning. I suppose my position has its obligations."

I was about to reply when Estíbaliz darted over and pushed between us.

"Good morning, Deputy Superintendent Salvatierra. I don't think we can do much more here. A few friends of the victim, all men, are here, but when we tried to talk to them, they scattered like teenagers caught in a broth— Well, you know what I mean. I don't think they wanted to be seen here. The mother doesn't seem too affected. She says it's been decades since they had anything to do with each other."

"Decades," Alba repeated. "So she really was completely independent. Do you have anything new to report?"

"There's a cold case that caught my attention because it's so similar. And it's good you're here, Unai, because I want your opinion. I started searching for similar victims: young, pregnant women, unmarried . . . But I also concentrated on the killer's modus operandi: hanging the victims by their feet, head down, hands tied behind their back, no gunshot or knife wounds, whose bodies appeared in places with historical associations."

And . . . ? I asked by raising my eyebrows.

Estíbaliz showed us some photos on her cell phone.

"I came across an unusual case that was never solved. I almost didn't notice it even though the press was involved, but it came up when I was comparing databases we share with other provinces. In April 1993, a fourteen-year-old girl disappeared in Cantabria. Her father believed she had run away from home. She was unstable, with a history of mental problems. Everyone thought she would return home or be found within a few days. Instead, an anonymous person sent these photos to the local newspaper, *El Periódico Cántabro.* They decided to hand them over to the police rather than publish them. It was determined that the photos were taken in—"

Fontibre, I thought, immediately recognizing it.

What I said aloud was something that sounded like a tuneless, strident "Foigbrre." Alba and Estíbaliz both turned toward me. I could have died of embarrassment.

"Unai, you're speaking again!" said Estíbaliz, looking like she'd won the lottery.

Alba said nothing, but for a split second I saw such relief on her face that I stared at her, stunned. I had no idea it would mean so much to her.

That's not speaking, Estí. That's all I can do right now, but next week I start my speech therapy, I wrote as quickly as I could on my cell phone.

I cleared my throat and pointed again to the photos Estí had shown us: the body of a young girl hanging from the bough of an ash tree, her feet tied with rope.

Her head was partially submerged in a river, and her hands

were tied behind her back. The photos were taken from various angles, and in one of them I could clearly see the distinctive colored ribbons left by the faithful at the ancient site.

"I spoke to the inspector who led the investigation back then, a man by the name of Pablo Lanero."

Paulaner, I thought.

I know him, I wrote.

During my profiler training at the headquarters in Santander, Inspector Pablo Lanero and I got along well. His beer belly gave many people the impression that he was a buffoon. Far from it. Paulaner, named after the German beer with the monk on the label, was good-natured, calm, and intelligent. He accepted his nickname stoically and went on with his life. He earned my complete respect. I knew he was close to retirement these days and was glad to hear about him again.

"He sends his regards. He gave me the official report on the case. When the police went to Fontibre, they found the rope still hanging from the tree, but no body. Someone had removed it. The girl was never found, but one thing about the photos worried me. It's not mentioned in the report, but the way her shirt hangs leaves her torso bare, and it's clear to me she's pregnant. Maybe it was relatively early on, but a slender girl of fourteen doesn't have a protruding stomach like that. What do you two think?"

Alba and I had more experience with pregnancy than Estíbaliz, and we both agreed that once again we were looking at a pregnant female hanging by the feet with her head submerged in water. It was twenty-three years earlier in another province, but it was a distinctive MO. When I'd first seen Annabel's body, I'd been afraid that this hadn't been the killer's first victim.

I didn't know if he left footprints or tire marks at the scene of the crime because the storm had erased everything. I didn't know whether we were looking for someone who had forensic knowledge or someone we could have caught in a few hours. But it seemed like a complex, well-executed ritual for a first-time killer.

"Do you have any more information? The name of the victim and her parents? Are they still alive? Can you interview them?" asked Alba.

"The girl's name was Rebeca Tovar Pereda. Her mother died a couple of years before she did, and her father was . . ."

Saúl, I said to myself, swallowing hard. Saúl Tovar, the director of our summer camp in the Cantabrian town of Cabezón de la Sal in the summer of 1992, less than a year before his poor daughter died.

12

THE ISLE OF MAN

Thursday, July 2, 1992

Unai had to admit that Annabel Lee took her work seriously. Every morning at six, she stretched out on her skull-decorated sleeping bag and started creating plots and characters in a tall spiral notebook, lit by a battered miner's headlamp that an archaeology student had left.

She drew every day. Without fail, even if the previous evening had lasted well into the early hours.

Unai, who usually got up before dawn with the lark, watched with one eye open as she juggled the black and gray felt-tip pens on her solitary bunk bed, set apart from the *cuadrilla*'s.

"I don't understand what you're doing in Cantabria," he whispered to her, after stealing silently out of his sleeping bag and crossing to her bed.

"I'm hunting crocodiles."

"It's far too early for me to understand the metaphor. Spell it out for me."

"It's not my metaphor. I heard it once from Angel Zapata, my creative-writing teacher. He used to say you have to put crocodiles into stories to keep the reader's attention."

"Crocodiles."

"Crocodiles. Imagine I'm drawing a story where someone

enters a hotel room. I carefully draw the drapes, a chest of drawers, a ten-foot crocodile asleep on the bed, a carpet, a mirror . . . What stays in your mind? What are you wondering right now?"

"What on earth is a crocodile doing sleeping on a hotel bed?"

"There you go. I'm hunting crocodiles for my stories. Every year I go to the Isle of Man with my mother for a dig. They give grants to people from all over the world: it's a tiny island in the Irish Sea, and you can find both Celtic and Viking artifacts there. It was on the Isle of Man that I realized I could find lots of crocodiles for my work in ancient history."

"And why do you visit the Isle of Man every year?" Unai asked. He hoped she wouldn't be able to tell that he had never heard of the place before. Despite the fact that they were probably the same age, Annabel had lived a more exciting life than he had.

She gave up shading the face of an angel she was drawing, frowning slightly.

"The thing is, my mother is the leader of a motorcycle club, an MC."

"Motorcycles."

"Harley-Davidson. Have you ever heard of them?"

"I didn't know there were female bikers."

"There aren't many female club leaders, but the ones out there are formidable, like my mother. I was born in Vitoria, where she keeps an apartment, but after I met you in preschool, I traveled all over Europe and Asia with her and her club. She's basically a nomad. For the past hundred years, they've held one of the most dangerous motorcycle races in the world on the Isle of Man, and every year tons of clubs meet there. We practically invade an island that's fifteen miles wide by forty or so long. It's hard not to fall off the edge of a cliff. Literally, there's not enough room for all of us," she said offhandedly, as if it were an old, well-worn joke.

"Wow, what a life you've led."

"I hate it. I'm fed up with being a nomad, I want to settle in Vitoria and never move again. I hate bikes, I hate the smell of gas and secondhand leather, beer . . ."

"You hate everything that has anything to do with your mother," Unai concluded.

"I do. They say there are two kinds of mother-daughter relationships. One is when the two are the same kind of woman: conformist with conformist, or rebel with rebel. And the other is when they're opposite: conformist mother with rebel daughter, or vice versa. My mother and I are oil and water."

"What about your father?" Unai asked. He didn't know whether she trusted him enough to let him pry into her personal life.

"I don't want to talk about my father with you. For all intents and purposes, he was never there for me," she said. "That's why I came to this camp. I want to save the money I'm making here, and as soon as I'm old enough, I'll leave my mother and stay in her Vitoria apartment. Ultimately, I want to live off my graphic novels. You don't need that much money to live."

At an age when Unai was still deciding whether to study agricultural engineering or forestry, Annabel Lee had seen it all and was ready to rest her weary bones.

As Unai crawled back into his sleeping bag, he realized the others had stopped snoring. They had probably all pricked their ears to listen.

Unperturbed, Annabel went back to drawing her granite angel.

Saúl assigned Jota and Annabel to replace the roof on the round Iron Age hut. They spent the first days a couple of yards off the ground, working closely together so they wouldn't fall off the narrow ladder. Annabel passed Jota the broom branches, and with painstaking precision, he laid them down like fish scales. Annabel was bored by repetitive manual tasks. If she didn't have to use her imagination, she ran out of patience quickly.

"Why don't you bring that swanky camera of yours to the settlement tomorrow, so you can take photos of everything we're doing?" she suggested.

"I've already taken group photos," Jota protested from the top of the roof.

"I'm not talking about photos for a souvenir album. I'm talking about photographing all the different textures we see here: ancient materials, wheat sheaves, wood, muddy hands . . . I mean artistic photos."

"I don't know how to take artistic photos. I'm not creative like you."

"Come on, we're all creative. I'll teach you how to take photos manually, to control the aperture and speed. We'll go to Santillana del Mar one day. I'm sure we could buy different ISOs or black-and-white film. Then you can take close-ups, capture gestures midaction . . . You just have to develop your eye, Jota. Anybody can do it."

"Well, if you'll teach me," he said.

Jota was finally enjoying himself. The Celtic village. Annabel Lee. He was enchanted by the story of her name.

Over the next few days, Jota took direction from his new creative mentor, who had him photograph every creature, living or dead. All signs of his bad temper, depression, and worry simply vanished.

The sky Jota saw in those first days was finally a deep azure, clear of the storm clouds waiting for him in Vitoria.

Jota was in such a good mood that he even managed to make time for Rebeca, Saúl's young daughter. They had sat next to each other on the first evening and now always ate together.

Jota was kindhearted, and he felt sorry for her. He could see how lonely she was. She seemed lost in a world that was too big for her. Plus, she was Saúl's daughter. Jota had already begun to worship Saúl—the cool professor, the young, devoted father, the attractive guy who pretended not to notice the way Annabel Lee and the female university students looked at him during their almost daily visits to the camp.

"Rebeca, can you come help Annabel and me tomorrow with the roof of the hut? We're stuck and need an expert like you," said Jota cheerfully.

Rebeca was taken aback, but concealed her surprise as she polished off the last piece of cake on the buffet table. She was still waiting for Sunday to arrive, when her father brought her favorite coconut *paluco* cookies from Cabezón.

"Of course I'll help you. I laid lots of roofs last year," she said, delighted. Smiling, her cheeks flushed.

Later that night, curled up in her sleeping bag, Rebeca thought, *Maybe I was wrong to tell Asier my secret. Maybe I should tell Jota. His family must have contacts who could help me.*

In his sleeping bag, Jota was thinking of her fondly: *What a remarkable girl Saúl's daughter is. And what a guy he is. If only he were my father, she and I could be brother and sister.*

The weekend arrived, and the far-sighted Saúl Tovar gave them some time off from adobe walls and Celtic roofs. He loaded them into the minibus and took them to Oñati in Guipúzcoa, close to the border with Álava. They were all grateful for the excursion and the chance to give their calloused hands a rest.

Saúl hadn't told Rebeca they were going to visit the cave at Sandaili. He didn't want her to refuse and cause a scene. Saúl couldn't tolerate anything that tarnished his public image. It had taken a lot to build up his reputation . . .

She sat beside him while he talked and kept her amused for the two-hour drive.

The landscape didn't change much. Eucalyptus and pine trees were replaced by oaks and beeches, their branches brushing against the windshield when the road narrowed. A magnificent summer's day for what promised to become an unforgettable memory.

"I'm really glad you came along," Saúl admitted to Rebeca, scratching the beard he always grew during the summer holidays. He considered the time a respite from having to shave, and his beard grew in so thick it soon covered his features. He lifted his right hand from the gear shift and extended it.

Rebeca stared at the hand. She looked at it a lot. It was big and rugged, the hand of an educated giant. For some time now, she had been obsessed by hands. She was embarrassed to admit that she classified people according to their hands.

If their hands are similar to my dad's, I don't like them.

If they're different, I'll give them a chance.

But at camp, her father was charming. He was always kind and helpful toward his only daughter, even though she could sometimes be capricious. *Buy me this book; why don't you take me here and there?* He constantly indulged her. Nothing was too good for his princess.

"Thanks for these past few days, Papa," she said, squeezing his hand. "Really and truly. Thanks for bringing me to the Cantabrian village and allowing me to do what I enjoy most."

"How could I not? It's you and me now. And your aunt. Just don't do it again, don't betray me. You and your aunt are all I have," he repeated. "Things wouldn't be the same without you. You know I love you, I love you very much, child."

Don't call me that. I'm not a child, she wanted to tell him. But she kept quiet and withdrew her hand instead.

He kept driving, and they both sat in silence. Rebeca was beginning to recognize the bends in the highway and was growing nervous about their destination.

"Where are we going?"

"To the Sandaili cave."

Rebeca swallowed. Her cheeks flushed.

Not to the Sandaili cave, Bluebeard, she thought. She tried to stifle her panic.

Not to Sandaili, not to that basin underneath the stalactites that shed their watery tears. That was where it had all begun.

13

TXAGORRITXU

SATURDAY, NOVEMBER 19, 2016

Kraken! Kraken! Kraken!" The shouts could be heard all the way down the long corridor. Two women, a redhead and a brunette, emerged from a screaming man's room, trying to appear calm.

That was a terrible idea, thought Estíbaliz as they hurried down the hallway.

She tugged on Alba's arm. Her friend had pretended not to notice how embarrassing the situation was when they were standing at the Alzheimer patient's bedside. But now the two women hurried into the metal elevator like souls coming up from hell for a breath of fresh air.

Alba had agreed to accompany Estíbaliz to the Txagorritxu facility on her weekly visit to her father. It wasn't that Estí didn't feel safe; it was just that her father wasn't as violent when strangers were around. Today she was spared the usual end to her visit—calling the nurse to give him a sedative.

As they descended the stairs to the entrance, Estí and Alba noticed a woman staring at them. Around sixty, she wore an enormous garishly colored scarf. She started screaming at them, shouting insults and waving her hands in the air.

"Unbelievable! You took us all in!" she shouted, pointing a finger at Alba.

"Are you talking to me?" Alba asked.

"Yes, I'm talking to you. You're Superintendent Salvatierra, aren't you?"

"Deputy superintendent," Alba corrected her.

"You came to the funeral of my son, Mateo Ruíz de Zuazo. You comforted me."

And with that, Alba and Estíbaliz instantly remembered her. Her son was one of the thirty-year-old victims murdered beneath the Virgen Blanca's marble niche during the August festivities.

"You promised me you'd catch the culprit . . . and you were sleeping with him the whole time," the woman continued, shaking with rage. "Why aren't you in prison?"

"Because I'm not guilty of anything, *señora*," Alba responded slowly and deliberately. Someone had to stay calm.

"And the judge believed you?"

"I was never a suspect. I didn't know about my ex-husband's crimes. I understand your pain, but—"

"You can't fool me! Until you lose a child of your own, you won't understand a thing."

Alba turned away. Her mind was on the house at Laguardia where she had hidden from the world, gazing at Unai's mountains. She protected her stomach with her hand unconsciously. "I'm sorry that you see it that way, but I kept my promise to you. We caught your son's murderer, at a high personal cost, I might add."

"Bullshit! You must have known something. Killers' wives always pretend to be innocent. Nobody can commit twenty murders without somebody suspecting something."

She's not going to listen to reason, Alba told herself. *This isn't personal. I'm the closest she's ever going to get to confronting her son's killer. It's not personal.*

"Again, I'm sorry that you see it that way. Good evening, *señora*," she said, politely but firmly.

They left the woman behind and entered a garden surrounded

by pines. The morning snow still lay on a few branches. They found
a bench covered in chipped green paint that was hidden from the
faltering gaze of the home's aging population.

"Is this the first time that's happened to you?" Estíbaliz asked.

"Don't worry about it. Let's just sit here. I need a break from
all this tension. I wasn't expecting this month to be so stressful."

Estíbaliz sat beside her. They stayed silent for a while, but Alba
didn't want to waste the opportunity.

In her line of work, she had to have uncomfortable conversations every day, and she knew Estíbaliz would be able to handle it.
"Estí, your father used to beat you, didn't he?"

Estí turned and took a small pine cone from the nearest tree
and began fiddling with it. She showed her nerves at her fingertips,
whether with a pen, a hair tie . . . they always gave her away.

"Is it that obvious?" she finally admitted.

"You didn't go near him. You sat there stiff as a board. I think
you're still afraid of him. I've seen it in lots of victims."

"I'm not a victim," Estíbaliz shot back. She had often repeated
that mantra to her reflection in the mirror. "My father has Alzheimer's. I could overpower him easily. I'm not afraid of him."

Alba wasn't convinced.

"Is that why you specialized in victimology?"

Estíbaliz finally surrendered. She let down her guard and
opened the gate to her fortress. "I wanted to know what made me
a victim so that I would never be one again, not with any man."

Alba put her hand on her friend's thigh, as though to say *I'm
here. You can tell me.* Her calm, warm touch helped Estíbaliz to
continue.

"You know," Estíbaliz said, after reflecting for a moment, "I
think that even if you're born with a survivor's mentality and you
try to resist being beaten or abused . . . the reality of childhood is
that you weigh forty-five pounds, and you can't stop an adult who

wants to hurt you. And I think that it goes on every day—domestic violence, abuse that is never detected or reported, mothers or fathers who look the other way. When they're so physically powerless, how can children avoid becoming victims? It's impossible. And then afterward there are psychological consequences for victims who would not otherwise have exhibited pathological traits."

Alba nodded. She knew all about pathological traits. "Your ex-boyfriend, Iker . . . he was a good guy, wasn't he?"

"He couldn't hurt a fly."

"That was why you allowed him in, because you felt safe in that relationship. You knew he'd never raise a hand to you. You were looking for a protector."

"Are you a psychologist?"

"To a certain extent in our line of work, we all are," Alba said.

"Well, you answered your own question, didn't you?"

"But you broke up with him a few months ago. So you must feel stronger now."

Estíbaliz nodded, raising her hand to the silver *eguzkilore* pendant around her neck.

"After Eneko died, I started feeling stronger. He protected me from my father, but he also introduced me to drugs. Really though, I was hooked on him, on the protection he could offer me. That's why I haven't taken any drugs since he died. I'm sure I'll never use again; they no longer hold any appeal to me. Unai still doesn't trust me, though, he doesn't understand that my addiction was inextricably connected to Eneko, and now I'm clean. My brother's death released me from him and from my need for protection.

"That was why I broke up with Iker a few weeks later. I realized that I've grown up because of this job and because of everything that I've experienced. Look at me: I'm just over five feet. I'll never be as strong as the guys we take down; anyone could beat me up. But I no longer live in a world where somebody who weighs a hundred pounds more than me can kick me every morning if I refuse to eat stale crackers."

"And yet you still choose good guys like Unai. You still love him, don't you?"

The pine cone slipped through Estíbaliz's fingers. What was the point in lying to Alba? "How did you guess?" she asked.

"When your father used to beat you, you yelled 'Kraken.' You wanted him to rescue you—that's how your father remembers his nickname. He remembers you screaming it."

"That's true, to an extent. Calling his name was like an escape, a way of getting through the worst of it. But I never expected him to come and save me. My relationship with him has never been about that."

There was no trace of bitterness, hostility, or rivalry in her tone. She considered Alba a friend she could talk to about anything. At last she could tell the truth. She'd found a confidante who wouldn't judge her.

"Unai is the only man I've ever loved. I've been in love with him since I was thirteen. Eneko and Lutxo used to go climbing together, and we would occasionally meet up with Unai. That was during the first wave of double crimes."

She didn't say *When your husband first started killing children* because she considered Alba to be one of Nancho's first victims.

"Unai was twenty," she continued, picking up another pine cone. "I had nothing to do with him. I tried for the longest time not to love him, especially when he started going out with Paula, who was one of my closest friends. I felt uncomfortable around both of them and tried to stay out of the way. When she died, I wanted to go with her. I could see Unai's grief, how that horrific accident destroyed him, how he took the death of his children . . . I thought I was going to die when I saw him grieving like that. He wanted it all to end, so he wouldn't suffer anymore. But together we all saved him—his grandfather, Germán, the *cuadrilla*, the peaceful rhythm of life in Villaverde. He leaned on us, and let us help him. That's how I know this Broca's aphasia won't be the end of him. He's no stranger to devastating setbacks. He just gets stronger and tougher, like his grandfather. Unai will live to be a hundred. When he retires, he'll go and live in his village, and no one will have been able to vanquish him."

Smiling, Alba put her arm around Estí and hugged her. Estí rested her head on her friend's shoulder.

"I always knew," said Alba. "What about him, does he know?"

"Unai's a man. He has no idea," said Estíbaliz with a smile and a shrug.

"That's true, he's so . . . unaware. That's why we can't help but love him, isn't it? Because he would never deliberately hurt us," said Alba.

"Yes, I think that's it. But listen, this doesn't mean our friendship's over, does it? Tell me it doesn't. It's such a cliché to think that women have to be rivals," Estíbaliz said.

"Not as far as I'm concerned. You care for him, and he cares for you. You're the best friend he could possibly have. I want you in his life. I want you to love him. It's not my place to say anything. He's chosen you: you're family to him, like a sister, and so much more than a friend."

"Yes, I've always been willing to take a supporting role," Estíbaliz sighed. Alba laughed. "I'm not joking. When he met Paula, he couldn't even see me. He kept telling me about the relationship, and so did Paula. They were crazy about each other, and I was in the middle, first as a confidante and then as the maid of honor—in a purple dress!

"You know what? I joined the Arkaute police academy because of him, so I could be at his side every day until I retired. Every single day. I saw him more than Paula did. He told me secrets he couldn't tell her. I love him too much to sleep with him and risk losing it all. I love everything about him, and I have everything I've ever wanted. I see him every day, I can call him any time. I can sit by his hospital bed, have lunch with him every day of the week. I have the person I love by my side, and I know that's how it's going to be for the rest of our lives. Believe me, it's not a consolation prize."

"And you deserve it. You're two good people who care for each other. If at some point I'm gone, if I fall by the wayside, I know you'll still be there, taking care of him."

"What do you mean if you fall by the wayside? . . . Is something wrong, Alba?" Estíbaliz pulled away from her.

"What could possibly be wrong? It's just an expression," Alba reassured her. "And that's enough about men. We said we wouldn't discuss them. Let's talk about something else, shall we?"

"Well, since we're confessing things, there's something I wanted to know . . . As my boss, you won't be angry, will you?"

"Spit it out, Estíbaliz. What's bothering you?"

"You've never asked me about my substance problems. Some of them are detailed in my file."

"I keep an eye on you. If you ever showed up under the influence, we would have a talk—I have zero tolerance. But I find the best way to deal with it is to bury you under mounds of work and responsibilities so you won't have time to think about anything else."

"Is that why you put me in charge of this case?"

"I assigned it to you because it's going to be complicated. And you have reinforcements. Use them. Don't burn yourself out like Unai did. Let's see if you can delegate better than he could, all right?"

"All right," said Estíbaliz.

She was happy to accept any advice Alba had for her. Her inspector's uniform felt too big.

"I assume that you need a goal to focus all your extra energy on anyway. I'm thinking about doing something with victimology. Maybe get you involved in a project to help protect young girls from abuse. I've been mulling over an idea for some time now. Maybe you and I could put it into practice."

"What kind of idea?"

"I'd like to create a Prevention Unit that would go into schools. We could start in Álava, where I'm based and have contacts. I'd like to educate the staff about how abuse occurs in the home. I thought we could use extracurricular activities to foster awareness among teachers so they recognize and act on the warning signs. I'd like to educate the boys so they don't become jealous, possessive, or machismo, and to boost the girls' self-esteem in the hopes that they won't put up with abusive behavior. I thought we could give talks, maybe run short self-defense classes in the schools . . . What do you think?"

Estíbaliz smiled, although her thoughts were far away. She was back in her house on the slopes of Monte Gorbea. Curled up in a ball, the little girl she had once been also smiled at her. Maybe she would never have to call out to Kraken again.

14

PORTÍO BEACH

MONDAY, NOVEMBER 21, 2016

Estíbaliz and I left for Cantabria early in the morning. We had two places to visit.

She was at the wheel even though I had felt confident driving since the first week of my leave in Villaverde. I might not have been able to talk, but I refused to make things more difficult for my family. I practiced driving for days on the farm tracks between Villaverde and Villafria, raising dust with the Outlander even though changing gears was difficult with my weak right side. Fortunately, it was like riding a bike, and things got easier the more I practiced.

Even so, I hadn't traveled outside Álava since then, and I was glad that Estí was driving our patrol car.

I put the address of the Cantabrian Archaeological Museum into the GPS. I wanted to talk to the head of the place, Héctor del Castillo, who was a historian and a friend. Tasio had been out of the profession for too long to have the information I needed. Héctor would help me.

He always had.

I trusted him.

We had also arranged to meet Inspector Pablo Lanero, Paulaner. We needed to figure out how we were going to work together on the investigation.

We headed for Bilbao, then passed by Castro Urdiales and Laredo. We skirted Santander Bay via El Astillero and turned off toward Liencres when we reached Santa Cruz de Bezana.

From there we drove to Portío beach on the Costa Quebrada, a spot I knew well. An imposing red building that had once belonged to the Marquis de Mouro, a nineteenth-century Spanish colonial returnee, was perched on the edge of a towering cliff. His initials were still legible on the wooden door that marked the entrance.

Estíbaliz was delighted by the view. She parked near the museum's front lawn and jumped out. I knew it was always windy there, but the sight of Estí near the jagged cliffs and the *urros*, as people in Cantabria call the sea stacks visible offshore, was too striking to ignore.

"Wow!" she said, standing on the cliff edge.

"Yes," I said. It was easy for me to say *yes*. The soft *Y* and unemphatic vowel didn't make me sound like a turkey.

Estí glanced at me sympathetically. I think she was pleased with my attempts to speak.

The wind was too warm for November, but it felt good to inhale the salty air. It looked as if the rain was going to start at any moment.

I was overwhelmed by the memories that came flooding back now that I was on this coast, a place that had been so important to me all those years ago. I had unfinished business with the god of that sea that I had avoided for two decades. The Cantabrian Sea was still a threatening, treacherous place. I tried to hide my discomfort.

Estí didn't know anything.

I had never told her.

And I was really annoyed that Lutxo had shared those secrets with her brother, the Eguzkilore.

Another car parked alongside ours, and Paulaner struggled out of it. He had put on a lot of weight since I'd seen him last, and he seemed clumsier. He'd grown one of those strange beards without a mustache that covered his whole jaw. The beard made him look even more like the monk in the beer ads.

"My dear Unai," he boomed, embracing me. "I'm so glad to see you again!"

I made a gesture meant to express the same thing. Paulaner looked at me in alarm.

"Oh, that's right . . . you can't speak. I knew that. I'm sorry, my boy. Really sorry."

I shrugged and smiled, trying to conceal how awkward I felt. I didn't like to see how my injury affected those who cared about me. It reminded me of how little I'd done over the last few months.

"I'm Inspector Gauna." Estíbaliz stepped in, extending her hand.

"Pleased to meet you. Take good care of our colleague here. We think a lot of him in these parts," he said, giving her a pat on the back that almost sent her flying.

"Yes, we make sure to do that," she replied with a smile.

"Well, then, let's go talk to Héctor del Castillo. I'm really grateful to you for solving the theft of the Cabárceno Cauldron. The media haven't given us much information about it, but if such an iconic piece hadn't reappeared, my superiors would have thrown me to the wolves."

"The truth is, we would have preferred to find the cauldron under different circumstances," said Estíbaliz. "We still don't know where all this leads. Oh, and by the way, thank your colleague for the file on the girl at Fontibre."

"That's what we're here for," said Paulaner, scratching his beard. "He said something about a cold case, but I didn't work on it back then."

"Let's go see if Héctor del Castillo can tell us more."

I had sent Héctor an e-mail the day before, as soon as Estí and I decided we needed to visit Cantabria, and he had replied quickly.

We entered the restored building and headed to Héctor's office on the fourth floor.

We found him staring out his office window at the spectacular view. He turned and gave me a pleasant, easy smile.

Several years older than I was, Héctor was short, with fair hair, light brown eyes, and a square chin. His formal style made him appear serious, even though his manner was relaxed. He was thoughtful, and nothing ever seemed to bother him. I wanted to discuss what I'd seen in the San Adrián Tunnel with him because of his archaeological expertise.

"Inspector Lanero," Héctor greeted Paulaner with a smile. "Inspector Ayala, you can't imagine how pleased I am to see you again. Welcome back. Did you miss us?"

We shook hands warmly, and I nodded.

He didn't seem to notice my inability to speak, but Estí came to my rescue before things became awkward.

"I'm Inspector Estíbaliz Ruíz de Gauna. I'm leading an investigation that involves an item stolen from this museum: the Cabárceno Cauldron. Inspector Ayala is one of our experts. He is still recovering from aphasia caused by a brain injury sustained on the job. He can't speak, sir."

"There's no need to be so formal with me, I'm not that old," Héctor replied, inviting us to take a seat in the chairs set in front of the huge walnut desk. He sat in a large leather armchair. "I was aware of Inspector Ayala's condition, but I thought it unnecessary to mention it when he contacted me yesterday. It's been impossible to ignore the media frenzy over the past few months about the crimes committed in Vitoria. Inspector Ayala, what's the best way for us to communicate?"

I'll write on my cell phone, show it to you, and you answer, I typed rapidly, and Héctor smiled.

"Where there's a will, there's a way," he murmured. "So be it."

"Last Friday we contacted you and the director of the Regional

Museum of Prehistory to inform you that the stolen object had been recovered," said Paulaner. "Our forensic unit and the Historical Heritage officers are coordinating with the technicians to return the cauldron and have it properly restored as soon as the Vitoria police have all the details they need for their investigation."

"Correct," replied Héctor.

"Inspector Lanero has given us a report that contains your sworn statement as well as the statements of all the museum employees, so we won't dwell on that," said Estíbaliz. "As far as I know, the cauldron was displayed in a glass case as part of a temporary exhibit on the Celtic-Iberian culture of the Cantabrian coast. The room doesn't have CCTV. I know you have made the recordings from the cameras at the entrance to the museum available, but there's nothing unusual there, just visitors and staff. We also took prints from all the window frames the thief could have escaped through, but have found no matches."

"That's right. This museum is family-run and financed by the estate of my deceased brother, Jairo del Castillo, who was a well-known philanthropist. But we don't have the economic resources of other public museums, so our security measures are limited to cameras at the entrance and security guards who make daily rounds. We don't have guards patrolling at night. We've never needed to. It was especially sad that we were robbed of that particular piece. Besides the sentimental value it has for me as a Cantabrian historian, it was on loan from the Regional Museum of Prehistory, so the theft put us in an awkward position. You can't imagine how relieved I am that you've found it. Although if two inspectors from the Criminal Investigation Unit have come all the way from Vitoria just to talk to us, I'm concerned about the circumstances surrounding its recovery. I suppose that's what you want to discuss with me?"

I nodded. Nothing ever escaped Héctor. You could say he had a panoramic view of events.

"What we're going to talk about here is confidential and classified. The examining magistrate has declared that nothing is to be made public," Estíbaliz warned him.

"I understand perfectly. You can count on my discretion. How was the cauldron used?" Héctor said. "In water rituals?"

"What did you say?" asked Estíbaliz.

"I was asking if the cauldron has been used in some kind of ritual involving water."

We don't know whether there was a ritual, but we found a body near the cauldron, I wrote, showing him the text.

"Hanging by the feet, possibly from the branch of a tree?"

"Possibly, yes. Possibly," said Estíbaliz. She was as stunned as I was.

Paulaner shifted uncomfortably in his seat.

Héctor glanced at us with concern and rose from his chair. He searched the thick tomes on the bookshelves and then placed a book on the desk called *Atlas of Archaeology*. He opened it to a full-color illustration of a cauldron that looked similar to the Cabárceno one, only with more decoration.

"This is the Gundestrup Cauldron, found in Denmark in 1891. Look at this silver relief: it shows the god Taranis, the main god of the Celts, and a warrior in a cauldron."

Estíbaliz and I saw an imposing figure holding a man by the feet and pushing his head into the cauldron.

Héctor turned the page and showed us a similar illustration, in which a figure was holding up a pair of cauldrons.

"If you want a more modern example, there's the Moñes Diadem, found in Asturias in the nineteenth century. It's also Celtic, but from the Castro Urial, dating anywhere between the third and the first centuries BC. These were propitiatory rites, related to fertility. Water symbolized sperm, and the creation of life."

"Does it have anything to do with the cult of las Matres?"

"The Three Mothers? Of course, that cult was common throughout areas influenced by Celtic culture, and the Cantabrian coast is no exception. The Romans later adopted the cult, which persisted in votive altars."

"Would it make sense for a ritual like that to be performed in the San Adrián Tunnel?"

Héctor took his time considering the question.

"The original chapel was built in honor of the Holy Trinity—*Sandrati* or *Santatria* in Basque. Due to a scribe's transcription, this became Sant Adria, and then finally Sant Adrián. The trinity . . . and the Three Mothers, yes, it makes sense. The choice of location fits. Once again, we see the number three, which is a constant in Celtic culture. There is also a prehistoric tumulus on the border of Álava known as the Alto de la Horca where they would hang bandits who pillaged the mountain villages. It's known as the Frontera de los Malhechores. And according to local legend, there are underground waterways that lead to other holy places for the cult of las Matres, in Zegama."

"Yes," I managed to say out loud. For some reason I didn't feel as embarrassed with Héctor as I did around others. But I knew my yes had been too piercing. *We know about that,* I wrote quickly.

Héctor pretended not to have noticed my struggle.

"What about Fontibre?" asked Estíbaliz. "Does that sound like a likely place for a similar ritual?"

"Fontibre: *Fontes Iberis*? The false source of the River Ebro, as Pliny the Elder called it? Water again, and nymphs, and Celtic gods . . . As you know, people still worship those waters, even today. Nowadays, it's usually devotees of the Virgin Mary. The faithful tie colored ribbons near the source of the river. But the ancient rituals would've likely been very similar. The Celts also used to tie colored ribbons on sacred trees around the sacrificial victim."

I was still pondering what he had said about "propitiatory rites."

Both victims, in San Adrián and Fontibre, were pregnant. That doesn't seem to fit the idea of a propitiatory rite.

The expression on his face changed immediately. A dark shadow flitted across his hazel-colored eyes.

"Pregnant? My God, in that case, it's quite a different kind of ritual. If they were found hanging, and I know you don't want to give too much about your investigation away, but my guess would be that their heads were immersed in the cauldron, or in the Fontibre case, in the river. Were they also burned?"

"Burned?" Estíbaliz repeated, horrified. "Not as far as we know, although we haven't seen the autopsies yet. Why do you mention burning?"

Héctor got up again. Seeing him this concerned worried me—a lot.

"Because then we're talking about the Celtic Threefold Death: drowning, hanging, and burning the victim. There are different versions. Here, read this," he said, pushing a small leather-bound volume in our direction. It was so worn and battered that I wondered when it had been published.

Estíbaliz looked at it, confused.

"It's in Latin. I don't know what it says," she pointed out.

"I'm sorry, I didn't realize," he said. "It's *Pharsalia* by Lucan, from the first century AD. It reads: 'Whom they appease with cruel blood, harsh Teutates, and wild, bristling Esus, and Taranis, whose altar is as insatiable as that of Scythian Diana.' For sacrifices in honor of Teutates, they drowned a man in a tub or cauldron. Esus was honored by hanging the sacrifice from a tree. And to honor Taranis, they burned their victim alive inside a wooden figure. I don't know whether you've heard of the movie *The Wicker Man*. The 1973 original starred Christopher Lee, and there was a remake in 2006 starring Nicolas Cage. The movie tells the story of a cult that sacrifices people inside a giant wicker doll, as the Celts did."

"Do you think these murders could have been committed by a neopagan cult or a sect inspired by the Celts?" asked Estíbaliz.

"Definitely not. There's been a resurgence of Celtic nationalism throughout Europe since the eighteenth century, and there are Celtic recreational and cultural associations, but I haven't heard of that kind of neopagan cult recently, at least not on the Iberian Peninsula. Besides, I don't think it has to be the work of a sect or an organized group for the connection to Celtic ritual to make sense. Anyone who knows about the Threefold Death might find meaning in that kind of punishment. As for the locations . . . that's open to interpretation. San Adrián and Fontibre have powerful meanings for those who live nearby. They're atavistic. There have always been rituals, ceremonies, prayers . . . and some of the most potent places of worship still exist. Religious practices adapt and survive. The Threefold Death is rooted in an ancient Indo-European myth from before the Bronze Age. It's included in Celtic imagery around the Atlantic and even in Hispania, as well as in popular Celtic literary traditions in Galicia, Asturias, and Cantabria . . . And it's not just on the Continent—it appears in medieval accounts of Celtic mythology in Ireland, it's mentioned in the Arthurian legends, and it's even in the *Libro de Buen Amor* by Arcipreste de Hita. The tradition has been passed down over the centuries: orally, textually, and symbolically."

He turned toward us. We were hanging on his every word.

"Have you ever heard of the bog people, the mummies found in peat bogs?"

"No," I squawked, then shook my head to reinforce the message.

"In the nineteenth century, archaeologists spoke of nothing else. Excavations became more professional and systematized. Rivers like the Thames were drained, along with marshes and bogs. In the peat bogs of temperate Europe—Ireland, Holland, Denmark, Great Britain—mummies began to surface that were perfectly preserved by the acidity of the water and the earth around them.

Have you heard of the Tollund Man or the Lindow Man? Forensic
scientists examined their bodies and determined that they were victims of complex ritual sacrifices. Evidence suggests that they were
burned, hanged, and submerged in water. For example, the Lindow
Man, discovered in 1984 near Manchester, England, was thought
to have died as a result of a threefold ritual sacrifice carried out in
the middle of the first century AD. He was a member of the local
elite: his fingernails and mustache were well groomed. A type of
cereal cake was found in his stomach, along with mistletoe berries,
which, according to Pliny, were sacred to the Celts."

"Were any of the bog people women?"

"Yes, in fact a lot of them were. There was one found in 1835 in
Gunnelmose, near the former medieval capital of Denmark. There
is some evidence that she was the legendary Norwegian queen
Gunnhild or Gunilda, the widow of King Eric Bloodaxe, born in
946. She was raped and drowned in the bog on Harald Blåtand's
orders. Blåtand is Harald Bluetooth, whose rune was adopted by
the Danish Bluetooth company and is now on your cell phones—"

"You mentioned punishment," Estíbaliz broke in. Héctor was
clearly about to go off on a tangent, and she wanted to bring him
back to what interested us most.

"That's right. The Threefold Death is seen as expiation or punishment for offending the gods. If your victims were pregnant, then
they were murdered because they offended the Three Mothers. The
executioner's message is clear: They should not be mothers—or
fathers, if the victim was a man expecting a child. They should not
bear those children. Instead the unborn children are offered to las
Matres, who can care for them better than their own parents. The
executioner watches over the babies who are about to be born. He
is a protector who rescues them from their parents."

But why were they punished? I wrote. *These victims you're talking
about—from the past, that is. What was their crime?*

"They were punished for breaking taboos or for serious crimes deemed worthy of capital punishment under the old Irish laws, like killing one's relatives."

I find it hard to imagine that a person today would kill pregnant women in order to protect the unborn, I wrote.

"There's a chain of violence stretching back to Paleolithic times," Héctor said in a sonorous voice, as if it were a mantra, staring out the window again. "By the way, it's going to rain. The *ábrego* has been blowing for three days now. I can lend you an umbrella."

What did you say? I wrote.

"*Ábrego.* 'Wind by day, rain on the third day,' they say around here. You Basques call it *hego haizea,* the wind from the south, or the madman's wind. But today's the third day."

I didn't mean the wind, I wrote. *What were you saying about a chain of violence?*

"It's an old theory our friend here likes to peddle," Paulaner explained. Apparently the inspector had heard this before.

"I'm speaking to you now as someone who has been examining human remains for years in excavations all over the world," Héctor began. "For as long as modern-day *Homo sapiens* have been around, we have used violence against our fellow humans—domestic violence, violence between clans, neighboring peoples, nations, states, kingdoms, and so on. In prehistory, patriarchs occasionally employed violence against the next generation while they were still weak; parents punished or abused their children. Those abused children in turn became abusers or torturers. Psychologists today claim that a normal person wouldn't torture. Only people who have themselves been tortured are likely to do the same to others."

I nodded. It was true. I studied it as a profiler, and it was widely accepted as an irrefutable paradigm.

"In recent years, archaeologists have uncovered evidence of violence between individuals dating to the earliest days of prehistory," Héctor continued. "The dates are being pushed further back all the time. In Kenya, archaeologists have found the bodies of children and a heavily pregnant woman dating back ten thousand years, and determined that they were beaten and pierced by arrows. Literally massacred. And if we look to the Middle Ages, a third of the population were killed by other people. Do you realize what a statistic like that implies?"

"That we're all grandchildren of a victim or a murderer," said Estíbaliz.

"That's right. If a third were murdered, then another third were killers. We likely have genes that come from both those who were killed and from the killers."

Héctor's words lodged in my brain.

They nested there, stoking what had become my greatest fear since Alba told me she was pregnant—that she might raise the son of a psychopath like Nancho.

I was terrified of bringing up a son or daughter who might have psychopathic tendencies. I just wanted a normal family—Alba as my wife, children born of our love. I wanted to go out to the country on Sundays, spend our weekends in Villaverde or Laguardia.

I didn't think that was too much to ask.

Just some normalcy.

Like Nancho, Tasio also had narcissistic psychopathic traits: extreme egomania, lack of empathy, manipulative tendencies, and charm when it suited him. In his case, this constellation of traits manifested in an obsessive need for social recognition.

On the other hand, Ignacio had the same genes as the other two and was not a psychopath. He had been brought up in the same environment as Tasio, and yet he had chosen to be compassionate, honest, upright. An honorable man. He cultivated a moral compass and decided to be a good policeman.

During my criminal-profiling training, I studied the controversial debate about the genetic component in psychopathy. Despite the fact that no single gene has been identified as the "psychopathic gene," it's believed that many genes contribute to that personality. But studies of twins also show that socialization and environmental factors interact with genetics.

So in a way, Héctor's assertion that we all have a murderer in our family history reassured me somewhat. Alba's visit to my apartment had left me with a question that tormented me: Would I be able to live with the uncertainty of what kind of person this child would be?

My mind drifted. I was aware of Estíbaliz firing questions at Héctor, and of him patiently clearing up her doubts, but mentally I was far away from that museum on the edge of the cliff. I was in my own entryway early one morning during las Fiestas de la Virgen Blanca, possibly conceiving a López de Ayala.

I was at the top of San Tirso, one day in October, unaware that I was saving a life that had just begun.

15

THE UNIVERSITY
OF CANTABRIA

MONDAY, NOVEMBER 21, 2016

Héctor came down to the staff parking lot with us to say good-bye. It had been raining gently for a while and showed no sign of stopping. He lent us a red umbrella with the museum's logo on it and offered to answer any further questions.

"I'll leave you for now," said Paulaner. "Keep me up to date, and we'll continue coordinating."

He gave me a gentle hug and a pitying glance, as though I were a hopeless case. It hurt. Then he climbed into his car and headed off to Santander.

What did you think of Héctor? I wrote to Estíbaliz as soon as we were back in our patrol car.

"I think I just fell in love," she said, following him with her gaze.

I pretended to look scandalized and nudged her with my elbow.

Inspector Gauna! Aren't your summer flings enough?

Estíbaliz kept me informed on her love life after things with Iker ended. She'd spent the summer and part of the fall dating around, which she told me about with casual amusement.

I was sometimes afraid she had swapped one addiction for another. She was a serial addict. But at least she seemed to be steering clear of drugs.

I kept my eye on her and she seemed healthier. She hiked more than ever. She also went out all the time and had new friends I didn't know.

Good for her.

"Héctor's not the kind of guy you have a summer fling with," she said. "As a profiler, you know that. Now, let's forget our fantasies, however tempting they might be. I want to know what you think."

I took my time. Héctor had given us too much information to absorb at once.

I think the Threefold Death would be an interesting line of investigation to pursue, except that neither victim was burned. If the murder at Fontibre 20 years earlier was committed by the same person, then that ritual was less elaborate, more improvised. The fact that the body was moved afterward indicates the killer was afraid something might be found on it. The deaths are very different. In fact, I'm still not convinced it's the same killer.

"Here's my take as the victimology expert: two unmarried women, both pregnant, hanged in places with historical ties to Celtic water rituals, in adjacent provinces, *and*—that's the key word here—the victims knew each other, because twenty-four years ago they both took part in an archaeological project in a Celtic settlement. Whichever way you look at it, my friend, both crimes and both victims are related. I didn't say anything to DSU Salvatierra about the fact that you knew the victims because I don't want to link the two crimes officially until we have something solid to go on. But I'm not going to jeopardize her trust in me by continuing to cover for you. I want you to explain to Alba that you went to the same summer camp."

I'll do it soon. I don't want to cause you problems. I promise I'll talk to her, but let me choose my moment.

She nodded.

"So now are you ready to visit the director of the unforgettable Cantabrian summer camp?" she asked.

I sighed, and Estíbaliz turned the ignition.

This was the other reason we'd come to Cantabria. To pay a surprise visit to Saúl Tovar. He was now a tenured professor and taught social and cultural anthropology at the University of Cantabria.

I had mixed feelings about Saúl. I always had.

He could have been the father figure we were all searching for that summer.

And he was for some of us.

But I hadn't been close to him, which was probably my fault, but our *cuadrilla*'s stupid rivalry didn't help. Now, after learning of the death of his daughter, I felt awful.

Poor Rebeca. She'd been dead for more than twenty years.

As usual, parking was difficult at the university, and the rain only made it worse. In the end, we had to wait for an unenthusiastic student to skip classes in order to get a spot. We left our car outside the redbrick interfaculty building with the striking deepblue columns.

It wasn't hard to find Saúl Tovar. Everyone's interest was piqued as soon as we asked, and they appeared to know exactly where he was.

But one reaction caught my attention. A slightly older boy, a senior student maybe, stared at us suspiciously and seemed upset when we asked about Saúl. He had one of those stiff quiffs that added a couple inches to his height, and an unusual feature: one eye was brown, the other light green.

"They're looking for Gray Beard," he whispered to another boy. I was close by and heard the exchange.

"Didn't you say he was Bluebeard, the wife-murderer?" the tallest in the group replied.

"Bluebeard is Gray Beard now, don't you know? Let's go," he said. They turned their backs on us and left. Estíbaliz was still listening to the directions two kind young women were giving us.

We found his office and knocked on the door. Saúl was perched on the edge of his desk, with several female students scattered in chairs around him. Barely glancing in our direction, he signaled to us to wait and went on with his tutorial.

It's funny what you notice when you haven't seen someone for twenty-four years. He had more wrinkles, just as I did, I suppose. He must have been fifty-something by now. Gray hairs in his once-black beard, deeper lines around his eyes . . . and his attitude. Above all, his attitude.

I remembered Saúl as a charismatic professor surrounded by young students, both boys and girls. He was still surrounded by students, playing the part of the cool professor, wearing jeans and an untucked casual shirt, but there was a distance and a weariness about his demeanor that seemed to me bitter or defeated. He seemed tired of pretending to be the young teacher.

I had first met him when Lutxo persuaded us to sign on as volunteers for a University of Cantabria–run project aimed at recruiting high schoolers from the autonomous regions to enroll in what was known as a history degree.

My friend had always wanted to be an archaeologist, and that summer all of us wanted to earn some money—we were also considering volunteering for the Expo in Seville or the Olympic Village in Barcelona.

In fact, what had really convinced Lutxo, Asier, and me to join was our feeling that as a *cuadrilla* we should support Jota during the worst time in his life by getting him away from Vitoria for a few weeks. His father was battling a devastating case of pancreatic cancer, and the once-strong student was going off the rails at breakneck speed.

He was drinking more and more *kalimotxos* every weekend and getting into fights. We wanted to get him back on track, and we knew he wouldn't be willing to go as far as Seville or Barcelona, so nearby Cantabria was the most realistic option.

It also helped that the program came with a fifty-thousand-peseta grant, as well as travel and lodging paid for by the university. So at sixteen, with the whole summer in front of us, we were all looking forward to a change.

The students were listening closely to Saúl, who was naming fossil deposits that correspond with the identities of Celtic gods such as Deba, Teutates, Tulonio, Lug, and so on. Two of the girls were taking notes, and whenever they raised their heads, they smiled at him with something close to adoration. He pretended not to notice.

We waited awhile, but Saúl was so focused on his talk that he seemed to have forgotten about us. After a few minutes, Estíbaliz's legendary patience was at an end. She cleared her throat.

"Professor Tovar," she said, holding up her police badge, "we've come from Vitoria police headquarters. We'd like to speak to you. There's no hurry. Whenever you can."

A shadow flitted across Saúl's almond-shaped eyes. We were getting off on the wrong foot.

"Patricia, Maite, Sandra . . . could you give us a moment, please? You can come back again on Thursday if you have any questions," he told them in a friendly tone that brooked no argument.

The girls gave one another knowing looks and filed out, scanning Estíbaliz and me from head to toe.

"What precisely brings you here?" Saúl asked once the girls had closed the door.

"Do you remember Inspector Unai López de Ayala?" Estí asked, making life a little easier for me.

"Of course. You've grown up now, Kraken, but your build is still very recognizable. Besides, I'm not going to pretend I didn't follow what happened in Vitoria a few months ago with interest. We do live on the same planet after all. In Santander, we talked of nothing else."

"Well, you should have been in Vitoria . . . ," Estíbaliz let slip. Then she cleared her throat again and straightened up. She was at work, after all, and we had to interview a witness about an old investigation.

"We're from the Álava Criminal Investigation Unit. We're here to ask you a few questions about the disappearance of your daughter, Rebeca Tovar."

"About Rebeca . . . so that's it," he muttered. He refused to look at us, his face twisting in a pained expression. "Is there something new? Have you finally found the body?" he asked after a moment.

"Unfortunately, no, but her case appears to be linked to a current investigation. We want to rule out any connection and leave you in peace," said Estíbaliz. "What do you think happened to your daughter, Saúl?" I wasn't used to this kind of confidence from her when she was interviewing witnesses.

"Something murky, involving several people. A botched job. That's what I think," replied Saúl. He was himself again, his voice warm. He looked Estíbaliz in the eye and leaned forward. "I think there were several of them, and that one took the photographs to incriminate the other or others, or that he regretted the murder and sent them to the press afterward. I think the body was never found because they were afraid of trace evidence or clues. By traces I mean biological evidence, semen or whatever . . ."

"Saúl, what about the pregnancy?" Estíbaliz asked cautiously.

"She wasn't pregnant."

"She was an adolescent. There are plenty of statistics that show that parents often aren't aware that their daughters are pregnant."

"I wasn't the kind of father who didn't know his daughter was pregnant. Rebeca couldn't have been, because . . ." He sighed and turned toward me. "Unai, do you remember her?"

Yes, I have fond memories of her, I wrote on my cell phone.

Until then I had not opened my mouth. Saúl put two and

two together, and realized I was not going to take part in their conversation.

"I mean physically," he insisted. "Do you remember my daughter looking like an adult woman?"

His question troubled me. To discuss with a father his deceased daughter's body was disturbing.

I don't remember, I lied.

"Of course, you only had eyes for Annabel Lee. Rebeca wasn't very mature at that point, either physically or mentally. She was still a little girl, and she didn't hang out with the boys. My sister was her endocrinologist and tracked her growth. The police asked me the same question twenty-three years ago, and she showed them reports proving Rebeca couldn't have been pregnant in the months leading up to her disappearance. They more or less dismissed the idea. Personally, I have two theories. First, she looked pregnant because of the angle those photos were taken. But when I still felt unsure, I consulted a forensic doctor in Santander. He thought that the abdominal swelling could have been due to decomposition, if she'd died several days before. Unfortunately, there were no other signs of decomposition visible from that distance. But the face . . . I've looked at those photos a thousand times, and there's no doubt it was my daughter. A father always recognizes his child's face."

You always used to talk about cult locations, I wrote. *What did you think of it happening in Fontibre?*

"That the Fates have very bad taste and a terrible sense of humor."

Did you ever consider it might be a colleague or someone in the field, maybe a group of your own students, or somebody with a special connection to Fontibre? The way your daughter was killed was unusual—in our modern culture, at least.

"So you're telling me that as the expert now, are you? Do you really think I didn't consider that?" he asked, raising his voice.

This Saúl was less in control of his feelings than the one I knew all those years ago. Back then, he seemed calm and strong, capable of mediating our conflicts.

Do you think somebody took their revenge on you, someone who had some vendetta against you?

"He harmed me, of course. But he harmed Rebeca so much more. What do you want? You come all the way from Vitoria, you ask me the same old questions, you don't offer me any progress in the investigation or any clue as to where Rebeca's body could be buried. It's obvious that they've killed again, that it happened in Álava, and that there was a similar MO. If that wasn't the case, Kraken, you wouldn't be here. I know that nowadays you're a criminal profiler. How many have they killed? Is it a serial killer?"

I didn't react, but I was struck by Saúl's hostility. I had never been one of his favorites: First, it had been Jota, whom Saúl had helped to cope with his father's illness. After that, it was Asier. And then, finally, Lutxo.

But he had also given me good advice, like when he'd told me to be proud of my nickname. He said I should take it as a totem, as the ancients had adopted the spirit of animals they admired and whose strengths they wanted to make their own.

So I'd stopped hating Lutxo for sticking me with the nickname and began to come to terms with it, at first begrudgingly and then with growing acceptance until I eventually identified completely with the Kraken.

I was still grateful to Saúl for that advice, and for the opportunity of that unique summer and for treading carefully around our adolescent egos.

I couldn't quite understand his current hostility. It was true we were dredging up difficult and painful memories and asking uncomfortable questions. I wouldn't have liked it either, but he seemed unusually combative.

"We don't know yet, Saúl," Estíbaliz said, when she saw I had no intention of writing anything. "We came to Santander to compare our current information with yours, and to see if there are enough commonalities to suggest it could be the same perpetrator."

"Perpetrators," Saúl corrected her. His voice was like a whiplash. "Perpetrators."

I see you have a clear idea of what you think happened, I wrote. *Hearing you now, it sounds like you have your own theory about who was responsible.*

"It's curious you should ask me that, Unai. Very curious."

16

THE PANDO-ARGÜELLES BUILDING

Monday, November 21, 2016

It was still raining in Santander. The rain had dispersed almost all the students, so the parking lot was empty. Without the hubbub of students chatting among its columns, the brick building looked even more imposing. Not too long ago I had been like them, worried about exams. Now I had other priorities: catching the killer, recovering my ability to speak, making sense of Alba's news . . .

"What did he mean when he said it was curious that you asked him about the suspects, Unai?" Estíbaliz asked, after Saúl had accompanied us to the door of his office, with the clear intention of getting rid of us.

I have no idea. I never heard about Rebeca's death, and nobody in the cuadrilla *ever mentioned it. But for years we didn't talk about that summer, for . . .* It took me a moment to find the right words. *For obvious reasons. Why didn't I know, Estí? I don't remember seeing the news of Rebeca Tovar's death on TV or in* El Correo Vitoriano *or* El Diario Alavés.

"I never heard about it either, but I must have been, what? Ten years old? Fourteen thousand people disappear every year, but most of them return. They're usually adolescents who run away, either from their own homes or from group homes. A disappearance rarely makes headlines—only when the circumstances are unusual,"

Estí explained as she drove. Vitoria would probably be as wet as Santander.

"I think the editors of the Cantabrian newspaper did the right thing. They contacted the police immediately and didn't make a media circus out of the death. Milán searched in our archives for news about Rebeca Tovar's disappearance, but only the initials of a fourteen-year-old who disappeared were mentioned. The newspaper report says nothing about the photographs. There was no public outcry. It didn't make the front page."

By the way, what do you make of Milán? I wrote when we reached Vitoria. I was curious about our new recruit.

"Well, despite seeming a little socially inept, she's a whiz kid with documentation and computers. She answers everything I ask in half the time I'd expect. She doesn't seem outgoing, and she's quiet. Sometimes she's a bit clumsy, but I get the sense that she's kindhearted. I'm really happy with the team I've been given. Peña is pretty nervous, and it drives Milán crazy that he can't sit still in our meetings. But I have a feeling they'll work well together. Outside police headquarters, Peña leads a curious life. He doesn't eat anything until seven in the evening. He says it suits him. And he's a musician. He plays the violin at folk festivals. But in the office, he's analytical and quick; thoughts seem to race through his mind. I don't see him as an emotional type, which will keep the team balanced when you return. You have more than enough passion."

"Look who's talking," I let slip out loud, ruffling her red hair.

What came out sounded like "uk-hoo-kin," and I felt my cheeks burn from embarrassment.

"You have to go and see that speech therapist, Unai," Estí said. "Alba made it a condition of your return to work, and I'm giving her periodic reports on your progress. We're sticking our necks out for you, so don't let us down. This is a warning, and I mean it."

Since when are you and Alba such close friends? I'm really glad, I wrote, shamelessly changing topics.

"Since I went to visit you in the hospital during your coma. For the first few days she was there as well, and I used to visit her. I thought it was incredibly tough that she had not only lost her husband, but that he was the murderer. Things at headquarters were really tense: Superintendent Medina didn't know whether to support her or to open an internal investigation. Some of our coworkers didn't trust her. They couldn't believe she'd never noticed anything suspicious about her husband's behavior. They thought she was complicit by sheer negligence. I was the one who killed Nancho. I killed her husband. I had to talk to her about it. I've always admired her, so I didn't want to leave it unsaid."

That's to your credit. And what happened?

"Since then, we've been meeting during the week in Vitoria. On weekends, we go to her house in Laguardia or go hiking together. She's tranquil and reflective, unlike me. She helps calm me down. She's a good listener and she doesn't judge me."

When she glanced at me, I nodded, but my initial reaction didn't escape her.

"You're jealous?"

Of course I'm jealous, I wrote. *I wish I could be friends with her like that.*

"We never talk about you anyway," Estí said. It seemed like something she wanted to clear up. "I mean apart from work. We've talked about your recovery, but always during the workday. When we're out of the office, we don't talk about men. We stick to our own lives. And though I'm not at liberty to say much about it, she has a really interesting past. She'll tell you if she wants to."

Now I really felt left out. I didn't know anything about Alba. Except that she and I had something together. I still got butterflies in my stomach whenever she appeared at headquarters. The chemistry had not evaporated, and neither had my desire to spend time with her, sleep with her, do just about anything with her.

"But this is about your recovery: either you start this week or I'll report you."

I have my first session this afternoon, Estí, I countered. *After what happened to Ana Belén Liaño and Rebeca Tovar, I'm the first to want my old self back.*

She smiled. We were nearing my apartment.

"That's exactly what I wanted to hear. I'll call you. Go on, give me a kiss," she said.

I gave her a loud smack on the cheek and went to have lunch in Toloño's. I didn't feel like cooking or staying at home with my thoughts.

That afternoon I mentally prepared for what was coming. I was hopeful and anxious as I headed for the nineteenth-century Ensanche neighborhood. My speech therapist's office was at the end of Calle San Antonio. You could almost see the train tracks from there. Elegant streets built for the upper classes. There were scores of offices in the area, but Doña Beatriz Korres's was particularly well chosen.

The Pando-Argüelles building was a mansion on the corner of Calle Manuel Iradier, one of the best streets in the city. During the Civil War, Grandfather said, its striking blue dome with orange stars had been an antiaircraft battery. At various times, the building had been the headquarters of the Francoist Sindicato Vertical trade union, the Nieves Canto school, and a hundred other things. I'd heard that a developer had bought it to renovate it into luxury apartments. That had failed, and now it was apparently used for offices.

Intrigued, I approached Number 4, where an imposing door

with black iron bars reminded me of the railings along the board-walk of the Playa de la Concha in Donosti. I pressed the intercom, and a steady voice invited me to the second floor.

As soon as I crossed the threshold, the smell of fresh paint and recent construction work filled my nostrils. It seemed my speech therapist was one of the first people to lease one of these chic apartments.

"So you've made up your mind, Unai," she said, smiling.

Her appearance took me aback. Beatriz Korres was like a 1940s diva, the kind of woman with elaborate makeup, eyeliner pointing to the heavens, and a dimple gloriously crowning her chin. She had cinnamon-colored hair, which was lifted off her face in curls with lacquer. Stiletto heels, a pencil skirt. She was slightly curvy, and proud of it.

I took to Beatriz immediately, although she didn't seem to notice my astonishment. Her extraordinary appearance was so per-fect that she looked as though she had stepped out of a haute cou-ture magazine. She must spend half the day getting ready. She knew precisely what she was: a hyperfeminine woman. It was impossible not to admire her.

I know I should have made an appointment a long time ago, I wrote, and showed it her.

"Come in. You're my last patient this afternoon," she said, inviting me into a small room that had almost no furniture or deco-rations. "I just started renting the office, so you'll have to excuse the lack of decor."

I smiled, and waved my hand in acknowledgment. On her desk were my neurologist's report and a jar filled with chocolate and vanilla Chupa Chups lollipops—my favorite.

"Please, take a seat. I'm really pleased you came. Doctor Diana Aldecoa told me a lot about you, and I'm glad she passed your case to me. Your recovery is going to depend on the hours you devote to your rehabilitation. It will be a challenge. We're working against the clock, Unai. If you dedicate two hours a day to it, that's all well and good. If you can make it three, we'll see results sooner, understood?"

It could be four, five, or all the time, I thought, but said nothing because she wouldn't have believed me. I didn't care. Learning to speak again and getting my life back had become my number one priority, and my speech therapist didn't know me when I was in overdrive.

Where do we start?

"This week I need to give you a series of tests before we can begin your rehabilitation. According to the team who operated on you, and from what Diana—sorry, I mean Doctor Aldecoa—told me, you were given medication. Are you taking it?"

I nodded. I might have been foolish enough to refuse speech therapy, but I wasn't suicidal or lazy, and I'd understood from the start that the prescription was vital for my brain to recover quickly. I didn't want to become a burden on Germán, and still less on my grandfather, who was nearing a hundred years old—even if he was the most determined person I'd ever met and was quite capable of bearing that burden and many more besides.

"That's good, Unai. The treatment you were prescribed is given for certain Alzheimer's and Parkinson's patients as well, and it has produced excellent results in cases of cranial trauma like yours. The source of the injury, the projectile, was removed quickly, so the prognosis, considering your age and your excellent physical and mental health, was quite promising. However, it is a prognosis that you have managed to complicate." She stared at me. I noticed again how perfectly her eyeliner was applied. I wasn't expecting to be reprimanded at my first consultation, but she wasn't saying anything that wasn't true. "Listen, I can understand your post-traumatic stress, but you should have gone to see a psychologist, which you evidently didn't do. So, Mister Self-Sufficient, it's time to show the world you were right, and that you can get out of this on your own."

Consider it done, I wrote. *And after the speech tests?*

"We'll start freeing up your oral capacities with some basic counting, naming the days of the week, the months of the year, and so on. We'll also do exercises together here, and at home you can practice repeating stock phrases. Are you religious?"

I shook my head.

"That's a shame. Prayers like the Lord's Prayer, for example, can be useful."

So what's the other way? I wrote.

"Music."

That works for me.

"Sing when you're on your own. In the shower, in your apartment, in your car . . ."

Free up my oral capacities, I repeated to myself. *Fine, I can do that. I spend a lot of time on my own. I'm not going to stay silent, not even when I'm underwater.*

"You also have to rebuild your pronunciation. We'll pronounce saying things together, whispering and out loud. And we're going to rehabilitate your active vocabulary. I'll describe an object, and you have to name it. Since I can see you like to use your cell phone, you're going to download two apps that present you with images and ask you to identify them out loud. Here in our sessions, we're going to practice speaking right from the start. At first, it will be basic two-syllable words and sounds, then three syllables, then four . . . After that, you'll repeat words with complex structures. As I said, you need to free up the language mechanism. In aphasia cases like yours, patients are very aware of their mistakes and of their telegraphic delivery. You have to overcome that sense of embarrassment. And you'll only do that if you practice a lot on your own and later with people you feel completely comfortable around or with your family. Do you have any volunteers?"

"Two," I managed to say. Again, it came out like a squawking bird. But she had to be used to all kinds of damaged voices, which took off the pressure, as she had said it would.

She took out a box of cards with pictures drawn on them and showed them to me.

"These are Nardil cards. You can use them to construct short phrases. I hope that within a few weeks you'll be able to start expressing yourself aloud. Maybe not as fluently as before, but my aim is to begin to minimize the number of errors in your speech. Your recovery will also require you to strengthen the right side of your body to improve the left side of your brain. Are you athletic?"

I used to run, I wrote.

In the early morning, but now I've lost interest, I added to myself.

"Start running again. It will help your stamina. You also need to do strength training. The left side of your brain now has to reconnect its neural pathways. Beyond athletic activities, anything that stimulates your right side is helpful. Roll meditation balls around the palm of your hand or on the soles of your feet, or use any object that works the sense of touch in your extremities. Become obsessive about your therapy. We'll work together every day to push you to get results. You're often going to hate me, but if you stop coming, I'll still be working with other patients, and you'll still be stuck with your Broca's aphasia."

No objection.

"Today I need to check your swallow reflex, the state of your buccofacial musculature, and your voice. But I'll also show you the exercises you need to do, and I want you to start this evening. Do them at least once a day."

I nodded, and my speech therapist smiled.

After an endless series of repetitive tests that I didn't understand, she concluded her evaluation and took a hand mirror out of her desk drawer. She used it to show me how to move my tongue from north to south, east to west, and in every other direction.

It was eight o'clock by the time we left the building together, after Beatriz had offered me a Chupa Chups to continue moving my tongue and then locked up her office.

It was no longer raining and had grown considerably chillier, but I wasn't expecting to see my brother waiting for us under a streetlamp. He was dressed in one of his immaculate made-to-measure suits, with three points of his handkerchief poking out of the breast pocket.

A day in court? I wrote on my cell phone.

"A day in court," he confirmed, but he wasn't looking at me. His eyes were fixed on my new therapist, so I quickly made the introductions.

Beatriz Korres, my speech therapist, I wrote, and showed it to both of them. *This is Germán López de Ayala, my brother. His legal office is in the Plaza América, and he apparently couldn't resist the opportunity to collect me.*

Beatriz extended her hand, and Germán bent to give it a courteous kiss, which usually delighted women. I looked at him in surprise. I hadn't seen him do that in quite a while. Also surprising was that Beatriz didn't seem to be taken aback by my brother's height.

"So how did he behave, Doctor Korres?" he asked her, as we headed toward Calle Manuel Iradier.

"Today I was simply starting to compile my preliminary report. But since you're here, I want to impress upon you that he take the therapy seriously not only when he comes to see me. If you can help him with the exercises I'm going to send him, he will make progress more quickly, and—"

"Not a problem," Germán interrupted her. "We're all dying to hear my pain-in-the-ass brother again. Unai and I were going to have a few *pintxos* in Saburdi's. Any chance you'd like to accompany us?"

Beatriz looked at him as though she would have loved to accept, and for a moment, I believed she was genuinely tempted to agree.

"Thanks very much, really, but our session is over," she said. "Unai, I'll see you tomorrow at seven. With your homework done. I want to see some progress immediately. Germán, delighted to meet you."

And with that, Beatriz and her maroon stiletto heels clacked away toward Calle Dato, my brother staring after her as though he had seen a vision of the goddess Mari.

What was all that about, Germán? I had to push the screen right in front of his face for him to take his eyes off her.

"What?" he replied, still hypnotized by her swaying hips.

That. I pointed to my therapist.

"Nothing. It's just that she gave me the impression that you're in good hands, and that makes me so happy, Unai. I want to see you well again, to turn the page, for this year to be over."

Brilliant. My brother was brilliant at avoiding the issue—and elegant as well.

He could have just told me that my speech therapist seemed like an interesting woman. But I suppose he might have been reluctant to express interest in another woman after Martina. I could understand that. I'd felt the same way after Paula died.

There was a sense of guilt at finding someone else attractive, the sense that you were being unfaithful to the dead. I'd always hated that feeling of disloyalty and it didn't seem to get easier with the passage of time.

I went home soon after we finished eating, but I got to bed late. I repeated the twenty-four exercises three times. That night I learned I could control my stiff masseters, the muscles that ran from my cheek to my jaw. My brain was numb after downloading the apps my therapist suggested and repeating the meaningless syllables over and over. I took my prescribed medication and fell asleep happy and satisfied.

Four hours. It was the first day of my new life, and I had dedicated four hours to my recovery.

I got up around eight and ate a leisurely breakfast. Since I had been on leave and no longer ran in the early morning, I had grown used to lazing around in bed when I stayed in Vitoria. In Villaverde, there was always a lot of hard work to do, and Grandfather got up before our neighbor's rooster Pruden began to crow, so in the city I allowed myself a little autumnal lethargy.

Turning on my cell phone, I saw I had a missed call from Estíbaliz. I was about to send her a WhatsApp when a number from police headquarters flashed on my screen. I heard the song "Lau tei-latu," the ringtone I'd had since the summer, one that reminded me of Alba and our time on those four roofs. I couldn't bring myself to get rid of the ringtone despite the pain I felt every time I heard it.

"Yes." That was my favorite word because I found it so easy to say. My speech therapist's instruction to unblock my language had made a big impression on me. I was hoping Estíbaliz was calling me from headquarters.

"Inspector López de Ayala?"

"Ye-yes," I repeated, not as confidently. I didn't recognize the deep voice.

"Officer Milán here. Inspector Ruiz de Gauna has left headquarters and asked me to bring you up to speed."

"And?" I asked. Another word that was both easy to say and useful.

"Well, she asked me to go through Ana Belén Liaño's bank accounts. Obviously, the one that interests us is the account she opened in Kutxabank when she won the three million euros. It was hard work, but we discovered that it was cosigned with someone by the name of Asier Ruiz de Azua."

She fell silent for a moment. I wouldn't have been able to reply even if I had recovered my powers of speech.

"I've done a small search of our databases," she continued in her rich baritone. "The curious thing is that this Asier is a married forty-year-old pharmacist. In fact, he's the owner of two pharmacies, one in Calle San Francisco, and the other in the Salburua neighborhood. As far as I can tell, he has no family or work connections with the victim. It occurs to me he could be the father of the child she was expecting. What do you think?"

I didn't think anything. My mind had gone blank when I heard her say that Asier, who only a few days earlier had denied seeing Annabel Lee in the past twenty years, had opened an account with her that would have given him access to three million euros.

17

CALLE SAN FRANCISCO

TUESDAY, NOVEMBER 22, 2016

A t that moment I received another call from Estíbaliz.

"Unai, you have to come to Asier's pharmacy in Cuesta," she insisted. "I found him on the floor."

I shot downstairs, still befuddled from my deep sleep, desperately trying not to anticipate anything.

I couldn't believe that something bad had happened to Asier. He was a rock, someone you could always rely on. In the nearly four decades I'd known him, I'd never seen him crack or fail.

No, nothing could have happened to him.

Five minutes later, I arrived at the pharmacy. From the threshold, Estíbaliz jerked her head to signal me to hurry.

Asier had inherited the pharmacy, and it was like a time capsule. It had a checkerboard floor, Limoges porcelain jars filled with active ingredients, and bronze scales. Seeing Asier facedown on the nineteenth-century tiles, his white coat spattered with blood, made my heart skip a beat. I rushed over to feel his pulse.

Estíbaliz was looking worriedly at me.

"It's okay, Unai. He's just unconscious. I don't know why on earth the ambulance hasn't arrived—I called for one a while ago. All the blood is from a big cut above his eyebrow. It looks like someone hit him and knocked him out."

It was a little after eight thirty in the morning, and Vitoria was slowly waking up: the stores in the Old Quarter didn't open until ten, and only a few people were out and about, sleepily heading for work. None of them realized that inside this building lay the bloodstained body of their pharmacist.

But I could see it, and I was paralyzed with fear. Thinking a childhood friend could be dead had knocked the wind out of me, making me doubt my decision to become an investigator again—at least in the Criminal Investigation Unit, where seeing dead bodies was a routine part of the job. Was I really ready to go back? Did I even want to?

Luckily, Asier had a harder head than me, or at least a harder occipital bone; a bump that was growing larger by the second proved that somebody had hit him there. Far more spectacular, though, was the blood pouring from his right eyebrow.

Then I noticed something on his hand. I took a towel from the staff bathroom to wipe away the blood around his eye, and surreptitiously hid his fist.

Let me talk to him first, I pleaded with Estíbaliz as we carried him into his office at the back of the pharmacy.

This didn't exactly please her, but it made sense, and she agreed.

We laid him on the sofa, and soon he opened his eyes with a grimace.

How are you? I asked with a wave of my hand. I hated not being able to speak. How could I tell him how worried I'd been about him, how frightened I was thinking that he was dead?

"I must be a sight right now," he moaned, seeing his bloody coat. "Help me take this off, will you? My assistants will be here in half an hour, and I don't want them to know anything about what happened. Not a thing, okay?"

So what did happen? I wrote on my screen.

"I didn't see him, but some bastard hit me hard on the back of the head and knocked me out. It must have been a junkie looking for drugs. I'm tired of that scum. Let's see if he stole anything," said Asier, struggling to get up from the sofa.

I held him down.

You didn't see him? I pointed to my screen.

Why are you lying to me? I thought uncomfortably.

"I told you. I was turning on the lights and was stupid enough not to lock the door before I went over to the switch. Somebody hit me from behind."

All right, you asked for it.

Your story doesn't make sense. Before you were hit from behind, you got punched in the eye—hence the cut—and you defended yourself. That's why your knuckles are skinned. You did see whoever it was. You know who it is, and you're not telling me. What the hell is going on? I wrote, losing patience.

"I told you. It must have been an addict. I didn't see a thing," he insisted.

This neighborhood doesn't see a lot of drug activity. And besides, we were coming to see you because we found something in the course of our investigation into Ana Belén Liaño's murder. Are you really going to keep denying it? I was weary of his obfuscation.

"Denying what?"

That you opened an account with her after she won the lottery.

"I don't have to explain that to you, Unai. It's a private matter."

Not when you're being investigated for murder.

"Do you have an arrest warrant?"

Don't be such a jerk. We're friends, I thought.

Not yet, but if you refuse to cooperate or explain what happened, Inspector Gauna may have to arrest you for obstruction of justice. I was disgusted that he was forcing me to write these things. *There's something else I want to ask you. After I told you the other day that Ana Belén had died, did you say anything to your wife?*

Asier's wife, Araceli, was a good woman, but she was pathologically jealous, and Asier had not been a saint after getting married. I was intrigued to know how he was handling the thorny issue of Annabel Lee's death with her.

"Don't bring Araceli into this, Kraken," he spat. His face, a few inches from mine, was contorted with rage. "Or you and I are going to end badly. Don't ever mention Araceli. And don't even think of talking to her."

Is that because you don't want me to see evidence of domestic abuse? I couldn't help thinking. *Did you cut her face with those knuckles?*

But at that instant, Estíbaliz, who had never been patient, came in with an expression that said we'd been left on our own for long enough.

"Hello, Asier. I can see you don't want to make things easy for us. Are you going to report this invisible junkie?"

"Would there be any point? Would you rush off to investigate and bring him to me handcuffed on a plate?" he replied, his voice as cold and flat as ever.

"Being funny won't get far with me," she snapped. "I'll get straight to it. Why did you take two hundred thousand euros out of the account you shared with Ana Belén Liaño two days before she died?"

Milán hadn't shared that detail. Two hundred thousand euros? Why did Asier need that kind of money?

"As I told our friend Kraken here, I don't have to explain that to you unless you have an arrest warrant," he said.

Seeing his frozen face, I knew we wouldn't get anything more out of Asier.

Nothing at all.

"How did Ana Belén feel about you going off with a sizable part of her winnings? Did she get angry, did you argue, did she call you a thief?" Estíbaliz pressed him, enjoying her interrogation. "Is that why you killed her? To be able to take half of the prize, money that's legally yours as the account's cosigner?"

"You're grasping at straws. Good luck with that," he replied.

At that moment, we heard the ambulance pull up. A broad-nosed paramedic stepped inside and began to attend to Asier's cut.

The paramedic went back to the ambulance for more medical supplies. "You two are unbelievable," Asier said. "The entire Old Quarter is going to find out now. Thanks, Kraken, for your legendary discretion. Many thanks." He gave me a sour look that bothered me for the rest of the day.

It had the taste of disappointment and evoked an ancient rivalry I thought had long since disappeared.

Estíbaliz and I left the pharmacy in the kind of bad mood that gives you ulcers.

"Come on, I'll buy you breakfast in the market. That asshole friend of yours made me so mad I felt like stealing some pills, but I kept my cool. Let's celebrate; today's a great day," said Estí gloomily.

We went to Txiki's, where she ordered a tortilla and then went up to the counter and returned with copies of the two daily newspapers, *El Correo Vitoriano* and *El Diario Alavés*.

"You know what, Unai?" she asked, as she leafed through the pages of *El Diario Alavés*.

"Hmm?" I managed to say out loud.

"Our friend Lutxo is as silent as the grave. His newspaper doesn't mention Ana Belén Liaño. Nor does *El Correo Vitoriano*. But he was at the funeral, so he must know. I know you told him."

In a personal capacity, not as an investigator. I told him, Asier, and Jota. She was a friend from our adolescence. They had a right to know.

"You take the cake when it comes to euphemisms, 'a friend from adolescence,'" she said, smirking. "But it's the first time I've seen Lutxo pass up a headline."

The judge slapped a gag order on the case. He has to respect that.

"Yes, but Lutxo could publish the news of the death of the graphic novelist Annabel Lee without linking it to the pregnant climber's body found in the San Adrián Tunnel. And he hasn't."

He could have stayed silent out of respect for Annabel Lee. But even I didn't believe that.

"Or he just didn't want to see it," she said, her mouth full of tortilla.

An hour later, with more than enough carbohydrates in our blood, we entered Doctor Guevara's office in the Palace of Justice, at the end of Avenida Gasteiz.

We had already received the results of the autopsy, performed on the Friday following our meeting. But after our talk with Héctor del Castillo in the Cantabrian Museum of Archaeology, there were several questions we needed answered.

Doctor Guevara was waiting for us behind her desk. She invited us to sit down.

"How were your weekends? How are you feeling after that hailstorm?"

"We just have to keep going. How are you?" asked Estíbaliz, taking a seat.

"I'm still in shock over Cuesta's death. We inspected a lot of crime scenes together. It's will be hard carrying on without him, but as you said, we have to keep going." She sighed. "How can I help you?"

"We have a question about Ana Belén Liaño's death," said Estíbaliz. "Our current line of investigation is leading us to suspect there was a ritual element to her murder—"

"And your job is to try to explain what they did to that poor pregnant woman," Doctor Guevara cut in. "I agree with you. I've never seen anything like this. To tie someone up, hang them by the feet, and drown them in a cauldron filled with water . . . Well, it's not exactly a typical murder."

What if it was three deaths instead of one? I wrote on my cell phone, and showed it to her.

"What do you mean, three? I don't understand your question, Ayala."

"We're looking into the possibility that Ana Belén Liaño was killed according to a Celtic ritual known as the Threefold Death, in which the victim is burned, hung, and drowned. In this case, we don't see any evidence of burning. We've read your report carefully and checked all the photographs of the corpse, the ones from the crime scene and the ones you sent us. We have just one question," said Estíbaliz, pulling out an image of Annabel's neck and showing it to her. "Could these two punctures have been caused by a Taser?"

The pathologist put on her reading glasses, which were hanging from a gold chain, and held the photograph at arm's length.

"I'm no expert in weapons that administer an electric shock," she said in an undertone, still calmly scrutinizing the photograph. "But you're right, these punctures are compatible with a weapon like that. They were beneath a bruise, and I thought they were small scratches incurred while she was flailing about in the cauldron. The victim was alive when her head was pushed into the cauldron. We found water in her lungs, which means she was still breathing, and of course she resisted. If she had been incapacitated by a Taser, the effect had worn off by the time she drowned. But that could have been what happened: The murderer or murderers tased her from behind, leaving her unconscious long enough to tie her up, hang her by the feet, and string her from a tree. Then they submerged her head in the Cabárceno Cauldron. Her muscles would have been working again when she tried to pull her head out to save her life and her son's."

I swallowed hard when I heard those last two words. Annabel had been expecting a boy. At twenty weeks, the fetus's gender was discernible to Doctor Guevara.

Learning this fact seemed to make the murders even more real and took us back to the inevitable question: Who was the father of Annabel Lee's son?

I knew we could extract the DNA. Doctor Guevara had kept a sample from both mother and fetus, and she could keep them for several months. We could use those samples for a paternity test, but we would need authorization from Judge Olano. He wouldn't agree unless we could present him with convincing proof of the suspect's identity, a plausible motive, and proof that the same person could be implicated in the murder of Ana Belén Liaño.

And presently we were nowhere near reaching that stage of our investigation.

For the moment, all we had was a bank account connecting Ana Belén with Asier. That wouldn't be enough to persuade Judge Olano to authorize a paternity test.

First, we had to find a prime suspect, and I knew just where to start. I sent a WhatsApp to Araceli. I wanted to know if she was responsible for Asier's cut eyebrow, and I also wanted to meet her face-to-face to look for any signs of violence. I wrote:

Kaixo, Araceli. Can I come and see you?

She replied:

Is something wrong, Unai?

No, nothing.

It was a lie.

I just wanted to have a coffee and
catch up. A bit of normality, I guess.

Of course. Let's see if we can meet up next
week. Until then I'm busy at Deusto. One class
after another. You know how it is.

Get in touch when you're
back and we'll meet.

Meanwhile, I returned home with Estíbaliz, as frustrated as she was. We didn't say much on the way. We both knew that if fire or something symbolizing fire was present in Ana Belén's murder, then we were likely dealing with the Celtic Threefold Death.

A ritual crime has more to do with the rite and the sacrifice than with the victim, which meant it could happen again.

I thought it was very unlikely that Rebeca Tovar had been tased. In 1993, Tasers were not widely used in Europe. Still, it was impossible to know if she had been burned after her body was taken down from the tree in Fontibre.

Perhaps that was why it was never discovered.

I had to stop myself from retching when I thought of Rebeca's burned body. It seemed too unspeakable an end for such a fragile girl.

18

EL PASEO DE FRAY FRANCISCO

WEDNESDAY, NOVEMBER 23, 2016

I set my alarm for six o'clock the next morning. I sprinted out of my building about half an hour later. Vitoria was frosty and dark, but it was all the same to me. I went into Florida Park, which at that early hour was like a cave under the trees' canopies. When I came to the Paseo de la Senda, I slowed down.

That's where I found her, running in her white leggings. She was surprised to see me. I supposed she had never stopped training and had gone back to the routes we had once shared.

Seeing her there before dawn was like returning to the previous summer, to the first days of August. To the chemistry that existed between us, to our innocence and ignorance of what awaited us.

Now life was on its way.

But I had to be fair with her. It was time for me to stop with the tricks, to lift the three cups to show what was underneath.

"Inspector Ayala or Unai?" she asked when I stepped in front of her.

Both, I wrote.

"As you wish," she said, trying to judge my mood.

We were standing under the yellowish glow of a streetlight. The sky had not yet turned the deep violet typical of Vitoria's dawn.

I don't want us to get cold. Let's jog slowly. I've got a lot to write.

"All right, start," she said, and we set off toward Paseo de Fray Francisco.

Inspector Gauna told you that the cosigner on the victim's bank account is Asier Ruiz de Azua, a married pharmacist. She also told you that yesterday morning he was attacked as he was opening the pharmacy, and that he was not willing to report the incident.

"Yes, I know all that. Is there something else?"

Yes, Alba. There's something I haven't told you because I didn't want to risk being taken off the case. I wanted you to count on me as an expert.

She didn't like the sound of this at all. She looked at me quizzically and came to a halt, arms folded across her chest.

"Unai, please tell me everything," she said sternly.

The victim was my first girlfriend—and Asier is in my cuadrilla. *As is Lutxo, the journalist at* El Diario Alavés. *And Jota, José Javier Hueto.*

Alba took it all in. "Are you telling me that four boys from your *cuadrilla* all went out with the same girl? I've heard the jokes about how the *cuadrillas* of Vitoria share everything."

Yes, it was the first time for all four of us. It happened in July 1992, when we all worked on an archaeological project on a Celtic settlement in Cantabria. Rebeca Tovar, the fourteen-year-old girl who was hung from a tree in Fontibre, and her father, Saúl Tovar, were at the same summer camp.

"Spill it, Unai. Now it's your boss talking, and I've put my job on the line for you."

Estí and I consulted an expert in Celtic culture. The murders of these two victims bear similarities to a sacrificial ritual carried out more than two thousand years ago in areas of Celtic-Iberian influence, which include Vitoria and Cantabria. This fertility sacrifice, known as the Celtic Threefold Death, required the victims to be burned, hung, and drowned. Since we believe that Rebeca was also pregnant, the two may have been punished because they were judged to be potentially unfit mothers. According to this ritual, the unborn child was then given to las tres Matres, *or the three mother goddesses.*

"My god, not again . . . Not another psychopath," Alba whispered, lifting her hands to her head in an unexpected, sorrowful gesture.

Alba didn't show her emotions, and I was caught off guard by this glimpse of her vulnerability.

"What do you think, as a profiler?"

As you know, to classify a suspect as a serial killer, three murders have to occur with a cooling-off period in between. However, we can't ignore the similarity in the modus operandi of these cases, and the victims fit a similar profile, too, as unmarried females who were pregnant. It doesn't look good. I would say we're at the start of a series and that the murderer or murderers lucked out when the storm washed away the evidence at San Adrián. If they were at Fontibre, too, then they may have taken the body because they were afraid the police would find it. With Ana Belén, the climbers found the corpse unexpectedly on a weekday in an inhospitable place. The murderer thought he could come back for the cauldron to use in further rituals. But the impunity that results when there is no publicity and there are no arrests could be fatal. The murderer will feel emboldened, invulnerable—and that could shorten the cooling-off period.

Alba read this and then sat down on a bench opposite the Villa Sofía, a nineteenth-century Moorish mansion that looked like something out of *One Thousand and One Nights*. Its appearance was completely at odds with the residence of the *lehendakari*, the regional president, that stood behind us. Alba stared at the villa's onion-shaped cupola and minarets as though they contained the key to the universe.

"You didn't tell me you knew the victim, and I allowed you to assist in the case. I stuck my neck out for you. You know what kind of pressure this puts on me, and the scandal that's going to break over my pregnancy, and yet you . . . you kept that information from me?"

I nodded.

"Unai, you cannot keep ignoring regulations and the chain of command for personal reasons. You're going to drag us all down with you, just as you did before. You can't hope to rejoin the team if you hide relevant information from me."

May I remind you that it was the two of us who enraged your husband, and that's why my sister-in-law and Estíbaliz's brother died. I don't want to be unfair, but you also ignored the rules.

"And I'm going to pay for it for the rest of my days," she whispered.

I don't want to talk about things outside our control now. The past is done, I wrote. *I am the right person to help solve this case. I know the context, the victims, and the probable suspects. Let me stay on as the profiling expert. Estíbaliz is as stubborn as I am, and she is conducting the investigation impeccably, but she didn't know either of the victims. Don't waste my inside knowledge on this case. Don't forget, our goal is to put those responsible behind bars.*

"I'm not forgetting that, Unai. Not for a second. You are one of the best profilers in Spain. I know we'd be losing a vital asset if you weren't part of the team, but this is the last time you can withhold information. I won't allow it. Do you understand?"

I nodded.

Alba looked at her watch and stood up. She disappeared down the path just as day was breaking.

19

THE POND AT VILLAVERDE

WEDNESDAY, NOVEMBER 23, 2016

I spent the morning waiting for a phone call from Estíbaliz, but when none came, I assumed she was busy cross-checking information and didn't need me in the office. So I drove to Villaverde, a small hamlet in the Montaña Alavesa, twenty-five miles south of Vitoria, where my grandfather lived.

Germán and I took turns checking on Grandfather during the week. He never asked for our help—despite being ninety-four, he knew how to look after himself perfectly well, and could tend to the fields better than any agricultural expert—but he was always glad to have an extra hand.

I found him sitting on his sofa in front of a fire that helped warm the enormous stone-walled house. He was snoring peacefully, his face shielded by his beret from the bright afternoon light streaming in through the open kitchen. But as I approached, just like a hare that sleeps with one eye open, he adjusted his beret and asked me jovially, "How are things, son?"

I gestured that my week was going fine. Although it wasn't exactly true, there was no need to worry him.

"Will you come with me to the vegetable patch? I want to see how my leeks are doing."

I nodded and followed him down the front steps that he had

cut from the riverbank. The vegetable patch was sad in winter. There were only a few plants that could withstand the frosts here. We walked around the stone wall leading to a pond that was used for irrigation; this time of year, it was only half full.

"Germán says your therapist is going to cure you quickly. He can't stop talking about how pretty she is," he commented with a sly gesture.

Yes, she's pretty all right, I wrote.

Grandfather didn't like looking at my messages on a screen. His poor eyesight meant he couldn't read them very well. He had never gotten used to putting on his reading glasses.

"And hasn't that doctor told you to forget about that damn cell phone yet?"

I was taken aback by his harshness. It wasn't like him at all.

No, I wrote, equally upset.

I'm trying, Grandpa. I'm trying, I wanted to tell him.

"Well, then, that doctor's no good. Anybody with an ounce of common sense knows that you won't ever speak again with that piece of junk as a crutch," he growled, standing in the middle of his garden.

Well, that's how it is. You have a dumb grandson and you're going to have to accept it. I wrote this in capital letters. My anger was near the boiling point, and so was his.

Grandfather read my message, and before I realized what was happening, he grabbed the cell phone and threw it into the pond.

"No!" I shouted, unable to believe my eyes.

I ran to get the old wooden ladder that was kept with the other tools.

"Now you'll have to speak," he said with his implacable logic.

Ignoring his comment, I carried the ladder to the pond, climbed a few rungs, and looked into the murky water. The pond measured about three yards by four, and the bottom was hidden by branches and weeds.

As I ran to grab a rake, I tried to concentrate on calming down. *He's trying to help you, in his own way,* I thought as I dragged the rake along the bottom of the pond.

I spent the next couple of hours pulling glutinous weeds and rotten branches from the water.

Grandfather reappeared at lunchtime, looking worried. "You have to eat something. Come inside now."

I shook my head and concentrated on an area I was sure I hadn't explored closely enough.

"It's a cell phone, son, and you don't switch it off even at night. You can't spend the rest of your life writing messages on it. People will get tired of it."

"No . . . is no . . ." I was trying to say *It's nothing*, but I still didn't have the skill to finish the sentence.

I went inside. He had a hot zucchini soup ready that comforted my soul slightly, but my mind was still at the bottom of that pond.

I resumed my rescue operation as soon as I polished off the chestnuts Grandpa had roasted. Changing tactics, I put on a pair of thigh-high rubber boots and stepped into the icy water. For once grateful for my long arms, I felt around every inch of the slippery, frozen bottom. It wasn't until the end of the afternoon, when the streetlights were about to turn on and my legs were numb from the cold, that I recovered what was left of my cell phone.

First, I removed the battery to avoid a short circuit, and then I carried the phone up to the house more carefully than if it had been a gigantic white truffle. I dried it off with a kitchen towel, but I knew I had to leave it in a dry, warm place for several hours, so I resigned myself to spending the night in Villaverde, unsure if my cell phone would ever come back to life.

Grandfather watched me in silence. He knew that we needed to talk.

I went to my bedroom and looked for a sheet of paper in my bedside table.

You've gone too far this time, Grandad. All my work contacts were in that phone, as well as lots of photos I haven't saved anywhere else. It was my office, my life, I wrote in gigantic handwriting so he could read it.

"You have your life in front of you, and you're throwing it away because you're a coward, son. And if I tossed five hundred euros into the water to teach you that lesson, then it was worth it. I'll pay for a new thingamajig," he said in a conciliatory tone.

It's not the money. Don't worry about that, I wrote on the sheet of paper.

Sometimes his lessons hurt—and it's possible they hurt him more than me.

And yet he was right. The cell phone was nothing more than an object. But I had given it so much power that it had become the center of my existence, my lifeline, or, as Héctor del Castillo put it, my crutch.

The next morning I awoke from troubled dreams and jumped out of bed to check on my phone. I put it back together, but it didn't turn on.

I opened my laptop and considered my options. I didn't want to race back to Vitoria to buy a new cell phone. Neither did I want to ask for help from my IT colleagues or Milán, who would have access to my phone's memory. I had kept Alba's messages from that summer, and I didn't want anyone to see them.

Finally, I decided to send an e-mail.

Golden, I need your help. Now.

Golden Girl, the country's premier hacker, always made me pay dearly for her expertise. The lively, white-haired old woman was an expert in computer security. She had worked at Cisco for decades and could run circles around many experienced hackers. I checked my e-mail.

Whatever you say, Kraken. I'm here.

I briefly explained my aquatic accident and agreed to meet her in an hour and a half in Vitoria to hand over what was left.

Golden lived in Cantón de las Pulmonías, a cluster of medieval houses that look out onto the interior courtyard of the Seminario Viejo, opposite the Plaza de la Catedral Vieja. She greeted me at the doorstep of her apartment, her white hair cropped short. Holding on to a pair of crutches, she looked much older than I remembered. She still wouldn't let me in. Golden didn't trust anyone, including me.

"What's this?" I managed to ask when I saw the crutches.

"I had a hip operation a month ago. I can hardly get around, and I'm dying of boredom," she said. "Thanks, Kraken."

"What's this?" I repeated, proud of myself.

"It's almost impossible to recover data from a waterlogged phone. But I love the challenge. I'll get in touch with you once I have an answer." She smiled, staring at my smartphone like it was a Fabergé egg.

Now that time has passed and I understand the consequences of that trip to see Golden, I realize that I am another link in the endless sequence of violence that goes back to the Paleolithic times Héctor del Castillo had described. But that was in the future. There was no way I could have known.

At least that's what I tell myself now to get to sleep at night.

20

SANDAILI

In the semidarkness of the minivan, the *cuadrilla* chatted and looked out at the landscape. Lutxo and Asier were in one row of seats, with Jota and Unai behind them. Jota was taking photos that turned out to be poorly focused, but they were his first uncertain steps in a new and exciting vocation.

All of them were a little too preoccupied with Annabel Lee's outfit that day: a deliciously short, loose black dress and yellow army boots that gave her a punk edge.

Asier fired the first shot, in his own inimitable style.

"Aren't you a little old to be doodling all the time?"

Annabel didn't even bother to raise her eyes from her forearm. Not having any paper, she was busy drawing on her skin a hanged man who was about to die. Her inspiration had come from the chestnut trees whose branches were scratching against the window beside her head.

"They're stories, you cretin," she said, while we held our breath. "You live in the material world."

"That's the only one there is. Come down to Earth, kid, your goth pose doesn't impress me. You're going to be a broke bum."

"Me, broke? Look at you in your bargain-bin jeans. I'll make a bet with you, Mister Hostile: I'll be richer than you the day I die."

Asier couldn't clench his teeth any tighter. He muttered, "Deal," and sank angrily back into his seat.

Unai watched anxiously as Annabel stared at his friend. He was surprised not to see any rancor in her gaze. Instead he saw determination, satisfaction, perhaps at some decision she'd made.

Saúl had silently watched the scene through the rear-view mirror. He did the same thing with his students at the university, observing them and then placing them into categories: alphas, betas, passive, aggressive, hostile, indifferent . . . They each had a defining trait that he could use to his advantage. At that age, they were so transparent.

At last, they arrived at their destination. Saúl and Rebeca led the group up a path that ran close to the peak. After a while, they saw the entrance to the cave and the chapel to San Elías built atop walls that had once been the *serora*'s hut, as Rebeca explained while they were climbing the narrow stone steps.

On their right was a basin, a rectangular hole cut out of the rock. They came to a halt. This was the reason for their visit, Saúl told them.

"The locals call this place Sandaili, but it might not be derived from Saint Elías, though that's what it sounds like. In fact, anthropologists think it may be linked to Saint Ylia, who in turn is related to the goddess Ivulia, a pre-Roman divinity who appears in an inscription discovered at Forua in Vizcaya. This is important. For the Celts, the goddess Ivulia is connected to the cult of water. Water rituals have been performed at this basin since time immemorial."

Some of us, like Lutxo, were listening with fascination, while others weren't paying much attention.

"Water rituals?" Jota repeated, anxious to please.

"Yes, the water dripping from the stalactites in the cave is said to collect in this basin. It is a clear reference to conception—the dripping water as sperm fertilizing the basin as a uterus. The

women from the Llanada Alavesa, the territory of the Guevaras who
ruled this region, came here to perform what were called 'fecundat-
ing ablutions.' The women from Oñati called it *beratu* in Basque,
or 'softening up.' These women entered this pool up to their
waist. Of course, these were fertility rites; they hoped to become
pregnant."

Saúl took his time telling his students about what fascinated
him most, how these Celtic rites had persisted to the present,
embedded in Christian ceremonies that barely concealed their
pagan origin.

Afterward, they climbed to the top of the cave. Weary from the
outing, they unwrapped their chorizo rolls and sat down against
the low wall surrounding the San Elías chapel. The building was
small, with whitewashed limestone, and the arch in the bell tower
gave it character.

It was time for a siesta. The horseflies were a nuisance, but the
cave offered a reprieve from the fierce heat, and everyone settled in
for a nap.

Almost everyone.

Asier was walking under the wall where rock climbers trained
and explored routes, but it was deserted in the merciless heat. He
was still annoyed at his conversation with Annabel. Maybe he was
too caught up in her, and maybe she could tell.

No, how could she? She's not telepathic, he kept telling himself.

Saúl appeared. He had come down for a stroll and found Asier
sitting against the rock wall, clearly irked.

"Hey, I saw your hand," Saúl said straight out. It was something he had been rehearsing for several nights.

"What about my hand?" Asier replied defensively, stuffing it
into his pocket.

"That badly healed knuckle on your ring finger. Did you
break it?"

"Yes, it was broken," Asier replied halfheartedly.

"Something similar happened to me at your age. When my father . . . Asier, what does your father do?"

"He stocks shelves in an Eroski supermarket." He paused. "This is where you laugh at me."

"Why would I laugh at you?"

"Because you're a university professor, and I'm the son of a shelf-stocker and a housewife."

"And how are your grades?"

"They're the best in my class." That was his plan A. His only plan, in fact. To study for a lucrative career, to escape from the mediocrity of an undistinguished, uneducated family. There was no way he would end up like his father in a poorly paid manual job.

"Well, then, I have nothing but respect for you."

Never in his life had Asier heard the word *respect* attributed to him.

"So, what are you going to study? History?" Saúl probed him, hoping to recruit a couple of the boys from Vitoria to his cause.

"No, something that will make me very rich."

Asier was tight where money was concerned. His friends in the *cuadrilla* knew that if he wasn't drinking on a night out, he wouldn't contribute to the pot, but then he would order a rum and cola or a *kalimotxo.* He was the same with cigarettes. There were always some to spare, and he made no bones about scrounging one. He usually picked on Jota, who was good-natured and had the most money.

Asier was obsessed with money, or rather the lack of it, and that was what motivated him to be a good student. It was his best prospect for long-term financial improvement.

"I understand," said Saúl. "Look, as far as your father is concerned—"

Asier stopped him. "As far as my father is concerned, it's—

never mind." But he also stopped himself from saying, *Better me than my sisters.*

"Don't worry, I won't say anything. These confidences shouldn't be shared. What happens in the family stays in the family. But, Asier, the day will come when he raises his hand to you and you'll be able to look down on him and stop him."

"I never said that anybody hit me," replied Asier, embarrassed.

"I know," said Saúl evenly, his voice cautious.

"I didn't say it!" Asier shouted, jumping up. He immediately regretted it.

Saúl watched him walk off toward the chapel steps.

He waited fifteen minutes, then silently climbed up to the chapel. He made sure everyone was still asleep and then approached his daughter.

"Come on, Rebeca. Let's go down to the basin. The goddess is waiting."

Rebeca looked at him, terrified. "Papa, please, not here," she whispered.

Saúl smiled at her. He couldn't understand why she was afraid. "Come on. Don't force me to . . ."

Rebeca knew there was nothing to be done. She swallowed, lowered her eyes, and without a word descended the narrow steps, her father following closely.

Unai woke shortly afterward, stifled by the heat and aching from the awkward position he'd fallen asleep in.

Looking around, he noticed several people weren't there.

Partly because he wanted to make sure everyone was all right, and partly because he really needed to pee, Unai rushed out of the cave and down the steps. He searched for a spot where he could undo his zipper with some privacy.

But he saw something unexpected.

Jota was on his back in the grass, pants down around his knees. Astride him sat Annabel, moving rhythmically like a wave. Even the hanged man on her forearm was dancing.

The famous little black dress hid their contact beneath its folds. A purposely lowered strap exposed a breast, whose size the four boys had been discussing every night.

Annabel was a good teacher, whispering instructions to Jota. And he obeyed, as if in a trance, as if he were looking at a water goddess.

Unai was dumbstruck, his zipper half undone. It took him a while to react. This was the first time he had seen two people being intimate, and for many years, that first vision of Jota and Annabel would still arouse him.

She was the first to notice his presence, but she didn't stop her movements until she began to pant and used Jota's obedient hand to cover her mouth so the others up in the cave wouldn't hear her moaning.

For both Unai and Jota, it was a glorious, almost supernatural sight. Afterward, Annabel simply climbed off her partner and resumed her apathetic demeanor. She looked calmly in Unai's direction without a trace of anxiety or embarrassment.

Jota had also reached his climax, a little more noisily and more quickly, as expected given that it was his first time. It was only when he finished that he realized his best friend was standing quietly next to a tree a few yards off.

Unai tried to justify his behavior as soon as he realized he had been spotted. "I'm sorry, I didn't mean to—"

"Shit, Unai! You didn't see—!" Jota shouted. His voice emerged as a comical high-pitched squeak.

"Sorry, sorry. I had to pee—I didn't mean to—" Unai apologized, and then he ran back up the steps, the need to urinate gone entirely—but with their image seared in his memory.

21

THE BARBACANA POOL

Sunday, December 4, 2016

More than a week had passed since the incident with my cell phone. I had to buy a new one, but Golden had managed to restore my photos. Fortunately, WhatsApp kept a record of all my conversations, and my service provider was able to duplicate my SIM card. My digital life had been saved.

At police headquarters, we were checking the CCTV footage from the cameras in Zalduondo close to the parking lot where Annabel and her companion or companions had begun their climb that morning.

She didn't have a car, so someone must have driven her. Despite the early time frame, we had to check at least thirty vehicles.

Annabel's phone had still not turned up, and although the service provider supplied us with a duplicate on Judge Olano's orders, Annabel turned out to be an infrequent caller. The only numbers on her call history from the evening before her death were to her editor. We discovered that on the morning of her murder she hadn't even switched her phone on. We weren't going to be able to follow the trail of her final hours.

After work I attended my speech therapy session. The whole hour consisted of pronouncing syllables and finishing words. During the week, I spent an average of five hours each day doing the exercises in front of the mirror, practicing with the apps Doctor

Korres had recommended, and I'd installed a horizontal bar across the hallway in my apartment. Every time I passed by, I did three pull-ups—about thirty a day. At first, this exercise left my arms stiff, but I was steadily strengthening my right side. I was also constantly using grippers to build the strength in my right hand.

At the rate I was going, I would soon become a Kraken for real.

On the weekend I felt too lethargic to go out with the *cuadrilla*, so I hid in Villaverde to get perspective on things. Grandpa refused to look at the screen if I typed something on it, so I communicated with him in monosyllables that he interpreted with the patience of a man nearly one hundred years old.

Early Sunday, Estíbaliz called. "Are you in Villaverde, Unai?" she barked. She was disturbed.

"Yes."

"You need to go to Laguardia right away."

"T-to . . . ?" I stuttered.

"To the museum. It's the Barbacana pool. Some locals discovered that the door to the visitors' center was forced open. A couple of officers checked to see if it was a robbery or just hooligans, and they found a young man hanging from the roof beams. This time there's no cauldron, but his hair and clothing are wet down to his shoulders, so he might've drowned. Milán, Peña, and I are on our way there now."

"Me . . . too," I managed to say.

I roused the Outlander from its sleep under Grandfather's balcony and raced to Laguardia. In less than half an hour, I was parking by the southern entrance to the town.

I had never been to the museum with the Celtic-Iberian pool. As far as I could tell, it was inside the medieval walls. I saw the Laguardia patrol car and pushed my way under the cordon.

I pulled out my badge, but they apparently already knew who I was. From the media, I suppose. I couldn't get used to being a legend in the force.

The judge had already authorized us to perform a visual inspection of the crime scene. I recognized the forensic team's vehicles and could tell that Muguruza had already arrived. I walked through the aluminum front door, which had been pried open. Going down a dark passageway, I came to the visitors' desk. Somebody had switched on the lights, and recordings of watery sounds echoed all around the room. The walls and ceiling were painted a deep blue, almost indigo; it was like walking on the bottom of the sea.

I could see panels describing the Celtic-Iberian culture that had thrived in this region 2,100 years ago. I knew that period well, both from the archaeological work I had done with Saúl Tovar and because of the double murders: Nancho had killed two five-year-old children in the Celtic-Iberian settlement at La Hoya on the outskirts of Laguardia.

An empty pool, the largest in Europe, spread out at my feet. A mannequin dressed as a Celtic-Iberian woman in a white tunic and headdress appeared to be approaching the pool, possibly to carry out a ritual or simply to retrieve some water.

I caught sight of the victim tied by the feet with a thick rope, hanging from one of the cement beams in the blue roof. The end of the rope was tied to the foot of one of the panels, keeping the bound man's body in the air. He wasn't very tall and seemed young. Muguruza handed me a pair of plastic overshoes, and I went up to the corpse.

I bent down on one knee as a mark of respect. Respect for accursed Death, and for the person that this corpse had been until only a few hours before.

Here your hunt ends, and mine begins.

His features were swollen, but he was recognizable. At least, I recognized him.

The dead man hanging in front of me was my friend Jota.

22

DOÑA BLANCA'S HOTEL

Sunday, December 4, 2016

I have no clear memory of what I did next. I don't know who I told about my dead friend. I do know that I sent a WhatsApp to Estíbaliz, because later on I was able to see messages.

On autopilot, I instructed her to ask the forensic pathologist if there were any Taser marks on Jota's body.

Barely a minute later, Alba called.

"I'm in Laguardia. Estíbaliz told me the new victim's identity. We need to talk. I'll send you my address. I have to meet Judge Olano, and then I'll go and visit the Barbacana. Wait for me here. Take that as a personal request or an order, but come here right away, okay?"

"Yes." I didn't care if it sounded like a screech. I didn't care what anybody said. Seeing Jota's blue-tinged face—the sorrow was too much.

I left the Barbacana without a word. The team was busy processing the evidence, and I wanted no part of analyzing the last minutes of my childhood friend's life. He was the golden boy we all looked after, the one we all betrayed.

The ruined Jota, his future wrecked by wine.

I can't remember the first time I saw him. It must have been the first day at San Viator elementary. You don't remember much about those years, do you? When do neurologists say that our first memories begin?

I had no idea. I no longer had any idea about anything.

I floated along. Alba sent directions to her house in Laguardia. I didn't want to take the car. I was in no state to drive, so I walked the cobbled streets, feeling the history under my feet as if I'd been transported to the Middle Ages. A stupid *eguzkilore* greeted me from the doorway to Number 96 in one of the narrow streets.

"Not now, you wretch," I whispered as I passed by. Nothing could protect me from evil spirits at that moment.

I crossed the medieval town square heading north. Alba's directions led me to the end of Paseo del Collado, and I saw that the address she had given me corresponded to a castle. Looking up from my daze, I could see that the castle had been turned into a hotel, the Doña Blanca.

It was an ancient building topped by an octagonal tower that dominated the promontory of Laguardia. I climbed the steep stone steps and entered a doorway crowned with a coat of arms.

One wall was covered with ivy. It was a bar with railings and big windows and was filled with people. I had no idea where to look for Alba.

At that moment, a woman intercepted me. A lady, I should say. Everything about her was distinguished: her short, thick blond curls, the warm cape around her shoulders that endowed her with a fashion-defying elegance. She must have been around seventy.

"Good morning, Unai. I was expecting you. I'm—"

Aurora Mistral, I thought, unable to believe I was in the presence of a titan of twentieth-century Spanish cinema and theater. The award-winning actress who would forever be remembered as the protagonist in the theater production of *The House of Bernarda Alba*.

I knew she had retired decades ago, but I had no idea what she was doing in Laguardia. Grandad would have gone weak at the knees if he had been there. She was a legend of the postwar years, a child prodigy. Over the course of her brilliant career, several generations had admired her and flocked to the movies to see her.

"Nieves Díaz de Salvatierra. I'm Alba's mother. She asked that you wait for her in the *El Amor y La Locura* room on the top floor. She just left on an urgent call. If you need to rest, feel free to use the bed. I'm busy with a Rotary Club event, so you'll have to excuse me. Here's the room key."

Aurora, or Nieves as she called herself, went behind the reception desk and handed me a heavy key.

She had a presence that came from more than being onstage, a special air that she had passed on to her daughter. They were not similar in appearance. Alba had dark hair and dark eyes; she was tall and slim. Her mother was blond and blue-eyed. Nor were the shapes of their faces, noses, or eyebrows similar. I would never have thought they were mother and daughter.

Stunned, I took the key. We shook hands again, and I climbed the staircase. I found the room, opened the door, and collapsed onto the bed. Burying my face in the pillows, I began to cry like a baby. My sobs were muffled, but I couldn't have cared less if the other guests had heard me.

Jota was dead. I was sick of so many deaths. Martina, Annabel Lee, my friend . . . too many for one year, too many cases one after the other.

I had to inform his family, his mother and uncle. I hated not being able to speak yet. It was not news I wanted to write.

I eventually stopped crying and felt more relaxed. I stretched out on the bed, in a honeymoon suite that was decorated for young, hopeful couples as they embarked on new lives. I was in a different space. At forty years old, I felt aged and weary.

————

It was quite a while before Alba arrived. She found me in a listless state, staring out the window at my San Tirso mountain range. But this time, I was looking at it with tired worry, not with hope and gratitude.

"How are you feeling?" she asked, sitting next to me on the huge bed.

I simply closed my fist and pointed my thumb downward, as Nero might have done on a bad day at the Colosseum.

She took my hand with infinite tenderness. It was like a small gift from the gods.

"I want you to know I'm here for you." She lay down beside me and hugged my back.

It was so good to feel her warmth on that cold morning.

"I don't want anything to happen to you, Unai. We've been through this before."

There was no point arguing. I had no desire to write or talk. All I wanted was to feel her caring for me, taking control. I wanted to be able to weep for the dead on that December Sunday.

"Let's go to the tower. The weather has cleared, and the fresh air will do us good. We have a lot to talk about, and down here there are too many temptations," she said, once she stopped stroking my hair.

She took my hand, and I followed her up the spiral staircase to the top of the tower.

The cool air was refreshing. We had a panoramic view of Laguardia and the sea of vines at our feet. We could see as far as the village of La Hoya, but that brought back painful memories. Wherever I might be with Alba, Nancho was never far from our thoughts.

"It was here that you saved the life of my child," she murmured, staring at the mountain range in the distance.

Perhaps the ancient gods of those hills are protecting him, I wrote.

She looked at me inquiringly.

We locals usually call them the Sierra de Cantabria, but they were originally known as the Sierra de Toloño, which comes from the pre-Roman Vardulo god Tullonius. He is the supreme Celtic deity, Teutates. There are even ruins of a medieval monastery dedicated to Santa María de Toloño. They say the monks had to abandon it because of the cold. I'd love to take you there. Maybe that day Tullonius protected your child. I hope that not everything is stacked against us.

"I hope so, too. It's the only way I can carry on . . . I know this is a bad day for you, and I'd like to change that, or at least help. Let me give you some good news."

"Tell . . . me," I managed to say.

"I went to the doctor this week and they did some tests. They're sure my baby doesn't have level-two brittle bone syndrome," she said, relishing the words.

I looked out at the old god's mountains. I felt a weight lift from my shoulders. The fear that my child might suffer from the same illness that had afflicted Alba's first baby had been another dark cloud hanging over me since she had told me she was pregnant.

Thank you, Tullonius, for looking after my loved ones, I prayed.

The way I embraced Alba, and the kisses that followed . . . they belong to my memories of that day, safely stored away. I prefer it that way.

Later that morning, feeling calmer but still resistant to the reality of what had happened, I questioned Alba.

You have to tell me about your mother. I can't believe you kept something so remarkable from me.

"I know." She sighed. "I know. So much of her life is already well known to most people. I'm sure you know the story of the poor provincial girl discovered by an agent from Madrid, a wily old fox, who turned up at a talent show because he'd heard about a little girl who was born to sing and dance. And her parents, who lived all their lives here in Laguardia, took the risk of sending her to stay in Madrid with an aunt and uncle who lived there."

I did know that much, apart from the Laguardia angle.

"The rest is history. An entire generation fell in love with her blue eyes and blond hair. She made film after film. After her first big flop, she turned to the theater. By then she was an adult, and yet her agent still controlled her career with a firm hand. She triumphed with her interpretation of García Lorca's *The House of Bernarda Alba*, but it meant I didn't see her very often. At least when she was filming for long stretches, I could see her on the weekends. But once she started working in the theater it was years-long tours throughout Spain while I was stuck at school in Madrid."

What about— I began to write, then stopped. I hesitated to ask such a personal question, but after all, she knew almost everything about me. *What about your father?*

"My father was my mother's driver, her agent's uneducated son. He never emerged from his father's shadow."

So your mother's agent was your grandfather?

"I've never called him that. He discovered her when she was a little girl. He molded her, paid for her dance, elocution, and singing lessons. But then he spent her money as fast as he could. He would go to the casino with four women and waste in one night what it had taken my mother a week of performances to earn. I hated his women. They had bags full of party dresses and high heels from the best boutiques, while my parents and I pinched pennies. I grew up in absolute austerity. It was around that time that my maternal grandparents died. My mother was left alone in Madrid in the only world she knew. Show business."

I looked at her without a word. I wanted her to continue.

"My father had no trade. He had what nowadays we would call a 'low ceiling.' I think my mother went out with him because they spent so much time together. They were the same age, and he didn't flatter her like the other actors. She didn't have to compete with his ego. Being with my father was a respite from her career. It was the only normal relationship on the roller coaster of her life. When they had me, I think at first my father's father hoped that the daughter of his protégée would turn out to be another gold mine. But I didn't inherit her big blue eyes, and I was chubby and talentless."

I never imagined you like that, I thought, waiting for her to go on. It was doing me good to escape from the present.

"Years later, the scandal erupted. My father's father was accused of tax evasion; he was liable for almost six hundred million old pesetas. My parents were financially illiterate. He gave them a tenth of what they asked for, and they barely knew how to make do with what they had. He took care of the rest. When the case came to trial, he ran away. A few years ago, I discovered he had changed his identity and left for Latin America. As for the poisoned chalice he left us, he had set up businesses in my mother's name. We were ruined. Almost all our assets were seized—the Madrid apartment, shops, and garages. My mother didn't want to go back to acting. She couldn't bear the attention from the press. She put that phase of her life behind her."

Did she like your husband?

I knew Alba had promised she would never talk about him again, but she was opening up. I wanted to see how much she was willing to reveal. I wanted to understand who she was, and what had brought her to that tower, that town, and that psychopath.

"She was never pleased I was going out with him. At first, she thought he was interested in getting close to her through me, to get a good scoop for an article. Or to see if she knew anything about where her agent had gone. Nancho handled it calmly, and tried to win her over little by little. In that unassuming way of his. You know what he was like."

I smiled. I did indeed remember that quiet man who had won my confidence with his patience and tact.

"Let's just say that my mother and I drifted apart after I married Nancho," Alba continued. "She never felt comfortable sharing her private life with him. When things fell apart, my mother developed a phobia of being in the limelight. She doesn't want anyone to associate her with her past, even though Laguardia is a small town. But the people here are discreet, and she's won their respect as a hotelier and a generous benefactor of the Vitoria and Logroño Rotary Clubs. And we're back in touch. As I told you, she was the first person to visit the hospital when she learned what he had done to me . . . done to us. She took care of everything during those first weeks when I was in a state of shock and worried sick about you in your coma. She brought me here, and the view of the mountains and vineyards cured me. Now I come here for the weekend, sometimes with Estíbaliz, and I sleep in the tower. I think I'm more settled now, and it's easier for me to understand my mother."

What happened after your mother quit her acting career?

"I was an awkward adolescent, overweight and shy. For a couple of years, we had a hard time. My father was basically housebound. He had no contacts, no work. When his father disappeared, he was completely stuck. My mother was much more mature, so she took the reins. She brought us a long way from Madrid to the safety of Laguardia, her parents' town, where we used to spend the summers. She set her sights on a property she wanted to rescue from disaster. She converted it into a hotel. You can ask me how much every flowerpot cost, because we scrutinized every expense. I started to teach classes after school and serve drinks here on the weekend. I think I grew up in two days. Until then I'd been a hopeless student, but once I focused I realized I was capable of anything. I was able to pay for my studies. I became a responsible adult overnight."

Did you change the order of your family surnames? Your mother said she's called Nieves Díaz de Salvatierra. I thought her real name was Aurora Mistral.

"No, that was her pseudonym. I don't want anything to do

with my father's name. I changed it with my parents' permission
when we came to live in Laguardia. I was still a very withdrawn
teenager. I tried to hide my mother's identity, first because I didn't
want to be treated differently, but more than anything I wanted to
leave behind the catastrophe of the financial scandal. The change
was in everyone's best interest because we didn't want to associate
that name with the hotel."

Did they name you Alba after the heroine of The House of Bernarda
Alba*?*

"We all have the right to a past, don't we?" she said, not without irony.

Was your mother as controlling and cruel as that character?

"No, she was only like that onstage. I think she was imitating
her father-in-law, who was similar. He wouldn't let her go out with
any one of the actors she knew. He wanted to safeguard her virtue.
He hated scandals, which was really rich, given his life and how
things turned out for him. I think he wanted to keep her a virgin,
and unmarried, like Elizabeth the First. My mother played that
role, too. But her first act of rebellion was to get pregnant before
she and my father were married. Her father-in-law had to accept a
shotgun wedding. He was a fervent Catholic, so he didn't believe
in abortion. He had no choice but to agree to it."

So you were born out of wedlock, I wrote. I've always liked illegiti-
mate children: their conception seems more authentic than those
born as the result of a contract. *But how did your father-in-law avoid
a scandal?*

"That was in the sixties. My mother disappeared from the stage
and the media for two years. No one kept count, and the date
of the wedding wasn't announced in the press. Her father-in-law
was friends with the magazine editors. When my mother reappeared, all anyone knew was that she had been married and had
a daughter. I never showed up in the magazines, partly thanks to

him, and partly because my mother wanted to shield me from the attention. She didn't want that kind of life for me. Then again, my father's father wasn't keen to show me off to his friends. He never treated me as a granddaughter. I was more of an inconvenience. I didn't know the meaning of the word *grandfather* until I heard it from my schoolmates. Their affection for one another seemed so odd I thought it was almost unnatural. I couldn't understand it. I thought a family was only a mother and a father, and that grand-parents were strangers."

Grandfather would laugh his head off if he heard you say that, I wrote.

At that moment, the screen lit up and I was dragged back to the real world. For a few minutes, Alba had helped me escape the event at the Barbacana pool.

It was a WhatsApp from the *cuadrilla*. Nerea had written:

Does anybody know where Jota is? We were supposed to meet at ten for a walk to Armentia. Jota, are you sleeping it off somewhere?

She and Jota had been close friends since our first year of high school. There was no sexual tension between them, and their friend-ship had lasted for three decades without the slightest hitch. They simply cared for each other. But Nerea, who ran the newspaper kiosk near my apartment, was a megaphone on legs, so I had to put a stop to this before it was all over Vitoria.

Unai, did you go out with him last night?

No, I told you all I was staying in Villaverde this weekend. I'll call you, Nerea.

I was still unable to pronounce the four syllables of the heart-breaking phrase: *Jota is dead.* I hated myself for having to write it so crudely.

Jota is dead.

A second later, Nerea called me. I imagine the shock made her forget I couldn't speak.

I answered. What else could I do?

"Tell me that was WhatsApp's predictive text, Unai. Tell me it was a typo," she screamed.

"Nerea, I . . . I . . ." I wasn't even able to console a friend. *Well done, Nancho, may you burn in hell.*

Alba came to the rescue. She snatched the phone.

"Good morning, Nerea. This is Deputy Superintendent Alba Díaz de Salvatierra, your friend Unai's superior officer. I'm sorry to confirm that José Javier Hueto has indeed been found dead. I would like to offer my sincere condolences." Alba spoke calmly and reassuringly, straight out of the book. She was an expert at relaying bad news tactfully. "We have already spoken to his family, and I imagine they will give everyone details about the funeral shortly. Be patient, these are difficult moments for them, and it will take them time to process and communicate. The investigation is confidential, so I beg you not to disclose anything or to speculate publicly about any aspect of his death. And . . . a more personal matter . . ."

Nerea responded with something I couldn't catch.

"Make sure you give each other support. Unai has taken the news hard as well. Thank you very much for listening at such a difficult moment."

Alba said good-bye to Nerea with infinite patience and handed my phone back.

Offering her a look of thanks, I went up to her, took her in my arms, and cradled her head against my chest. I wanted her as close as possible. I was sick of distances.

She was the one who broke the spell. Something was troubling her, and she had to get it out.

"We have to talk about what I saw at the Barbacana pool, Unai."

"It's . . . up . . . to . . . you . . . ," I managed to say, and she pretended not to notice how flushed I was.

"I saw Doctor Guevara. Your friend José Javier—"

"Jo . . . Jota . . . ," I cut in. Jota hated to be called by the name he shared with his father. We could at least respect his wishes on the day he died.

"Jota had a black eye. Estíbaliz has mentioned the possibility that it was your friend Asier who punched him, and that the mysterious addict Asier blamed for his attack never existed. Did you see Jota at all after the incident at the pharmacy?"

No, it didn't occur to me, I wrote uneasily.

Why hadn't it occurred to me?

I hadn't seen Lutxo, either. How had I been so careless as not to interview Asier's friends? All I had done was contact Araceli, who had put off meeting me.

"You told me that four of you from your *cuadrilla* went with Ana Belén Liaño as teenagers. And now we've discovered that at least one of the four was still in touch with her, to the extent that she trusted him enough to share three million euros. And that friend was beaten up and attacked by an invisible man."

Where are you going with this, Alba?

"Estíbaliz is analyzing this new twist from the point of view of a victimology expert. The profile of the victims, as you know, has changed."

Yes, I realize that. The murderer or murderers isn't killing just pregnant women. They're going after all of us who were in that Cantabrian settlement in 1992.

"We don't know that for sure. This may still be a punishment related to fertility. This could be another example of the Celtic Threefold Death for somebody they believe doesn't deserve to have children."

I'm lost. Jota isn't a pregnant woman.

"No, he isn't, but he could be expecting a child."

Jota? I don't think so.

"Unless, that is . . ." Alba trailed off with an eloquent gesture.

Unless my friend Jota was the father of the child Ana Belén Liaño had been expecting.

23

EL CANTÓN DE SAN ROQUE

SUNDAY, DECEMBER 4, 2016

Night had fallen by the time I reached the Plaza de la Virgen Blanca on my way home. It had rained in Vitoria that afternoon, and the yellow light from the streetlamps was reflected on the granite pavement slabs.

I took out my key ring with Grandfather's carved wooden fob and pulled up the zipper on my jacket.

I couldn't wait to go to bed. To go to sleep. To escape for a little while. It's the sort of thing you do when your childhood friends are dying and the responsibility for arresting their killer falls on your aching shoulders.

Just as I was putting my hand back in my jacket pocket, I felt another hand.

It brushed quickly against my fingers and deposited a scrap of paper in my pocket. I whirled around, unsure whether I was being groped or mugged.

A teenager ran off with a huge skateboard under his arm, his face hidden beneath a white hood, a few strands of blue hair peeking out. His white down jacket had no distinguishing marks. The only thing that would have helped me identify him was the painting of an old man with a white beard on the underside of his skateboard.

"Hey!" I shouted angrily. "What are you up to?"

Five syllables, I suddenly realized. When I wasn't self-conscious, I could string together more words than ever. It seemed like I did need to step outside my comfort zone.

I ran down the square. No one was out. It was after eleven on a Sunday night in December, and everyone in Vitoria was indoors.

When we passed the Dublin café, the mysterious skateboarder saw I was gaining on him, so he jumped on his board and turned into Calle Diputación. It was completely deserted.

When he reached the narrow Cantón de San Roque, an architectural gem that was little more than a yard wide, he jumped off his board, slung it over his shoulder, and disappeared into the darkness.

By the time I reached the alleyway, I had lost him. I didn't know whether he had turned onto Calle Herrería, or if he was already in Calle Zapatería or in La Corre.

I had to let him go.

I returned home, walking along the streets named after the medieval guilds. Closing the front door behind me, I finally took out the crumpled bit of paper and read the message I had been given:

Kraken youre making such a mess I cant believe it. Tomorrow you and me at 13:13 in the New Cathedral crypt. Not a word of this to anyone.
    For gods sake dont bring your phone

The note ended with the ornate signature of MatuSalem.

MatuSalem? Now I understood the drawing on his skateboard: Methuselah, the biblical patriarch who'd lived more than nine hundred years.

I had met MatuSalem a few months earlier when he was helping Tasio Ortiz de Zárate as his man on the outside. Despite the fact that Matu looked like a cherub, he was in fact an adult, and kindhearted Tasio had protected Matu when he was in jail.

The young hacker had resisted assisting with my investigation of the double crimes of the dolmen, but his gratitude toward Tasio won out, and he ended up working reliably as an unofficial adviser.

After that, he had disappeared.

Tasio's Twitter account had fallen silent.

Any sign of him in my inbox was a distant memory.

I didn't hear anything about MatuSalem after I came out of my coma. It wasn't that he was discreet—he could be careless, too. But he was the king of conspiracy theorists, and if he didn't want to leave any trace, he didn't, neither in the virtual world nor in the real one. He was good at making himself invisible. I had tried to find him, and found nothing. Only Golden Girl could serve him up on a platter, but that's another story.

Estíbaliz called the next morning for an urgent meeting at police headquarters. I knew we wouldn't have Jota's autopsy report yet, but there was still a lot to discuss. After doing my exercises in front of the mirror, I got into my car and headed over. The day was overcast and rainy.

Alba, Estí, Milán, and Peña were waiting for me. A screen projected a blank Word document on the wall.

I smiled thankfully at everyone. That projection would make it easy to contribute to the conversation. It had been a long time since I had taken part in a discussion among colleagues. I could finally contribute again. My damaged ego needed that.

Estíbaliz, who never beat around the bush, came straight to the point.

"Here is what we have. Because of this investigation's unique circumstances, we're calling it 'Water Rituals,'" she began, handing out the folders. "Unai, Doctor Guevara still has to confirm it in her autopsy report, but José Javier Hueto's body did have two punctures that correspond with a Taser's probes."

"Understood," I said out loud, pleased with myself when I heard my voice again. I had practiced it in front of the mirror, and it sounded almost normal.

"Peña," Estíbaliz continued, "what did you learn from the staff and the neighbors?"

"Not a lot, boss," he said, sighing. "There is no CCTV inside or outside the visitors' center, which means we have no photos at all. The neighbors didn't hear or see anything unusual. They're elderly. On Saturday night and early Sunday morning, everyone was in bed, except for an eighty-one-year-old insomniac, Doña Regina Montauco, who didn't say much. She was restless early Sunday morning. Looking out her living-room window, she saw a vehicle parked outside the Barbacana, blocking the front entrance. Unfortunately, she couldn't say whether it was a car or a van. All she could say for certain was that it was a dark color. We tried to spark her memory, but basically all she could give us was that it had four wheels. It's infuriating—"

"Let's concentrate on what we do know," Estí butted in. "What can you get out of her statement, Peña?"

"In my opinion, from the second-floor window, she could see a vehicle blocking her view of the center's entrance and what was taking place. The entrance has a thatched roof, which makes it a blind spot. Take a look at the photos," he said, spreading images of the front door from every angle. "The perpetrator or perpetrators could have parked the vehicle before daybreak, when the street was empty and the old folks were asleep. Then they forced the door open with a crowbar and dragged the body to the pool. The victim probably was already dead because, if the cause of death was drowning, there just wasn't enough water in the pool. It must have happened earlier, maybe in the murderer's home, in a bathtub, or in a basin in the hills. The victim could have been stunned with a Taser. The rest could have been carried out in an hour or two, especially if it's not the first time the killer has used this modus operandi.

"Like the first victim, we haven't found his cell phone. Judge Olano is going to ask the service provider to make a copy of his SIM card, so we'll see if that sheds any light on his last movements. We know from statements by several members of his *cuadrilla* that he went out in Vitoria's Old Quarter on Saturday night, and that he left the group around four in the morning. He never made it home, which means it's possible the murderer intercepted him during his night out."

I imagined an inebriated Jota on foot. He was always a simple, trustful soul. I cursed the person who killed him for preying on my vulnerable friend.

"One more thing about the crime scene," Estíbaliz said. "We're still waiting for any clues from the forensic report, although they had none when I left. But curiously, the attacker or attackers swept the floor from the entrance to the spot where they hung the victim, which complicates things. Forensics couldn't identify any footprints. The perpetrators left the broom, but there were no fingerprints on it. The broom's bristles are being analyzed. We'll see if it has anything to offer."

"So the guy is tidy as well," Peña muttered.

He does at least have some forensic awareness, I wrote on the laptop. *It could be that he's becoming more careful and avoiding mistakes he made with his earlier crimes. There's no Celtic cauldron. I think that the Cabárceno Cauldron was too big a risk, and, besides, archaeological artifacts must be hard to come by. This time he simply drowned his victim in a place with water.*

I was being understood in real time on the big screen. It worked a treat.

"Let's move on to the second point in our investigation," said Estíbaliz. "The connection between Asier Ruiz de Azua, the cosigner of the previous victim's bank account, and José Javier Hueto. They have been in the same *cuadrilla* as Inspector López de Ayala since childhood."

I nodded.

"We haven't been able to link José Javier's murder with Asier's attack on November twenty-second in his pharmacy, but they both had cuts near their eyes," Estíbaliz explained. "Doctor Guevara is looking into the timing of José Javier's black eye. It's possible that it developed at the same time as the assault on the pharmacist. It could be useful in establishing a connection."

"Inspector Gauna, tell us about the other possible victim who may have been killed with a similar modus operandi," said Alba.

"Rebeca Tovar, aged fourteen. She disappeared from her home in Cantabria in 1993. Her body has not been found, but these photos were sent anonymously a few days later to *El Periódico Cántabro*. They were never published. As you can see, the young girl is hanging from a tree with her head half submerged in the river at Fontibre, a sacred space for aquatic deities since time immemorial. The police found the rope but not the corpse."

"Anything else?"

"Inspector Ayala and I visited the father, Saúl Tovar, a cultural anthropology professor at the University of Cantabria. He is convinced there were several attackers, and that they hid the body because they were afraid they had left trace evidence on it that could implicate them. He thinks that one of them felt remorse and sent the photographs to the newspaper, maybe to at least give the family some closure or to give the police a lead on the other murderers. In my opinion, and from what the photos show, Rebeca Tovar was pregnant, although her father categorically denies this. He told us that twenty years ago the girl's endocrinologist backed up his statement. Nota bene: the endocrinologist is his sister."

"Let me dig a bit deeper into the professor and his sister," Milán butted in energetically, despite the hour.

"Go ahead, Milán," said Estíbaliz. "You can ask Inspector Lanero to help you. Our collaboration with headquarters might prove useful. If you want, you can go to Santander to meet him, although I'm sure you can handle it on your own."

"I don't think that will be necessary. If I need to, I'll definitely contact him," she said gruffly, shrugging as her cheeks flushed bright red. It was touching to see how embarrassed she became when she was praised.

"What's the victimology say, Inspector Gauna?" asked Alba, glancing at her watch.

I was sure she had a day filled with meetings before the December break. With la Fiesta de la Inmaculada Concepción coming up, it wouldn't be a very productive week.

"Unfortunately, we are looking at two different victim profiles. All the victims may have been expecting a child, if it turns out that José Javier was the father of Ana Belén Liaño's baby, and if Rebeca was in fact pregnant. But if we discount both those things, the only connection we have among the three victims is that they spent the summer of 1992 at a Celtic-Iberian settlement in Cantabria. That fact is consistent with the location of the crime scenes. San Adrián, Fontibre, and the Barbacana center all have connections to Celtic culture. We have no proof that the three of them stayed in touch. A few days before he died, José Javier told Inspector Ayala that he had not had any contact with Ana Belén, although obviously he could have lied if he was trying to hide something."

"How do you think the murders were carried out?"

In the case of Ana Belén, she was burned, hanged, and submerged in water: the Celtic Threefold Death. The same was true for José Javier, although as you said we need to confirm the use of a Taser. As for Rebeca

Tovar, it's impossible to confirm or rule out the use of a Taser, because that kind of weapon was uncommon when she died. However, we cannot disregard the possibility that the body was burned postmortem and that the murderer or murderers altered the modus operandi in their later crimes. Burning a corpse requires an isolated spot where you can build up a fire that will burn for hours. It's slow and extremely unpleasant. Maybe the experience scared the perpetrator, so he didn't repeat it for twenty years. He might have wanted to maintain the ritual of the Threefold Death and simplify things more recently and, for that reason, began using a Taser.

"Why do you think there was a cooling-off period of twenty years?" Peña asked.

If this is a punishment ritual, the murderer or murderers don't know when they will strike again. They would simply have to wait until the victims they have chosen are expecting a child.

Alba went white. She looked at me with terror in her eyes—real terror, not the stuff of nightmares.

"All of you," she said quickly, clearing her throat, "tell me, at this stage of the investigation, and with two or three corpses on our hands, do you think we're talking about one or several murderers?"

"Saúl Tovar is convinced there were several killers involved in his daughter's death," repeated Estí, casting a brief sidelong glance at me.

We were both silent, despite what we knew. For some reason, Saúl believed it had been the four of us from the *cuadrilla*.

You're wrong, Saúl, I imagined telling him. *What would you say now, now that one of us is no longer here?*

I think the perpetrator would have to be incredibly strong to raise a body on a rope, as we saw with Ana Belén or José Javier. Either he's an extraordinarily strong man or there was more than one person involved.

"Inspector Ayala, do you think we're up against a serial killer?"

I'm not sure about that yet. That depends on whether the perpetrator or perpetrators were the same in Rebeca Tovar's murder. I've also been considering that it might be a spree killer—someone who kills in fairly quick succession. Serial killers differ because they have a cooling-off period in which they go back to their normal lives before their next murder. We can't forget that if they are psychopaths, they are likely to be perfectly integrated into society. A spree killer doesn't return to his usual behavior. I'm worried that there are only seventeen days between Ana Belén Liaño's murder and José Javier's. I only hope we're not facing a spiral of violence like the one we experienced in Vitoria only a few months ago. I don't know whether the city could bear to go through that again.

I glanced quickly at my watch. MatuSalem was expecting me in the crypt at 13:13. Fortunately Alba drew the tense meeting to a close, and I raced off to the New Cathedral.

The city's most elusive hacker was waiting for me.

24

THE NEW CATHEDRAL CRYPT

Monday, December 5, 2016

I made my way between the highly polished wooden pews in the crypt. I was surrounded by stone columns as thick as sequoias and resplendent rainbow stained-glass windows. I was sitting at the empty altar when I heard someone behind me.

"No cell phone, I hope. Otherwise, I'm outta here," whispered MatuSalem in his high-pitched voice.

"Uh-huh," I murmured.

There was no one else in that underworld lined with arches and granite reliefs. Still, I didn't raise my voice.

"I think you'll need this," he said, handing me a notebook and a pencil.

So why have you brought me to this sepulchre? I wrote without looking at him.

"I brought you here to warn you."

"About what?" I said out loud.

"You've made the biggest mistake of your life by allowing Golden Girl to see what was on your cell phone."

Why would that be?

"Because, friend, Golden is asking very strange questions on the deep web—and nothing on the deep web is to be taken lightly. Golden wasn't in the habit of spending much time down there until now. But she found something—I don't know what—on your cell phone and began to spend hours searching for who knows what."

The deep web is the 98 percent of the Internet that doesn't appear on search engines. All of it is illegal—the biggest crime supermarket in the history of humanity, with contract killers, drugs, weapons, trafficked humans. It is where the darkest parts of the human race conduct their business. Venturing there, if only out of curiosity, will take its toll on even computer experts. Although their owners might be unaware of it, their computers and cell phones are left at the mercy of crackers, the black-hat hackers. Connecting with the deep web is a kind of suicide—any device can become part of huge networks of botnets or zombie computers, making photos, contacts, credit cards, and passwords vulnerable. The price of admittance is beyond expensive. It would be naive to think you could emerge unscathed.

And how do you know this, Matu? Don't tell me you're still snooping on me, because that would make me really angry.

MatuSalem pulled down his hoodie so I couldn't see his eyes. He had let his hair grow and dyed it an angelic blue. He looked like something out of a manga drawing: perfect features, eyes as big as a fawn's, flawlessly smooth skin. Annabel Lee would have found him a perfect muse for her graphic novels.

"As I told you once in front of the *Triumph of Vitoria* mural, Kraken. *Fidelitas*. That's my thing."

It took me a while to make the connection.

I get it. Tasio asked you to do it, I wrote.

"Let's just say that before leaving for the Americas, he entrusted me with a sacred mission. He cares about you, man. And that's to his credit since he distrusts half the world. After all, you locked him up when he was innocent."

His twin locked him up, kid. His twin, I reminded him. *But the point is, you two are spying on me.*

"We look after you. I'm your cyber nanny. Don't mention it."

I never asked for that. My privacy isn't your or Tasio's plaything. I want it back, Matu, or I swear I'll take you down.

"Don't mistake your target. I've been squeaky clean for a while now, making a living as a white hat, but finding a job is difficult when you're not even twenty and your criminal record is everywhere. Anyway, it's Golden you have to keep an eye on."

"I trust Golden," I said out loud. It came out something like "E . . . st . . . goold," but I was realizing the importance of pushing past my self-consciousness.

"How well do you really know her?" he challenged me.

Well enough, I wrote.

She had helped me arrest a fugitive accused of gender-based violence who was renting a room from her. In return, I kept quiet about the pension she was drawing as the widow of a man she had been living with for forty years but never married . . . That was how well I knew her.

"Maybe not as well as you should. All this stuff gives me the creeps. Did you know she even pretended to be an adolescent girl in a suicide chat room?"

Suicide rooms? Isn't that an urban myth?

MatuSalem stared at me like I was an imbecile.

"You live in a very innocent world, man."

Yeah, very innocent, I thought, bitter. *Today I have to bury a friend. So don't mess with me. Satan has already screwed me.*

"Just a word of advice, and let's see if you can get it into your thick skull that I'm telling you the truth. Don't confront her directly; she'll curl up into her shell. Let me keep tabs on her, and I'll report back to you. Golden has a long history, longer than you think. When the Internet was just getting off the ground in the late nineties, she was already pushing the envelope for Cisco. Golden was part of the original group that launched the World Wide Web in Europe. But just because she's on your side now doesn't mean she's always been white hat. She's gone to the dark side more than once. Look, she visits the deep web as if it were nothing, and it takes a strong stomach to go trolling around there. Let's be clear. If you get involved with it, it's because you want to commit a crime. That's all there is to it.

"Sometimes you think you know everything, but there's something blocking your view," he said. But I still didn't understand. "Sometimes we draw conclusions from part of a picture even when we don't see the whole thing. Take Cisco, for example. At Stanford, there was a sign opposite the founders' office that read SAN FRAN-CISCO. But a tree obscured part of it, and all they could see was CISCO. They took that as the name, and now they're on Wall Street."

Do you have any technical advice for me?

"Buy another cell phone with a new number for everything you don't want monitored. Get a new SIM card that's not linked to your ID. I'm sure one of your colleagues can help. The investigation, your private life, your security . . . Keep offering Golden a few crumbs so that she doesn't catch on. And regardless of what you want, I'm going to keep track of her as she delves into the deep web. That's just the way it's going to be. I don't take orders from you anyway."

His insolence was starting to make my blood boil.

Give me just a shred of proof, Matu. Just a single piece of evidence.

"You want proof? Ask your Golden Girl what she's doing ordering Tasers at the gates to the underworld."

That was enough to shut me up.

That really was proof that Golden Girl was asking too many questions.

Glancing at his watch, MatuSalem got up from the bench.

"They close at two, so I'm out of here. Now either burn those sheets of paper or eat them. I'm not one to give you advice on how to live your life, Kraken, but you need to start speaking again, because right now all your conversations appear on a screen. Whatever precautions you take, it's not safe. As we hackers say, the more you know, the more paranoid you become. The danger is real. Don't make yourself such an easy target. You've had your life ruined once already."

With that, he tore out the pages I had written on, left them on the bench beside me, and took back the notebook and pencil.

And Jota's funeral?

Better to leave it unsaid. The rites were the same as ever; there's nothing to add. Our *cuadrilla* was in a state of shock, speechless.

Once again, we were three hooded figures in the rain, a hellish trinity who had not known how to protect him.

Jota was the weakest of us.

Always.

He was the first to fall.

But Lutxo, Asier, and I were as hard as rocks, as ice, as oak.

We remained standing.

A black crow, a bird of ill omen, settled on my shoulder. No— it was just a daydream.

As my grandfather's grandson, I'm going to finish this. I'll make a pact with any god who hears me that no one else here is going to die.

Every statue in the cemetery laughed as I walked past.

25

THE SUMMER OF THE KRAKEN

WEDNESDAY, JULY 8, 1992

Their early-morning routines hadn't changed much since their return from Sandaili. Around six o'clock, Annabel Lee lit the miner's lamp, crawled out of her sleeping bag, and began to draw in bed. Unable to sleep, Unai joined her and they talked in increasingly intimate whispers.

One thing had changed, though, or perhaps had simply been added to Annabel's rituals.

Once she had finished her drawing, before the sky began to lighten, she would put on her boots and hike the nearby sequoia forest.

She didn't go alone. In recent days, Lutxo went with her. At about seven they set off from the mansion in silence and plunged into a dark, still-sleeping Cantabria.

Lutxo was the latest of Annabel's projects. She had stared at him fixedly one night while he was polishing off some fried bacon.

"What?" he had asked, his mouth full, when he realized he was being observed.

"You are what you eat," she said caustically. "You eat fat; you are fat. And people see fat. We'll go for a walk in the hills tomorrow. In a couple of months, you'll be in shape."

Over the years, Lutxo kept up the early-morning habit of walking the hills. He also became a fan of rock climbing after seeing two climbers on the wall at Sandaili. Annabel told him that she had visited rock-climbing schools and indoor walls. She explained handholds, magnesium, and climbing shoes. They practiced on boulders, and even climbed the walls of the Conde de San Diego palace, crawling ten feet straight up like spiders to strengthen their grip.

But this new alliance between Annabel and Lutxo brought problems. Lutxo was more abrupt than usual with Unai, perhaps because he couldn't bear the whispered conversations, the laughter, and the secrets that Unai and Annabel shared each morning.

Lutxo found the perfect insult in a newspaper headline:

THE SUMMER OF THE KRAKEN

At least three specimens of giant squid have been found dead on the Asturian coast near the town of Luarca. The latest was a male *Architeuthisis dux* that, at the age of 17 months, had reached a length of almost 60 feet.

"Unai, doesn't that squid look a lot like you?" Lutxo had taunted him at breakfast.

Saúl, Rebeca, Annabel, and the four boys from Vitoria were all there. At first, none of them understood the joke.

"What are you talking about?"

"Just look at the tentacles—they're twice as long as its body. How long are your arms?"

"Bigger than your brain cells, obviously."

"Don't get mad, Kraken."

"I'm no Kraken. Get off my back, Lutxo, or you'll get what's coming to you."

"The Kraken is upset," Lutxo goaded him.

He repeated the same joke the next morning, and the next.

Unai couldn't find his towel when he stepped out of the shower. Some joker—Lutxo? Asier?—must have taken it. So Unai, naked and dripping with water, had to go into the bathroom and find a hand towel to tie around his waist.

He headed downstairs cursing, hoping he wouldn't run into anyone on the way. It wasn't even nine thirty yet, and it was already stifling. The boys' dormitory was deserted. They had all gone down to breakfast.

He was about to unwrap the towel and get dressed when he sensed someone behind him.

"Where's Lutxo?" asked Unai.

"Having breakfast. Are you annoyed about your nickname?" asked Annabel Lee.

"No," he lied.

"Well, I really like Kraken. You're luckier with your nickname than I am."

"I doubt it."

"Seriously. I chose my name, Annabel Lee, because I didn't like the one my mom's biker gang gave me," she said.

He turned and sat on a mattress, holding his clothes in one hand.

"What did they call you?" he asked.

"Poison. They said that I'm like poison ivy, that I cause trouble for girls, even grown women. I can't help that their boyfriends or husbands follow me with their eyes. My friends' mothers don't invite me to their parties, and as for boys . . . I sow the wind and reap the whirlwind, as they say. I can't help it. I don't mean to. Even my mother's boyfriends have pursued me, and it's hurt her. Sometimes she took my side, but other times—and they were times that really hurt—she blamed me for leading the guys on. I couldn't care less about any boy in the world, apart from you. I am faithful only to you. I have been waiting for you since I was four."

Unai sat there, with the hand towel covering his privates. Preferring not to say anything, he clutched his clothes to himself, and ran out of the room.

A few hours later, Jota, Annabel, and Rebeca, their hands cut to ribbons, were putting the finishing touches on the roof of the Iron Age hut. Jota was keenly aware that Rebeca was tense and silent. Some people, like him, are empathetic. Others are self-absorbed, like Annabel, who didn't even notice the other girl was there.

Jota left to fill their canteen with some much-needed water. Rebeca took advantage of the opportunity to try to talk to Annabel.

She knew that Jota and Annabel had seen something in Sandaili. When they came down from the cave in search of a bit of privacy, they ran into Saúl and Rebeca on their way back up. Completely ashamed, her heart pounding, Rebeca began to broach the subject.

Annabel stopped her in her tracks. "I don't want to hear another word. You're imagining things."

"You don't believe me?" asked Rebeca faintly. She couldn't even look at Annabel. The girl was so . . . cold. She reminded Rebeca of her aunt.

"Of course not. Saúl Tovar? My God! If it were true, you'd be the luckiest person in the world."

Standing in the doorway to the hut, Jota had caught the last words.

"What's going on here?" he asked, noting the tension between the two girls.

"Let her tell you—I'm done with this stupid hut," said Annabel, snatching the canteen from him and storming out.

Rebeca was left trembling, on the point of collapse. Her heart was racing. It happened fairly often to her.

"What's wrong, Rebeca? You can tell me."

"Nothing, Jota. Nothing's wrong," she said quietly. The last thing she wanted was for her father to find out, although she knew he had gone back to the mansion for cold drinks and a cooler.

Jota came over and sat next to her on the wooden bench. He took her hand.

"Seriously, Rebeca. Whatever it is, you can tell me." His voice was trustworthy, affectionate, like an older brother.

Rebeca looked down at his hand and immediately liked it. It was still small like a child's, innocent.

And so Rebeca told her story once more. She didn't leave anything out. She even told him about her aunt.

Twenty minutes later, Unai found Jota throwing up beside the path.

"You don't look so good. The heat getting to you?"

I hope you aren't drunk already, Unai thought.

Jota laid a hand on his shoulder, looking for support. Unai had a lot of common sense, but this situation was too much for him.

"It's Saúl's daughter; she's not well. She's got real mental health problems. Saúl already told me she's on medication, and that she was hospitalized for depression."

"What did she say to you?"

"A load of garbage. She told me a really sick story. She's only thirteen. I don't know how she could think like that. Seriously, it blows my mind. Saúl told me to tell him if I noticed anything strange. He's very worried about her. Listen, don't mention any of this to the *cuadrilla.* I really like her. She lost her mother last year, and I feel sorry for her."

"Good lord, that's awful. At the age of twelve," Unai thought out loud.

If there was anybody at the camp who could relate to Rebeca's sadness, it was Unai, having lost both his parents. And Jota, who was about to join the club.

"Saúl told me that she was diagnosed with something more than just depression, but I can't remember what he said. I didn't really get it. They gave her pills and kept her in the hospital in Santander for months, drugged to the eyeballs. Saúl is in a real state. He brought her here so she could get some fresh air and forget all about it. He says the last thing he wants to do is to have to send her back there."

"So what are you planning to do, Jota? Don't worry, I'm not going to tell anyone."

"What can I do? I have to tell her father. It's the least I can do to help her, isn't it?"

26

THE COLLADO GARDENS

December brought frosty mornings and cloudy dawns. I was still running despite the early-morning mist. I was following my speech therapist's instructions to the letter, strengthening the right side of my body and obsessively practicing out loud at home.

Being obsessed wasn't a problem for me. I could be quite good at it.

I was cruising along with my recuperation. In little more than a fortnight, I could pronounce three-word phrases and had grown more comfortable speaking in front of others. My life as it used to be was at stake here, and that was far more important than other people's pity.

I intended to follow MatuSalem's advice and buy another cell phone. I would ask Milán to help me figure out how to obtain a number that wasn't linked to my ID.

It was an atypical week with two holidays, so I put on my sweatpants and hoodie and ran toward Florida Park.

Alba and I had returned to our previous routes. Our city's darkened streets offered us anonymity and privacy that was impossible in police headquarters.

Once again, I found her running along El Batán, focusing on her rhythm. Her stomach was less well-defined, her speed had diminished, and her strides were more tentative. These changes worried me, but I filed them away and stopped in front of her.

I was equipped analogically, as MatuSalem would have said, with a notebook and pen. We ran toward Avenida San Prudencio.

"Will you come . . . ?" I said riskily.

"Go on."

"To the meadows . . . ?"

"Of Armentia?" she said, finishing my sentence.

"I wan . . . want . . . to . . . tell you something."

It's important, I conveyed with a look.

"If you say so, Unai. Do you want us to stop?"

"Yes, it's better," I replied, taking the notebook out of my pocket. Alba looked at me, puzzled.

We'd better sit on a bench, I wrote.

On our left, the lights of the villas were beginning to come on. The low mist was thick as I searched for a bench. We had reached the stone arch containing the statue of San Prudencio, Vitoria's patron saint. The aged bishop stared down at us with a worried expression.

It was cold, and the damp air clung to our running gear. It wasn't going to be a peaceful day.

I'm afraid my cell phone has been hacked. Two weeks ago, Grandfather threw it into the pond, and I asked my extraofficial computer adviser to help me recover its contents . . . She goes by the name of Golden Girl. I've always trusted her completely, but another of my collaborators, MatuSalem, the hacker who helped Tasio Ortiz de Zárate, warned me that, ever since I gave her my phone, Golden Girl has been going on the deep web asking about Tasers and other things related to the Water Rituals investigation.

Alba read the paragraph and asked me to go on.

I turned the page and wrote: *We should keep an eye on her, but we'll need a strategy because she's an experienced hacker. First, though, I'm going to buy a new phone. Estíbaliz, Milán, Peña, and you will have the number. Outside the unit, I'll only share it with my brother and my grandfather. We'll have to establish what kinds of messages to send on my original cell phone, and what to keep for the new number, so that Golden Girl doesn't suspect anything. But from now on, I can't run the risk of writing any confidential information on my screen or making any calls related to the investigation. We've got two hackers reading everything.*

"Two questions. What do you think she has to do with the Water Rituals?"

"No . . . idea," I said out loud. "The . . . second question?"

"Why didn't you hand your SIM card over to our computer people, or to Milán?"

I stole a quick look at her. She had gained a few pounds, and her long face looked fuller. Her slender hands were swollen. I could see dark lines under her eyes. I wanted to ask her to come sleep at my place for a while, as we did that summer morning.

Because I kept all the WhatsApp messages we sent each other in August, I wrote. *I'm sorry, Alba. I didn't delete them. Every once in a while, I would read them again and they gave me strength. I didn't want our colleagues to know, they would've found out. I couldn't do that to you.*

Alba blushed, then took my hand, and thanked me with a look. But DSU Salvatierra quickly regained control.

"Do you think she's a suspect?"

"Golden Girl? Of course not," I protested.

Not on your life, I thought.

She's an elderly woman who just had a hip replacement. Not even in her wildest dreams could she be the murderer.

Alba took her time absorbing what I had written. She unzipped her top and with an automatic gesture stroked her belly, as if I weren't there. She must have seen the tenderness in my expression because a smile lifted the corners of her mouth.

It'll soon be obvious. Are you going to mention it at work?

"Yes, it's almost time for me to talk to Superintendent Medina before the gossip starts. I never imagined I'd have to explain my personal business at work, especially given the kind of work I do."

I've always wanted to ask. How did you get into all this?

"Do you really want to talk about my life right now?"

There are still things about you that I don't know—and I'd like to know everything.

Alba leaned closer to my notebook than I expected. Her swaying worried me.

"Are you all right?"

"Yes . . . no . . . I'm not sure, everything is a bit blurred. I think it's the running."

"Should we go back?" I asked, concerned.

"No, I'm fine," she insisted. I was glad she was sitting down, because she looked so tired. "You were asking how I got into this . . . It was in my last year of high school. I was seventeen, shy, plump, self-conscious about the scandal in Madrid and about our family's finances. We had moved to Laguardia for a normal life. There was a boy in my grade named Alvaro, and everyone was crazy about him, including me."

It's not that I was jealous about Alba's past or had any right to be, but I still felt a tickle in my throat.

"There was another girl, Marta. She was a bully and had a gang of girls who followed her everywhere. She was crazy about Alvaro, too, but despite all my problems, he preferred me. I think he played us against each other to make us jealous, but you never know. One day he asked me out—on a proper date, the first I'd ever been on. We agreed to meet that night in the park below my mother's hotel, in the Collado gardens next to the statue of Samaniego, who was famous for his fables. I put on a skirt and a pair of high heels, used my mother's lipstick. I don't know how Marta found out. I've always thought maybe Alvaro told her so that she would sleep with him. Alvaro didn't show up, but Marta did with her gang."

Alba gave a sad smile. I squeezed her hand encouragingly.

"I didn't see them until they came up behind me. They followed me through the park, insulting me. I sped up, and they started chasing me. I was not in shape. I weighed two hundred forty-five pounds and was five feet, seven inches tall. I was gasping for breath. My heart was pounding so hard, I thought it was going to burst. They jumped me. Marta kicked me in the stomach, and I threw up. I shouldn't have been walking alone in a deserted park in the middle of the night. It was stupid, but I was so eager to meet Alvaro that I didn't even think about where I was. All my life, my father had gone everywhere with me. But that night I was alone.

"That summer I walked the Camino de Santiago on my own. I lied to my parents and said I was going with a group. It took me twenty days to cover almost five hundred kilometers, at a pace of forty a day. When I reached the Plaza del Obradoiro in Santiago, I had lost more than fifty pounds. I never put them on again, and I've never missed a day's exercise since. I took some self-defense courses in Logroño, and I realized I wanted to be useful. I also wanted to see my mother's agent behind bars. I wanted to make him pay his debts so the hotel wouldn't be seized. Eventually I was chosen as a member of the regional police, the *Ertzaintza*. I've been following my grandfather's trail in Chile for years, but it's gone cold. I think he's dead, but I don't know where the money is. My mother has no idea I've been investigating him."

Alba took her time telling me this. She didn't look well, and it worried me. Whenever she took a breath, she clutched her belly.

"It turned out that Marta was involved in one of my first arrests years later. We got a call from a neighbor in Laguardia, and when we turned up at the house, there they were, Marta and Alvaro, married. She had aged and her face was covered with bruises. I had to arrest Alvaro, the same boy I wouldn't have hesitated to date in school. The beating that night had persuaded me to run away from that date all those summers ago. By the time I arrested him, Marta had a daughter, and Alvaro was abusing her as well. I made sure Marta and her daughter moved into a safe apartment for victims of domestic violence. Now she has a restraining order against him. She calls me occasionally to have coffee, and we pretend to be friends. I listen to her efforts to remake her life, but she struggles. She didn't go to university and never had a job because Alvaro insisted that what he earned was enough. He isolated her. She got married early, she has no education, and she never worked. It's a hard life."

Even so . . . why do it? She attacked you once, I wrote, feeling uneasy.

"Because Marta needs anchors, friends, even the most basic social life so that Alvaro doesn't draw her back into that toxic relationship. I could never forget that night, but I don't want Alvaro to win. I don't know whether I do it for her, or for her daughter. More than anything else, I can't bear the idea that it could have been me, and I don't want him to win."

"You . . . cause trouble for men," I said out loud. But was I just making trouble for myself?

"You included?"

Yes, me included, I wrote in the notebook. *Everything in the past three years has been too intense to feel normal. I'm addicted to the problems that go hand in hand with being a profiler. Investigating serial killers only exacerbates my obsessive nature. I don't have the right temperament for a profiler—I can't disconnect, and I lose objectivity too easily. Living with me is a constant drama while we hunt the killer and then wait for the next one. Does that kind of life appeal to you? Is that how you want to live? Wouldn't you prefer somebody quieter?*

"I've already been married to somebody quieter, the king of tranquility, of peaceful coexistence—"

Is that what you're running from? Yet another deception?

Maybe I shouldn't have said that. The truth is that I'm sorry now that my question upset her. She glared at me and stood up, still clutching her belly.

"What you feel for me," she said pointedly, "what I produce in you, is authentic. It's visceral, instinctive. When I'm around you, I can see you stiffen. Your body language shouts that you're there for me. At least what you feel is real—it's not a trick to deflower a reticent classmate the way it was for Alvaro, or to get inside information on an investigation the way it was for Nancho. You don't need me. You don't need anybody apart from your grandfather and your brother, and yet you're here, despite all the complications."

Do you only want to be with me because of what I feel? I wrote, angry. *Because I don't need to be needed by you. But I also can't be a strategy, a refuge, a Band-Aid for you.*

"My God, a Band-Aid . . . ," she whispered. "You get me pregnant with a daughter, and you call yourself a *Band-Aid*—"

Alba couldn't finish her sentence. She cried out in pain and collapsed before I could catch her.

Then she began to convulse on the icy path.

27

TXAGORRITXU HOSPITAL

WEDNESDAY, DECEMBER 7, 2016

I couldn't even call an ambulance properly. I dialed 911, but only managed to mumble "San . . . Prudencio." I hung up, frustrated and distressed, as I held on to Alba's limp hand. I sent a desperate WhatsApp to Estíbaliz, praying she'd have her cell phone on this early in the morning:

> **Send an ambulance to Avenida San Prudencio. Pregnant 40-year-old woman suffering convulsions, semiconscious.**

A thumbs-up emoticon was enough to assure me help was on the way.

It was a long, agonizing day. Alba was admitted to Txagorritxu hospital, where she underwent a battery of tests. In the meantime, I didn't know if she'd lost the baby. I was surrounded by silence and reassuring looks.

I called Alba's mother in Laguardia, and with a great deal of patience on her part and stumbling on mine, I managed to explain to her what happened. She was there less than an hour later, and we stayed at Alba's side.

I was worried sick, but I was also reeling from a new revelation: Alba was expecting a baby girl. I knew that she was mine the instant she said she was going to have a girl. It didn't matter if Nancho was the biological father. Nancho wasn't there to raise her. I was.

The diagnosis came in as it was getting dark. Alba had a rare complication due to preeclampsia. The doctors had pointed to her high blood pressure as a sign. She had known about the condition, yet she hadn't told me. It seemed as though I hadn't earned her trust.

Both mother and baby were out of danger once she had taken antihypertensive medication. Yes, we could visit. No, we shouldn't tire her out. Yes, Nieves could spend the night at the hospital. No, there was no need for me to stay. Go home and rest, Alba told me in a shaky voice. As if I could sleep a wink on the day I was told I was going to have a daughter.

Estí popped in to see her after work. I'm sure the Goya truffles she brought were intended for Alba, but that didn't stop me from pocketing a few for the sleepless night ahead. The two of them laughed, clasped hands, exchanged whispered confidences. Right now, Alba was no longer Estí's boss, she was a relieved mother-to-be. No amount of love and support was too much. I could have kissed Estí, enveloped her in a Kraken's embrace.

I suppressed the urge.

I was on my way out when I bumped into Superintendent Medina in the polished hospital corridors.

"I only just heard," he said, in a low, cautious voice. "Is it possible to see her?"

I shook my head, pointing at my watch. It was already dark, and visiting hours had been over for a while. Besides, Alba was sleeping when I closed the door to her room.

"All right, I'll come back tomorrow. I wanted to see how she was, but I also came to discuss a professional matter. You led the investigation into the case involving her husband, didn't you?"

I nodded uneasily. I wasn't sure where this was going.

"The police station is buzzing with rumors, and I need to know how DSU Salvatierra wants to handle the situation. What I'm trying to say is that, well, if she's been pregnant for nineteen weeks, since August, then her child—"

Daughter, I typed on my phone, and showed it to him. I forgot MatuSalem's warnings about communicating with my phone. I was in no mood for trouble, caution, or strategy. I was a first-time father, and I was worried sick about the woman I was madly in love with and the daughter she was expecting.

"Her daughter," he corrected himself, "might be the progeny of our serial—"

"I'm the father," I interrupted. I said it out loud, like a whip cracking. My pronunciation was firm and clear, fierce and self-assured. "I'm the father," I repeated.

I invented a white lie to protect them. I wrote on my phone, as the superintendent watched with interest.

DSU Salvatierra had begun the process of separating from her husband, although it wasn't official. All along, she and I were in a relationship, and she is pregnant with our daughter. We kept it a secret because of the special circumstances. DSU Salvatierra was intending to inform you about it in the near future. I'm sure you'll understand that this situation isn't easy for either of us. I would ask you not to let this information go any further, until DSU Salvatierra is well enough to discuss it with you in person. Although it goes without saying that you must do all you can to stop any suggestion that our daughter might be Nancho's.

I didn't want this to affect Alba professionally—and it wasn't fair to the baby to come into the world branded by the possibility that a serial killer was her father.

I didn't know whether Alba would allow me to be part of their lives. Perhaps my part in this tragicomedy had been unclear because I hadn't been equal to the task. But I needed to protect them both from the shadow that Nancho had cast over Vitoria, and this was the only way that occurred to me.

Had I only realized I was signing my own death warrant.

28

THE HOSPITAL GARDENS

THURSDAY, DECEMBER 8, 2016

Even though it was a public holiday, I showed up at the hospital first thing in the morning, when the nurses were making their rounds. Alba's mother lay curled up on a green leather sofa, elegant even in sleep. Had someone carried her off slumbering like that, she still would have retained her poise.

I woke her gently, trying not to disturb Alba. Nieves understood my intentions when I gave her a pleading look, and she left me alone with her daughter. I brought a hard chair over to perch on.

I was in no hurry to wake Alba. I was absorbed by the discreet bump discernible beneath the sheets. I had an overwhelming urge to run my hand over Alba's belly and tell our child not to be afraid, but I didn't dare.

Perhaps this strong little girl was already able to sense my presence, because at that very instant, Alba opened her eyes slowly, as though she was returning from exile.

"Good morning, Alba. How are you feeling?" The sentence came out smoothly, but it was, admittedly, rehearsed.

"Seven words. You spoke seven words." She smiled, despite her exhaustion and the shadows under her eyes.

"One more month and I'll . . . make a speech."

She laughed, but I didn't want her to laugh. Not yet. Now came the hard part. And I wanted to have this conversation unaided, without my notebook. I'd spent the night preparing a series of pithy sentences, the kind that define a life and that you remember when you're old.

"The superintendent knows," I told her.

"What does he know?"

"He came here last night."

"What does he know?" she insisted.

"You had separated, and we were together."

She considered the idea. I hadn't expressed it very well, but my verbal prowess didn't extend much further.

"Why? Why did you tell him that?"

"I said she's my daughter, for certain."

Alba looked at her belly, as though engaging the baby in a conversation from which I was excluded.

"You did it for her sake," she finally said.

"People are talking, Alba. No one—"

"That she could be Nancho's daughter."

"She doesn't deserve that burden."

"You're protecting her. You don't even know she's your daughter, yet you're protecting her."

"Let me do this. You and I . . . You have to decide if there is a you and I. But let me do this."

"So we're going to tell everybody that Nancho and I had already separated, that you and I have been in a relationship since August, and that there's no doubt this is your daughter."

"One story. Forever. No cracks." Like a mantra. We had to make it watertight; our story needed to last a lifetime. Two lifetimes. Hers and her daughter's.

"What if she takes after Nancho?"

"He was okay when he wasn't killing people," I blurted out.

She looked as if she wanted to stab me with the needle from her IV, then she laughed a deep belly laugh.

"You're right, he wasn't such a bad guy after all," she said, nodding.

I laughed with her, even though deep down I begged Martina to forgive this sacrilege. But we needed to laugh, to see the humor of our situation, in order to overcome the challenges ahead.

That brief moment wasn't enough, and I brushed Alba's hand intending to squeeze it, to give her strength, but she pulled away.

"Unai, about you and me . . . I can't give you an answer today, okay? Right now, I have other things to think about. I need to build up my strength for when I leave the hospital and go back to work. I want to face the situation at the police station alone. After that, I'll decide about us, all right?"

What choice do I have?

"Of course," I said. "May I come back this afternoon?" I asked before leaving.

"You may see your daughter whenever you want, Unai. Come whenever you want."

And those words were enough to light up my universe.

I went out into the corridor and found Nieves leaning against the wall waiting for me.

"Come on, Unai. I'll walk you out."

"Of course," I replied.

Here and there, a patient wandering around with an IV drip on wheels gave us a sidelong glance.

I wasn't sure if they'd recognized Kraken or the former actress.

Nieves pretended not to notice, so I followed her lead. We passed nurses and staff until we reached the main entrance. Then we went outside and crossed the parking lot. Cars rolled by, their drivers protected from the morning chill, focused on the workday ahead.

I wasn't jealous as I watched them. I'd soon be one of them.

Suddenly, Nieves said, "I admire her."

"Sorry?"

"I admire Alba."

I was going to agree, but it felt inappropriate.

"I've always admired how strong and grown-up she is. Do you know what it's like to have a daughter who never complains?"

I smiled. Her description of Alba was spot on. Quiet and tough.

"Of all the things I've accomplished in my life, she's my greatest achievement. She won't break. This pregnancy won't break her, however tough it is. She's already lost one child. That loss was much more difficult. She's decided. You strike me as a good man, so I'll spare you the lecture about not hurting my daughter. That's up to you both. She'll make sure you don't hurt her."

"I know."

"What I will ask you is to not hurt my granddaughter. If you're going to be part of her life, if Alba wants that, then be a father to her. But if one or both of you decide that you aren't going to be, then leave. Don't get involved. Don't barge into my granddaughter's life and turn things upside down. I don't know if she'll be strong like Alba, or weak like her grandfather, acquisitive like her great-grandfather, or psychopathic if she's Nancho's daughter. All I know is that having a part-time father will only make her suffer, as it would any of us. You and Alba must be absolutely clear about the role you're going to play in my granddaughter's life. Fatherhood isn't a license they give away, Unai. You'll make mistakes and mess up the way all parents do. But decide now what role you're going to play. From now on, you're no longer just a couple. You're a family, and a child's life is in your hands."

"I hope Alba lets me, Ni . . . Nieves. I want my daughter to have a father."

Nieves seemed satisfied with my reply, or maybe with the determination she saw in my eyes.

I wasn't putting on an act. I was standing in front of her showing her everything and I didn't mind her seeing my nerves, my inability to converse.

Despite everything, I knew I could be a good father.

We kissed each other on both cheeks, and Nieves turned toward the entrance steps.

"See you this afternoon. Tell me if . . . if you need anything," I said.

She turned to face me. "Unai . . . I just want you to know something," she said.

"What?"

"I'd love you to be my granddaughter's father."

"Th . . . th . . . thank you, Nieves," I said, touched.

Now I knew where Alba got her strong character.

29

THE ALTAR OF LAS MATRES

Friday, December 9, 2016

At seven in the evening it started to pour. I narrowly escaped into my speech therapist's doorway, my shoulders and hair dripping wet. I shook the excess off in the stairwell. Beatriz Korres's consulting room had no heating and poor insulation, and I wondered how she would fare against what threatened to be a harsh winter.

We repeated the eight-word sentences, and she urged me to keep practicing on my phone. I seemed to be progressing more quickly than she'd expected. There was no secret to it: I simply spent four or five hours doing rehabilitation exercises on my own. I was desperate to return to normal.

My apartment had become a boxing ring. My main opponents were inertia, the ups and downs of the investigation, and mental fatigue. I got to know them better every day, and every day my muscles grew stronger. Every day I threw another punch, won a small battle. The key was persistence.

The clock in her consulting room struck eight. It was dark and the intense downpour had eased.

"That's enough for today, Unai. If you carry on like this, I won't have any time with my other patients," she said with a placid smile.

She put on her blue leather coat and picked up a matching umbrella, and we headed out.

I saw a surprising thing outside, and I was so touched, it gave me back my belief in humanity.

My poor brother was waiting for us on Calle San Antonio, soaked to the skin and shielding from the rain what must have been an elegant and expensive bouquet.

In a nearby trash can, I spotted a familiar umbrella, the ribs bent out of shape. The rainstorm hadn't been kind to Germán's romantic intentions.

"What are you doing?" I asked out loud.

This was one of the stock questions I'd been working on with Beatriz. It was a useful phrase.

Germán cleared his throat, composing himself. Clearly, this meant a lot to him.

"I brought this small gift as a thank-you to my brother's speech therapist for helping him. Beatriz, I'll bring you a new bouquet tomorrow, I—"

"Why didn't you buzz up to bring this"—she interrupted him, stepping forward to take the bedraggled blooms he was cradling—"small gift?"

"I didn't want to interrupt your session. That's what matters . . . more than anything."

Beatriz looked at him tenderly. She seemed genuinely touched. My brother was soaked down to his briefcase. His stubby fingers, trembling in the cold, were wrinkled like an old man's.

I cast a sidelong glance at my speech therapist. She was quiet, possibly a little disconcerted. I couldn't tell for sure, but I suspect this was the moment she fell in love with him. Something had broken through her professional exterior.

She had let Germán in.

From then on, Beatriz was all sweetness and light with him.

"You're freezing, Germán. Let's go to a café and I'll buy you both something hot . . . I don't need warming up, but I'll go with you."

We headed toward Calle Dato, Beatriz still carrying the bouquet even though it was dripping onto her leather coat and designer bag.

"Are you sure you aren't cold?" Germán persisted.

Beatriz laughed off his concern. "I've always been on the heavy side. I was plump as a little girl and then as a teenager. I guess it has some advantages because I don't feel the cold," she said, smiling.

I watched them in silence. How sweet. Love's shy blossoming.

My brother's doubts and misgivings and my speech therapist's decorum ended up in the trash can, alongside his umbrella, vanquished by the rain.

There were enough pheromones in the air to rouse the libido of even a gray wolf, the most monogamous and faithful of creatures. I was impressed by how compatible they were. Germán talked continuously, a veritable volcano of verbosity, while Beatriz, a good listener, gazed at him like the heaven-sent gift he was.

I accompanied them as far as Usokari's, where I took my leave, giving a convenient excuse neither of them questioned, even though it sounded like a well-intentioned lie. They said good-bye, promising that we'd get together another day, and I left them in their paradise. They'd earned it; they were good people.

I wandered down the deserted, wet Calle Dato, where the only person who greeted me was the bronze El Caminante statue. The temperature had plummeted, and the city stayed inside, helping their kids with their homework, slouching in front of the television, making supper.

I was passing the monument to the Battle of Vitoria, heading for my building, when I remembered I needed to call Héctor del Castillo. I pulled out my new phone from Milán. I didn't want Golden tracing this call. To differentiate it from my old phone, I'd given it the ringtone "Love Me Again" by John Newman. I know, sometimes my subconscious decides these things for me.

I dialed Héctor's number.

"Héctor, it's Unai López de Ayala. New phone."

"Inspector, I'm pleased to hear how well your speech is coming along," he replied in his calm, affable voice.

"I know." I smiled. "May I ask you something?"

"Yes, by all means."

In a child's simple sentences, I told him about the Barbacana pool. I knew he would assume another body had been found. There was no need to go into detail.

"Is there another altar there?" I asked.

"Yes, in fact, it's dedicated to the three mothers. It was discovered in an orchard wall outside Laguardia, yet another example of a place connected with the worship of water as an element of fertility and with rituals and offerings made to las Matres. You haven't mentioned the circumstances of your latest find, but as a place to carry out the Threefold Death, the Barbacana pool is ideal. Does that make sense in terms of your investigation, Inspector Ayala?"

I sighed. I dearly wished it didn't make sense. More water rituals were not what I wanted. I preferred a personal motive or a single murder, not the possibility of more murders. They had only just started and didn't seem about to end.

"Yes, it . . . it does," I said at last, opening the main door to my building with my free hand. "Thanks, Héctor."

"Don't mention it, Inspector Ayala. I'm as concerned as you are about this affair. I'm happy to help, although I hope you won't need me again. Take care."

I went up to my apartment to practice the new batch of exercises. The Nardil cards Beatriz had given me had successively longer sentences: *The girl goes down the stairs. The boys play with the girl. The girl draws a big white moon* . . .

As I was going through them, Estíbaliz called my new phone.

"I've made some headway in the investigation, Unai. Connected with Cantabria. Sit tight," my colleague said.

"I'm . . . listening," I told her. I waited a good while.

I took off my damp pullover and put on a loose sweatshirt. I went over to the window and pressed my forehead against the glass, training my eyes on the white balconies opposite.

"Milán found Saúl Tovar's sister, Sarah. She holds a senior position at Valdecilla hospital and is apparently untouchable. I think we should pay her a surprise visit, just like we did with Saúl. I don't know what kind of relationship they have now. They were both young when their parents died. She's four years older and took care of him through childhood. They shared a house until he got married. She is single and has no children. She doesn't have a partner and appears to be celibate. She belongs to a dozen or so religious associations, a few with charitable enterprises. A devout soul, people say."

"Why . . . why Saúl?"

Estíbaliz understood my question. I wanted to know why she was focusing on Saúl when we had suspects in Vitoria. We had more reasons to investigate Asier and Golden Girl than him. They both had a lot of explaining to do, and they were both going to be evasive. We'd make more headway if we focused on them.

"Why Saúl? Well, get this—Milán discovered something we overlooked. She's amazing, that girl; we have a whiz kid on our team."

"Estí . . ." I was getting impatient.

"I don't know if you've been up to speed on the recent suicides this year, but three people have died by suicide under mysterious circumstances, each on a different mountain on the Cantabrian coast. Last September a twenty-three-year-old girl from Santander was found on Monte Dobra, in Cantabria."

"How . . . how did it happen?"

"That's the mysterious part about these deaths. The victims are teenagers or young adults. Some have antisocial tendencies, living like recluses, but no history of violence or drug abuse. One day, they leave home wearing only the clothes on their backs, climb the nearest mountain, strip naked, spend the night in the open, and are found dead the next day. They seemingly let themselves die of exposure, an extremely unusual act of self-directed aggression. Apparently, they prefer to freeze for several hours rather than end things quickly with a razor blade or pills or by jumping off something. From the victimologist point of view, I'd say these are people phobic about blood, reserved, almost fearful, despite having the courage to stay out on a dark mountainside for hours."

"Who was the girl?"

I understood what she was saying about the suicides. What I wasn't sure about was the connection between the victim and Saúl.

"Her name was Gimena Tovar, Unai. She's Saúl Tovar's daughter. Rebeca Tovar isn't the only daughter your teacher lost."

What? I couldn't express my astonishment.

Saúl had a daughter other than Rebeca? He hadn't mentioned her when we visited him at the university.

For a father to lose two daughters under such appalling circumstances . . .

In all honesty, I wasn't sure whether to pity him or to start suspecting that these tragedies were more than what one might expect someone to suffer in a lifetime.

Be that as it may, we had to pay another visit to Cantabria.

30

THE MONTE GORBEA CROSS

SATURDAY, DECEMBER 10, 2016

A young woman set off for the cross on Monte Gorbea in the early hours. She didn't mind walking in the dark. The path was familiar, and she wouldn't be long. She was just visiting her brother. She carried him with her everywhere, hidden, a silver *eguzkilore* kept warm next to her chest, but she needed to speak with him. He was the only one to whom she could unburden herself. Alba was no use. Not for this particular conversation. She'd been worried sick since the shock of Alba's convulsions, and, for the first time, a tiny bit jealous of the sympathy and attention Unai gave her, despite her efforts not to be. She felt proud of her stoic attitude. She'd managed to control herself with Paula, and, to her relief, Alba was better for Kraken than Paula. More mature, more focused. She would do more to protect him from himself and his obsessions.

Why did you get yourself pregnant now of all times? Haven't you realized what this ritual is all about? Can't you see that the people dying aren't equipped to be parents? she reproached Alba.

Like that cynical Annabel. How could such a cold person be a good mother? And Jota . . . Estí had firsthand experience of the way an alcoholic parent brings up his children. Not to mention Rebeca. Eneko had told her about the things Lutxo hinted at . . .

Unai had told her as if he were making a confession. Yes, the girl was his, yes, there was no doubt about it . . .

Would it work? Would he persuade an entire city to swallow this unlikely explanation?

Estíbaliz had said, "I'm happy for you both." What choice did she have? And in a sense, she was happy. She wanted Unai to have a family. She'd been through this already when he and Paula, desperate because they couldn't get pregnant, had made an appointment with a fertility expert. Estíbaliz had accepted it.

But not now, for God's sake, not now.

She had parked her car at Murua and, a good while later, arrived exhausted and worked up at the foot of the cross. This was the last place she had seen her brother, touched his ashes, watched them float away to mingle with the mountain.

"I know you never liked Unai, and you'll say I deserve all I get for being a masochist, but seriously, they don't realize what they're getting into . . ."

Estíbaliz listened to Eneko's sarcastic response.

"Hey, I didn't come all the way here to be yelled at."

Eneko said something more. Her brother's spirit was having a bad day.

"Stop being so rude or I'll leave you all alone up here in the cold."

Eneko changed the subject, but that didn't go too well, either.

"Dad's not good, as usual. More stressed out, more violent, more medicated. You already know, so why ask."

Estíbaliz pulled out a ham roll she'd made for the trip and, leaning back against the base of the cross, started nibbling at it.

"Eneko, I'm thinking about helping other kids like us. So they don't . . . you know what I mean. So they don't have to go through what we did. Alba is eager to set it up, and, well, we're all destined to do something in this life that touches us deeply, that we're driven to do. You protected me, saved me from hell even if you did introduce me to drugs to do it. I want to be that person, to help other people out of their private hells, by giving them strength. I know

this sounds like a lot of baloney to you. Hey, don't look so skepti-
cal, or I won't continue."

But it was no use. Maybe it was the day, or the wind, or the
negative ions, but that morning Estíbaliz couldn't connect with
her brother the way she had before.

Frustrated, she kissed the stone cross and started back down.

Twenty-five kilometers south, on the Alavese plain, Vitoria
was still asleep.

31

THE HANGMAN GAME

Thursday, December 15, 2016

The rumor started on Twitter that morning. There was talk of hanged bodies in the San Adrián Tunnel. Someone connected that event to what had happened at the Barbacana pool.

By the time we traced the first tweet and discussed whether to press charges for a breach of the gag order, it had been retweeted by thousands of other accounts and was completely out of our hands.

To me, this was a perfect example of the butterfly effect. Was it Nerea or Lutxo? A friend or relative of the climbers from Araia? Or someone peeping through their curtains across the street from the Barbacana pool in Laguardia?

Maybe Nerea told her sister and started a chain of promises not to tell, which the sister broke with her husband, who scored points with a few trusted colleagues around the coffee machine at the Mercedes factory. The story was repeated, rebooted, and replicated countless times in bedrooms, in bars, and on the streets of Vitoria, until some attention-seeker far removed from the initial source launched it into the social-media stratosphere.

Maybe it was Lutxo, who opened a Twitter account with an anonymous handle, anxious to tell the story simply because his newspaper couldn't. Maybe he felt frustrated because his editor refused to run the story. The question that plagued me was whether

Lutxo had any interest in the news spreading. How deeply, if at all, was he implicated in this? How much did he know? Was he withholding any information about the deaths of Annabel and Jota?

After reading and analyzing all the related tweets, we realized that not all the details had been revealed, like the bodies being hung upside down, although the location of the crime scenes at the San Adrián Tunnel and the Barbacana pool had leaked as well as the fact that one of the victims was pregnant.

The collective mind, in an inventive flourish, had baptized the crimes "The Hangman Game."

For simple souls, there was a pattern to these murders.

The *A* in San Adrián.

The *B* in Barbacana.

Where would the next person be hung? What historic locations began with *C*?

We knew about the two locations in Cantabria that could be added to that list.

The *D* in Monte Dobra and the *F* in Fontibre.

But we couldn't prevent the city from waking up to a headline that dropped like an atomic bomb: LUNATIC KILLER PLAYING HANGMAN WITH US ALL.

32

VALDECILLA HOSPITAL

FRIDAY, DECEMBER 16, 2016

It was open season on the streets of Vitoria again. I was the prey and the stranger's glares felt like the ammo.

On Friday, I decided to take a tram to the police headquarters in Lakua. It turned out to be an unpleasant ride. A pregnant woman protected her belly as I walked past while her partner scowled at me. An older woman shifted to occupy half the empty seat next to her so I couldn't sit down. I guessed she was about to become a grandmother.

I had become the public face of a police unit that was expected to produce immediate results, even though we had few clues from forensics, no clear motive for the killings nor profiles for the victims, and were unable to predict the killer's next move.

I welcomed Héctor's impromptu call, even though he was ringing my old cell phone. So when I heard him tell me he'd remembered something that might help the investigation, I quickly cut in:

"I'm headed to Santander today. I'll stop by . . . Tell me then." I concentrated hard. Eleven words.

I followed up with a text from the new phone to arrange a time, and Héctor sent me his home address in Santander. He also wanted some privacy; all these police visits didn't look good for his museum.

Two hours later, Estíbaliz and I were navigating the corridors of the impressive Marqués de Valdecilla University Hospital in Santander in search of Sarah Tovar.

At the reception desk, a snub-nosed woman with a breezy manner directed us to the hospital chapel. "You're more likely to find her there than in her office," the woman said, shrugging.

After losing our bearings several times amid the maze of corridors, we finally entered the empty chapel with its light polished floors. A lone woman in a white lab coat was praying in the front pew.

She wore her hair pulled back into a low bun and looked old. I didn't think she could be Saúl's sister.

Even so, we approached the pew and stood discreetly beside her. Estíbaliz extended her hand and introduced herself in a hushed voice, seeing her name badge.

"Inspector Gauna, Vitoria police. This is my colleague, Inspector Ayala, an old acquaintance of your brother. Could you spare us a moment of your time, Doctor Tovar?"

The woman gave a start, as if her direct line to God had been rudely cut off.

Sarah Tovar rose, tall and willowy as a paschal candle, and extended a long, slender hand. She invited us to take a seat, giving the impression that the chapel, as well as being God's house, was hers, too.

"We can talk here. We'll have more privacy than anywhere else in the hospital. My brother already warned me that you were asking questions about my niece. What do you want from me? I told the detectives investigating the case at the time everything I knew."

Sarah looked at us with unconcealed hostility. Her raked-back hair lent a harshness to her features, which a few years ago must have been as splendid as her brother's: the dark complexion, the black hair with a bluish tinge, the green eyes like a cat's, the angular jawline that was now a little flaccid.

She dressed like a fastidious widow, complete with an elegant little pearl necklace. The contrast between her and her brother was striking, and yet I now detected a distinct family resemblance.

Estíbaliz and I had gone over the questions I wanted her to ask, and, anticipating that the doctor wouldn't give us much of her time, my colleague made a tentative start.

"Then you know that we're looking into the disappearance of your niece again."

"Her murder," she interrupted. "She was murdered. Didn't you see the photographs of Rebeca suspended from a tree?"

"Of course, but her body was never found."

"No, it wasn't. No thanks to your blundering. But anyone can see the girl was dead when those pictures were taken."

Estíbaliz sighed. The two women had taken an instant dislike to each other, and my colleague was doing her best to prevent that hostility from cutting the interview short.

"In any case, we would like to ask you about Rebeca's medical history. Your brother told us that as an endocrinologist you were monitoring her growth, since she was small for her age. He also said that the results of routine blood tests in the months prior to her disappearance ruled out the possibility that she was pregnant."

"That's correct, and anyway such an aberration was out of the question."

"Sarah, we know that Rebeca was admitted to the psychiatric wing of this hospital. Could you tell us why?"

Doctor Tovar gave us a withering look, folded her arms in a defensive gesture, and shook her head.

"As you both know, I'm not at liberty to provide medical information concerning a minor. With Rebeca's father's permission, I revealed the results of her blood tests to the police to prove she hadn't been pregnant, but this is a different matter. You will need a signed warrant, and, assuming you get it, you'll need to speak to Doctor Osorio, the head of the Children's Psychiatric Unit. Rebeca was his patient. Good luck."

Estí and I exchanged a quick glance: a dead end. We needed to take a different approach.

"We also came to ask you about the suicide of your other niece, Gimena."

A grimace of pain threatened to shatter Sarah Tovar's steely expression. The kind of pain you can't fake.

"What Gimena did was a mortal sin, and I'll never forgive her for taking her own life. It is such a pity because she was a good girl. Very studious, top of her class in history. She was pure; she never stained our family's reputation by having a boyfriend."

"There's one thing I don't understand," said Estíbaliz, treading carefully to prolong this unexpected confession. "Saúl lost his wife, and Rebeca two years later. He wasn't in a relationship with anyone after that, so who was Gimena's mother?"

"Didn't you know? Gimena was adopted. My brother and his wife thought it would be good for Rebeca to have a sibling, and as generous people, they decided to adopt a child who hadn't had the good fortune to be born into a loving family like theirs. Saúl and my sister-in-law were considered an ideal couple and were placed on the waiting list.

"When he was widowed, it never occurred to him to take his name off the list. He had enough on his plate coping with his loss and an unstable daughter. Even though he had become a single parent, Saúl was still considered an ideal candidate—he earned a good salary, lived in a big house, and had time to raise a child.

"Gimena arrived like a blessing soon after Rebeca died. She was a beautiful baby when she came into my brother's shattered life.

He gave her all the love and attention she deserved, and she . . . I still don't know how she could have done this to us, gone up that mountain and stayed out in the cold. Not after all the love we gave her. Rebeca was a different story—rebellious, capricious, manipulative . . . She lived in a fantasy world; her soul was blackened with lies and falsehoods."

"What do you think might have led her to take her own life?" I asked.

"Gimena had just finished her degree. She was so happy at graduation and had a bright future. But she was also a little depressed those last few months. Understandably, Saúl was spending less time with her. While she was still at university, they were constantly together, at school and at home. Perhaps she was too dependent on him, I don't know. My brother was a wonderful father, so it was only normal that she adored him."

"Do you . . . do you have a photo of Gimena?" I asked tentatively.

"Yes, I bring it with me to the altar every day, and I pray for her soul. Altars are important, you know. They bring us before God. Look at her, was she not a child untouched by the evil of this world?"

She showed us a photograph of a girl who did not look twenty-three. She was childlike, androgynous, with a sweet, short haircut, and an innocent, timid expression.

"Yes," Estíbaliz agreed. "Yes, she looks like a nice girl. And can you tell me—"

My colleague didn't get to finish her question. Sarah was tired of our questions and our company. She looked at the vintage watch on her slender wrist.

"I need to get back to work, as I'm sure you'll appreciate," she declared in a tone that brooked no second attempt. She rose from the shiny pew.

"Of course." said Estíbaliz. "Perhaps you can show us the way out—it took us ages to find our way here."

Sarah smirked, and I glimpsed a sense of her satisfaction at having the upper hand.

She escorted us to the elevator, and the three of us stepped inside its shiny steel interior. Sarah Tovar was about to press the button when an elderly gentleman, who despite his white coat looked well beyond retirement age, appeared in the door.

"Oh, I'm so sorry," he said in a smoker's husky voice. "If it's going to be a squeeze, I'll wait for the next one."

Sarah and the man exchanged a look. It was only a fraction of a second, but I could tell something was going on between them. I couldn't help forcing the situation to find out what.

"Get in, get in. There's plenty of room," I urged him.

I stepped out of the lift and—as politely as possible, with an angelic look on my face—all but pushed him inside, giving him no choice.

Unwilling to create a scene, he reluctantly joined us and stared uncomfortably at the ceiling, while the four of us were whisked down to the first floor.

I prepared a seventeen-word sentence, my longest to date, and launched it like a grenade, hoping it wouldn't backfire.

"So you know where to find us, Doctor Tovar . . . to talk about Rebeca. At Vitoria police headquarters."

It was worth the effort to see the horrified expression of the doctor whose initials, embroidered on his spotless white coat, matched those of the psychiatrist who had committed Rebeca Tovar.

Sarah shot me a look of hatred.

The elevator opened and spat us out. Estíbaliz and I said polite good-byes to Sarah Tovar, while the old doctor headed off in the opposite direction, looking a little lost.

Back in the patrol car, Estíbaliz dished out the praise. "That was the old you, Kraken. And that was the most I've heard you speak since your recovery!"

Having noticed the curious stares we got on our first visit, we had taken a marked car on this trip so there was no mistaking who we were. We desperately needed the locals to take note in the hopes it would encourage them to talk about the past. We didn't want to pass up this opportunity to loosen a few tongues.

"Instinct, Inspector Gauna," I responded. I felt like myself again.

"Clearly Doctor Osorio warrants further investigation. But Sarah Tovar also made it perfectly obvious that she adored Gimena and detested Rebeca. I wonder why when they were both her nieces," Estí said.

"Rebeca was a blood relative, and Gimena was adopted," I suggested.

"That theory makes sense, but the adoption story doesn't add up. It was wrong on every level. Waiting list or no, there's no way that twenty years ago a widowed father would be given a newborn to look after."

"Unless . . ." I looked at Estíbaliz. We'd both come to the same conclusion.

"Unless Saúl, his sister, or Doctor Osorio pulled some strings."

Estíbaliz was picking up her phone to get in touch with our team when Milán called, as if she'd been reading our thoughts.

"Milán, good timing. Is Peña there by any chance?" Estí asked.

"Yes, we're both in the office—there have been some developments."

"Put your cell phone on speaker."

"Sure."

"Inspector Ayala is with me here in Santander," she told them. "Peña, I need you to look into the adoption of Gimena Tovar in Santander in 1993."

"What are we looking for?"

"Any irregularities, and also whether there's any mention of Doctor Sarah Tovar, or Doctor Osorio, a psychiatrist at the Marqués de Valdecilla Hospital."

"I'll get on it right away," Peña replied.

"What's your news?"

"Things on the Internet have gone crazy, boss," said Milán. "Annabel Lee's editor at Malatrama posted an official announcement this morning on their Twitter account confirming her death."

"And why the hell did he choose to do that right now?"

"For weeks Annabel Lee's fans have been demanding to know why she's stopped updating her social media. When the stories appeared on Twitter this morning about a pregnant Alavese woman found dead on November seventeenth, people put two and two together and started asking her editor if the dead woman was Annabel Lee. He confirmed it in a tweet, out of carelessness I think as much as anything else. After that, it's all been memes and condolences, and—" Milán broke off, as though unsure whether to continue.

"And what, Milán?" I urged her, getting impatient.

"I don't quite know how to tell you this, Inspector Ayala."

"Yes you do, just say it."

"Annabel Lee had a lot of fans who . . . would kill for her. Literally, or so they claim. They refuse to accept that their muse is dead, and that the killer is still on the loose, and—"

"Milán, tell us what's going on right now," Estíbaliz cut in.

"They've put a price on Kraken's head."

33

SAN JUAN DE GATZELUGATXE

SATURDAY, JULY 11, 1992

On Saturday, midway through summer camp, they set off for San Juan de Gatzelugatxe, the legendary church nestled on a tiny, idyllic islet on the coast of Viscaya. That weekend, a few older students had joined them, and Saúl decided to celebrate the occasion with mead. He had tried without much success to teach them how to make Celtic recipes like gruel and roasted meats.

They were interested in learning how to brew mead, the liquor of the Celts dating back some 2,500 years, though. They poured several liters of water mixed with clear honey into a copper cauldron, which Saúl produced from somewhere. Then they added an herbal blend, which would be removed later, that consisted of cinnamon, cloves, ground pepper, ginger, and dried elderberry leaves. Rebeca stirred the mixture patiently, caught up in her own thoughts, already detached from everything around her.

Mead needed to ferment for at least three months before it was ready to drink, so Saúl had brought the unopened bottles from the previous year. In the same way, the following year's students would enjoy the mead they were making now. The strongest of the bunch, Unai and Asier, were tasked with carrying the bottles.

Asier's attitude toward Saúl had changed radically. He never left the professor's side, sitting next to him in the evenings when Saúl told stories around the fire.

They didn't need to return to the conversation they'd had about Asier's father. Now they communicated with looks. Saúl made Asier feel strong. They were inseparable, and Lutxo had joined them, too. Three alpha males who were more dynamic than Jota or Unai, the laid-back members of the *cuadrilla*.

It was already dark when they began celebrating the success of summer camp, sitting outside the church, a little tipsy from the mead. Following tradition, they rang the bell three times and sat staring at the choppy sea. All except for Saúl, who did not join in the festivities. He had a two-hour drive back to Cantabria.

He had been entrusted with his students' lives and would not endanger them.

Jota stood up, stumbling, and looked around for Annabel. He hadn't seen her in a while.

"I hope she hasn't wandered off in the dark, with all these cliffs," he whispered to Unai.

Unai was also a little worried. The two friends decided to look for her. Jota unzipped Annabel's skull-design backpack, pulled out her headlamp, and slipped it on. Inside the backpack he also found some condoms. Possibly excited by the prospect, he set off with Unai to find her.

They tried to keep count as they descended the two-hundred-odd steps, laughing and exulting in this moment of friendship.

Little Jota went ahead, illuminating the coastal night with the circle of light that jerked around as he reeled drunkenly. Unai took more care and walked behind him, glancing to either side in search of the missing girl.

They found her farther down, on step number two hundred and five.

They were fucking the same way they spoke to each other, contemptuously, with furious gestures, and without any trace of tenderness in their caresses. Theirs was a violent, thrusting copulation.

"Jota, don't look," Unai whispered, fearing the worst.

And there was Jota, unable to turn off the headlamp. Unai reacted more quickly this time, maybe because he'd been through it before and it hurt less this time. He put his hand over the light and pulled Jota away to prevent an ugly scene.

What had Saúl been thinking giving everyone mead?

Jota had already proved he couldn't handle alcohol. That Friday when his father had been diagnosed with terminal cancer, the group had been in Bar Okendo. Jota, drinking heavily, had become convinced that people walking by were stepping on his feet on purpose. Unai had no choice but to drag his friend out of the bar before something happened.

So Unai left the pair in their seated position and pulled Jota back up the steps.

34

LA CUESTA DE LAS VIUDAS

FRIDAY, DECEMBER 16, 2016

The pale sun hidden amid clouds struggled to warm the wary city of Santander.

The fact that a mob of gothic-comics fans wanted my head on a pike wasn't exactly a relaxing way to spend Christmas. More sidelong glances, more belligerence online, more hostile whispers in my wake.

Fine. I'd been through this before.

What would Grandfather tell me? *Stop moaning and get on with it.*

Quite right, Grandad. Quite right.

We decided to tempt fate and pay a second visit to the University of Cantabria in search of Saúl.

Estíbaliz was suppressing her rage, her knuckles turning white. I knew she worried about my safety, but even so, her reactions touched me.

We left the car in the student parking lot the same way we had the last time. Walking through the corridors, we noticed the students' cautious glances.

I knocked on the door to Saúl's office, but there was no answer. It was locked. I asked Estíbaliz to call him.

She waited impatiently for him to pick up, but Saúl's phone was either switched off or out of range.

"His sister must have warned him we're in Santander, and he's avoiding us," she said, pacing the corridor like a caged cat.

"It's very likely."

Then Estí noticed the student with the different-colored eyes watching us from around a corner. He had called Saúl Gray Beard and wife-murderer.

Losing no time, Estíbaliz called out to him. But her shout frightened him, and he ran down the corridor.

We both took off, and despite my morning workouts, Estíbaliz proved to be the true gazelle. She quickly caught up with him, but the boy with the quiff ducked into the men's restroom, leaving Estí flustered for a second.

"You go in," she said when I arrived.

I entered and swore quietly to myself. The boy had escaped through a window. Why did they install such big windows in bathrooms? I always remembered them being small and high off the ground, not made for jumping through.

"There was a window," I explained as I came back out.

A handful of students had gathered and were openly curious. There must not have been much going on at the campus that day, because we'd turned into the star attraction.

"You," said Estíbaliz, picking out the least conventional-looking boy among the bystanders. "Do you know that boy?"

"Osorio. He's a good kid; he's not into anything sketchy, that's for sure," the boy replied. "You've got the wrong guy."

"Thanks. You can all get going, the show's over," she ordered, raising her voice slightly.

The small crowd dispersed, happy to have something to gossip about, and we were left alone in the corridor.

Estíbaliz said what both of us were thinking:

"It remains to be seen how much of a coincidence this is, but this elusive Osorio shares a surname with the psychiatrist who locked up Rebeca."

I pulled my little notebook out of my pocket and wrote, *Yes, but we shouldn't start looking for coincidences everywhere. Still, I don't think our trip has been a complete waste of time. Come on, we're meeting Héctor del Castillo next.*

Estí brightened. "This is turning into a rather pleasant day," she said, grinning, as we climbed back into the car. "We're making headway in the investigation, visiting a person of interest . . ."

"Our redhead is in love."

We drove up a tree-lined street the locals called La Cuesta de las Viudas, or Widows' Hill, although I couldn't recall why.

In any event, we were in the most beautiful part of Santander, and Héctor's coordinates had brought us to a tall old mansion overlooking Los Peligros beach. Ivy crept up the façade.

Estíbaliz responded with an appreciative "Wow."

We pressed the polished brass buzzer at the entrance and entered a beautiful garden. It must have been a lovely place to read, especially in the evening among the spectacular night-blooming queens of the night cacti.

Héctor waited for us in his luxuriant library. He was seated before the fire. Two empty armchairs stood next to his.

"It's nice and cozy in here," I said.

"How pleased I am at the progress you've made, Inspector Ayala," Héctor replied, shaking my hand warmly. He greeted Estíbaliz with kisses on both cheeks.

"So what have you got for us, Héctor?" she asked.

"Please sit down," he replied, and offered us a bowl of hazelnuts. "I remembered an incident that I think might help your investigation, and I wanted to tell you about it."

"We appreciate anything you can tell us," Estíbaliz encouraged him.

"You see, I can't stop thinking about how unusual it is to come across the ritual of the Celtic Threefold Death. I really thought it had vanished. We rejoice when the violence of the past is put behind us, when progress makes us abandon cruel practices. But then I remembered a story one of my fellow archeologists from Holland told me a few years ago."

"Holland," Estí said, confused.

"Yes, he worked at the Amsterdam Museum, which used to be the municipal orphanage, perhaps you know it. Doctor Groen is his name. He oversaw the ancient history section and was responsible for organizing temporary exhibitions. The museum borrows pieces from larger institutions, since they don't have an extensive collection."

"We're following you," I said supportively, after taking a few hazelnuts and warming my hands near the flames.

"I told you about the Gundestrup Cauldron—the most famous of the Celtic cauldrons. Well, it belongs to the National Museum of Denmark. My colleague organized an exhibition featuring various Celtic artifacts that were on loan, among them the Gundestrup Cauldron and the Trundholm Sun Chariot. Well, a few days before the exhibition opened, amid the rush of final preparations, the cauldron disappeared."

"Disappeared?"

"Someone stole it. He's sure. Just like what happened at our museum with the Cabárceno Cauldron. It too was a small museum without security cameras."

"What did they do?"

"The Amsterdam Museum owned a rather crude replica, but it was better than nothing. The museum's director contacted his Danish counterpart to inform him of the theft. Copenhagen wanted to avoid a scandal. I shouldn't really be telling you this, but I feel I should be completely honest with you. Museums don't always report thefts immediately. Sometimes the stolen items turn up because the thieves abandon them."

"I don't understand," said Estí.

"I'll explain. You see, if the thieves want to sell the piece on the black market, broadcasting the theft draws the attention of prospective buyers, making it more likely the piece will disappear. That's why the director of the National Museum of Denmark asked his Dutch counterpart to wait a few days before alerting the police."

"I don't like the sound of your Danish colleague," Estí blurted out.

Héctor pretended he hadn't heard. "The preparations for the exhibition continued, and a few days later, the original Gundestrup Cauldron was found lying in a gutter near the museum. Groen retrieved it after a neighbor told him."

"So the theft wasn't reported, no fingerprints were taken, no investigation was opened, and there were no suspects."

"Unfortunately, that's how these things sometimes go. However, the part that really disturbs me is what took place in Amsterdam during those few days. You see, the people in Groen's neighborhood started to complain that their pets had gone missing. Cats, dogs, small domestic animals. Some of them were found . . ." He sighed. "Well, the images are rather unpleasant."

"Believe me, we've seen all kinds of unpleasant things," said Estí.

"I can imagine. Then I'll get to the point. They were found burned, hanging from trees strung up by their back legs, their heads drenched . . . My colleague immediately thought of the Celtic Threefold Death. He'd analyzed one of the bog bodies, the woman from Huldremose, and so he was familiar with the ritual and knew that the cauldron played an important role in the ceremony."

"I see," I said out loud.

"Groen has always felt bad about this, because he believes that whoever took the cauldron wanted to perform the water rituals."

"Do you know if any of these neighbors reported their pets' deaths?" asked Estí.

"I don't know, this was simply an anecdote a fellow archaeologist told me. I didn't really want to dig any deeper, so I never thought to ask. I just wanted to show you how unusual it is for anyone in modern times to carry out the ritual of the Celtic Threefold Death."

"Are you saying you think it was the same person?" I asked.

"I'm not sure, these incidents took place a long time ago and a long way from here. And yet . . . it's hard not to think there's a connection."

"Héctor, I have an important question," I managed to say. I was terribly worried by what I'd just heard.

"What is it?"

"When did it happen?"

"In 1998. Does that tell you anything?"

It certainly did.

It told me something I didn't want to hear.

Golden Girl was living in Amsterdam, the European headquarters of Cisco Systems, when somebody started to dabble with the Celtic Threefold Death.

35

THE ATTIC ROOM AT VILLAVERDE

TUESDAY, DECEMBER 20, 2016

We'd planned for the whole team to meet in Villaverde. I was fed up with the imbroglio online. I felt watched wherever I went. I needed a rest from Big Brother.

Alba, Estí, Milán, and Peña agreed to meet me at six o'clock at Grandfather's house.

Villaverde was a lonely village in winter. Its seventeen inhabitants rarely even met in the streets during the week, preferring to hunker down inside their thick stone walls.

It was bitterly cold, but early in the morning, Grandfather had lit the stove in the little downstairs kitchen so that the heat rose up the old staircase, and we were able to gather around the enormous Ping-Pong table.

I'd instructed everyone to park in different places outside the entrance to the village to avoid an accumulation of vehicles, which I knew would arouse the suspicions of the few neighbors who might see strangers climbing the steep streets.

All the information we shared at the meeting was typed and printed using offline computers.

Grandfather came upstairs with a fresh, sweet-smelling batch of sugared almonds, and firmly extended his hand to Milán, Peña, and Alba. He gave Estí a warm and familiar pat on the back.

He offered us some home-brewed *zurracapote*, but I sent him back downstairs with an imploring look that said, *Please, not now.* He quietly withdrew, closing the attic door behind him.

Milán had spread out several yellow, pink, and green Post-it notes, causing Peña to roll his eyes.

I went over to the cardboard boxes that contained all my memories, the ones beneath the two fox pelts that had been hanging on the walls since after the war. I opened the box marked 1992 and selected a handful of photographs. I spread them out on the table, and my colleagues leaned in to examine them.

There were Lutxo, Asier, Jota, Annabel Lee . . . Saúl appeared in some, always with a protective arm around Rebeca. I even had a group photo that included the students from previous summers, who showed up on weekends to help out.

"This is so you have a photographic record from that time," I said, in one breath.

"Okay," Estí began, rising to her feet, "we're here to update one another on our progress in the investigation and to establish the leads we're going to follow. As you know, due to the special nature of the case, Inspector Ayala has a new cell phone, which you can use to share confidential information with him. Use his old number for everything else. We know it's been hacked by at least two different people. We'll talk about that more in a minute. Peña, let's start with José Javier Hueto's autopsy."

Peña passed out the report. It was still deeply troubling to see Jota's body. We had grown up together, friends since we were little. We came of age together, and as he continued to grow, I saw him stumble with alcohol and bad habits. I didn't want to see his mottled skin, his blue face, his bloated belly.

Even so, I read the report carefully, eager for anything that would help me find his killer.

Estíbaliz summed it up: "The deceased was shocked by a Taser.

Here we can see the two marks on his neck from the probes. We also know that the cause of death was drowning: water in the victim's lungs indicates that he was alive when his head was submerged. We're currently analyzing the water to determine whether it was potable or untreated. Finding out where the victim died is more problematic, although there's no doubt that José Javier was moved postmortem and strung up by his feet at the Barbacana pool."

We all nodded.

"These details lead us to believe that the killer was following the ritual of the Celtic Threefold Death," she added, "which is the same modus operandi as in the Ana Belén Liaño murder. This case, however, didn't involve a stolen cauldron—possibly because this type of archaeological artifact is rare on the Iberian Peninsula. We believe that after killing Ana Belén Liaño, the perpetrator or perpetrators intended to continue using the Cabárceno Cauldron to carry out subsequent murders, but their plan was foiled by the swift discovery of her body. We know that killers follow a cost-benefit rationale: although the cauldron was an essential part of the Celtic ritual, the risk involved in attempting to steal it again was too great, since it is currently in police possession. The killer has changed his or her modus operandi to accommodate the new situation. This is not unlike the murder of Rebeca Tovar in Fontibre, assuming we're looking at the same perpetrator, since she was submerged in the river, not in a cauldron."

"How many murders do we have so far?" asked Alba.

"Rebeca Tovar in 1993, Ana Belén Liaño on November seventeenth, 2016, and José Javier Hueto on December fourth, 2016. Inspector Ayala and I have discovered another possible connection among these three cases, dating back to 1998 in Amsterdam. However, in this case, the victims were pets that were sacrificed using the ritual of the Celtic Threefold Death, and it involved the theft of another archaeological artifact important to the Celtic repertory—the Gundestrup Cauldron."

As she finished, Estíbaliz scooped up a handful of Grandfather's sugared almonds. Like me, she had a sweet tooth, and I made a mental note to give her some of my wine-preserved pears and baked apples. They were irresistible.

"I think we need to continue investigating our suspects. What leads are we currently following, Inspector Gauna?"

"Asier Ruiz de Azua, the hacker known as Golden Girl, and Saúl Tovar."

"Let's start with Asier," said Alba. "What do we have on him?"

"He knew all three victims," Estíbaliz noted. "The nature of his relationship with Ana Belén Liaño is still unclear, but he is the cosigner on her multimillion-euro account. Asier was attacked at his pharmacy a few days before José Javier's death and has not been forthcoming about his assailant. We have physical evidence that he hit his attacker. It's possible he fought with his friend José Javier, whose facial bruising occurred before his death."

"Motive?"

"In the case of Ana Belén Liaño, he might have wanted the money to bail out his failing business, but also possibly to prevent his wife from finding out he was the father of the victim's unborn child, if indeed that was the case. It's conceivable that his friend José Javier knew too much, and after a violent altercation, he dumped him at the Barbacana pool. As for Rebeca's murder, it's possible he got her pregnant. They had met at the summer camp in 1992. He might have killed her because he didn't want to have a child with a fourteen-year-old girl. Asier would have been about seventeen back then, and a pregnancy would have wrecked his future. Her father would have been able to report him for having sex with a minor—a crime that would still carry a sentence even if she said it was consensual."

I was shocked.

Estí had never presented the case for Asier's possible guilt so clearly. She hadn't said anything I hadn't already thought of, yet hearing it summed up like that, with her cold reasoning . . .

For Asier, who was part of my *cuadrilla*, to kill Rebeca, Ana Belén, and Jota . . .

He had motives; he lacked empathy; he even had a smattering of knowledge about the Celtic world. But was that enough for him to commit three murders?

"What's your strategy?" Alba asked.

"We're going to look into his social circle, check out his alibis for November seventeenth and December fourth, possibly interrogate him, step up the pressure to see what he says—"

"Let me try," I interrupted. "It can't hurt."

They turned with a piteous look. I detest that look.

"Let me try," I repeated. "I'll talk to him. Then he's all yours."

"Okay," said Estíbaliz. "Talk to him this week. If you're making no headway, maybe we'll call him in as a suspect. Let's see how far you get, Unai."

I nodded silently. Asier was a block of ice, but his wife, Araceli, and I had always gotten along well. Maybe she could provide me with some clue that Asier was refusing to give us.

"Whether we want to talk about it or not," Estí said, "I think the most urgent thing we need to establish is whether all three victims were expecting a child. Because if Rebeca, Ana Belén Liaño, and José Javier were going to be parents . . . everyone else who was at the Cantabrian settlement in 1992 and who is now expecting a child could be a target. That's my theory."

"Do you think it's that clear-cut?" Alba asked.

"If the victim profile is an expectant parent who attended that summer camp in 1992, then Inspector Ayala is in grave danger—and I'm not talking about the online threats he's been receiving. I have a feeling a lot of that is just hot air. I'm talking about whoever in Inspector Ayala's circle has already committed murder," Estíbaliz said.

Although I found it extremely awkward for my private life, and my relationship with Alba, to be discussed in front of our colleagues, I was touched by Estíbaliz's unfailing desire to protect me.

Milán held her breath, while Peña blushed to the roots of his hair. Alba stepped up with her usual aplomb.

"Well, in that case you must make every effort to discover the true motive behind these murders, because my daughter doesn't deserve not to know her father."

They turned toward me as one, but I was too stunned to feel embarrassed.

This was the first time Alba had referred to me unequivocally as the father of her daughter.

Our show of unity was for the protection of the child. It was the only thing that could save her from being known for the rest of her life as the daughter of a serial killer.

"Asier and Lutxo could also be in danger, if either of them is expecting a child," the ever-pragmatic Peña volunteered. "We need to rule that out, don't you agree?"

"Of course," said Milán, jotting down this directive on a pink Post-it note.

"Shall we talk about the other suspects?" I proposed, ready to move on from the awkward topic.

"Golden Girl. She's collaborated unofficially with Inspector Ayala on previous cases," explained Estíbaliz. "He received a warning from MatuSalem, another security expert with a criminal record, that Golden has been looking into elements of our investigation on the deep web—specifically, Tasers and forums relating to young people's suicides. She was already looking at those forums before Milán discovered that Gimena Tovar, the adopted daughter of Saúl Tovar, who led the 1992 summer camp, took her own life in similar circumstances. She intentionally died of hypothermia on Monte Dobra, a place that has numerous archaeological remains, and therefore links to all our current crime scenes."

"Just a moment," I interrupted. "Okay, Golden is suspiciously following the . . . the investigation, but since when is she a murder suspect?"

"You don't suspect her, Unai?" asked Estíbaliz. "Not even a little bit?"

We're talking about a retired 68-year-old woman with a hip replacement, I replied in writing. I was running out of lengthy sentences. Can you really imagine her stringing people up on top of a mountain?

"You need to tell them everything, Kraken," Estíbaliz said after reading my note. "Tell them about Amsterdam."

"You tell them, we . . . we don't have all day," I said grumpily.

Estí acquiesced.

"She worked for the RIPE cooperative in Amsterdam, as an employee of Cisco Systems. She was part of the first group of IP network administrators in Europe, and there's nothing she doesn't know about cybersecurity. That was back in 1998, the year when the Gundestrup Cauldron was stolen from the Amsterdam Museum and domestic animals were sacrificed using the Celtic Threefold Death ritual."

"I understand where you're coming from," said Alba. "How can our unit investigate her when she has the edge in computer technology, and she'll find us out no matter what we do?"

"In my opinion," Milán said after loudly and endearingly clearing her throat, "our best plan is to proceed as normal and keep two channels of communication, one protected from Golden and one for less classified information."

I had another plan in mind—something more analog to find

out why Golden was poking her nose into this investigation. But I knew that my boss and my colleagues wouldn't approve, so I kept my mouth shut and snatched up the last of Grandfather's sugared almonds.

"Isn't anyone going to ask about MatuSalem? And what about Tasio?" Peña ventured.

"Here we go," I said. "That case is over. He's innocent. He's suffered enough."

"Tasio's no saint."

"He wasn't a murderer, and he's in Los Angeles anyway. Let him be. The guy is trying to rebuild his life," I insisted.

"Officer Peña," Alba said, "are you suggesting this could be a trap set by MatuSalem or by Tasio Ortiz de Zárate?"

"I'm suggesting that MatuSalem has already been to prison, so we know what he thinks of the law. And Tasio . . . Well, fine. Let's drop it. He was framed, but it's difficult to see him as anything but guilty when you've grown up believing he was a serial killer. Regardless of their pasts, they're still hacking a detective's phone, which is an offense despite the fact that they claim to be protecting him."

"Then we need to look into it," Alba said. "But, as far as the Water Rituals case goes, there's nothing to suggest that either MatuSalem or Tasio has any connection with the victims or the crime scenes."

"That's not entirely true," Peña insisted. "The archaeological element of the crime scenes could implicate Tasio, who is or was an archaeologist."

"Not again!" I said, leaping up. I grabbed my paper and quickly wrote, *That was the main evidence against him last time and it was baseless then—haven't we learned anything?*

Peña sighed as he read my words.

"All right, calm down, I was just playing devil's advocate—it's something we used to do in the brainstorming sessions in Donostia. I'm sorry if I went too far. I don't even believe it myself. As far as I'm concerned, it's a dead end. I think we should focus on other suspects who can tell us a lot more. Like Saúl Tovar."

Estíbaliz took the floor again.

"I agree. There's a lot more to him. He didn't tell us that his adopted daughter, Gimena, took her own life a few months ago. We also have reason to suspect that the adoption was illegal. He was awarded the child based on an application he and his wife submitted together, and after she died in 1991, Saúl failed to update his status. We've asked for the Santander police's cooperation in reviewing some aspects of the deaths of both Rebeca and Gimena. Inspector Lanero didn't see the connection between the two cases, despite the girls having the same father, and none of the officers currently stationed at Santander worked on the Fontibre case back in 1993. It seems nobody picked up on Gimena's death because they were treating it as another suicide. We should also look into Saúl's wife's death. We're unsure how she died."

"Good, let's get working on that," Alba said, nodding. "Do you see Saúl Tovar as a suspect?"

"It's early days yet," replied Estí. "We can't go around accusing people just because their immediate family members have died, and right now that's all we have. But I think digging in that direction might yield something helpful for our case."

"What about everything happening on Twitter?" Milán piped up, a green Post-it note in her hand. "Are we giving the Hangman Game theory any credence?"

"It's bullshit," snorted Estí. "People with nothing better to do than peddle crackpot theories. Let's be adults, shall we?"

"I agree," Alba said. "We're professionals. This isn't a guessing game. The computer crime unit is monitoring social media to see whether the situation escalates, and Judge Olano has agreed to extend the gag order for another four weeks. Our press office is busy ensuring that the media we *are* able to oversee—the papers, radio, and television—respect this blackout. We haven't been contacted by foreign press agencies, and I don't believe any have picked up the story. So far so good."

We all nodded.

"On the other hand, there isn't much we can do to prevent public hysteria on social media, and especially the mounting pressure on Inspector Ayala, who has the highest media profile of all of us. The fans of Annabel Lee who made death threats against Inspector Ayala have been identified and reported, which has helped calm things down a little. But if you feel, Inspector Ayala, that public pressure is adversely affecting your private life and you'd prefer to step down, now is the time to speak up."

"No chance," I said out loud.

And on that note, the meeting ended.

It was eight o'clock, and the streets of Villaverde were dark save for the streetlights. Vitoria was an hour's drive away.

Grandfather intercepted the five of us as we came down from the attic, and began handing out jars of roasted peppers, chili peppers in brine, and sloeberries for making *patxaran*.

"Grandad, you'll clear out your larder," I said, although I knew his generosity would outpace my objection.

I gave Estí several jars of pears poached in red wine, and she looked at them as if they were top-grade marijuana from Chaouen.

Outside, Milán and Peña were already walking down the hill when I overheard an exchange between Grandfather and Alba.

He was clasping her hands, as though fearing she might disappear in a puff of smoke.

"As his boss, you'll have to take good care of him for me. Please don't send him on another dangerous mission that puts him in the line of fire. Can you do that for me?"

"I'll try, Grandad. I promise."

I got goose bumps hearing Alba call him that. In her family the word had been taboo. I had hoped he and I could change that and give Alba the grandfather she deserved.

He cleared his throat, glanced at Alba's growing belly, and handed her another jar.

"It's a little jar of honey, from here, from the hills. Take it. It'll give you strength, and you're going to need it. And if there's anything else, you know where to find me."

36

THE ICE RINK

TUESDAY, DECEMBER 20, 2016

On the road back to Vitoria, close to San Vicentejo, it began to snow. The fine, treacherous, powdery flakes whitened the tarmac, slowing all five cars until they formed a caravan that broke up only when we reached Aretxabaleta.

I took the opportunity at the first red light next to the Urssa Steel plant to text Alba from my new cell phone.

Are you going home?

She responded instantly.

That was the plan.

**Vitoria will be empty now. This is
the last snowfall of autumn.
Come for a walk with me?**

She made me suffer—she didn't respond until the next red light at the turnoff to Batán.

Okay.

That one word felt like a blessing.

> **We can park in the New Cathedral lot. I'll**
> **meet you at the pools, by the sculpture of the**
> **crocodile with human hands.**

She didn't reply, which I took as a yes.

Inside my Outlander, I was singing "Chasing Cars" at the top of my lungs. I had been following the prompts from my speech therapist, my possible future-sister-in-law, and this daily exercise of shouting the lyrics to my favorite songs was helping me speak more fluently and reel off set phrases.

> *If I lay here*
> *If I just lay here*
> *Would you lie with me*
> *And just forget the world?*

The snow was falling softly and quietly, settling on the pine trees and bushes in the gardens surrounding the New Cathedral. I found Alba next to the bronze crocodile.

"Let's go for a walk. There's nobody out." I said the words I'd rehearsed as I came up the steps from the parking lot.

Alba locked her arm in mine, and we walked in silence toward Florida Park.

"So it's official, we're parents."

"It's official," she confirmed, smiling. "Come on, I'll buy you some hot chestnuts. I saw the way you were looking at them."

Alba went over to one of those stands that look like black carriages and presented me with a generous cone of beautiful, big, sizzling chestnuts.

Almost without realizing it, we'd arrived at the entrance to the

Plaza de la Virgen Blanca. In the snow it looked whiter and more pristine than ever. No footprints disturbed the deep frosty blanket as the snow continued to fall quietly over our peaceful city.

A lone skater glided around the ice rink set up in the plaza under the monument to the Battle of Vitoria.

The song from the car still echoed in my head. I walked Alba to the top of the square, opposite my apartment block, on the far side of the snow-covered monument with its sword-wielding angel.

"If I lay here, if I just lay here, would you lie with me and just forget the world?" I asked, quoting Snow Patrol.

She rose to the challenge, and we both let ourselves fall onto the white ground like a couple of kids.

We held hands and gazed at the sky, lightened by the white clouds. We didn't need anything, not even the Perseids.

We made snow angels the way I had in nursery school in Paseo de la Senda, in another life. And we laughed when we saw that the shape our bodies had left looked more like a many-limbed deity than an angel.

"I think we've made a Kraken," she whispered, laughing.

"Let's go to my place and dry off. I don't want you and my daughter catching cold," I said with concern. Maybe I'd gotten a bit carried away, and we'd gone too far.

We ducked into the entrance where everything had started that summer night, where perhaps we'd even created a new life, and we climbed the stairs, giggling and anxious to be alone together.

As I stepped forward to open the front door, Alba waited on the landing, her breath on my neck.

Had my tongue allowed it, I would have said, *Put your arms around me, and hold me tight, because when I turn around I never want to let you out of my sight again,* but I couldn't trust my brain to make such a long sentence work. I slipped the key into the lock and turned it.

I spun around, and as I picked her up, she wrapped her legs around my waist. The apartment was warm and inviting, and the air inside electric with the energy between us.

"I thought you didn't want me anymore," Alba murmured in my ear.

"The hell I don't."

"Prove it, then."

"I fully intend to."

She undressed and stood naked in front of the picture window, her curvy figure shielded from the outside only by a diaphanous curtain. She was a goddess. I went into the bedroom, stripped the blanket off my bed and spread it over the living-room floor. I pushed the table to one side and cleared a space for us.

Alba made love gently, as if in slow motion. How good it was to be inside her.

She seemed even more powerful, and at that moment we were the white city's beating heart, rhythmic, engrossed, and silent.

My hands touched her navel, and I realized that a layer of skin was all that separated me and my daughter. She was there, aware that her parents loved each other.

And the baby girl we're carrying will be protected by us both. Together we're unstoppable. Let me share your white goddess's niche, I thought.

But that was too much to ask.

In no time at all, Alba had put on her clothes again, and she was Deputy Superintendent Salvatierra again.

"Just one night. I have my own home, Unai."

"Just one night. You have your own home." I nodded. What else could I do? "I hope that whatever arrangement we come to—whether it's two homes or one, whatever you wish—we'll be a family."

"A family," she replied before vanishing downstairs.

And, coward that I was, I was left wishing I'd told her just how badly I wanted that, that I was teaching myself lullabies so I wouldn't be a silent father, so I could comfort my daughter when she started teething, when she fell taking her first steps. I wish I had told her that nobody, nobody had ever made me tremble the way she had on that December night.

37

THE NIGHT OF CANDLES

FRIDAY, DECEMBER 23, 2016

December was speeding by. The holidays would soon be upon us and that meant the investigation would slow down for several weeks. Unless, that is, another body showed up to put a black cross on our calendar.

My days had started filling up with a series of routines, all of which I welcomed. Peña, who rented an apartment in La Corre, rang my buzzer some mornings, and we'd walk together to police headquarters.

For all his fastidiousness during the investigation, he was outgoing and amusing outside the office, and his creative mind was on full display. Judging from some of the looks he got as we walked to work, women found him attractive.

Germán picked me up every day after speech therapy. Occasionally, I had a *pintxo* with him and Beatriz, but often I excused myself and left them to their own devices.

Finally, my brother plucked up the courage to bring her to Villaverde.

Beatriz seemed captivated by our village and our hills—and the village seemed captivated by her. In our small town, she stood out with her high heels and pencil skirts, her perfectly lacquered auburn hair. Their relationship brought back to life the witty, loquacious brother I had been missing since Martina left us.

Alba made unscheduled visits to my apartment, and after walking around the city center, we'd end up panting between the sheets.

In short, life wasn't so bad.

I had also been tying up a few loose ends. I called Araceli, Asier's wife, from my old number. I needed to keep feeding information to Golden in case she began to suspect I was onto her.

Araceli was busy one afternoon helping with the Night of Candles, an event in which fifteen thousand tiny candles lit up the Old Quarter and transported the city to another time. She persuaded me to help her, so I met her at the Escoriaza-Esquivel Palace.

Araceli was one of the newest members of our *cuadrilla*. She and Asier had met a couple of years earlier and were attracted to each other's strong personalities. They married almost immediately. Araceli worked for an innovative technology company with an unpronounceable name and taught at several universities in the north, which unfortunately meant she and Asier didn't see much of each other.

We got along from the beginning. She was forthright and guileless, and striking with a dark complexion and long hair.

But that day, seeing her walk through the arched entrance in the medieval wall, I noticed something different about her appearance. She had cut her bangs. She reminded me of someone, but who was it? Dead straight, just above the eyebrows. An ample bosom. She was in black as usual. She looked like a posh goth. Then it hit me.

Annabel Lee.

It was one of those things you notice, but never really become conscious of until it's staring you in the face, and occasionally, when it's too late.

"Do you like it?" she asked coquettishly.

"Yes," I said, mussing up her bangs a bit.

I did my best to conceal my bewilderment. It was impossible not to see Ana Belén Liaño when I looked at her.

It was her appearance and possibly her personality as well.

Love and hate. Why hadn't I noticed it before? Is that what turns you on, Asier?

"I wanted to talk to you about something, Ara," I said, but my words were stifled by a frenzy of activity. She thrust a lighter into my hand and opened her backpack, which was stuffed with hundreds of candles.

All around us, scores of volunteers and friends of the local storekeepers were lighting candles and torches to illuminate the Old Quarter.

We walked to the courtyard of the Renaissance palace, which shared a wall with Cantón de las Carnicerías.

Approaching the ancient city gateway to Vitoria-Gasteiz, I felt a shiver run down my spine as I recalled the two murdered fifteen-year-olds whose bodies Nancho had left beneath the archway, garlanded with three *eguzkilores*.

Like many locals, I was in the habit of avoiding those black spots in our city.

Nevertheless, I followed my friend's wife and helped her place the candles around the edge of the courtyard. It had been built long ago by the physician to Henry VIII, history's most infamous wife-murderer.

Enlivened by the candles' warm, contrasting light, we must have looked like Caravaggio's signature chiaroscuro.

We dedicated half an hour to the task and eventually ran out of small talk. Araceli finally asked me the question that had been hovering between us all the while.

"Is it work-related?"

"I'm afraid so."

Araceli stooped to line up another batch of candles and discreetly signaled for me to move away from another group of storekeepers.

"Don't scare me, Unai," she said. "We've had quite enough already with Jota. What's going on?"

"It's about Asier. I'll come straight to the point, okay?"

"Okay."

Although it wasn't a long sentence, I was already getting tired from chatting with her, so I pulled my notebook out of my back pocket.

What do you know about the assault at the pharmacy?

Araceli grimaced, but her pat answer seemed to indicate that she'd been expecting the question.

"That it was a junkie and Asier didn't see his face. Why, have you arrested the guy?"

"We think Asier is lying," I said.

And so do you, I thought.

"I hate to have to ask you this, Ara, but—"

"But what? What's this about, Unai?"

"Did you have a fight that day?"

I studied her reaction. Her surprise was genuine this time.

"You think I hit him?"

"In self-defense, maybe."

"Look, Asier can be a total jerk, but he's never laid a finger on me. Not on me or on anyone else. That would be the last straw. I simply wouldn't tolerate it. I'd call the police and pack my bags. Is that clear enough for you?"

Yes, coming from you, I wrote.

A dead end. No marital brawl after all. I was running out of leads, but I wanted to see how much she would reveal and how much she knew.

I took the candle out of her hand, lit it, and held it up to her face.

It's more difficult to hide a lie in the light. If you know what you're looking for, you can detect even the smallest tell when a person is lying—their eyes move up and to the right.

You can detect every gesture they attempt to conceal—a flicker of the eyelids, tension in the jaw, pursed lips that refuse to tell the truth.

"Who was it, then?" I asked.

"I have no idea, Kraken."

Kraken. Very good, Araceli. You're creating distance. I'm not Unai anymore.

"Ara, I can tell when you're lying. And right now you're lying to me."

She folded her arms across her chest, standing firm. Then she dropped her chin.

She surrendered.

"It was Jota. Asier and Jota had an argument. Jota was drunk, and things got violent. Asier won't tell me why. 'Unresolved issues' was all he said. He told me they have a long history. Things to do with the *cuadrilla* that I wouldn't understand. When Jota was found dead at the Barbacana pool, he made me swear not to tell anyone. He doesn't want everyone to think he killed Jota, because he didn't. I was with him that Saturday. We left Cuesta at four in the morning, you can ask Nerea. We went home and slept until ten the next morning. We were in bed, Unai. He couldn't have gone out, killed Jota, taken him to Laguardia, and driven back to Vitoria."

"In six hours? He could have."

Yes, he could have.

"Look, Asier snores, and I swear I heard him snoring all night long."

"In your sleep?"

"I don't know what to tell you, Unai. I don't think he murdered Jota."

How about Thursday, November 17? Were you home all night with Asier, or were you away teaching? I wrote.

Araceli didn't understand the reasoning behind my questions. Confused, she consulted the calendar on her phone.

"I wasn't teaching that week. I was in Vitoria. Why do you ask, Unai?"

Just try to remember, did Asier sleep at home all night, or was he at the pharmacy? Did he do anything out of the ordinary?

Araceli consulted her calendar again. I had already checked Asier's schedule, but I wanted to study Araceli's reactions.

"No, the pharmacy was closed that night, but I don't remember exactly what happened that day. It was over a month ago, and if I don't remember, it's because nothing unusual happened. Asier never goes out late on weekday nights. It bugs me that you aren't telling me the reason for all these questions."

A woman died. Ana Belén Liaño—does the name ring a bell?

I observed her face, but she registered no reaction. Not even surprise. It was curious.

"No, should it?"

Not if you and your husband don't talk about your pasts.

No, I wrote, *we're simply looking for possible links between her death and Jota's.*

"Just promise me that if Asier's hiding something, you'll tell me first," she implored. I saw no pleading look in her eyes. Rather, she had the staid look of a woman who wasn't easily hurt.

You and Asier don't seem close, I thought.

"I'll do what I can," I promised, and gave her a peck on the cheek before I left.

I walked quickly through the cobbled streets, the candle flames flickering in my wake. It would have been a perfect evening for a stroll around the Old Quarter, but I had a date with Alba at my apartment, and I was not going to arrive a second late.

A couple of hours later, Estíbaliz called with a surprising piece of news. Alba and I had switched off the lights, and were lazing in bed, enjoying the spectacular display of candles around the Plaza de la Virgen Blanca through the window.

I tried my best to ignore Estí's call and just enjoy the moment, but the ringtone wailed so insistently that I finally picked up.

"Is it urgent?" I asked. I felt like strangling her for her timing.

"It's very interesting."

"Go ahead then," I said, my eyes gliding over Alba's thighs. I'm nothing if not simple.

"Do you remember the student we ran after in Santander?"

"Yes, I remember."

"Do you remember that he called Saúl Bluebeard, like the character in the folktale who kills his wives?"

"Come on, Estí, spit it out."

"Saúl's wife. Milán found her obituary in the archives of *El Periódico Cántabro*. Her name was Asunción Pereda. I've spoken to Paulaner and he's going to look through the Santander police records, although, with it being Christmas, I doubt he'll get back to us before Monday. Here's the thing, Unai—the obituary said she died from an unusual domestic accident. I don't know about you, but I think a man who loses his wife and two daughters in the bloom of youth, and in such odd circumstances, has some explaining to do."

38

LA CUESTA DEL RESBALADERO

SATURDAY, DECEMBER 24, 2016

Every year, the *cuadrilla* meets in the Old Quarter on Christmas Eve to drink mulled wine.

In the winter, the hot wine is infused with cinnamon, lemon, dried apricots, figs, and other delights and joyfully consumed by the crowds who pack the old part of the city, evoking the summer's las Fiestas de la Virgen Blanca. It's one of Vitoria's most cherished traditions.

This year was different. There was tension in the air. The looks, the shoves when we entered Bar Rojo or El Segundo . . . I was a head taller than most, and people stared at me openly.

Some gave me nods of reassurance, while others looked at me as if they wanted to hang me from the beer tap.

The mood in the *cuadrilla* was tempered as well. We were still mourning Jota. This was the time of year when he would head home for Christmas dinner a little worse for wear, and we would chaperone him for fear he might mistake the garage for the front door. But not this year. There was no need. He had struggled greatly, and his loss was almost too much to bear.

But Germán was shining, more talkative than ever. His relationship with Beatriz was blossoming, and I was delighted for them both. This evening he was coaxing Nerea into relaying bits of gossip she'd read in the press or heard from her customers. Ara was distant, Xabier and Lutxo had gone skiing, and Asier and I were keeping up appearances, but avoided each other.

In the men's bathroom of Bar Extitxu, Asier cornered me. "I've been waiting for you. Let's step outside."

"Sure."

We were nervous walking down what had once been known as la Cuesta del Resbaladero because you could easily crack your skull open on the ice, especially if you were drunk.

When we reached the Plaza de los Fueros, I nodded toward the granite steps of the amphitheater. We would have some privacy up there overlooking the square. Below us were a stone maze and an empty fronton court, where many kids had split open their heads playing jai alai.

Asier and I sat at the highest point, warm from our drinks despite the early-evening chill.

"Why the hell have you been grilling Araceli?" he began.

"As you know, Asier, it's my job—"

"Well, she's been pissed at me since yesterday. What did you say to her?"

Let me be honest. I know you've been lying, my friend, so I checked your alibis for Annabel's and Jota's murders, I wrote in my notebook.

"You shouldn't have talked to her. You don't know her like I do. Araceli has two sides—in public she's charming and confident, but underneath she's morbidly jealous. She knows nothing about Ana Belén Liaño, but she's beside herself now that you've mentioned her name. She knows I'm hiding something. And now I'm in deep shit, and it's your fault."

"If you hadn't lied to me from the beginning, I wouldn't have had to talk to her," I retorted.

"I've already said all I have to say to you and your colleagues. So unless you have an arrest warrant, I'm not sa—"

"Stop it! We're going in circles," I cut in.

"Good, because I have nothing more to say."

You hit Jota, and he hit you. Your wife confirmed it. I can make life difficult for you, Asier. I have enough to put the screws to you. Is that clear, or do you want me to draw a diagram? I showed him what I'd written and gave him time to absorb it.

"Fuckin' Araceli," he muttered.

"You'd better explain. Everything. Starting with Annabel Lee."

Asier thought it over for a moment. He looked as if he might talk, but he didn't seem distressed. He was always calculating the odds, weighing the costs, but never emotional.

"Last spring, Jota bumped into Annabel, and they started meeting regularly. She encouraged him to take up photography again, told him he should have an exhibition, reconnect with his creative self . . ."

Jota had been talking about digital photography a lot lately. I had hoped that he had grown tired of the life he was leading and wanted to make some changes. How could I have associated this with Annabel Lee when we hadn't spoken about her for twenty-four years?

"It never occurred to me that she was behind this."

"I bumped into them in a bar in Calle Judizmendi. They looked like they were together. Well, as 'together' as anyone can be with Annabel Lee—you know what I mean, you've been there. I joined them for coffee, and she slipped me her number. So I called her."

Nice going, Asier, I thought. *Classy.*

"I've heard enough. It's your life. Just tell me who the father is."

"Jota maybe, definitely not me," Asier replied brusquely. "Annabel and I didn't sleep together."

"Don't lie to me."

"No, seriously, we—"

I was done. I'd heard enough lies from my childhood friends.

I seized him by the lapels and threw myself onto him so that his upper body was tilted precariously over Calle Fueros below us.

If I let go, he fell.

"Don't . . . lie . . . to . . . me . . . ," I whispered slowly.

I pulled him back toward me. He got the message.

"Okay, okay, we had sex. But there's no way I'm the father of her child. I took precautions. Come on, Unai, I'm married."

"That doesn't mean you're not the father."

"It's impossible. It couldn't have been me."

"You think it could have been Jota?"

"Maybe . . . Jota was careless, and he was always drunk. Their affair had been going on for months, but then in the summer the double murders took over everything. You were all conveniently caught up in that, and you and Lutxo never caught on to us. We weren't sure how you'd react. It could have reopened old wounds."

"Why didn't you tell me about this sooner if you knew I'd find out?"

"Hell, I don't have the imagination to improvise. That day when you asked us to meet you in the park by the old wall, my mind went blank . . . Annabel hadn't called me that Thursday, but I didn't expect she'd turn up dead."

In which case, as far as the killer's concerned, you or Jota could be the father.

"Do you know if she hiked up the mountain with somebody that day?"

"I know Annabel liked to hike early in the morning, and she'd leave Vitoria before dawn, but I have no idea if she went on her own or with other people."

"Do you know if she had any new friends?"

He thought for a moment.

"Yes, as a matter of fact," he said at last. "She mentioned

someone a few times, but I never met the woman. What was her name? . . . Oh, I don't know. All I remember is that Annabel said the woman had been supportive about her pregnancy."

"Really?"

"It was a few months ago, around the time Annabel announced the pregnancy on social media. I think the woman was a fan of her work, and she wanted Annabel to sign all her books. They hit it off. I was surprised because Annabel didn't have many female friends. It's possible she made new male friends, but obviously she didn't talk to me about them and I didn't ask. Anybody could have gone up that mountain with her."

"I didn't notice any female friends at her funeral."

Asier shrugged. "As you know, I didn't go."

"The rest of us did."

"And how was I supposed to explain it to Araceli?" he snapped. "I didn't want to be interrogated, or risk her hearing that the dead woman was pregnant and then putting two and two together."

"What about the money, Asier? You need to explain that."

"I was furious when Annabel won the lottery . . . It happened just when I was thinking of cutting things off. I think the pregnancy changed her. She wanted some stability for her kid, and Jota couldn't give her that. She insisted I leave Araceli. She told me the kid was probably mine, despite the precautions we'd taken. She said it was possible, but you know how she was—she would lie to herself until she believed it, and she thought it worked on everyone else. I wanted to leave her. I was fed up with the situation, with the fact that Jota was getting more and more out of control. I don't think he knew about us, but he suspected something, and he was very tense around me. He was acting oddly, but he didn't have the balls to confront me about it."

"So you were planning to break it off with her, and then she won the lottery," I said, looking at him.

"Don't you remember when she taunted me all those years ago at summer camp?"

"No, what happened?"

"She said, 'I'll be richer than you on the day I die.'"

"You're kidding, Asier. That stuck with you after all this time?"

"I'm not kidding. It made me who I am today. That's why I became a pharmacist, not because I enjoy filling prescriptions. It gave me a goal. It made me realize I didn't want to be a loser like my father. I never wanted to go without. I wanted to be rich. I swear those words have stayed with me since July fourth, 1992, the day that bitch said them."

That bitch . . . I made a mental note.

"And she didn't win the bet. The day she died she wasn't richer than me. We were equal. We both had a million and a half euros in the bank."

"She won the lottery, so you hung around."

"I told her that I'd leave Araceli and that we would be a family. But I needed some guarantee that she was ready to make that commitment, too."

"The shared bank account."

"Yes, she agreed more easily than I'd expected. Money wasn't important to her. She would have been perfectly content with nothing; she earned more than enough from her novels. Annabel wasn't greedy; she didn't care about material things. She had everything she wanted inside her head. She didn't mind sharing those three million euros with me."

I stared straight in front of me, my mind spinning. I glanced at my watch.

Grandfather was expecting Germán and me to join him for Christmas Eve dinner in Villaverde. Alba and her mother were eating together in Laguardia. They'd invited Estíbaliz, who had no family and would otherwise have dined alone or with us. It was already half past seven, and I needed to end this conversation. But the more I probed Asier, the more questions I had. I knew my friend well, and it was rare for him to open up—I needed to keep him talking. I wouldn't get many more opportunities like this.

"Didn't she get annoyed when you immediately withdrew two hundred thousand euros?" I pressed him.

"You won't believe this, but we didn't discuss it. It never came up. Maybe because she didn't check the account. I took the money out on Monday, and she died the following Thursday."

"Don't you see how guilty that makes you look to a judge?"

"And don't you see that I'm telling you the truth, at the risk of incriminating myself. For fuck's sake, Unai."

"What are you going to do with the money?"

He paused, as if considering it for the first time. But I was sure he had it all planned out.

"Once you've caught the real perpetrator and I'm in the clear, I'm going to leave Araceli—and I'll take all the money. Luckily, we signed a prenuptial agreement, so she has no claim to it. I'll pay off my debts and take some time to decide what to do with my life."

"I didn't think you needed to take stock, you seem so . . ."

Self-satisfied, I thought to myself.

"I'm not sure I want to be a pharmacist. It was a way of making money, but now I barely break even. I don't want to waste my fortune patching up a leaking ship. Maybe I'll sell the two businesses and invest the money, or spend the time until I retire managing my assets. All I wanted out of life was to have money and not to end up like my father, and it was Annabel who gave me that. Funny, isn't it?"

I'd heard more than enough. My stomach was churning.

"We're finished here, Asier. You can go."

"About time," he said, rising to his feet and starting down the steps. "Do you know something, Kraken? You've turned that mulled wine sour and wrecked my Christmas Eve. Araceli and my parents are expecting me. Merry Christmas."

I sat watching him descend the stairs, bristling as he wove among the people hurrying home to their families.

I wasn't sure whether to give him police protection because he was going to be the next victim, or to ask the judge for an arrest warrant. Asier had both the motive and the temperament to have killed Rebecca, Annabel, and Jota with his bare hands.

39

EL PICO DE DOBRA

WEDNESDAY, JULY 15, 1992

Tensions among the *cuadrilla* were running high, and they were evident in the smallest details.

Shared secrets, private jokes, all the old camaraderie began to disintegrate as the days passed, and the four friends competed for the attentions of Annabel Lee, who seemed to live in another, far more interesting universe than the one they had known until then.

Unai watched Jota with concern, watering down his wine when he wasn't looking and trying to take him out of the tense atmosphere that surrounded Annabel and his former closest friends.

Lutxo was probably the worst. In front of Annabel, he hounded Unai ruthlessly, taunting him with the Kraken nickname and jeering.

Saúl had been observing these scenes every morning, and by midweek, he realized he had to do something. He decided a change of scenery might help, so he drove them to Puente Viesgo, an area covered in Cantabrian forts. As they began their ascent of Pico de Dobra, Saúl explained that Dobra was actually a theonym—a place named after a deity. The word came from the Celtic *dubrón*, meaning "place of much water." An altar to the god Erudino had been discovered nearby.

Saúl was also keeping a close eye on Jota, who was always whispering with Beca. Were they holding hands? They were too far away for him to see, so he quickened his pace.

Seeing Unai up ahead, Saúl approached him.

"You don't appreciate your friend's humor."

"I don't like nicknames," said Unai. "They're never innocent."

"You don't strike me as the type of kid who's bullied at school."

"Well, no, not me . . . It's my brother, Germán. He's eleven and has achondroplasia."

"Dwarfism."

"Whatever you want to call it."

"And you feel you have to stick up for him."

"That's not the problem. One day I won't be in the courtyard, and he'll have to stick up for himself."

"I see."

"I hate nicknames," Unai repeated. "They're always mean."

"I'd say Kraken is a totem rather than a nickname."

"A what?"

"The ancients also had aliases. They would choose animals whose qualities they wanted to appropriate and make the animal their own. Why not do as they did, and wear the name with pride?"

"I don't really see myself as a squid."

"In the Middle Ages, drawings of the kraken appeared on the portolan, ancient nautical charts, and in the bestiaries, alongside sea snakes and leviathans. The kraken was a mythical, but fearsome, creature. They also showed up in Nordic texts, in the *edda* recited by the Viking *skálds* or poets. And a thousand years later, it turns out they really do exist. They wash up right here on the Cantabrian coast. I think the kraken is an extraordinary creature, a quiet survivor, a powerful force of nature that has no need to show off. I wouldn't see the name as a problem at all."

What would you know about my problems? thought Unai.

The boy was right. In fact, they knew nothing of each other's problems.

They continued the climb in silence, each thinking about the couple walking a few yards ahead. Saúl about Rebeca, and Unai about his friend Jota, whom he'd been worried about since the scene at Gatzelugatxe.

At last, they reached the summit of the mountain and sat down for a rest. Not one to share confidences, Unai was hesitant to approach Jota, but found him seated out of earshot of the others.

"Hey, are you okay?" Unai asked, sitting down.

"Yeah, never better."

"And the thing with Annabel and Asier?"

"For me, it was just sex. And for Asier, I wish him luck. It won't last long."

"That's what I think, too. There was something strange about it, like it was more about hate than love. But I'm not worried about Asier, he has a heart of stone. I worry about you. Are you sure everything's okay? You can tell me, you know."

"I am telling you, Unai. Annabel Lee dropped me so fast I'm still reeling. And I'd be lying if I said I wasn't upset. But I'm dealing with something else, too. I spoke to my mother yesterday, and my father has taken a turn for the worse while I'm here having fun. I offered to go to Vitoria, but she won't hear of it. She insists everything is under control, and that I should rest and prepare myself for the weeks ahead, when we'll have to take turns sitting with him in the hospital. She's right. I'm doing better here than I would at home, and I'm working up the courage to . . . Don't tell anyone, Unai, but I've decided not to study architecture."

"How come?"

"Because I want to be a photographer, take a fine arts course."

Unai pinched the bridge of his nose. "Are you sure?"

"I felt so good this morning in Santillana looking at my photos. I never imagined I could take pictures like that. They're powerful, in a way that's . . . I don't know, it's hard to explain. It's like there's part of me in them. The hostile world, the feeling of being trapped—it's all there for anyone to see. I'm going to be a photographer, Unai. To hell with elevation plans and refurbishing structures."

"To hell with them, then," Unai declared, pleased and concerned in equal measure.

Back at the mansion, Unai was dawdling in the boys' dormitory. He could hear clatter from below, the sounds of people setting the table for dinner.

He sensed her footfall on the stairs. Nobody moved quite like she did in that centuries-old mansion.

"Funny about you and Asier," Unai remarked as Annabel Lee came into the room. He tried to look busy folding a pair of jeans.

She looked at him with pity. "I didn't do it to pacify him if that's what you think. I actually like his hostility. It keeps me on my toes."

Unai's brows furrowed. He didn't know how she did it, but Annabel Lee constantly disconcerted him. And worse, he was becoming addicted to that feeling.

"Why did you, then?" he asked, setting his clothes aside and turning to face her.

"To show he isn't invulnerable."

"To what?"

"To someone like me coming along and lighting a fire under you all. None of you are."

"Don't talk to me like you know me," he retorted.

"But I've known you your entire life . . . And, Unai, now that we've cleared the way, and your friends are out of the running, will you listen to me for once? Can we pick up where we left off?"

"That's not how things work."

And with that he barreled downstairs, his heart racing.

40

BLUEBEARD

Monday, December 26, 2016

On Monday, after all the festivities were over, Estí and I met to discuss the case. I picked her up from her apartment. Number 1 Portal de Castilla. After she broke up with her ex, Estíbaliz had chosen to live in a place famous for being the narrowest building in Vitoria. It was her way of telling the world that she didn't need company, that she was fine in an apartment that could only take one occupant.

We walked in silence toward Calle Florida and entered the park, where we saw a life-size Nativity.

Whole families whose children were on break ambled among the effigies of washerwomen, potters, and sheep. They photographed Roman legionnaires and took selfies next to Herod.

Hiding from passersby on a small slope behind the building where Parliament meets, we found refuge on a stone seat in the shape of a tree trunk.

Estí was wearing a T-shirt with a Lao Tse quote: WHEN YOU REALIZE THERE IS NOTHING LACKING, THE WHOLE WORLD BELONGS TO YOU.

"What's that?"

"A Christmas present from Alba."

"Is she your mentor now?"

Estí shrugged. "She saw it, liked it, and gave it to me at Christmas dinner. That's all."

So maybe friendship really does make the world go around. I'm so glad, I wrote. *How did the evening go?*

"Pleasant, cozy . . . friendly. Alba's mother welcomed me like family. She has a kind of inner peace, as if, after losing faith in the world, she's chosen to accept things as they are. The complete opposite of my mother."

"Nervous, like you?"

"Weak."

She changed the topic.

"Did you interrogate Asier?"

"I did."

I filled her in on everything I'd learned about Araceli and Asier, including the fact that, assuming Araceli wasn't hiding anything or covering for him, Asier had an alibi for both murders. I also told her about Annabel Lee's relationship with my two friends.

The long explanations left me exhausted, even though I had practiced at home.

"Unai, even if he denies paternity, Asier has admitted that he and Jota were both having sex with Annabel, so either of them could be the father. I think we should ask Judge Olano's permission to compare José Javier Hueto's DNA with the fetus Ana Belén Liaño was carrying."

Do you think that's necessary? I wrote. *Jota is dead, and there's no evidence linking Asier to either crime scene since his wife corroborated his alibi.*

"It would help if we knew that Jota was the father. At least, then, Asier would no longer be in danger."

That depends on how much the killer knows about the paternity question, I pointed out. *Either way, talk to Alba about getting a court order. We need to make progress fast.*

I also told her about the new friend Annabel Lee had made after she announced her pregnancy on social media.

Estí made a note to ask Milán to search for possible candidates. She had been monitoring Annabel's accounts since the investigation started and would be able to find information much faster than the rest of us.

"Tell me about Saúl's wife's death. Has Paulaner given you the report on the accident yet?" I asked.

"Yes, first thing this morning. Apparently, it was strange and tragic. Asunción Pereda Argüeso went for an early-morning stroll along the coast by their cottage. It was still dark and, according to the report, Saúl was asleep inside. The couple's twelve-year-old daughter, Rebeca, was away that weekend with her mother's sister; apparently, the two were very close."

"What was strange about Asunción's death?"

"Saúl's wife fell into an open well in the fields behind their house. The police concluded she must not have seen the opening and was knocked unconscious when she fell. She drowned in the water at the bottom of the well. By the time Saúl woke up, discovered his wife missing, and called the police and neighbors to help look for her, she was already dead."

Estí paused, waiting for me to react.

"Don't you see?" she asked, puzzled.

"See what?"

"A woman drowns upside down in a well. Don't you see the link to the other victims?"

"To date, her death is accidental. She wasn't murdered," I reminded her.

"Give me a break, Unai. That's too many tragedies in one family. First his wife dies, then his daughter, and then his adoptive daughter dies by suicide?"

Call them family tragedies; call them whatever. Look at your family,

and mine. Maybe they're tragedies, or maybe life is just a bitch sometimes.
Either way, Saúl doesn't fit the profile of someone who could carry out these
murders, especially not in the case of his daughter and Ana Belén. That
was what I wrote, but my head was spinning.

"Why do you say that?"

"Because I lived with the guy. He really cared about us. He
adored Rebeca. You can't fake that."

Estíbaliz rose to her feet. She began pacing back and forth,
unsure whether to believe me. It was hard for her. I don't think
she wanted to.

"In that case, poor guy. What a life . . . ," she conceded at
last. "Either that or someone has it in for him and he's kept quiet
about it."

"Maybe his repressed sister, a rival professor, a love affair with
someone who's married . . . I don't know."

"One thing strikes me as really suspicious," she declared, stopping in front of me and crossing her arms. "Saúl is an incredibly
attractive, charismatic guy. He exudes sex from every pore. Have
you seen the way his female students look at him? And he knows
it. He doesn't fit the profile of the eternal widower or the celibate,
and yet his wife died more than twenty-five years ago and he's never
remarried."

"He must have had affairs, as we all do. He's probably discreet.
That doesn't make him a suspect."

"No, but the fact that a student would call him a wife-murderer,
and then there's the nickname Bluebeard . . . I've been doing some
research. Do you know the story behind the real Bluebeard? It's
enough to make your hair stand on end."

"No, I don't. Is it relevant?"

"There are some interesting comparisons at the very least.
Bluebeard is the subject of a folktale written by Charles Perrault
in the seventeenth century. A wealthy nobleman was adored by

women for his bushy blue beard. Thanks to his vast fortune, and despite his ominous reputation for having been widowed several times, he marries and remarries repeatedly. Disobeying his wishes, his last wife enters a forbidden chamber where she discovers the hanging corpses of her predecessors. She manages to send word to her brothers, who save her in the nick of time. It's yet another fable punishing women for being curious, just like Eve, Lot's wife, Pandora . . ."

"I'm listening," I said.

"Perrault's fable is based on the true story of a French baron, Gilles de Rais, who was born in Brittany in 1404. He was ferocious on the battlefield, a companion-in-arms to Joan of Arc. However, if we look at him more closely in the light of twenty-first-century criminology, he appears to have had a psychopathic personality and probably suffered from a severe form of schizophrenia."

An elderly lady walked past holding her granddaughter's hand, and Estíbaliz fell silent until they had disappeared in the direction of the crèche's stable.

"Experts now believe that he took part in the Hundred Years' War to satisfy his appetite for butchery," she went on. "He was a hero in France, but when Joan of Arc was burned at the stake, he snapped. He began carrying out ritual sacrifices. Hundreds of peasant children in the villages surrounding his castle at Tiffauges disappeared. This went on for years, until finally the Church intervened, and the Bishop of Nantes sentenced him to death. He was hanged and burned at the stake, in what was, incidentally, close to being a Threefold Death."

"I'd advise against focusing too much on that," I said.

"Okay, but listen to the torments he subjected those children to, all of which he admitted. Thanks to the detailed accounts of his trial, these have been saved for posterity. You won't be able to get to sleep tonight."

"All right, tell me everything."

Estíbaliz told me what I wanted and didn't want to hear.

A comprehensive account of what one man can do to a child simply because he's bigger and stronger.

I'd rather not go into details. What would be the sense in that?

The story of the real Bluebeard made me feel physically sick. That someone could torture, rape, dismember, and slaughter hundreds of children over a period of eight years with absolute impunity, even if it did happen in fifteenth-century France, appalled me, because it implied that the authorities of the day were extremely lax.

Too willing to look the other way, not willing enough to act.

Was I doing the same thing?

Was I failing to stop the person responsible for all this death?

I was coming face-to-face with one of my biggest weaknesses: my trust in other people's goodness.

Right from the start, I'd been avoiding confronting Golden Girl.

Despite MatuSalem's warning, for days I'd been evading a physical confrontation, no hiding behind a screen, just two people looking each other in the eye and explaining themselves.

It was time I paid a visit to the Cantón de las Pulmonías.

41

EL CANTÓN DE LAS PULMONÍAS

Monday, December 26, 2016

I wanted to catch her by surprise, and since I assumed she was still tracking my old cell phone, I left it at home. I approached her lair with my new phone instead, concealing it in my inside pocket. As if Golden was in any way dangerous . . .

Perhaps we were all overly paranoid. I was at the point where even the statues on Calle Dato seemed suspicious.

I strolled through the Old Quarter, absorbed in planning the best way to tackle the situation with Golden. Finally, I entered the gardens next to the archway on Cantón de las Pulmonías. The thick surrounding walls trapped the cold air and turned the space into a freezer. There were patches of white in some of the flower beds, vestiges of the last snowfall.

It was an idyllic setting, a place of calm, an urban oasis that helped steady my nerves and mitigate the image of Bluebeard.

Few people would have believed that beyond this peaceful exterior lay the headquarters of one of Europe's most infamous hackers.

I knocked on the door and heard her shuffle down the hallway, hampered by her recent hip replacement.

"Who is it?"

"It's me, Unai. I need your help. I think my SIM card is playing up again," I yelled through the door.

She hesitated for a few seconds. Then she unlocked the door, but left the steel chain in place.

"Let me see . . . They don't make these cards like they used to," she murmured through the crack.

She held out her hand.

I seized her wizened fingers and kissed them, as Germán might have done.

It worked.

She softened.

She let me into her bunker.

I knew she'd be wondering why she hadn't been able to track my approach, but the faulty SIM gave me an alibi of sorts.

"Aren't you going to offer me some pretzels?" I purred, grinning like a Cheshire cat.

I wanted Golden to invite me into her living room. I wanted to talk to her face-to-face, so we could clear the air about her suspicious behavior.

"I see you've made great strides with your speech, Kraken. I'm happy for you. But I'll be less happy if the neighbors see you prowling around here. Everyone in Vitoria knows who you are. It does neither of us any favors. Come in and sit down."

I followed her down the hallway. Her white hair swayed as she moved.

Her apartment didn't look like a typical retiree's. The decor was functional and modern, no porcelain figurines or crocheted doilies here. In fact, there was nothing that hinted at the occupant's personality—it was almost as if the apartment had come furnished. The most personal touch was the thousands of CDs and DVDs that crammed the shelves. I sat on the sofa, which sank beneath me, and waited for her to sit down on a dining-room chair nearby.

I didn't want to skirt the issue. Golden had a knack for drawing people out, and would usually get more information out of you than you got from her.

"Is your life so bad that you're searching for answers on teenage suicide forums?" I asked point-blank.

The explosive question ricocheted around the room, leaving silence in its wake.

Golden grimaced for a nanosecond, and then her face straightened. She would have made a fantastic poker player.

"It's none of your business," she snapped.

"Yet what you're looking for *is* my business. And let's not even mention the Tasers, Golden."

She glanced at me tenderly, the kind of look a farmer might give a calf being taken to slaughter.

"This is a bigger threat to you than you could possibly imagine, Kraken dear. So you're better off answering my next question with a simple yes or no. In the long run, you'll understand that I'm trying to save your life. Now, tell me, did MatuSalem warn you?"

"Let's leave him out of it. You still haven't answered my question."

Golden took her time. Then she relented. "All right. I haven't been honest with you, and I owe you an explanation."

"I thought so. Now we're starting to agree on something. Maybe because it's Christmas."

"Maybe it is because it's Christmas. Well, it's a long story, Unai, so make yourself comfortable. I'll get those pretzels and some wine to wash them down."

I had no intention of drinking wine in a hacker's lair, but I nodded, and she hobbled off toward the kitchen.

I have almost no memory of what came next.

I don't remember her hitting me, or what she used.

I can remember what she said after she hit me, though, unless I simply imagined it. I remember her gazing down at me from above, without any regret. "That fuckin' kid," she muttered. "On the run again. What a life. That fuckin' Matu."

With hindsight, I know that Golden didn't want me to die.

She left the door of the apartment open as she fled, so that her nosy neighbor from the third floor would walk in and see my body lying on the living-room floor. She must have known the neighbor would call an ambulance.

And yet I don't forgive her. I don't forgive her.

No one hits someone with a brain injury over the head.

42

SANTIAGO HOSPITAL

MONDAY, JANUARY 9, 2017

Judge Olano issued a search warrant for Gloria Echegaray, alias Golden Girl, whereabouts unknown.

I spent the next thirteen days in Santiago hospital, where my medical team kept me more or less immobile until a CAT scan confirmed that the traumatic brain injury I'd suffered was mild. There was no internal bleeding, and the rusty taste in my mouth, once I'd regained consciousness, was determined to be the result of a ruptured blood vessel close to the temporal bone—dramatic, but not unheard of with a superficial head wound.

For the first few days my head throbbed, and after that I had cramps in my legs from lack of movement. Toward the end of my stay, I was trying the nurses' patience. The inactivity was making me restless and irritable. Now that we had made this giant leap forward, I was eager to get on with the investigation. It hardly mattered that I'd paid for this new lead with a nasty bruise on my right temple.

Once I felt marginally recovered, Estíbaliz showed up with the paternity test results, which confirmed that Jota was indeed the father of Annabel Lee's unborn child.

It took me a few days to digest the news, maybe because I was reluctant to accept that Jota's death and his future as a parent were so intricately linked.

Being in the hospital had some advantages. Alba visited first thing in the morning, during her lunch break, and then again in the evening. Every single day. Her belly grew apace as our relationship deepened.

Occasionally she brought her tablet and we watched our favorite films. *The Usual Suspects*, *Wicker Park,* a few B-movies. The time together brought us closer. I finally felt as though I was getting to know the inscrutable, mysterious Alba.

I took advantage of the time between her visits to improve my speech and invent practice sentences. I broke my record of twenty-five words in a row, making it to thirty-eight by the time I left the hospital. I constantly set new goals, and while I was certainly doing it for myself, I was also doing it for my daughter. I didn't want her to have a father who was incapacitated.

I was discharged on January 9.

At that point, my tiny family had doubled. My grandfather and Nieves Díaz de Salvatierra, Alba's mother, exchanged recipes for squid ink sauce, while Germán, my speech therapist, and Alba visited the bars in Calle Dato. They didn't tell me they were going, probably because they knew that I'd be jealous and unbearably grumpy, thinking about how badly I wanted a slice of tortilla.

Still, there was a kind of euphoria in the air; we had a suspect at last.

Someone tangible, although she had vanished into thin air.

Golden was apparently used to fleeing with just the clothes on her back. We found no trace of computer equipment during the search of her apartment in Cantón de las Pulmonías. My colleagues in the computer crime department had removed all her CDs and were busy trawling though them, but they were only copies of work files from her time with Cisco Systems, and it was unlikely that she had infringed any law by keeping them.

But the morning I got out, there was another development in the case.

Our whiz kid Milán brought me the news as I was getting dressed to leave the hospital.

"Inspector Ayala, I couldn't let this wait. I know Golden Girl's true identity," she said, gasping for breath as though she'd run up all three flights of stairs.

She probably had. She caught me while I was in the middle of taking off my drafty hospital gown, which barely reached my thighs and was open in the back.

"Calm down, Milán," I said. I leaned over and put my hand on her shoulder.

Milán leaped away from me as if an electric current had passed through her.

I stepped back, slightly embarrassed. It didn't take a profiler to realize that Milán wasn't used to physical contact, and I wondered what had happened to make her reject a gesture of support.

Milán pulled several Post-it notes out of her thick overcoat, blushing as she avoided looking at me in my gown.

"Okay," she explained nervously, "you told us that Golden Girl was born Gloria Echegaray in Vitoria in 1948, and that she lived for nearly forty years with a Don Benigno Larrea Ruiz de Eguino at Calle Fray de Zacarías in Cantón del Seminario. The first thing that set off alarm bells for me is that the guy she lived with doesn't exist; his name isn't on any of our databases or in the National Statistical Institute. He does have a social security number, though. A fake one. Someone forged the necessary documentation."

"That's impossible." I sat down on the bed, stunned.

I had looked the other way when Golden forged a marriage certificate to prevent the city council from evicting her from the apartment she had shared with her partner for several decades.

I kept quiet because Golden was renting out a few rooms in the apartment to a man wanted for domestic violence. Golden cooperated with us, and I was able to arrest the bastard who was beating his wife and kids.

I didn't have the heart to report her. But I did occasionally ask her to use her computer knowledge for help off the record, and for several years now we had been doing favors for each other.

Not a healthy relationship, admittedly.

Even so, it came as a shock that her partner of forty years didn't exist. She had lied to me from the start and had played on my emotions by casting herself as a poor, helpless old woman in order to secure an apartment in the city's historic Old Quarter. She'd been lying to me from the beginning.

"Go on," I said. "You said that she was also using a false identity."

"Yes, you asked me to search for a Gloria Echegaray. There is a woman with that name on the register of employees at Cisco Systems, but there was no trace of her before 1993. So I looked at her ID card fingerprint, which is also false, and found a match to a Lourdes Pereda Argüeso whose ID card has expired. She isn't registered as deceased, but she disappears from the system after 1993, the same year Gloria Echegaray appears with a driver's license, social security number—"

"What did you say her real name was?"

"You've probably already made the connection: Lourdes Pereda Argüeso, born in 1949 in Santillana del Mar, Cantabria, sixty-seven years ago. She has the same surname as Saúl Tovar's deceased wife."

"The shared surname could be a coincidence."

"They also share the same place of birth, I checked. Saúl Tovar's wife, Asunción Pereda Argüeso, was born twelve years after Lourdes Pereda Argüeso, in 1961, the same year as Saúl. I think the two women are sisters. I haven't had time to confirm it, but if we can determine that they had the same parents, we'll know for sure."

I felt dizzy, sitting on the bed, naked beneath the flimsy hospital gown.

"So Golden Girl could be Rebeca's aunt," I managed to say, concealing my confusion and anger from Milán.

Now I understood why Golden had started digging around when she saw the news of Annabel Lee's curious death on my cell phone. She recognized the same modus operandi used by her niece's killer or killers.

Or at least, that's what I wanted to believe at that moment.

43

THE SEQUOIA GARDEN

MONDAY, JANUARY 9, 2017

I should have gone straight home to rest, but Milán's discovery made me veer off the path of common sense, and I walked straight past my building in the Plaza de la Virgen Blanca, on my way to the New Cathedral.

A group of young skateboarders practiced their tricks on their customized boards on the main steps leading up to the entrance, across from a row of fountains.

I liked to watch them out of the corner of my eye when I walked past the cathedral, on my way for a snack at Bar Sagartoki, or when Alba would let me walk her home to Number 22 Calle del Prado. Occasionally, I had noticed a young boy with blue hair wearing a white hoodie. The skateboarder named after the biblical patriarch wasn't above strutting his stuff.

On that icy morning, I went straight there to find him in the thick fog.

He had his back to me as I approached, and I waited for him to finish his acrobatics. The other skaters indicated my presence with a nod, and I noticed he was about to flee, so I seized his thin arm.

MatuSalem looked daggers at me.

"Do you want to sabotage all my offline personas?"

"I need your help," I whispered.

"Let's go somewhere less public," he replied reluctantly. "Don't you know how to be discreet?"

"That's funny coming from someone who knows what I eat for breakfast every morning."

"Hey, at least you're talking," he said, pulling his hood over his face.

"Come on," I said, "we'll go to the sequoia garden. This is important."

The boy clenched his teeth, his angelic eyes trained on a gargoyle on the New Cathedral.

"Okay, but you can't do this again."

"Agreed," I said, marching him around the side of the building to the tiny enclosure next to the old Ursulinas convent where the gigantic tree stood.

There were no security cameras, and no one ever went in there. I ushered him inside next to the sequoia.

"What do you want?"

"Golden ran away," I told him.

"Correct, but imprecise."

"Meaning?"

"All we really know is that Golden has gone offline and erased all trace of herself, even on the deep web."

"Since when?" I asked.

"Since December twenty-sixth. She's gone dark."

"Can you use your superpowers to find her?"

"First, tell me what happened in the real world. Does that ugly bruise have anything to do with her?"

"She attacked me, hit me over the head. There's a warrant out for her arrest. The identity she used was a cover, and she hasn't used it again."

"The old witch."

"Can you find her?" I asked again.

He sighed, as if I were hopeless.

"I know it can be difficult for grown-ups sometimes, so I'll explain it to you slowly, and if you pay attention, maybe you'll understand: Golden is no longer online, so there's nothing for me to find."

"Are you telling me the world's number one hacker can't locate a has-been like Golden?"

"Ego games won't work with me. You know I'm only doing this for Tasio. I'll keep protecting you online, but I'm warning you, if you invade my physical space again, and my friends find out I talk to cops, it's over."

"All right. Keep checking my balcony window, and if you see a white cross, we'll meet the next day at one thirteen in the New Cathedral crypt. Okay?"

"Okay," he replied, and for a second I thought he was going to tell me it was a cool idea, but he stopped himself.

"Then we'll leave it at that. *Agur*, Matu."

"*Agur*, Kraken."

And I went home, weighed down by frustration.

I sensed the exasperation hidden behind MatuSalem's posturing. He had done everything he could to trace Golden and hadn't found her. He'd come up against a brick wall. We weren't going to find Golden unless she wanted us to.

Little did I imagine that the mild-mannered retiree was again pulling her strings to trap me in her web.

When I entered my building, I checked my mail. Among the flyers that had accumulated in my absence was a letter addressed to Kraken. There was no return address and no stamp, so someone had to come inside the building and put it in my mailbox, which was unmarked for security reasons.

I picked the letter up gingerly. It looked innocuous. It was white and weighed nothing. I imagined it contained a single sheet of paper. I held it at arm's length and opened it cautiously.

Kraken, I know you get out of the hospital today. Twelve o'clock sharp at Atxa Park, this is a one-time offer. Don't mention it to anyone, or I won't show. No phones, no tracking devices. And do me a favor: DON'T shoot at anything that moves.

Golden Girl

44

THE THREE WAVES

SATURDAY, JULY 18, 1992

Summer camp was coming to an end. The three weeks were almost over, and Saúl had decided that on the last weekend they would visit Deba beach, on the Guipúzcoa coast.

"Deba," he explained to them the night before, as they all sat around the hearth at the mansion, "is a Celtic theonym that is repeated all along the Cantabrian coast: in Asturias, in Galicia, and in the Basque Country. Rivers, mountains, villages, and beaches bear the name of the deity Deba. The word derives from the Indo-European *deywo*, and in the language of the ancient Celts, it simply means 'goddess.'"

"What a beautiful name," Unai said to Annabel.

"Yes. I want to do something special there," she replied in a low voice. She didn't go into any detail, but the look she gave Unai was pregnant with promise and sent a shiver up his spine.

And it wasn't just Annabel Lee. Unai sensed a certain excitement in the air, a tension that he couldn't quite identify. He knew Jota had decided to tell Saúl what Rebeca had confided in him, all the stories she had made up.

Saúl, for his part, was acting strangely.

Distracted, pensive, irate. Once again, she had betrayed him; the girl was beyond hope, as much as he loved her. Rebeca didn't understand the notion of family, how they needed to look out for each other, that this stayed between them and would outlive them. It made him furious. He had raised her to understand these values. He despaired at having to go through it all again. The threat of scandal, suspicion, public ridicule. He couldn't afford to let that happen.

He reassured Jota, "She's having a relapse. They warned us about it. Try not to talk to her or fuel her fantasies. I'll do what I can to avoid having to leave camp to recommit her."

Sweet-natured Jota did not want Rebeca to be recommitted or for the camp to end abruptly because their leader was forced to leave. Jota wanted to extend the time he had before he was forced to confront the reality waiting for him in Vitoria.

Rebeca's survival instinct meant she could always detect the subtlest change in Saúl's mood, so she understood immediately that her relationship with her father had changed. No more smiles or knowing gestures, just Bluebeard and his terrifying gaze.

"Papa, are you all right?"

"Tomorrow night, Beca. Tomorrow night."

They arrived at Deba in the afternoon. A few of the volunteers from previous summers came as well, and the large group scattered among the various bars in the town. Later they congregated on the beach, where they relaxed in a companionable circle. It was their way of saying good-bye to the summer. This was the last weekend of camp. They all knew this chapter in their lives was closing. They would return to Santander or Vitoria and would never see some of these people again.

Unai sat near the front of the minibus on the drive. He needed to be alone to reflect on what he thought was going to happen later that night. But he immediately noticed that something was off between Saúl and his daughter. They hadn't said a word to each other during the two-hour drive from Cabezón de la Sal to Deba. Saúl was distant, and Rebeca's leg couldn't stop twitching in a nervous gesture that nearly drove Unai crazy.

When they got off the bus at last, Saúl unloaded the bronze cauldron and bottles of mead.

Unai took the opportunity to approach Rebeca.

"Hey, are you okay?"

"Sure, Unai." Rebeca forced a smile. She saw no reason to be unfriendly. Unai had always been kind to her. He'd stayed behind every evening to sweep the kitchen and help her carry out the trash.

Maybe she's sad to go back to Santander because it reminds her of her mother, he thought.

"We can talk later if you feel like it, okay?" he offered.

"Okay," Rebeca accepted.

At least someone talked to her. As for Lutxo, Asier, and Ana Belén . . .

Best not to dwell on that.

These were the last few hours of camp. She wouldn't see them again. Ever.

They could burn in hell for all she cared.

Saúl had a story lined up for the occasion, a traditional oral folktale that had been collected in 1865 from an old woman who lived in the village of Deba.

"The curse of the three waves. Has anyone heard it before?"

They shook their heads. None of them came from the area.

"According to this old woman, around that time, the mid-nineteenth century, there lived in Deba a fisherman, his wife, and their daughter. The fisherman's nephew also lived with the family, as did a young sailor by the name of Blinich. The fishing was poor, and the boat returned to land with empty nets several days in a row. But then, one night, when the three men were sleeping out at sea

Blinich dreamed that two women appeared before him. They are referred to variously as witches, lamias, or water nymphs. In any event, the women warned Blinich of an impending shipwreck and said that their vessel would have to confront three enormous waves. The first was of milk, the second of tears, and the third of blood. The older woman also told him that the only way to conquer the waves was to harpoon the wave of blood, but that if he did that, she would die. Blinich woke up in an agitated, excited state and told the fisherman his dream, but the man ignored it and they continued to fish as usual—"

"And they met the three waves," interrupted Jota, the most impressionable, the one who would carry these stories into his dreams.

"So they did. No sooner had they left the harbor than a big white wave came toward them, the one made of milk. Then they had to confront the wave of tears as best they could. By the time the mighty red wave of blood arrived, the fisherman understood that the only way to lift the curse was to harpoon it. So he did. The sea calmed again, and his nets filled with fish."

"A happy ending, then," said Lutxo, hanging on every word from the man who he hoped would be his mentor.

"Not at all. The man arrived home, his baskets overflowing with fish, to find his wife dying. The woman swore at him for killing her with a harpoon. His daughter was also angry with her father, for killing her mother. The daughter disappeared and was never seen in Deba again. When the fisherman asked Blinich who the two women in his dream were, the young sailor admitted that they were the fisherman's wife and daughter. The fisherman was left alone in the house, sick with sorrow. A sad ending, you see."

After a theatrical pause for effect, Saúl pointed toward the beach.

"Look at the sea. This is the perfect night for you to wait for the three waves."

"Why tonight?" asked Unai.

Yes, why tonight? thought Rebeca, curled up next to her father, her legs crossed on the sand.

"Tonight's full moon will look huge from where we're sitting. There's a beautiful word used to describe the silvery phosphorescence that a shoal of fish creates on the ocean surface: *ardora*. In Galicia, this word is also used to describe the way the moon reflects on the water. It'll be like a wide, white carpet of moonlight."

A *night of* ardora, thought Annabel Lee. It was a good theme for her latest graphic novel. She made up her mind. She smiled at Unai, and they agreed, through furtive glances, to meet later.

Saúl resumed his final lecture. He liked to have an audience; he was addicted to holding the attention of a crowd.

"This folktale contains elements of ritual, the water rituals I'm always telling you about. Once again, we see the female element: the wife who dies and the daughter who disappears. Then we have the milk, tears, and blood—liquid elements connected with human life. Milk for a mother's milk or a father's sperm, tears for the unavoidable struggles that occur in life, and blood as a symbol of death and rebirth . . . The ancient place-name *Deba* or *Deva* refers to one of the most significant deities in the Celtic pantheon: the triad of Celtic goddesses, Nabia, Reva, and Deva. And the folktale contains ancient elements of fertility and purification."

The students nodded and passed around the bottles of mead Saúl had brought. Soon thoughts of fertility and purification were the furthest things from their minds.

"There is one idea I'd like to leave you with, and I hope it stays with you whether or not you go on to study history: Virtually all of our celebrations, all the festivals in your towns and villages, have evolved out of much older traditions. From the Celtic Samhain, which Irish immigrants took to the United States as Halloween and which became La Noche de Samaín in Galicia, to the Roman harvest festival of St. John's Eve, which celebrates the summer solstice, and Christmas Eve, the winter solstice. The significant times of year in our ancestors' culture—solstices and equinoxes—correspond to important feast days in the Catholic Church's calendar. Every time you visit a place of worship, think about the hidden ruins beneath, the power of the place your ancestors chose. I'd be happy with that."

It was growing dark; a few wispy clouds slowly disappeared above them.

Saúl stretched, looked at his watch, and declared camp officially over for another year.

"I'll leave you to your own devices for a few hours and we'll meet back at the bus at eleven. Go into town, have a few drinks at the local bars. Enjoy yourselves. You've earned it."

As everyone else stood up to go, Annabel took advantage of the general excitement to seize Unai's wrist and hold him back. "Don't go into town with the others. Stay with me on the beach."

Unai nodded. He'd wanted this moment to arrive, the moment he'd been thinking about for the past twenty days, ever since boarding the train.

"I'll make up some excuse. Wait for me on that rock," he whispered in her ear.

She smiled.

Unai ran to catch up with his three friends.

Jota was already weaving a bit. He was partial to Saúl's mead and had drunk a fair amount, knowing he'd probably never get to have it again.

Lutxo and Asier, thick as thieves, were excited about the prospect of meeting some local girls to top off the evening.

"Hey, guys!" Unai shouted from behind them. "I think I'll wait in the bus. I feel sick after all that mead."

"Make yourself throw up," said Jota, the expert.

"No, it's okay," insisted Unai. "I'll sleep it off. I don't want to ruin the trip back."

"Suit yourself," Asier and Lutxo replied as one. In fact, they welcomed the idea: *Less competition,* they each thought.

And the three friends headed off toward the center of Deba.

Unai wheeled around and returned to the beach. He peered ahead, looking for his nymph in the distance, even though it was almost dark.

There she was, by the rock as agreed. He hurried to meet her, scarcely aware of the other figure.

"Hey, Unai. Did you stay behind to talk to me?" a voice asked, relieved. "Thanks a lot, I mean it. Thanks a lot. If you want, we can sit by the shore."

Unai stopped dead in his tracks, unable to take his eyes away from the silhouette of Annabel Lee.

"Rebeca . . . er . . . tomorrow. Tomorrow we'll talk about whatever you want. That way we can say a real good-bye. If you'd like, we can write to each other this summer, and when I'm in Santander I'll come visit you and your dad. But right now I've got to go, okay?"

"Yeah . . . sure." Rebeca turned around, trapped on the beach where Saúl had asked her to help him with the bronze cauldron.

Finally, she was accepting the awful reality of her life. *Nobody can protect me. Nobody wants to protect me. This is going to happen, and I'm all alone.*

As she watched Unai walk toward his own rite of passage, Rebeca tried to make sense of what Saúl had whispered to her when the group stood up to leave:

"The goddess awaits us."

It had a double meaning, which she suddenly understood. She was terrified.

Her imagination spiraled into panic.

The seconds ticked by. Darkness descended on Deba beach, and Rebeca knew that as soon as the moon rose, she was going to meet her fate.

45

SAN MIGUEL DE ATXA

MONDAY, JANUARY 9, 2017

Where the hell was Atxa Park? I looked at my watch: twenty past eleven. I didn't have time to get a team in place, or even warn Estí and work out a strategy. I had to go on my own or Golden would slip through our fingers.

I bounded up the stairs to my apartment, where I rummaged through the top shelf of my wardrobe for my bulletproof vest, put it on, and then pulled a high-necked down coat on over it.

If Golden was thinking of attacking me with a Taser, the way she had Jota and Annabel, I wasn't going to make it easy. I also wore gloves and a hat, although I would have preferred a helmet. I was sick of being hit on the head. I left both my cell phones behind.

I grabbed my piece. I didn't like carrying a weapon, but . . . well, no explanation needed.

I sprinted from the Plaza de la Virgen Blanca to the Plaza Nueva in less than thirty seconds, went into the visitors' center, and asked one of the friendly assistants, "Do you know where Atxa Park is? It's urgent."

"I'll look for you," she replied, which made me think she didn't have a clue, either.

Meanwhile I went through a mental list of the archaeological sites I knew in and around Vitoria. Atxa didn't ring any bells.

The girl, who had short hair and wore black-framed glasses, worked quickly on the computer and then beckoned to me.

"It's in the Green Belt, between Yurre and Gobeo, in the north of the city. Not your usual tourist destination. Do you want me to print out a map?"

"I'd rather look at it," I said. "Can you find some photos to give me a sense of what it looks like?"

To give me an idea of what to expect.

I swallowed hard when she showed me the photos. The park was nothing more than a few stones demarcating the walls and rooms of what had once been a pre-Roman settlement and later an important Roman military camp.

What worried me most of all was how close it was to the River Zadorra, which had an abundance of poplar trees and holm oaks on its banks.

It reminded me of Fontibre, the scene of Rebeca's murder.

After thanking her for the information, I hurried out to find my car. I glanced at my watch: twenty minutes to twelve. I was going to be late.

I parked outside the villas on Avenida Zadorra, crossed the road, and entered Atxa Park. Much of the vegetation had been killed by the harsh morning frosts. It was almost noon, and the pale sun had no intention of warming things up. Fog clung to the ground.

I saw a park map on a signpost and set off along the narrow path in the direction indicated. No one else was walking that day. I climbed a small slope and found another rustic sign pointing the way to the park.

Emerging from the small labyrinth, I saw a patch of weeds below me obscuring what looked like archaeological remains. The area scarcely measured twelve square yards. Ignoring the pegs marking off the site, I walked onto it. I wasn't quite sure what I was expecting to find.

Then I heard the noise of an engine.

I swung around nervously.

A 50cc scooter was barreling toward me up the narrow path.

I reached for my weapon almost without realizing it. I was sweating despite the fog.

The big, blond dispatch rider rode a ludicrously small scooter with a red trunk. He made a face as he came to a stop beside me.

"Are you Unai López de Ayala?" he squawked.

"Who's asking?"

"Joserra, I work for the express courier Poliki. If you are, I've got a package for you. It was supposed to be for twelve o'clock sharp, but it took me forever to find this place."

I looked at him suspiciously. "I've never heard of you. Your company, I mean."

It sounded like a lousy joke. *Poliki* means "slow" in Basque. Who would use a name like that for an express courier company?

"We're new. Look, just sign this piece of paper, will you, and I'll get out of your hair."

"Show me the package first, but open the trunk slowly," I commanded, slipping my gun out of its holster.

I couldn't be sure this guy wasn't going to pull out a Taser.

"Shit! Hey, I'm just the messenger," he exclaimed when he saw my gun. He raised his hands meekly above his head, even though I hadn't asked him to.

"I'm a detective," I said, showing him my badge. "Now, do as I say . . . Very slowly."

He opened the trunk of his scooter, extracted a padded envelope, and tried to give it to me.

I glanced at my watch: five minutes past twelve. This could easily be a letter bomb. I knew the proper procedure. I should have asked him to place the package gently on the ground, made sure both of us got the hell out of there, and then called in the bomb squad.

But instead I moved a few yards away, my gun trained on the dispatch rider. I was still wary of him. "Now, very slowly, open the package and tell me what's inside, assuming you don't already know."

As I edged my way toward the embankment, I noticed a wet stain spreading down the leg of his red uniform. The big guy had pissed himself.

Ignoring my command, he ripped open the envelope like a kid on Christmas morning.

"It's a tablet!" he shouted. "With a pink Post-it note that says, *This is not a bomb.* God, I wish they'd put that on the outside."

Me too, I thought.

I walked back to the messenger and grabbed the tablet.

"Fuckin' zero-hour contracts. What did I tell my mom . . . ?" he muttered. "You need to sign this paper."

I passed him my notebook as I scrawled a signature for him.

"Write down your name and ID number," I said, feeling slightly more relaxed. "And don't mention this to anyone at work or at home. Gag order."

"As if they'd believe me . . . ," he replied peevishly.

He clambered onto the scooter, his bulk dwarfing the minuscule vehicle, and hotfooted it out of there as if I had rabies.

Alone at the ruins, I switched on the tablet. A private chat room popped onto the screen.

Hello, Kraken. I'm sorry about the blow to the head.

I accepted her invitation to chat and began to write.

You're strong for a woman your age.

Take it as a warning never to
underestimate me.

Roger. It won't happen again.

It was a promise to both of us.

And apologies for the method of
communication, but I have nothing to gain by
getting myself arrested.

What do you want?

Despite the way it looks, I want to help.

Help with what, Golden?

You need to stop Rebeca. She isn't finished
yet. I know her.

Rebeca?

Why was Golden talking about Rebeca as if she were still alive
when the poor girl was murdered back in 1993?

46

AMSTERDAM

Monday, January 9, 2017

Let's start from the beginning, but keep it simple, because you've just blown a hole in several of my theories. I'll go first: we know you're Rebeca's aunt.

That's quite an achievement. You have some good people on your team. I never thought you'd figure that out.

Top marks for Milán, I thought. I didn't respond, though. I didn't want to give anything away. I needed to pressure her.

Now it's your turn. What can you tell me about Rebeca's disappearance?

You know my brother-in-law, Saúl. Everything begins and ends with him.

Now you're going to tell me you think he's Bluebeard.

Wait until you've read what I have to say,
then judge for yourself, Kraken.

> All right, go ahead.

My sister, Asun, died under very suspicious
circumstances. I've always been convinced
that Saúl pushed her down that well,
although I've given up hope of ever proving
it. But at least I can stop what he's unleashed,
all this bloodshed.

> And what did Saúl unleash?

It's a long story . . .

> The sooner you start . . .

There was always something strange about
Saúl's relationship with Sarah, his older sister.
They came from one of the oldest families in
Santillana de Mar, and there were rumors.
The mother was disabled, and in the last few
years of her life, she took to her bed, the way
women did in the old days. Their father was
strict and religious, in an old-fashioned way:
Spartan habits, biblical names, twelve o'clock
mass on Sundays. Both parents died early.
Saúl and his sister became VERY close after
that. Nobody really knew why Saúl started
courting my little sister, Asun. She was young
at the time, a slip of a girl. She found Saúl

fascinating, as did all the girls in the village.
They married young. Asun was eighteen
when Rebeca was born.

I'm following so far.

Saúl was as controlling as he was charming,
and he isolated my sister. He used Rebeca as
a pretext to keep Asun away from our family.
I used to visit Asun and Rebeca at their villa
without Saúl's knowledge. He'd always
disapproved of me and tried to separate us.
I thought about leaving them alone, but I just
didn't trust him. I didn't trust the image Saúl
painted for us of his idyllic world.

Why not?

After my sister died, I kept in touch with
Rebeca without Saúl's knowledge. I was her
godmother, and we were very close, even
though we didn't see each other much. The
girl was deeply unhappy and turned to
her father for comfort. He started to isolate
her, too, and an unhealthy relationship
developed among Rebeca, Saúl, and Sarah,
who became a kind of evil stepmother.
Rebeca was an imaginative child, and her
father filled her head with stories about the
magic of the past settings and its rituals.
Rebeca took refuge in an imaginary world.
She immersed herself in the books her father

made her read. She wanted to please him.
Without my sister, their relationship became
extremely unwholesome.

Up to this point, I agreed with Golden. I'd seen it for myself
at camp: their mutual dependence, the way they kept constant tabs
on each other.

Sometimes I wouldn't see Rebeca for months.
I visited her after the trip to the Cantabrian
settlement you and the other victims went
on. I found her changed, distant, almost
grown-up. Very unhappy. I was worried
about her. She wouldn't confide in me, but
seeing her alarmed me. One day, in April
1993, I went to see her at the villa. Her father
was at the university, and I found her packing
a small backpack. She looked terrible. She
tried to hide it, but I could see that her belly
was swollen. When I lifted her sweater, I
couldn't believe my eyes, Kraken.

                                        Was she pregnant?

No, but she had given birth a few days
earlier, at home, assisted by Saúl and Sarah.
The baby was a boy. He had been born
prematurely and died, they told her. Rebeca
was fourteen at the time and small for
her age.

                                        Who was the father?

Saúl.

                              Saúl?

Yes, Kraken. He liked prepubescent girls.
There had always been sordid rumors
circulating in the village.

                         Define "sordid."

About Saúl and Sarah holding hands when
they were little, kissing and touching each
other in the hay barn. Salacious village
gossip. Stories about incest. But the rumors
stopped when Sarah grew into a woman.
She and Saúl didn't seem to be as close
anymore, as if he had lost interest in her.

I encouraged her to go on, although I wasn't sure how much
I could take.

That's why he married my sister when she
was so young. And why he lost interest in her
sexually when she matured. My sister told
me that months would go by without Saúl
showing the slightest interest in her. When
Rebeca turned twelve, my thirty-year-old
sister became unnecessary.

                    Did Rebeca tell you that her father got her
                                      pregnant?

Yes, Unai. Beca adored her father, she worshipped him. Imagine the shock for a thirteen-year-old. You love your father, you idolize him, and yet he sexually abuses you.

What did you do when she told you?

I helped her escape.

You faked her disappearance.

I faked her murder. I wanted to implicate Saúl, to make him pay for what he'd done to her. I persuaded Rebeca to leave the country with me and to never see her father again. I promised her a new identity and a passport, but for the plan to work we needed to convince Saúl that Beca was dead.

So you sent those photographs to the newspaper, and you staged the whole Celtic ritual in Fontibre?

Yes, I did. I thought that would be enough for the police to investigate Saúl. But they never arrested him, they never even considered him a suspect. He's a natural-born manipulator. It was Rebeca's idea to replicate a Celtic ritual by suspending herself upside down with her head in the water. All her life her father had been filling her mind with stories like that, so she knew exactly

what to do. I thought this modus operandi
would incriminate him, but I was wrong.

You do realize that staging a crime is a
criminal offense?

Why else would I be communicating with you
using a stolen SIM card? Tracing it will lead
you nowhere.

That figures, I thought.

Then you took her with you to Amsterdam.

You've gotten further than I expected. I tip my
cap to you, Kraken.

I ignored the praise; I hadn't earned it.

What happened over there? Why wasn't
anyone suspicious when you turned up with
a fourteen-year-old girl?

I won't reveal my black-market contacts.
Suffice it to say, I bought new identities, and
Rebeca became my adopted child. I started
working for Cisco Systems, and for a few
years we were happy, at peace, removed
from the past.

Did Saúl ever try to get in touch with you
after his daughter disappeared?
Were you interviewed by the police?

No, Saúl and I never got along, and I moved
around a lot in those days. The police saw
no reason to contact me. I was an estranged
relative.

Continue.

Rebeca was an excellent student, a bit
of a loner. She was shy and rejected
boys. I thought this was normal, given
the circumstances. She was focused.
Occasionally, because of my job, we spent
time in other European cities: Paris, Milan,
Geneva . . . I loved Rebeca like the daughter
I never had, and I did my best to be a good
mother to her, but I failed.

What makes you say that?

I wasn't there when she
started to go off the rails.

Do you know where Rebeca is?

That's what I've been trying to find out ever
since you came to me with your broken
cell phone and I recognized her modus
operandi, the Celtic Threefold Death. I've
looked into every illegal Taser purchase, but
I can't trace her. I know she's behind these
killings. That's her signature. You have to

understand that she learned a great deal
about cybersecurity when she was living
with me.

The noble art of hacking, you mean.

Call it what you will, but take it seriously.
Beca is stalking you.

Am I in danger?

Everyone she considers unfit to bring a child
into the world is in danger. I'm sorry for
intruding on your private life, but I've seen
a lot of your exchanges with Alba Díaz de
Salvatierra. If your boss's child is yours, then
you're in danger. And if it isn't, then you
aren't. Go public, state openly that the child
isn't yours and you'll live. Isn't that better than
for your child to grow up fatherless? To have
to lay flowers on the graves of two supposed
fathers.

I'll make that determination, I said to myself. I asked my next
question to change the subject more than anything else.

What about Asier? Is he in danger?

If Asier isn't already dead, then he's no
longer in danger. I'm sure Rebeca managed
to persuade Annabel Lee to reveal the
father's true identity, which is why she killed

Jota. As for Lutxo, he's safe, too, as long as he doesn't get anyone pregnant.

A wonderful method of contraception known as Rebeca, I thought.

I'm writing to warn you, Unai. I need to tell you about the Rebeca that I knew.

I'm all ears.

Rebeca inherited her father's charm and his manipulative side. She never did anything just to do it: all her plans and actions had a motive. I quickly realized how spoiled she was. Saúl had pampered her, indulged her every whim. This was something I couldn't afford and didn't want to do, especially not while living among the austere Dutch. Rebeca continued to study history on her own. She visited museums. One day, she saw an advertisement about an upcoming exhibition at the Amsterdam Museum. She became terribly excited after reading the brochure. They were going to exhibit the Gundestrup Cauldron.

I've heard of it.

Not long afterward, Beca told me she was going to volunteer at the museum. She had been stalking the students hired for the exhibition and had knocked one of them down with her bicycle, breaking her ankle

and forcing her to drop out. The next day
Rebeca showed up at the museum's human
resources department with a fake resume.
She worked there for a few weeks, and
during that time, she stole the cauldron. She
did all of that just to perform that damned
ritual on our neighbors' pets. She presented it
as a prank, and she assumed I'd be proud of
her audacity. Then she returned the cauldron,
leaving it in a street near the museum.

How could you have let her get away with
it, Golden? You're not the kind of person who
condones that kind of behavior.

You have no idea how angry it made me.
But Beca didn't understand—those animals'
lives weren't important to her, and she was
proud of her exploit. But I threw her out of
my house.

What?

She was an adult. I'd provided her with an
education and the means to earn a living, as
well as a new identity. While she was living
with me, she respected the one condition I
had: she must never track down her father,
not even look him up online, or get in touch
with him ever again. Saúl was dangerous,
his sister had a great deal of influence in
official circles, and I risked going to jail for
abducting a minor. But Rebeca was obsessed

with what had happened that summer. She
blamed the four teenagers from Vitoria and
their girlfriend for allowing it to happen.
When you brought me your phone, I made
the connection and realized you were one
of them.

            So you haven't heard from her since . . .

Since 1998. It's my fault. Instead of throwing
her out, I should have taken her to see a
psychologist, to try to stop that behavior.
Let's be realistic, Unai, do you think she's
changed? After I kicked her out, she was
on her own, and she had somebody else
to hate, in addition to the five people from
summer camp. When I looked at your phone
and discovered that she had started to kill
people, I was convinced she was settling
past scores and would be coming for
me, too.

          Listen, Golden, in every murderer's life there's
          a trigger, a traumatic event that pushes them
          past the point of no return, that prompts their
          decision to kill. After all these years, what do
          you think Rebeca's trigger was?

Golden reflected for a few seconds at the other end of the line, wherever she was hiding.

I think that it was the young people's
suicides.

You mean Gimena Tovar?

Yes, Saúl's adopted daughter. I think Rebeca
heard the news and assumed Gimena had
killed herself because her father had been
abusing her as well. I think that was the
trigger, the moment when Rebeca decided
to act, when she started to contact all of you,
assuming she hadn't already.

I thought about the first time I was expecting a child, in 2014.
Was Golden's theory right? Had Rebeca been watching us then?
Would she have tried to kill me if Paula's pregnancy had gone to
term? I thrust the thought aside. I needed to focus on the present,
on what I could try to prevent.

Is that why you created false identities and
entered suicide chat rooms?

I haven't found Gimena Tovar yet, but I think
I will. I want to know what made her do it.
Those young people are often quite open
when they're hiding behind a screen. I met
all kinds on the forums I visited: kids who
are suicidal because they're being bullied
at school, girls with anorexia, adolescents
who are brokenhearted . . . and also several
cases of young people suffering sexual
abuse that goes undetected by anyone
around them.

But why would Rebeca take revenge on us,
and not on Saúl?

Didn't you receive training on how to deal
with victims of sexual violence, Kraken? Show
me one who doesn't have feelings of guilt.
"I shouldn't have accepted a ride, I shouldn't
have let him into my house, I shouldn't have
worn that skirt, I shouldn't have given my
dad a kiss, I shouldn't have . . ." For years
I listened to her defend him whenever I
accused him. She justified his behavior. She
hated him, but he's her father. She has an
Electra complex and she knows it, hence
the guilt. So she has directed all her hatred
against you. She would never hurt Saúl; she
loves him too much. She's convinced herself
that she is still in love with him. To her, he
will always be the handsomest, cleverest,
most wonderful father in the world. She's still
under his spell.

Golden was right. Rebeca fit the profile of our perpetrator, and
Annabel Lee's and Jota's deaths fit her modus operandi.

Then give me some information I can act
on, because I have nothing to show to my
superiors. Can you tell me
who Rebeca is now?

I still haven't found out, but you can be sure
the four of you who were at that summer
camp have either met her or she's watching
you.

Where do I start?

With anything that might give her away.
Names, for example. But it will be hard.
Beca left nothing to chance. She inherited
that Machiavellian trait from her father.
Remember, she is manipulative, a
chameleon . . . Until you've connected all the
dots, there'll be lots of Rebecas.

You haven't given me anything tangible,
Golden. Just a story you can't back up on
the pretext that you're a fugitive from justice.
They aren't going to believe that at police
headquarters. And the investigating judge
won't make things easy for me, either.

Well, that's all you're getting, Kraken. I've
already stuck my neck out, and I'm not the
charitable kind. From now on, you're on your
own. I want to live out my old age in peace,
if Rebeca doesn't find me first. So long,
Kraken. This is good-bye.

I had to protest.

Wait! If I need you for something, I'll put a
black cross in my balcony window, okay?

But a second later the screen went dark, and I was left wondering if that was the last I'd ever hear from the elusive Golden
Girl.

I walked back through the park the way I'd come, climbed
into my car, and drove home, my head spinning. So I was facing a
standoff with Rebeca.

If I was the father of Alba's daughter, she would kill me. If it was Nancho, she would spare me.

A standoff. With my daughter in the middle.

As soon as I closed the door behind me, I picked up my new cell phone and called Tasio in Los Angeles.

"How is the series going?" I asked.

"I'm still getting used to the life of a producer and the crazy pace of the writers' room. Do you know what time it is in California?"

I ignored his last comment, although I did some quick mental math and realized it was five in the morning.

"Tell me something, have you finished writing the script for *The Silence of the White City*?"

"I'm still working on it. Why do you ask?" His tone of voice had changed. I'd managed to wake him up.

"There's something you don't know, and I need to tell you about it, because I want you to include it in your script."

47

DEBA

SATURDAY, JULY 18, 1992

I t happened one calm night by a silvery sea on a beach named after a Celtic goddess.

For Rebeca, it occurred just like in the story: a wave of milk followed by a wave of tears and finally a torrent of blood.

"Is this what you wanted? Is this what you dreamed of?" Saúl had whispered in her ear. His rage felt like molten lava.

Rebeca said nothing. She couldn't have, even if she had wanted to.

"You can't keep doing this, my girl. You can't keep telling these tales. You're going to destroy the family, and me. I don't want to have to commit you again. You need to get better. Promise me you'll try when we're back home."

Rebeca nodded convincingly enough to persuade Saúl.

He stood up and looked at the time.

There was no one else on that dark stretch of beach.

"Go and wash yourself in the water," he ordered his daughter. "Three waves will be enough."

Rebeca hated him for that.

Not just because of the pain he'd inflicted, not just because of the betrayal.

But because in his cynicism, Bluebeard had ridiculed the legends, tainting what had united them. Rebeca swore to herself she would never be a historian. Never. From then on, she would detest history, the Celts, the folktales, the past . . . The past. It had just happened, but Rebeca knew even then that she would never stop hating her own past.

Unai's first time was a different story.

Annabel was a shadow waiting for him far down the beach. Not even the silver moon reflected on the sea was enough to illuminate her face.

Unai had no desire to be cast in the role of inexperienced virgin. He had purloined some seashells from the shore and ran them over the bits of her the dress didn't cover. His initiative caught Annabel off guard and she purred softly, delighting in their touch. Unai used the opportunity to clasp both her wrists with one hand. He didn't want her taking charge the way she had with Jota and Asier; he wanted it to be different with him. He wanted to tear off her cold mask, to see what was beneath that silvery skin: a beating heart or an uncaring carcass.

And when, impatient, she tried to undress him, he stopped her.

"Without hands, Annabel."

He noticed a glint of surprise in the girl's dilated pupils.

"All right," she agreed. "It won't be so perfect, but—"

"Forget about perfection."

Annabel began to pull up his Nirvana T-shirt with her teeth, and they giggled at her clumsy attempts. She explored Unai's stomach with her lips, teeth, and tongue, a tickling sensation that aroused him intensely. Undoing his pants proved more difficult since the crotch was bursting at the seams.

Then it was Unai's turn. He lowered the straps of her dress with his teeth, lingering over her neck, shoulders, breasts, and navel.

Sand stuck to their bodies as they rolled on the ground, but when he finally penetrated her, he saw what he'd hoped for: someone enjoying herself as much as he was.

After they finished Unai felt drowsy, and he would have fallen asleep on the beach, but Annabel was already thinking about something else, looking at her watch.

"I want to do it again, Unai, somewhere more comfortable, without sand. Let's go to the minibus. Saúl left me the keys, and the others won't be back for an hour and a half."

What could he say? They shook the sand out of their clothes and got dressed again, relaxed and laughing. Two shadows headed for the parking lot where the locked minibus was waiting. Annabel Lee opened the rear door and they climbed the steep steps into the vehicle. The darkness inside was so welcoming that they only had to look at each other, strip off again, and they were writhing in the middle of the aisle. Unai hadn't even noticed that Annabel Lee had lied to him about the time and that she had left the door open.

In a moment of lucidity, he sensed when Jota, Lutxo, and Asier climbed aboard in the dark, half drunk, and caught them in the act.

48

LA ARNÍA

That was a crazy thing to do. You should have told me," Estíbaliz repeated as she drove us back to Santander.

She was angry, yes. And upset, too.

"Alba has already taken me to task, can we change the subject?"

"No, we can't. You're not playing by the rules, and you took a big chance yesterday. What if it had been a trap? Do you realize you could have ended up dangling upside down from a pine tree?"

"A poplar tree."

"What?"

"From a poplar tree. The trees I saw on the riverbank were poplars, and there were some holm oaks, too."

"This is no laughing matter, Kraken, I'm close to taking you off the investigation."

"Golden made the conditions. If I hadn't . . . if I hadn't accepted, we wouldn't have the information that she gave us."

"And what did she give us, Unai? We don't have a shred of evidence to take to the presiding judge, just another line of investigation we need to verify, which just slows things down further. I'm beginning to understand why Alba is pressuring us for results. I have nothing. We have nothing," she corrected herself. "Only cauldrons that vanish and reappear, crime scenes with hanging bodies but no DNA to corroborate our bizarre theories. So far, the only progress we've made is to confirm that Ana Belén and Jota were expecting a child."

I chose to keep silent for the rest of the journey. Estíbaliz had been under an absurd amount of pressure these past few weeks, and her nerves were frayed. Alba and I had already had an almighty fight when I filled her in on what had taken place at Atxa Park.

I had the impression neither of them appreciated how significant Golden's revelations were; they were more worried about my safety. It was exasperating. For my part, I couldn't wait to see Saúl's face when we told him Rebeca was still alive.

We drove back to the university and asked to see Saúl Tovar. We were told he was in a lecture and were directed to one of the classrooms. We slipped in through a door at the back of the hall and heard his closing remarks.

The topic was sacrifice among the Cantabrian tribes. How appropriate. I studied his appreciative audience, nearly all women. And they had excellent taste; Saúl sparkled when he was speaking about his subject. He seemed to grow younger and to fill the auditorium the way an actor fills a stage. He had *presence*.

But there was a moment, just as he was concluding the lecture, when his eyes slid over the room, and he saw us leaning against the wall. His face stiffened. I couldn't tell whether anyone else had noticed.

"That's all for today," he said, breaking off without explaining what exactly the Cantabrians did with the goats they sacrificed. "More tomorrow."

A few of the students looked at each other, mystified; then they collected their things and started filing out of the auditorium in silence, some approaching Saúl to ask questions, to thank him, and to arrange a time to meet with him during his office hours.

Saúl stayed behind to gather his notes and switch off the projector. We waited until the room was empty and then approached him.

"Here you are again, after I told you I didn't want you coming to the university. I'm going to lodge an official complaint. This is harassment," he whispered angrily, without looking at us. He locked the projector's remote control in a drawer.

"Saúl, we have important news for you about Rebeca," Estí declared, looking straight into his beguiling eyes.

Saúl took one glance at her solemn face and realized this must be something enormous. He stood still, as though waiting for a lightning bolt to strike.

"Finally, some news about Rebeca?" His voice held a mixture of tension and relief.

"Yes," I said.

Saúl sighed, took a deep breath, and stood staring at the floor, arms akimbo, as if to steady himself.

"Then it's best we go somewhere more private. Come to my house. Follow me in your car, and we can talk about this calmly."

Estí and I exchanged glances. Naturally, this sounded like another trap. And, alas, I knew where he was taking us. It was burned into my blackest memories.

"All right, I'll go with you, and Inspector Gauna can follow us," I commanded.

My tone brooked no protest. Estí glowered at me as we walked out of the lecture hall, and I managed to show her discreetly, while Saúl wasn't looking, that I was armed beneath my jacket.

Just to be on the safe side.

Less than twenty minutes later, we were at Saúl Tovar's villa on the Costa Quebrada. The area was sparsely populated and overlooked the cove at Arnía beach.

It had been almost twenty-five years, but nothing had changed.

The house was clearly too big for Saúl alone. It was very masculine—there was no trace of the daughter who, until only a few months ago, had lived there with him.

The vast living room, which was more of a library, was brimming with books, some of which were in stacks on the floor. I felt as if I were visiting his brain. Saúl looked uncomfortable as we discreetly inspected his home.

On the mantelpiece above the fireplace was a Cantabrian stone disk, or stela, and a small collection of daggers and spearheads, which could have been genuine Cantabrian weapons, over two thousand years old, or humble reproductions based on a lifetime of archaeological finds. I wasn't enough of an expert to know.

"Let's talk out on the terrace. A sea breeze always helps relax the atmosphere," he said nervously.

Estí and I nodded and walked out through the doors at the back of the villa, which opened straight onto the beach. To the east were the Urros de Liencres, a cluster of sea stacks protruding from the water, and Castro Island. I could tell that my colleague was exhilarated by the landscape of jagged cliffs, but I recalled that violent sea all too well. I still hadn't made peace with my past, and the growing tension I felt at being back in that accursed place was causing the bullet wound in my head to throb.

It was probably the moist air. Annoying sensations, nothing more.

We sat outside on wooden chairs that were too big for Estí, who looked tiny among the voluminous cushions, and waited for an offer of refreshments that never came.

"Let's get it over with then. Did you find Rebeca's body?" Saúl said, rubbing his hands together in an involuntary nervous gesture.

"No, we haven't. And given the turn our investigation into her disappearance has taken these past few days, I doubt we ever will. We have a witness who was close to Rebeca and who claims she's still alive."

Saúl's large, ever-expressive hands froze.

"What . . . What do you mean she's alive?"

Saúl leaned back in his chair, and a relieved smile spread across his face, the most genuine expression I had seen on him in a long time.

"But . . . what about the photographs? We saw her dead body, don't you remember? That was my daughter, I'm sure, not some other girl. That was my daughter . . . and she was dead."

"According to our witness, Rebeca ran away from home and faked her own death so she couldn't be found. She staged the pictures and sent them herself."

"Then it's true, she's alive. You've brought my daughter back to me, after all these years . . . I thought the police were incompetent. If you knew how often I've dreamed of hearing these words, of having this conversation—" His voice cracked with emotion.

He raised his hands to his face and wiped away his tears, a little ashamed. He was the living embodiment of relief, of happiness, of a father witnessing a miracle.

He rose rather shakily to his feet, and came over to embrace me. I stood up hurriedly to receive him.

It was a powerful, unrestrained show of genuine gratitude. We didn't get much of that in our job, and I wasn't quite sure how to respond. I was well versed in giving good and bad news, but my skills were useless in this situation.

"And . . . where is she? Can I see her? Can I talk to her? I have so much I want to say to her—"

"Saúl, perhaps we haven't been clear," Estíbaliz cut in somberly. "You'd better sit down again."

"But she is alive, isn't she?" he said impatiently, bewildered. "Please don't play games with me. I've suffered enough."

"As we were saying, the witness has given a version of events that we haven't corroborated yet. So far, there's nothing to prove that this person is telling the truth. However, we felt we should inform you first, because the witness is someone you know, a relative of yours, in fact. We'd like you to tell us about her, to help us determine whether we can take what she told us seriously."

"A relative? Surely not my sister? Sarah would never . . . Sarah wouldn't have told you such a—"

"It wasn't Sarah, Saúl," Estí interrupted.

Too quickly. I would have liked to have heard what he was going to say next.

"Who, then? I don't have many relatives."

"Your sister-in-law, Lourdes Pereda."

"Her? You believe that con artist?" he yelled, his flushed face stiffening.

I had anticipated this response. Golden didn't seem too enamored of Saúl, either.

"Your sister-in-law claims she came to this house in April 1993, on the day Rebeca disappeared. She says she found her packing a backpack, preparing to run away from home. She also discovered that Rebeca had recently given birth and had decided to leave after losing the baby. According to Lourdes, she and your daughter staged her death with the photographs so that you wouldn't try to look for her. They didn't want the police to think there was a possibility that Rebeca was still alive and had simply run away from home."

"What did she do with Rebeca? Where did she take her? It isn't easy to hide a fourteen-year-old girl without somebody noticing."

"She obtained new passports and identities on the black market. They lived for several years in Amsterdam, where Lourdes worked for Cisco Systems. She claims she falsified the necessary papers for Rebeca to be registered as her adopted daughter."

"Amsterdam . . . I was grieving for her in Fontibre and you tell me she was living and growing up in Amsterdam."

"Is this . . . plausible?" I ventured, faltering slightly. Saúl wasn't the only one who was feeling tense and emotional.

"I find it hard to believe that Rebeca would have abandoned me."

I didn't know how to respond to such a candid statement.

"Could you elaborate?" Estí insisted.

"No, I don't want to talk about that now. What you need to know is that your witness, my sister-in-law, was the black sheep of the family. She and my wife were barely on speaking terms. Lourdes was always a manipulator and a swindler. For all I know she's spent time in prison. I haven't heard from her in decades, but everybody knew she was mixed up in counterfeiting and had no fixed address because she was constantly trying to keep one step ahead of the law. Lourdes caused my wife a lot of grief and sent her parents to an early grave. So the answer to your question is, I don't know. I don't know whether you can give any credence to what she told you."

"Funnily enough, your sister-in-law claims you isolated your wife from her family by marrying so young."

"Asun and I were very much in love. Don't defile that," he snapped.

"We aren't here to judge you. We simply wanted to tell you what Lourdes said to give you a chance to respond to her version of events," Estíbaliz explained patiently. "She went so far as to claim that your wife's death was not an accident."

"Let's end this right now. Who are you going to believe, a known con woman who has admitted to kidnapping a minor and holding her for years in a foreign country with a fake identity, or your colleagues from the Santander police department who examined the well Asun fell into and found no evidence of foul play?"

"We believe you, Saúl," I interjected. It was important to gain his trust since the hardest part of the conversation was yet to come. "We aren't taking her suspicions seriously."

My words seemed to calm him.

"But we do need to speak to you about an extremely delicate matter. I'd like to pick up on what you said about finding it hard to believe that . . . Rebeca would have abandoned you." I paused for breath. "Your sister-in-law claims that Rebeca told her you sexually abused her."

Saúl tossed his hair back and looked out at the sea. He took his time replying. "Here we go again. It looks as if this story will haunt me forever," he murmured, as if to himself.

"Could you explain?"

"Rebeca has told this story to other people before, and nobody believed her. That's why we had her committed a few months before the summer camp you attended, Unai."

"And at the camp she told Jota. He was vague about it, but that's what Rebeca told him, isn't it?"

"I think you should look at some documents," he said, rising from his chair.

Saúl reentered the house and went upstairs.

Estí rushed after him. I knew she was also armed, but I was still alarmed when I heard her call to Saúl, "Wait, I'm coming with you."

I followed her cautiously into the living room, my hand on my gun.

I didn't slip it out of the holster, but listened for any sound or cry for help. The silence that followed seemed, if not endless, too long.

Stop all this nonsense and go on up, Grandfather would've told me. I decided to follow his advice and started toward the staircase.

But there was no need, they were already on their way down.

Saúl had a file full of papers under his arm. The look in Estíbaliz's eyes told me to leave my gun holstered.

And just then I understood that whatever Estíbaliz had seen or read in those papers was about to change the course of our investigation yet again.

49

EL URRO DEL MANZANO

SUNDAY, JULY 19, 1992

Morning brought the threat of storms. The oppressive heat of the past few days was exacting its price, and the air was charged with electricity. A single spark would have blown everything sky-high.

Unai was feeling similarly explosive. At seven he climbed out of his sleeping bag for the last time, and his heart sank when he realized that Annabel and Lutxo had gone off for their habitual predawn walk in the sequoias. He told himself it didn't matter. Last night Annabel had made her choice; what was between them had been different from what she'd had with Jota and Asier.

Special, unique.

At least that was what Annabel Lee had whispered to him.

He went downstairs and entered the empty dining room, deep in thought, remembering the caresses, Annabel Lee's thighs, the thrusts, and bites—oh, the bites. He headed for the pantry and grabbed the last remaining bar of handmade chocolate they had bought for everyone to share, going through the motions like a robot.

Unai wasn't selfish by nature; his grandfather had taught him to respect other people's property and to behave politely. But he wasn't even aware of what he was doing when he sat down and munched his way through the entire chocolate bar. He was absent-mindedly focusing on a patch of wall that had once been white while his mind replayed the events of the past few hours, over and over, like a broken record.

He was slightly in shock.

Life could be so beautiful when it wasn't being a bitch.

Rebeca also spent the night in a state of shock, curled up inside her sleeping bag. Alert to every noise in case Bluebeard came back.

She heard several cars pull up outside the mansion. She was familiar with the rituals of the camp: on the last day, all the university students who had worked there over the years gathered to mark the end of another summer.

She didn't want to go downstairs to have breakfast with the others. Nobody called her—even her father left her alone.

She listened quietly to the hubbub coming from the kitchen, laughter and excitement over the last breakfast. She tried to make herself tiny so no one would notice her presence or absence.

Finally she heard car engines outside again, and then the noise died away. The day before, Saúl had told them all about his plan: they would spend this last morning on the cliffs near his villa, between Portío beach and Arnía beach, about half an hour's drive from Cabezón de la Sal.

Fine, they can clear off, thought Rebeca.

Good riddance to them all.

She just wanted this damned camp session to end, yet she was also terrified of going back home alone with Bluebeard.

She heard heavy footfalls on the stairs and instinctively stiffened.

"Is someone still in there?" Rebeca heard a voice call out.

A girl's voice, she didn't know who.

"Me . . . ," she said weakly. She didn't have the strength to speak up.

When the girl entered the room, Rebeca recognized her: Marian, a third-year history student who had been to camp a few years before. She was faintly masculine, big and awkward. Like Rebeca, Marian didn't attract the interest of boys. In the cataloguer's brain she had inherited from her father, Rebeca had always found her a bit strange, too outspoken and impulsive.

"Who is 'me'?" Marian asked, puzzled.

"Rebeca, Saúl's daughter," she identified herself from deep inside her pink Hello Kitty sleeping bag.

"Rebeca, you should come! We're all going for a walk on the beach. Come on, I'll take you in my car. I can't believe your father left you here on your own. I stayed to clean up, and he gave me the keys. Come on, get up," said the giantess, seizing the girl's arm.

"No, I'm not going." Rebeca curled up inside her sleeping bag like a chrysalis.

The two girls looked at each other. Marian in her boxy red Barcelona Olympics T-shirt, and Rebeca, who would rather die than leave her eiderdown womb.

"Hey, what's wrong?"

"Nothing . . . ," the girl protested in a faint voice that suggested the opposite.

The kindhearted student perched on the edge of Rebeca's bed next to her sleeping bag. She was proud of the fact that she had a way with young girls—she was practically bringing up her little sister single-handed.

It didn't take her long to win Rebeca over with a little sweet-talking and cajolery, to get her to open up . . .

Twenty minutes later she stormed out of the house. This happened to her sometimes when she got upset. She was like the bison from the Altamira caves—susceptible to rage and, once she was angry, unstoppable.

And the things poor Rebeca had told her . . . well, of course she'd heard rumors at the university about Bluebeard, his wife, his sister. For all that Marian appeared inattentive during lectures, she heard everything that was said in the university's hallways.

She told the girl to stay in the dormitory, locked up the mansion, and headed toward the Costa Quebrada in her beat-up Ford Fiesta.

Unai was relaxing at the sea's edge. Directly opposite were the three sea stacks, their columns and arches evoking fanciful shapes: Urro Mayor, Urro Menor, and the Urro del Manzano, bent like a bonsai in the wind.

A few yards away, his friends pretended to be talking and taking a walk.

He didn't have to refuse an offer to join them, because not one had extended an invitation.

He assumed they were embarrassed at surprising him and Annabel the night before. And he understood . . . completely. He had felt the same way with Jota and then with Asier . . . It had been awkward looking them in the eye after catching them with their pants down.

He let it go, and assumed they would get over it, too. Still, he intended to speak to Jota, because their friendship was important to him, and he wanted to be sure things were okay between them. As for Annabel . . .

She had refused the *cuadrilla*'s invitation to go for a walk on the beach. The heat was stifling, and huge gray clouds were looming. You didn't need to be Unai's grandfather to realize that the skies were going to erupt into a summer storm at any moment.

Out of the corner of his eye, Unai saw one of the older students, a girl as tall and robust as him. She was striding resolutely toward the far end of the cliff, toward Arnía beach, where Saúl had wandered off alone. Maybe she'd had enough of all the teenagers and needed a break.

But Unai quickly forgot about the student and Saúl. Annabel Lee came and sat between his legs, leaning her head against his chest. She seemed to bring the storm with her—in some distant cloud, thunder rumbled, echoing just moments before Annabel spoke.

"I brought you a drawing," she whispered in a voice that sounded like the sea.

She pushed a sheet of paper torn from her sketchpad into his hand. It showed a tomb facing the sea, and the outline of two lovers sitting on a cliff. It could have been them.

Unai took it from her the same way he might have received the tablets inscribed with the Ten Commandments. In awe and with a sense of duty, as if it were a sacred object.

"I'll keep it . . . ," he was able to say.

"Promise me you'll keep it always. At least until the day I die," she murmured solemnly, her lips brushing his earlobe.

Of course, thought Unai. How could he refuse when she put it like that?

And then it began to rain—big, hot, heavy drops of water.

"I promise," he replied. He knew Annabel Lee wouldn't accept any other response.

She looked at the clouds and the rain with irritation, as though reproaching them for ruining her carefully planned scene. She took the drawing back from Kraken and put it inside the hard cover of her sketchpad to keep it from getting wet.

"Do you want to go?" suggested Unai. "I don't mind the rain. I've always liked it, especially in the summer. But we can go if you want."

"No, let's stay. It's like something out of *Wuthering Heights*," she replied.

"I wonder what will happen tomorrow when we get back to Vitoria. Will we see each other again?" he said tentatively.

Or will you forget us and go back to hanging out with your mother's biker gang?

"Of course we'll keep seeing each other," she replied, sounding slightly annoyed. "It's always been you and me, since preschool, I told you. This was just the start. We'll keep dating in Vitoria."

Relieved, Unai embraced her. He couldn't contain his feelings. He and Annabel were both a bit wet, and water dripped from her dark bangs onto his face.

"I was afraid . . . I was afraid I might be just another guy you met at summer camp."

"That's what you get for not trusting me," she murmured to the sea. She yielded to his embrace but seemed absent.

Unai relaxed as he gazed at the horizon.

Only then did he see her. A red dot in the water.

He leaped to his feet. Annabel wasn't happy about the interruption of the romantic moment.

"Did you see that?"

"*That* meaning what?" she snapped. She was still sitting on the beach, drenched.

"A red bag, or an enormous buoy! It was definitely something, I saw it . . . ," he cried, anxiously scanning the white-crested waves.

"Well, I can't see anything," she replied, but Unai realized she hadn't even looked.

He ran in the direction the history student had disappeared earlier.

"Saúl, Saúl! Did you see that? Did something happen?" he shouted as he ran along the cliff.

The rain made the ground slippery, treacherous.

What had started as a shower had turned into a downpour. The sea was churning, and Unai stopped to scan the coastline.

Then he saw it again, and a shiver ran down his spine as he realized it was the body of the girl in the red T-shirt. She was being tossed toward the sea stacks by the waves, getting pulled under and then bobbing back up repeatedly.

Saúl came running in response to Unai's calls, a look of horror on his face.

"Marian fell in the sea!" his professor cried out when he was a few yards away. "A gust of wind knocked her over, and she slipped over the edge of the cliff. She must have hit the rocks on the way down. She could be unconscious or even dead. We can call emergency services from my house—they'll send a rescue team."

"It'll be too late by then, Saúl! Come on!" Unai knew exactly what to do.

Rather reluctantly, Saúl obeyed.

Unai ran to where his friends were sitting on the beach. Asier, Lutxo, and Jota stared at him blankly as he came hurtling toward them, followed by Saúl and then Annabel, who was more concerned about her sketchbook than anything else.

"Marian fell into the sea! We need to make a human chain! Come on, she's not far from the shore!" he shouted at them.

The expression on the three friends' faces changed. They followed him out onto the rocks until they were facing the sea stack against which Marian's body was being buffeted like a rag doll.

But then she moved, her arm lifting vertically as if she were attempting to swim, or to grab hold of the vast rock. Unai felt a surge of hope. He pulled off his hiking boots before wading in.

The water hit him with greater force than he had anticipated. The sea was like a brick wall that day, and a huge wave pushed him under for longer than he would have liked.

He struggled to the surface and gulped for air. Training his eyes on his objective, the red T-shirt about fifteen yards ahead of him, he started swimming toward it, his powerful arms cutting through the water. It was the first time he was glad to have earned the nickname Kraken.

If my long arms help save a life, then Lutxo can laugh all he wants, I don't give a damn, he thought as he gasped for breath.

And then he remembered Lutxo. *Where is he?*

He should have been a few yards behind him by now, forming a chain back to dry land.

Unai turned his head toward the shore as he fought the next big wave.

After a few strokes, his strength proved no match for the waves. He was getting closer to Marian, but he began to think that he might need help getting back to shore.

As Unai made one last effort, he caught a fleeting glimpse of Saúl, Annabel, and his three friends watching the scene from the beach. It was clear they hadn't the slightest intention of going into the water, let alone forming a human chain.

He fixed his sights on the red Barcelona Olympics T-shirt and reached the body of the student being tossed against the base of the rock. Her clothes were caught on its craggy surface.

He examined Marian. She was unconscious and had a huge gash on her forehead. He started to feel desperate. The passive stares of his friends, his new girlfriend, and his conscientious teacher didn't help. For the first time, he thought he was going to die.

50

LA COSTA QUEBRADA

TUESDAY, JANUARY 10, 2017

W e'd better sit down," Estíbaliz said. "You have a lot of explaining to do, Saúl."

"I know," he murmured solemnly.

I gave Estíbaliz a searching look. *What the hell is going on here?*

"I'm listening," I said.

"Here," said Saúl, handing me a patient's file. The hospital's name was printed across the top of each page. "You'd better read it yourself."

"Summarize it for me," I said, flipping through the thick pile of reports and assessments, some typed, most handwritten in a doctor's illegible scrawl.

"Rebeca suffered from, suffers from, suffered from . . ." He pursed his lips in a gesture of despair. "Rebeca's case was extremely complex. She was diagnosed with acute paranoid psychosis accentuated by her unresolved grief over her mother's death and an unresolved Electra complex."

"In plain language please, Saúl," I implored.

"All little girls go through a phase when they become enamored with their father. It's called the Electra complex, after the Greek myth: Electra was the daughter of King Agamemnon of Mycenae. The phase usually starts around age four, when little girls begin to fantasize about being their father's partner and their mother becomes redundant. It's a normal part of development; in fact, it's essential because it breaks their dependency on their mother, who becomes their rival, their enemy for a while.

"The same thing happens with little boys. Only it's referred to as the Oedipus complex, after the myth by Sophocles. This is universal. My daughter went through an Electra phase when she was tiny, just like every other little girl. But after she lost Asun, Rebeca's Electra complex resurfaced, fueled by her powerful imagination. What's more, her mother's death triggered a chemical imbalance in her fragile psyche. Her fantasies took over and she lost touch with reality. It was a textbook case of psychosis."

Estíbaliz and I exchanged a brief glance; we weren't expecting this.

"There was a huge gap between reality—a normal relationship between a widowed father and his daughter—and Rebeca's interpretation of that reality," Saúl continued. "My daughter didn't grieve the way a normal twelve-year-old would. She carried on as though nothing had happened—happy, smiling, and bubbly. Her behavior was abnormal. I was devastated by the death of my wife, but my daughter insisted we go to the movies holding hands, that we stroll down Paseo Pereda eating ice cream from Regma's. She became capricious and domineering, and I confess, I was too lenient. I was a pushover. I asked my sister for help, because she was always stricter than me, better about setting boundaries. But Rebeca reacted badly to Sarah coming to live with us. Then the horrors started . . ."

"What horrors?"

"She told my sister that I touched her inappropriately. I still find it too upsetting to go into any detail about her claims. My sister knew she was lying, and she spoke to a colleague at Valdecilla hospital. He explained that Rebeca was gravely ill, and following an assessment, he strongly advised that we commit her. That was the worst moment of my life. They gave her antipsychotic drugs—dopamine and serotonin inhibitors—that turned her into a zombie. It destroyed me to see her like that. My world imploded."

We looked at him.

We believed him.

The poor man.

"It's all in there: the assessments, her medication, the dates she was committed and released. I tried to be as discreet as possible in order to protect her. I hoped that she would have a normal teenage life once she was released, but she missed three months of school, couldn't catch up, and failed her final exams. In the end, she had to repeat a grade after you met us that summer."

"But her pregnancy was real," I interrupted. "And you lied to us about it."

"Yes, I did. It was real, and she hid it right up until the end. I lied because, well, once she was dead, I didn't think it was relevant. Also . . . it isn't easy to admit that your teenage daughter was pregnant. What was the point in raking all that up?"

"And the baby?"

"A boy, stillborn. Her fourteen-year-old body couldn't carry the child to term. It was all very quick, the boy was tiny, and she gave birth as soon as she dilated. My sister had contacts at the hospital and was able to have the fetus incinerated at the crematorium there. There was no record of him, something that I regret. I should have reported it to the police—maybe they would have discovered who the father was—but at the time I was afraid that would only cause further harm to Rebeca, who was still unstable. I didn't want to see her committed again. A few days later, she disappeared. I always assumed she ran off with the father of her child and possibly the others in his *cuadrilla*, and that they had killed her to keep her from talking. Maybe she threatened to tell, I don't know."

"You say with the others in his *cuadrilla*," Estíbaliz remarked. "Is that because you think you know who the father was?"

"Well, I have my suspicions, of course. Rebeca got pregnant in July 1992, during the three weeks we spent at the Cantabrian settlement. The only males she came in contact with were the four volunteers and me. So tell me, Inspector Ayala, which of you four got her pregnant?"

"I can assure you I didn't touch her. It never even occurred to me."

"I'm inclined to believe you. You were too obsessed with Ana Belén Liaño. I trusted you all, and yet one of you seduced my daughter. I've always suspected that one or all four of you killed her, but if that's not true, if she staged the ritual herself—"

"Ritual?"

"The Celtic Threefold Death. Rebeca was always fascinated by it, by the peat bog people. I took her to see Lindow Man at a temporary exhibition in Milan once. It was a wonderful trip, memorable for us both."

"Saúl, several people have been killed recently after being subjected to this ritual of burning, hanging, and drowning. Do you think your daughter might be responsible for those deaths? You knew her better than anyone. Please take a minute to consider it," Estíbaliz said.

Saúl took his time. He went over to the sideboard and picked up a photograph of him and Rebeca smiling, in a snug embrace, with the nearby cove in the background.

"I want to believe you . . . to think Rebeca is still alive," he said, staring at his daughter's picture, "but you have only the word of a con artist."

"Do you think Rebeca fooled your sister-in-law, too?"

"If what Lourdes says is true, then Beca obviously used her. She told her the same lies about abuse to get Lourdes to help her run away. My daughter knew that her aunt and I didn't get along, and that she could turn her against me relatively easily. Rebeca could convince anyone of anything. She was a good-natured, intelligent, spirited girl. And yet, according to her psychiatrist, the sick part of her mind actually believed that she and I had a sexual relationship, that when we went to the movies, it was as a couple. She felt humiliated because she was a child, and she couldn't wait to grow up."

"I'm obliged to ask you, even after what you just told us . . . Have you ever thought your daughter was trying to contact you?" Estíbaliz ventured.

Saúl looked at us sorrowfully, like we were a couple of immature kids who had disappointed him. When he replied, he sounded like an old man.

"Contact me? Forgive me for being blunt, but my daughter disappeared when she was fourteen years old. You have no evidence that she's still alive other than a statement from a known criminal. I don't want to go through all this again . . . I don't want to get my hopes up. You have no idea how painful this is."

"We're just asking you to look back, and—" my colleague began, but Saúl didn't let her finish.

"Enough! That's enough. You barge into my class and drop this emotional time bomb, under the pretext of pursuing this mockery of an investigation. This has been going on for more than twenty years now. I lost another daughter recently. How much grief can a father take?"

I didn't know, and I had no wish to find out.

Saúl rose. The interview was over. "I think you should leave now. And, please, Unai, if you ever had any respect for me, don't do this again. I don't want to know anything more about your inquiry unless you're bringing me my daughter's remains."

"I promise. I'm really sorry about today," I said, placing a hand on his shoulder.

We looked at each other. I never wanted to inflict suffering, and I had no desire to trifle with what he held most sacred.

Estíbaliz and I crept back to the car, heads bowed.

It was the kind of experience that made you hate your job.

Saúl didn't even say good-bye. He closed the door on us quickly, and I had the impression he was holding back tears.

We got into the car and sat facing the inlet on Arnía beach.

I drove, only a hundred yards or so, to the far side of the cove, out of sight of Saúl's villa. I didn't want him to see us, but we needed some fresh air before returning to Vitoria.

"Let's sit here for a while," I said to Estí.

She welcomed the idea.

Once we were sitting out on the cold grass, I said, "If what Saúl says is true, then we have a psychotic killer on our hands—"

"Uh-huh."

"Who invented a story about Saúl raping her at the camp that summer," I continued.

"Go on."

"When in fact, one of my friends got her pregnant."

"So . . ."

"She convinced Golden to take her away by telling her that Saúl had raped her. She left in order to get away from him and from the threat of being committed again. And now, she's started killing."

"But why now? Why start killing after all these years?"

"Let's assume that at fourteen she was too young," I said, thinking out loud.

"Okay."

"Golden thinks that hearing the news about Gimena's suicide was the trigger. Maybe she identified with her, maybe she convinced herself that, like her, Gimena was being sexually abused and was pregnant."

"Or maybe she assumed that Saúl had stopped desiring Gimena because she was too old, just like Rebeca's mother. She was twenty-three, a woman, so Saúl was no longer interested. In any case, Gimena's suicide pushed Rebeca over the edge," Estíbaliz said, playing devil's advocate. "You're the profiler, Kraken. Does it sound convincing? Doesn't what we've seen at the crime scenes suggest a cold, calculating killer? Didn't I once hear you say that killers suffering from psychosis tend to have sudden violent outbursts? They listen to voices that tell them to do things," she said hoarsely.

Something was troubling her. Estí always cleared her throat when she was perturbed.

I pulled my pad from my inside pocket. I wasn't in the mood to force myself to speak, nor did I feel like giving a master class in profiling.

First of all, I wrote, *experiencing psychosis doesn't equate to being violent. It's a common misunderstanding that prevents mentally ill people from being fully accepted in society and that hinders their recovery. Only a small percentage of mentally ill people commit crimes, no more on average than the general population. It is true that those who do commit crimes are often obeying delusional voices or fantasies. There's a disconnect between reality and the distorted world that exists in their own mind. Up until now, we've assumed that the crime scene is complex, an elaborate representation or fantasy, but maybe it's simply the reflection of a mission. That would fit the profile of a patient with a messianic complex. Rebeca believes she has a duty to punish expectant parents, to decide whether they deserve to bring up their unborn babies, and, if she determines they aren't worthy, to sacrifice them to the Three Mothers. She has carried out the Threefold Death according to the descriptions of our ancestors who lived alongside the Celts. But these aren't her fantasies. Rebeca fantasizes that her father desired her sexually and raped her, and that her pregnancy was the result of incest. That's what she told Golden, and maybe she believed it, but perhaps the person she actually slept with was . . .*

I reflected. Who were the leading candidates?

I can't imagine her sleeping with Lutxo, I wrote, thinking back to that summer long ago. *Or Asier. They didn't even notice her. Possibly*

Jota. He was the baby of the group, and they spent time together. She could have slept with Jota. After Annabel Lee dumped him, I thought. *Maybe that's why she killed him.*

"But why kill Ana Belén Liaño?"

Maybe she saw Annabel as a rival because she slept with Jota, or because she was having his baby. Maybe what happened back then stayed with Rebeca forever. It's impossible to predict how her mind would respond to the trauma in her life. She became unbalanced after her mother's death, which is when she started having unhealthy fantasies about her father, her only remaining role model. That gave weight to the idea that the child she was carrying was theirs, that they would be a family again, and that she would usurp the role of her absent mother. After she lost the baby, she had another breakdown and ran away, afraid of being committed or of what might happen if they discovered Jota was the father.

"Or maybe she did it to protect Jota from the scandal," Estí suggested.

Possibly. Jota was a child himself and had recently lost his father. Something like that might have destroyed him. He was already under a lot of pressure from his family, and Rebeca knew that.

"If so, that's excellent news for anyone else who might have been a victim. The crimes aren't the work of a psychopathic serial killer. Rebeca murdered Jota and Ana Belén, but she isn't planning on murdering anybody else. That means you're out of danger."

I hope you're right. But we can't rule anything out. This is merely speculation, I reminded her.

"I know, I'm just wishing out loud," she said pensively. "Tell me, Unai, after everything we've seen today . . . do you think Rebeca could be our killer?"

I still can't believe that a woman would have the strength to hang somebody upside down from a tree.

"Golden managed it twenty years ago with Rebeca," protested Estí.

Rebeca was a fourteen-year-old girl and Golden was an adult. I'm not convinced.

Estíbaliz looked at me defiantly. I wasn't sure why.

"The other day when you told me friendship makes the world go round, I started thinking. You're wrong. It isn't friendship; it's a lever. Archimedes said, 'Give me a long enough lever and I will move the world.'"

I don't follow you, Estí, and believe me, I'm trying.

"We're going to Villaverde. I'll explain after I've hung you upside down."

51

GRANDFATHER'S GARDEN

TUESDAY, JANUARY 10, 2017

Grandfather lent Estíbaliz a length of rope and she went down to the vegetable garden. I had been ordered to join her in fifteen minutes. I stayed in the kitchen with Grandfather, who was even more taciturn than usual.

"What's the matter?" I asked.

"Come upstairs with me, son. I have something to tell you," he said in his flinty voice.

I followed him along the hallway and up the rickety wooden stairs to the attic.

He stood staring at the fox pelts nailed to the beams and then pointed at them as if they should tell me something.

"I think somebody's been nosing around up here," he said at last.

"What do you mean, somebody?"

"If I knew I'd tell you, son."

"Please explain, Grandad," I said, slightly alarmed.

"Those pelts have been there for fifty years. Nowadays you, your brother, and I are the only people who come up here, and none of us has moved them. But somebody must have been up here recently because now two of them aren't straight."

He was right. I hadn't noticed it before, but two were askew.

"The wind?"

"The wind, my eye," he scoffed. "They're as stiff as boards, and the wind has never shifted them before. No, son. I don't like worrying you, but somebody outside the family has been up here. Come with me," he commanded, and we went over to the boxes where I stored my memories.

"They're all closed, the way you left them, except the one from the summer of 1992."

"You're right," I said, looking more closely.

I was sure I had closed the box properly after briefing the team. I always made sure the boxes were sealed so dust couldn't get inside.

"This one has something to do with the case you're working on now, doesn't it?" I heard him say behind me.

"Yes, it does. This is no coincidence," I said, picking up the first photograph pensively.

It was a group photo of our *cuadrilla*, Saúl, Rebeca, Annabel, and some of the university students, among them Marian in her red Olympics T-shirt.

Grandfather moved closer as if to take a look, but he didn't pull his glasses out of his pocket.

"Grandad, what's your take on a man who has been widowed and lost both his daughters?"

Grandfather tensed slightly, then cleared his throat before speaking.

"I thought that you and Paula were expecting twins, a baby boy and a baby girl."

At first, I didn't understand. I hadn't realized that Saúl and I had similarly tragic pasts, and that Grandfather had conflated our biographies.

"No, not me. I'm talking about the case I'm working on," I explained awkwardly.

I gave him a brief account of Saúl Tovar's life and then

asked him to put on his glasses so that he could see the picture clearly.

"You want to know if I think your teacher is a murderer because he lost three women in his family?"

"How does it look from the outside?" I asked.

Grandfather thought for a moment before replying. "He could have been responsible for their deaths without actually killing them. A weak or evil man can bring devastation to those around him without firing a shot, if you know what I mean."

"Not really."

"Well, before I left for the front in '36, I used to deliver grain, in Laguardia. I did business with a man there. He wasn't a bad man, but he was weak, a drunk who couldn't say no to liquor even if it was vinegar. He went bankrupt, and after the Civil War, his family went hungry and his wife contracted tuberculosis. His eldest son became a trucker in Irún, but he started smuggling contraband over the border and was killed in a brawl somewhere far from home. The younger boy suffered from depression. They found him in the River Ebro with a rope around his neck. A stone was tied to the other end. That man didn't kill his family, he didn't want them to die, but still they ended up in the cemetery long before their time. Do you understand what I'm saying? This Saúl seems like that man. I've never mentioned it, but you were different when you came back from that summer camp in Cantabria."

"Different in what way?"

"You left a boy and came back a man. I realized that you weren't going to be an engineer. Whatever happened with that girl . . . you need to let that go, son. You've got too much weight on your shoulders."

"You might be right, Grandad. But then again, maybe now isn't the time to let go. Maybe it's time I found out the truth about what actually happened on the cliffs that Sunday."

"Is this the girl who was in the accident? Didn't you tell me that once?" he said, replacing his glasses and pointing at Marian.

Grandfather had an excellent memory for faces. At the annual August 15 gatherings, when all the villagers in the Alavese hills came together to celebrate mass in the Church of Our Lady of Okon, my grandfather remembered that So-and-so from Navarrete was a cousin of the baker in Urturi, and the kid from Villafría couldn't possibly be the son of Antonia and Mauleón because he looked nothing like them.

I nodded as I looked at the picture.

"Are you sure this girl died?"

"Of course, Grandad, they took her to the morgue. Nobody walks out of there alive."

"The thing is . . . I've seen that face recently, or one that looked remarkably similar. I couldn't tell you where. But I've seen that face."

I believed him. It didn't seem possible, but experience had taught me never to question Grandfather's unflinching comments. I stored the information for future use.

"Is everybody suddenly deaf?" Estíbaliz sang out like a sparrow from behind us. We turned around at the interruption and saw her propped against the wall.

"Sorry, Estí. We didn't even hear you come up."

"I've been calling you for a while from outside. Of course, with these thick walls . . . Come on, Unai, to the scaffold. Grandad has to come, too, in case it all goes horribly wrong and I need a pair of strong arms."

"You're the boss."

We followed Estíbaliz down to the garden, and she told us to stand underneath the big pear tree. It had been there for decades, maybe even a hundred years. It was already huge when I was a boy and had boughs thick enough to play hangman on.

"Imagine I Taser you. You fall to the ground," Estí said. "Your central nervous system is shutting down, you can't move. You're at my mercy. Lie down on the ground."

"Is this really necessary?"

"You have to remember that you're completely powerless; otherwise, this isn't going to work."

I stretched out between two rows of leeks.

With nimble fingers, Estí tied the rope around my ankles and pulled it tight. I was unable to move, and I hated the feeling. It reminded me of what Nancho had done to me, and I didn't want to be reminded of him.

"Good, now I'm going to roll you onto your stomach and tie your hands behind your back."

She did so, rather roughly, and I took in a mouthful of dirt. I looked past the cauliflowers to where Grandfather was guffawing at the sight of me.

"If I had known it was this much fun, I'd have become a policeman myself."

"Don't encourage her," I implored.

"Now to the practical part of the experiment, where I prove that by using the tree as a fulcrum, a featherweight like me can lift a kraken like you," said Estíbaliz. She hurled the rope over the thickest bough of the pear tree, the one I had clambered onto hundreds of times as a child, my hands sticky from the resinous knots.

She pulled on the rope, hauling me up with relative ease.

"If you get dizzy or your head starts hurting, tell me right away," she shouted, straining to keep a grip on the rope. "We don't want to stir things up in there."

She left me hanging above the ground. I was seeing my world upside down. The dark purple mountains were level with my eyes, and the overcast sky was at my feet.

It was strange to look at things from a different perspective, but maybe the world was telling me I needed to do just that.

"QED!" Estíbaliz declared proudly.

"Good, now get me down from here! Gently, please, very gently!" I yelled.

I hadn't counted on gravity making the blood rush to my head. My cheeks were burning, and I felt an unpleasant throbbing sensation in the place the bullet had once been lodged.

Estí must not have heard my request—either that or the laws of physics took over and she wasn't able to lower my body gradually. I felt a sudden yank on the rope as she let go, and then I plummeted into the leek beds.

"That was some landing, son. There goes tonight's dinner," said Grandfather, rushing over to help me. He seemed torn between smiling and looking worried. "Are you all right?"

"I'm fine, Grandad. It was nothing."

Estí gathered up the rope and brought it over. She was triumphant. "I just lifted someone three times my size, which means I've proven that the killer could be a woman acting alone. Forget the theory of the three hooded figures. The Taser allows the killer to take control without a struggle, and by using the tree as a lever, she can overcome the difference in weight. Before she dunks their heads in the water, or whatever it was she did to Jota, she neutralizes them. She doesn't need to be that strong. Those Celts weren't nearly as clever."

Grandfather took the coiled rope from Estíbaliz and disappeared quietly up the stone steps, discreet as always.

He always said that was how he would leave this world: whistling quietly. I knew it wasn't true, that he would never leave, but none of us dared contradict him.

"This is what I think happened," said Estíbaliz. "Rebeca contacted Annabel online when she found out Annabel was pregnant. They became friends. They went on a hike up the mountain together. Before killing her, Rebeca persuaded Annabel to reveal the identity of the father. And then she killed Jota. It isn't hard to imagine him going back to some girl's house on a drunken Saturday night," said Estíbaliz.

I was convinced by her argument. *I need to rethink the killer's profile,* I thought. *Leave male suspects aside, and start accepting the possibility that Rebeca, or whoever she is now, could have killed Ana Belén and Jota.*

But how do you unmask somebody who has spent years preparing to hunt you down?

52

THE CONDE DE SAN DIEGO PALACE

SUNDAY, JULY 19, 1992

A final wave slammed into him, propelling him closer to the sea stack. Unai clung to the girl's body as best as he could with one arm. He used his other arm to thrash through the water until he made it to the rock. As he pulled Marian's inert body toward him, he realized with horror that she was either dead or unconscious.

He also understood, in a moment of strange lucidity, that he was going to die unless help arrived.

He didn't have enough strength to swim back to shore, especially if he had to drag the girl's bulky body . . .

And if the rain kept coming . . .

Unai clung to Marian. This life-and-death embrace was so different from the way he had held Annabel Lee moments before, which now seemed gratuitous and trite.

When he had enough of a purchase on the rock, he looked up and saw that there were only three people left standing in the group on the shore.

Unai imagined, wished, hoped that Saúl and Annabel had gone for help.

And help did arrive: forty minutes later, they said.

By that time, the skin on Unai's arms was flayed from clinging to the jagged rocks, holding on to Marian's cold body.

He was kept under observation at the hospital for a few hours, and Marian was delivered to the mortuary.

Unai insisted that they not inform his grandfather. They bandaged his arms, and then Lutxo, Jota, and Asier came into the room to see him.

They couldn't look each other in the eye. They were too mortified.

Lutxo tried to make a joke about a kraken and a mummy, but it fell flat.

"They said you can get dressed and leave. Saúl and Annabel are coming to pick you up, and they're bringing dry clothes," Jota whispered to him. His tone was almost reverent, like he was at mass.

Unai shot him a sidelong glance and knew immediately that he had gotten into their stash of red wine back at the mansion; they had planned to make *kalimotxo* but had run out of money for the Coca-Cola.

He felt like yelling at him. *Go for it, Jota. Today's the day! Why hold back?*

But there were too many battles raging in his head. He didn't have the energy to start another one with the guy who had been his best friend until three weeks ago.

The members of his *cuadrilla* left, sullen and silent. Unai lay sprawled on the bed, waiting for his next visitors.

"The doctors say Marian suffered a severe head injury when she fell. That was the cause of death. She didn't drown," Saúl Tovar informed him from his perch at the bottom of Unai's bed. "You couldn't have saved her. She was already dead. Apparently it's quite common when people fall off cliffs."

Unai felt like Saúl's empty, incisive words were condemning him. He couldn't meet Saúl's gaze that day, either.

Saúl sensed the boy's unspoken irritation. "Not everybody possesses the heroic instinct you do. You could be a police officer. But you shouldn't begrudge the others, they have the right to be cowardly," he said, his big paw clasped around Unai's ankle. He meant it as a gesture of support, a way of bonding, but it made Unai uncomfortable.

Really uncomfortable.

"What about you?" he asked bluntly.

"I have a thirteen-year-old daughter to consider. I can't risk leaving her alone in the world, abandoning her to the foster system."

Unai blushed to the roots of his hair.

"I'm sorry. I've judged you too harshly."

"Apology accepted," Saúl replied. His tone was rather abrupt, but perhaps he was weary after the dark day they had all gone through. "Come on, get dressed."

Saúl passed him a pair of boxers, jeans, and a T-shirt that didn't fit. *Who cares,* Unai thought, *all I want is to get out of here and take off these bandages . . .*

He dressed in front of his professor's frank stare, and a moment later Annabel, who wasn't shy either, walked in. She had seen it all before.

"I'll leave you two alone, but don't keep me waiting," Saúl said, stern. "We're running late, and you have a train to Vitoria to catch."

He left the new lovers alone. They were both silent. They didn't really know what to say.

"You almost ruined everything," Annabel declared at last.

"What?" Unai asked, confused.

"You could have died in that sounding sea, but that's not how the poem goes. I'm the one who dies first. And yet you dove in to save a dead girl."

"She wasn't dead!" he yelled.

"She was dead. You risked everything for nothing."

That's it. I've had enough for one day, Unai thought.

"You sound insane!" he exploded. "How can you be so selfish? A girl died today and none of you lifted a finger to save her."

"But you did. You couldn't stand by; you had to play the hero."

"No, I had to save her, period."

"Ah, so that's it," she murmured to herself, wrapped up in her own thoughts as always. "That's what you are . . ."

"I'm not in the mood for your cryptic comments, Ana Belén," he said, getting off the bed and moving toward the door.

He wanted to leave everything behind: the white room, the summer camp, the stench of cruelty and cynicism that trailed behind Annabel Lee.

"Don't you see? You were made for this. I'm not suggesting you should become a lifeguard, but you were born to save lives."

In fact, that's how Unai spent the rest of the summer. He walked into the offices of Bernedo's local council and secured a job as a lifeguard at the town's swimming pool. There on the northern side of the mountains, the water was rarely warm, and there were some summers when only the bravest took the plunge. That year the water was bitterly cold.

And then, much later, after Unai finished university and was feeling rather unmotivated about his career prospects, the double crimes of the dolmen happened.

He became obsessed. First, by the historical aspect of the murders, which became apparent when the second pair of bodies were discovered at La Hoya, the Celtic-Iberian settlement near Laguardia. Then by Tasio Ortiz de Zárate, his hero. Before he knew it, the police investigation was all he thought about, talked about, and dreamed about.

And he remembered Annabel Lee's words: "You were born to save lives. It's part of who you are; it's your calling. I should know—some of my mother's boyfriends were policemen, and that's all they lived for. Everything else came second."

Besides, Unai's obsessiveness worried him.

So he decided to channel it into a cause that let him sleep at night. Better that than some uncertain path, like Jota with his creative urges or Asier with his love of money. Or Lutxo, whose inferiority complex forced him to compete with everyone and everything, including himself.

Unai couldn't care less about creativity, money, or what others thought of him. As a result, and because the death of his parents was still an open wound, his mind was made up: criminal investigation.

When they got back to the Conde de San Diego palace in Cabezón de la Sal, the atmosphere was somber. It didn't seem like the time for fond good-byes, and indeed there was no appetite for them.

Annabel and the four young members of the *cuadrilla* from Vitoria loaded their backpacks into the baggage compartment beneath the minibus, and a nervous, silent Saúl drove them to the train station.

The truth was they couldn't wait to leave the mansion behind. They wanted to forget the past few hours, the past few weeks. They all swore never to return. It was as if the place was cursed, as though it was somehow responsible for everything that had happened.

Unai had a few seconds to say good-bye to Rebeca, who looked aghast at the bandages around both of his arms.

"I'm really sorry about what happened to you, Unai," she said in her high, childish voice.

"It wasn't your fault," he replied with a shrug. It was painful to raise his shoulders, but he didn't wince.

"I know, of course . . . ," she said, lowering her eyes.

"Hey, you and I still have to talk . . . ," Unai remembered.

"No!" she gave a little cry. "Don't worry, it was nothing, honestly. I'm fine, everything's fine. There's nothing to talk about."

Unai was puzzled by her flustered response, but he smiled at her because that seemed to be what she was expecting, and he kissed her on both cheeks.

Being shy, she flinched. But her father was also watching her intently while he pretended to chat casually with Lutxo and Asier.

Just then, Jota walked up to them. He had already retrieved his Levi's backpack from the belly of the minibus, and he wanted to say good-bye to Rebeca, too.

"Hey, thanks for showing me how to thatch the hut and fix the adobe walls . . . Thanks for everything, Beca," he said sincerely. He felt sorry for her. He moved forward to offer his hand and help her off the bus.

Saúl didn't appreciate the gesture, or the complicity between them.

But that was only natural.

No father, no matter how young and open-minded, likes to see his thirteen-year-old daughter holding hands with a sixteen-year-old.

53

EL PORTALÓN

TUESDAY, JANUARY 10, 2017

Estíbaliz was darting around my grandfather's garden like a restless little snake. I eventually put my hands on her shoulders to slow her down, and she came to a halt and looked me in the eye.

"Is there something you're not telling me?" I asked, confronting her.

"Yes, Unai, I do need to talk to you about something. But all this stuff about hackers getting into our cell phones is making me paranoid," said Estíbaliz.

"Go ahead."

"I'm not showing you this online in case somebody's hacking my phone, too, so you'll just have to take my word for it."

"I always do," I replied, incredulous.

"Well, then, given how off the grid your grandfather's house is, this is probably as good a place as any for me to tell you about it. Let's sit down."

I indicated the low wall separating Grandfather's plot from Aquilino's, and we perched on it, even though the moss was dry like an old sponge, and the January frost that had settled overnight had left the stones icy.

"It's about Annabel Lee's Facebook account. I asked Milán to look for the mystery friend Annabel made a few months before she died, and she still hasn't come up with a name. Usually when I ask her to run a search, she gets back to me almost immediately, as though getting me an answer were her main mission in life. This is a first."

"Yes, I've heard that she's good."

"She's more than good, she's exceptional. That's why I don't understand how she could have missed one name in particular: Geneva. Someone with that username started to post comments on Ana Belén's wall right after she announced that she was pregnant. It took some patience, but I was able to follow the thread of their conversations until they started to communicate privately. Here's the thing: Geneva's profile is obviously fake—there's almost no activity on the account, and there's nothing linking it to anyone who might be able to corroborate the profile. It's filled with goth photos, which I suspect were uploaded to cater to Ana Belén. Geneva's profile does say she is from Vitoria, but that's all."

"Where is this leading?"

"Milán could have easily discovered this fake account—it only took me a few hours. So I can't help wondering why she hasn't gotten back to me about this mystery friend who may have accompanied Ana Belén on her last walk to San Adrián."

"Golden said something about . . . about names." My memory was hazy.

"Names?"

"Yes, that I should start by looking at names, that names held special meaning for Rebeca. Don't you see?"

"What?"

"Golden told me that she and Rebeca spent time in Milan and Geneva . . ."

"Their names . . . *Milán, Geneva* . . . correspond to the places where Rebeca lived."

"And also, Saúl . . ." I paused. The cold was getting to me. "Remember when Saúl told us he and Rebeca went to Milan to see an exhibition about the bog people, and that the trip had been special for them both?"

Estíbaliz nodded. She thought for a minute, then looked up. The pear tree's bare branches were sighing softly in the breeze.

"Milán is worth her weight in gold. These are all bizarre coincidences, and we're being paranoid," she said slowly, eyes closed, head tilted toward the old tree.

"Milán is worth her weight in gold. These are all bizarre coincidences, and we're being paranoid," I repeated after her.

I said it partly to convince myself, partly in the hopes that if I said it out loud, I would speak it into existence.

Milán reminded me of someone. I'd felt it the first time I met her. But I still couldn't pin it down.

"Let's head back to Vitoria, then," said Estí. "I'll call Alba because she has access to Milán's file. I'll tell her about our . . . they aren't exactly suspicions, are they, Unai? We're just covering our backs."

"Right. Yes, let's go. I want to visit someone, too."

I called him on my old cell phone as soon as I arrived in Vitoria. Asier was not on the list of people I trusted implicitly.

"Asier, I'd like a word with you. Now."

"Impossible, my friend," he replied abruptly. "I'm at El Portalón having lunch with my pharmaceutical rep."

"In that case stay where you are, I'm on my way. I'll drop in and we can talk." I hung up so he couldn't wriggle out of it.

I set off toward the end of Calle de la Correría, on the north side of the Old Quarter. Opposite to the Plaza de la Burullería was El Portalón, an old coaching inn that had been serving thirsty Vitorians for six hundred years. It was just the kind of discreet venue I needed to talk about equally sensitive topics.

I crossed the stone threshold and asked for my friend. A waitress wearing the traditional Basque *neska* costume sent me upstairs to an old dining room lined with oak beams that was next to what was once the inn's chapel.

Asier had gotten rid of his rep and was waiting—somewhat impatiently if his expression was anything to go by. He looked pale. The new year disagreed with him, or perhaps it was the burden of his new wealth, or maybe his marriage was cracking under the strain. I couldn't know for sure.

"How's your head?" he greeted me. "You spent New Year's Eve in the hospital."

"Watching *The Usual Suspects*." I refrained from adding *with Alba*. "It wasn't a bad way to spend the evening."

"Sure, it's a great movie! I especially like the line about the devil."

I didn't get the reference. It was time for my nap, and I was feeling less sharp than usual.

"What line about the devil?"

"When Verbal quotes Baudelaire: 'The greatest trick the Devil ever pulled was convincing the world he didn't exist.'"

I contemplated his words in silence. So Asier wanted to talk to me about the devil and his tricks? Fine.

"I need to ask you a few questions," I said, clearing my throat.

"I figured as much. We're not likely to just meet for a coffee these days, are we? Fire away, but I need to be back at the pharmacy in an hour," he said, irritably.

"I want you to tell me everything you remember about Saúl's daughter Rebeca."

"Oof . . . that kid." He made a face. Thinking about her evidently didn't bring back pleasant memories.

"What about 'that kid'?"

Asier twisted a paper napkin between his fingers until it looked like a piece of rope.

"I didn't have a lot to do with her. What do you want to know?"

"Why you disliked her? Why you avoided her? You were really cold toward her."

"Are you going to arrest me for that?" he said, arching his eyebrow contemptuously.

"Relax, Asier."

"Okay, sorry. It's just that the whole thing makes me sick. The past should stay in the past, don't you think?"

"Tell that to Jota."

He sighed. "Fine. The kid was weird. Our first night there she took me into the kitchen and burst into tears. She told me some sick story. It made me want to go straight back to Vitoria. I actually wondered what the fuck I'd gotten myself into. How could a twelve- or thirteen-year-old girl have such a sick imagination . . ."

"What did she tell you, Asier?"

"That her father touched her. She said it just like that. 'Hi, my name's Rebeca and my father touches me in places he shouldn't.' She said that Saúl and his sister, her aunt, had been boyfriend and girlfriend, and that when she told her aunt, who was a doctor, what was happening to her, her aunt had her committed to the psychiatric wing at Valdecilla hospital."

"Yes, I knew about that," I said. The waitress had brought me a cappuccino, and I was already draining the last of it.

"The kid was hysterical. She told me that her father and her aunt were liars, and that she wasn't making it up. She said that she knew her father and his sister had been together after their parents died. I don't remember much of what she said about the family history, I wasn't really listening. I just wanted to get out of there as fast as I could, in case Saúl walked in on us while she was sobbing uncontrollably."

"Try to remember. It would really help me out."

"She said her grandmother had been bedridden for years because of a promise she made to who-knows-what virgin, and that she'd never met her grandfather, but that people in Santillana said he was very strange. The grandparents died just as Saúl's sister was finishing medical school, so Saúl went to live with her. Rebeca told me about the sexual abuse and incest in the family, but it sounded like a fantasy. And she kept contradicting herself. One minute she's talking all this shit about him, and then the next she's telling me how much she loved him. To be honest, I thought the kid was nuts. Saúl had warned Jota not to believe what she said, and later Jota told me that she had gone to him and to Annabel with the same story. You could tell that Saúl was upset and worried about it. Would you have believed her? Did she try to get you involved, too?"

"I think she tried, but we never got a chance to talk."

Marian's death put a stop to everything, I thought.

"That kid sounded crazy. She was crazy."

"Yes, I believe she was suffering from mental illness. Saúl confirmed that she was diagnosed with acute paranoid psychosis." I took a deep breath to try to put my words in order. "She had an Electra complex. She was in love with Saúl. She said all of that to get attention."

"Yes, that much was clear at camp."

"You were right not to believe Rebeca," I went on. "She invented the story of sexual abuse, as well as the incestuous relationship between her father and his sister."

"Shit, the chick had a twisted mind."

I nodded. I might not like the way Asier said it, but I basically agreed with him.

"Why is this relevant now? Didn't you tell me she was killed a year later?"

"Because she's alive, and she might be coming after us."

"What do you mean she's alive?"

"I'm going to ask you something personal. You told me you weren't the father of Ana Belén's child, but are you and Araceli expecting?"

I didn't want to reveal that Jota was really the father, partly because of the gag order but also because right now I knew more than Asier did. Our conversation was quickly turning into a game of chess, and I was willing to take any advantage I could get.

"Not that I know of. I already told you what I plan to do about my marriage once you get around to solving this case and I can get my hands on those millions without you sending me to jail. I don't want to end up like that Tasio guy who spent twenty years in the slammer because of your screwups."

I gritted my teeth. I couldn't tell him to go to hell, not yet.

"Just answer my question. I don't want to argue with you. Are you sure . . . that you aren't going to be a father?"

"Completely. Unless Ara is pregnant and just hasn't told me."

"What about with someone else?"

"No way. This is Vitoria, Unai, everyone knows everyone else's business . . . Anyway, you didn't answer my question: How do you know Rebeca's alive?"

"We have a statement from Saúl's sister-in-law, Rebeca's maternal aunt. According to her, Rebeca didn't die." I took a few breaths. Too many consecutive sentences. "We believe she's alive, and we think she killed Annabel and Jota. Have you met any women lately who might conceivably be her? Thirty-eight, educated, she had dark hair back then, but she's probably changed her appearance."

"My wife," he hissed. His voice sounded like a whip cracking, and he tensed.

"Araceli? How could it be her?"

"My wife," he repeated in a hushed tone. "Araceli, she's here . . . be discreet, will you? She doesn't need to know about any of this."

Then the penny dropped. Araceli was a few feet away from us, in the dining room's doorway. How long had she been there and how much had she overheard?

We stood up as she approached, like a couple of kids caught with their hands in the cookie jar.

"What are you doing here?" Asier said, kissing her awkwardly on the lips.

Araceli folded her arms. With her new haircut, she looked more and more like Annabel Lee. Hadn't Asier noticed?

"Can't I drop by to see my husband?"

"I thought you were in Donostia today?"

"Bilbao, I was in Bilbao. My classes were finished, so I thought to myself, *I'll pay my husband a surprise visit at the restaurant where he has lunch every Tuesday, and maybe we'll see each other for a change.* Was that so wrong of me? Hi, Unai," she said, giving me two floral-scented kisses. "Sorry I didn't say hello earlier. I was too busy having to explain my agenda to my husband."

"Hi, Ara," I said. I would limit myself to polite small talk. I didn't want to get too involved.

"Is everything okay?" she asked. "Did something happen? Why so glum?"

"Everything's fine," I said, putting on my best poker face. "I was feeling nostalgia for my old *cuadrilla* buddies, that's all."

"So am I. We're all acting strangely these days. We never get around to meeting up the way we used to. I guess it's to be expected with all these funerals . . . Our *cuadrilla* has the highest mortality rate in the north. First Martina, then Jota—"

"Was that supposed to be funny?" her husband cut in.

"Okay, forget it. You obviously got up on the wrong side of the bed this morning."

"Well, you two, I'm going to head out," I said hurriedly.

Thankfully, I was saved by my cell phone buzzing. I smiled

apologetically as I left the inn and went outside to take Estíbaliz's call.

"Unai, I've spoken to Alba about Milán Martínez. According to her file, Milán was born in Santander. Strange, don't you think? She never said anything to us about it, and she avoided accompanying us on our fact-finding trips to Cantabria."

"Yes, but that's not enough to make her a suspect," I said. "Come on, Estí, what are you thinking?"

"Look, someone hacked into your cell phone, so you had to get a new one. What if, and I'm just saying we should keep an open mind here, what if Rebeca is following the investigation using your new phone?"

"You're saying Milán could be Rebeca? Fine, let's ask her right now then, so we can clear this thing up," I said, trying to bring a little common sense into play.

Still, I couldn't help remembering the quote Asier had told me: *The greatest trick the Devil ever pulled was convincing the world he didn't exist.*

If Rebeca was still alive, anyone could be her. Including . . . Milán.

"Where are you now, Unai? I'm heading for Torre de los Anda. That's the address Alba gave me for Milán Martínez."

"I've just left El Portalón, so I'm nearby. I'll wait for you."

Soon afterward, Estí and I met at the entrance to the imposing medieval building in the Plaza de la Burullería.

She pulled out her cell phone and called Milán.

"Inspector Ayala and I just had lunch at El Portalón, and I said to him, Hey, let's go see Milán. She told me she rented an apartment in Torre de los Anda."

"I never told you where I live," Milán's throaty voice answered.

"Really? Then it must have been Peña."

"I doubt it," she replied curtly.

"In any case, we're downstairs. We're curious to see inside the oldest building in Vitoria, and you're the first person we know who's ever lived here. I'm going to ring your buzzer, could you let us in, please?"

Milán took forever to open the door.

When we reached her apartment on the top floor, we could hear the sound of someone frantically cleaning up. It didn't sound like they were being too careful.

Estíbaliz tentatively rang the bell on the landing.

Milán opened the door. Her hair was wet, and she was wearing a bathrobe. I suddenly understood the odd feeling of familiarity I had whenever I saw her, and I understood Grandfather's comment, too: Milán couldn't possibly be Rebeca, because she was the spitting image of Marian Martínez, the history student whose life I had been unable to save twenty-four years ago.

54

LA TORRE DE LOS ANDA

TUESDAY, JANUARY 10, 2017

I instinctively took a step back. I felt a sudden pang seeing Milán with wet hair. It brought back the last image I had of Marian, in my arms, by the sea stacks off the Cantabrian coast.

"Marian? Are you Marian?" I said to no one in particular.

"I'm not Marian," replied Milán, her hand still hesitating on the door. Was she going to slam it in our faces?

"You look so much like Marian. I understand now why you look so familiar," I persisted. "Older than she was, but—"

"I'm telling you, I'm not Marian."

"Can we talk inside, Milán?" Estí interrupted. She already had one foot over the threshold.

"Of course. Sorry about the mess, I wasn't expecting anyone," she murmured, tightening the belt on her bathrobe.

We walked down the hallway in the centuries-old building, but as we passed one of the rooms Estí and I both froze.

It looked like a simple study, empty except for a laptop on a table. But spread across one of the walls was a mass of photographs and dozens of pink, green, and orange Post-it notes. The pink Post-its corresponded to pictures of Saúl Tovar. Saúl as a child, a youth, at our summer camp, at lectures he had given over the course of the twenty years or so when I had lost track of him. I may not have been following him, but Milán had, judging by that strange wonderwall.

The green ones were for Asier, Jota, Lutxo, and me. She had printed pictures of our *cuadrilla* dinner meetings that had been uploaded onto social media, as well as my media appearances during the double crimes. Her study was adorned with photographs I thought were private.

The orange Post-it notes mapped the timeline of Annabel's life and death. Milán had tracked her entire career, from the moment she was first published twenty years earlier. There were photographs of her at book presentations and signings and pictures of her with her fans. Milán had a lot more photographic material than we did.

I went up to the wall and pulled off the photo that matched the one that had been taken from the attic at Villaverde. There we were—younger, carefree, oblivious to what was going to happen to us in just a few days . . .

"Milán, you need to explain this," I said, turning toward her, photograph in hand. "Or should I call you Marian?"

"Will somebody please tell me who Marian is?" Estíbaliz erupted.

"Was."

"Who was she?" my colleague insisted.

"She was my older sister. She died, or was killed, at the summer camp in Cantabria in 1992."

Then it dawned on me. It was a family resemblance. Milán had familiar features: close-set eyes, a body like a Spartan's, prepared for battle.

"Your sister? I didn't know Marian had a sister."

"She had a family, Inspector Ayala. Maybe you all were able to go on with your lives without asking too many questions. But my parents' questions were never answered. They were older, and her death devastated them. But they didn't want to bother the police, so they said nothing. I was young, and I was left without . . . Marian took care of me. I need to know if it was an accident, if someone killed her, or if she threw herself off the cliffs on purpose . . . At the time, nobody seemed to care what had happened. One Sunday afternoon, they just gave us back her body with no explanation."

"Hold on, hold on . . . what do you mean if someone killed her? She fell off the cliff."

"Did you see it happen?" she murmured angrily, snatching the picture from me.

"No."

"Did anyone?"

"Saúl."

"Exactly. Saúl."

"Do you think that Saúl lied, that he pushed her off the cliff?"

"You're the boy who went into the sea, so you must have been nearby. What really happened?"

I forced myself to remember, but my only recollections were intensely physical: the fury of the waves that flayed my skin, the weight of her sister's dead body. That was all my brain had registered. How could I tell her that?

"Annabel and I were sitting on top of the cliffs overlooking Portío beach." I had to concentrate to get such a long sentence out. "Your sister . . . asked us where Saúl was. She was furious. We pointed him out and she stormed off to talk to him. Soon afterward, we saw her floating in the water, next to one of the sea stacks."

"How could she have fallen in? She wasn't stupid, and it doesn't make sense as a suicide. Why would she have killed herself in front of her professor, especially with young students so close by?"

"Saúl said it was a gust of wind."

"Was it windy that day?"

"It had started to rain, but no, there was no wind where we

were sitting. Then a summer storm blew in and whipped up the waves."

"And you think a gust of wind could have blown my sister over?" she yelled, unable to contain herself.

My mind went blank. I had never stopped to think about how strong the wind would need to be to knock over a person weighing around a hundred and seventy pounds.

"That's enough!" Estíbaliz cut in, stepping between us. "Let's go into the living room and discuss this calmly. I want you to tell me the whole story, from the beginning, so that I know what's going on."

Despite the fact that Milán and I were two heads taller than Estíbaliz, who barely took up space in the room, we listened to her. She had earned her stripes.

We ended up sitting in Milán's small living room. From the windows you could see the Plaza de la Burullería, El Portalón, and the Museum of Archaeology. This was the medieval heart of the city, and we could easily have been distracted by the view, but Estí and I had no time for distractions.

"I guess I have a lot of explaining to do," Milán murmured, her head bowed to the collar of her bathrobe.

"I assume you're going to tell us that you asked to join our unit when Ana Belén Liaño was found murdered."

"Yes. I already knew who Inspector Ayala was. There were all the Kraken stories in the press, and besides, the only name they gave my parents in connection with my sister's death was that of the boy who went into the water to rescue her dead body."

"She was alive," I said. It was an automatic response even now, twenty-four years after the fact.

"Are you sure?"

"No . . . ," I had to admit. "I was always told that she wasn't, but at the time I went into the water because I thought she was alive."

"Let's move along," Estíbaliz broke in. "You two can go over this later. Milán, I need to clear up a few things with you. I found a fake profile on Annabel Lee's Facebook account, somebody calling themselves Geneva. This person fits the profile of the woman we're looking for, the woman who befriended Ana Belén after she announced she was pregnant. Why didn't you tell me about her?"

"Because it wasn't the only fake profile I found. There were others: Brianda, Alana . . . And Inspector Ayala said to pay special attention to names, so I thought I should search for anyone with a Celtic name who had contacted Ana. I found two: Linett, which means 'nymph,' and Begoña Kortajarena. Both profiles are obviously fake, but they didn't lead anywhere. I don't like to bother my superiors until I have something substantial. Was I wrong?"

Estíbaliz waited a few seconds before replying. "No, I think I'm the one jumping to conclusions here. But, Milán, I still have to ask you: Where were you in the early hours of November seventeenth?"

"I was at home, asleep. Like most other people."

"And you have no way of proving that you're telling the truth."

"No. Like most other people," she repeated. Her logic was impeccable.

"Okay. How about December third, a Saturday night? Did you go out? Did anyone see you?"

Milán made a face, ill at ease. She leaned back into the sofa.

"I can't tell you," she replied, folding her arms over her chest.

"What do you mean you can't tell me? Did somebody see you or not?" Estíbaliz insisted.

"I said, I can't tell you."

"Milán, this is simple. You just have to tell me whether anyone can verify that you weren't out partying in Cuesta, where you could have bumped into José Javier Hueto and killed him at the Barbacana pool."

"And I'm saying that I can't tell you my whereabouts, or whether anyone can corroborate them," she insisted.

"She won't say anything because she doesn't want to embarrass me," said Peña, who emerged, stark naked, from the bathroom opposite where we were sitting.

After recovering from the shock, Estí stared at the pale blond, nearly white hair on Peña's anatomy with great delight, for a few seconds longer than strictly necessary.

"Explain yourself, Peña." I was forced to interject when nobody else spoke up.

"Because she was here with me most of Saturday night and all of Sunday. We can prove it, although the photos are a little raunchy. Will that be necessary?"

55

LA MALQUERIDA

FRIDAY, JANUARY 13, 2017

It was one of the worst days of the year, and it was only mid-January. The fact that it was Friday the thirteenth had nothing to do with it. Nothing whatsoever.

It was a cold, dark morning, one of those days when the bitter wind gets under your clothes and you can't put on enough layers to keep your body or your spirits warm. My white city was whiter than ever in the early-morning frost.

Alba sent a WhatsApp to my new phone saying she didn't want to sleep over at my place that night. She gave some excuse, I can't remember what. She didn't even respond to the rest of my texts.

She had seemed cold and distant at work over the past few days, too. There was zero chemistry between us: no winks, no meaningful glances.

Maybe the pregnancy was beginning to get to her, or she was worried about another attack of preeclampsia. I reassured myself with these likely explanations and persuaded her to have lunch with me at a bar called La Malquerida that was close to my place. I refused to take no for an answer. Desperate measures.

I bought a bag of roasted chestnuts for her and waited in a corner of the bar, warming my cold hands on the bag. I wondered nervously whether she was going to stand me up.

But then she appeared. Alba looked as beautiful as she was sad. In her perennial white down jacket, she resembled the lady of the lake in a medieval fable.

She greeted me distractedly, and my attempts at making small talk fizzled one by one, until we were left in a dense silence.

"Do you know why they call this place La Malquerida?" she asked coldly. "It's because of one of your illustrious ancestors, Pedro López de Ayala, the Comunero."

"There's a bit of him in you, too," I reminded her. "He was the count of Salvatierra."

"It seems like he was a real piece of work. He even sued his own mother, María Sarmiento, over some land. His second wife left him, despite having his children, and was forced to go to his rival, General Álava, for protection. And they say La Malquerida lived in this alley overlooking Puerta de San Miguel," she said. There was a hint of bitterness in her voice.

"You seem very hostile, and I . . . I have no idea what's going on," I said, extending my hand, warm from the chestnuts, to her. She withdrew.

"Let's go up to your apartment. I don't want anyone to hear what I have to say to you."

I nodded. "Okay, let's go. I wasn't sure if you wanted to come up."

We paid the bill and went up to my cozy nest on the third floor.

I closed the door behind me, but my home was missing its welcoming warmth that day. Alba was icy and there was no way to melt her.

I stood across from her in the living room, and she gazed wistfully out the big window, as though she were saying good-bye to the view of the plaza.

"What happened, Alba?" I asked. It was obvious that it was something very serious.

"Tasio Ortiz de Zárate, one of my dead husband's triplet brothers, called me . . ."

"I know who he is," I interrupted. I didn't need her to remind me of that tragedy.

"He sent me this." Alba thrust her phone at me.

The screen showed an old photograph. Two identical newborns snuggled close together.

"What's this?"

"Tasio and Ignacio."

"But why did Tasio send it to you?"

"You tell me, Unai."

Yes, I did need to tell her. I should have told her already—and I knew it.

"You called Tasio and you told him about us, you told him I was pregnant and that I'm expecting our daughter. You asked him to include this part of my private life in the screenplay he's writing for a TV series that thousands of people are going to watch, for God's sake!" she yelled.

"I did it to protect her," I spluttered.

"That is how you protect my daughter?" she demanded, raising her voice.

"If Tasio doesn't mention our affair, the whole world will assume Nancho is her father. She'll grow up with the stigma of being a serial killer's daughter."

Alba looked at me with despair and disbelief. I'd never seen her this furious.

"You should have discussed it with me first!" she yelled. "That's what couples do, Unai. But apparently you've forgotten what it's like to be with somebody else. Your actions have repercussions for my daughter and for me. Tasio didn't stop with your request."

"What do you mean?"

"When my daughter is born, he wants me to allow a DNA

test. He and his brother want to know if she's their niece. He says that since neither of them plan on having children, they want to bequeath the entire Ortiz de Zárate estate to her. Apparently, they have no direct heirs, and despite the fact that they are the bastard sons of Doctor Urbina, they have chosen to keep quiet about that and hold on to the family fortune."

"What . . . what did you say to him?"

"I explained to him that I don't want to do a paternity test, that I intend to bring up my daughter as though she is yours, and that that is the story she will hear. I don't want my daughter to doubt for a second who her father is. But Tasio insists he wants to be part of his niece's life. And if Tasio and Ignacio insist on playing the role of uncle . . . how in the hell am I going to stop them? You didn't think about that when you decided to call him without consulting me! It didn't occur to you that he could destroy our lives, did it?"

"I was just thinking that I'd rather have everyone think that she's my daughter, even if it means I become a target for crazy Rebeca."

"Crazy Rebeca! I can't even think about that now, about how stupid you can be sometimes, exposing yourself like this. You want to end up hanging from a rope with your head in a cauldron."

"Be careful, Alba," I warned her.

"You tell me to be careful when you're the one who needs to be careful. Since I agreed to let you work on the investigation, not only have you failed to give me a credible suspect, you've endangered all of us with your mistakes."

"Well, that's who I am, Alba! As you can see. When it comes to you . . . I'm reckless, I can't think straight . . . It's always been like that." I took a deep breath and tried to concentrate. It didn't work. "I apologize for the way I did it, but not for what I did," I said, plowing forward—why stop now? "I won't allow half the world to think she's a serial killer's daughter."

"Well, I've had enough! We're not a couple. We've never even managed to be that, much less a family. You insist on acting alone, and not just on this investigation. You don't know how to work as part of a team, in your professional life or in your private life. I won't let you make decisions that affect me and my daughter without consulting me. You and Tasio are treating her as if she were a picture card or a trophy. Are you really thinking about her, or is this about what you need?"

"Don't tar me with the same brush as Tasio!" I roared.

She picked up her white coat, draped it around her shoulders, and stood at arm's length, facing me.

"This is good-bye, Unai," she said, and I knew that she had made up her mind. "I'm tired of trying. You can see the girl. You can help bring her up. We'll do that together, but we'll live our own lives, like parents who have separated."

Great, I thought. *We were a couple for a minute, and now I'm going to be an estranged father.*

Alba disappeared, whiter than ever, and once again she was the stranger I'd seen during an early-morning run, a few yards below, on the esplanade outside San Miguel Church.

I grabbed my old cell phone, blinded by rage. Tasio's number wasn't in my new one, and I didn't want MatuSalem tracking the call anyway.

"Is there no way you're going to let me get a full night's sleep? . . . Do you know what time it is in LA, Kraken?" asked Tasio in a croaky voice, from six thousand miles away.

"I don't know and I don't care."

"Ah!" He paused for a few seconds and then the penny dropped. "Alba, I suppose."

Yes, indeed, my friend. Alba.

"I'll get straight to the point," I told him. "You have no right to barge into this child's life."

"I can obtain a paternity test through the courts if I need to."

"Would you go that far?"

"I want to be part of her life, Kraken. I want to give her what we refused to give her father, Nancho."

"Don't use my daughter to assuage your guilt."

"Prove to me that she is your daughter, and I won't have any claim to her."

"Alba told you she doesn't want to do the test. Believe me, I wish she would. But I want to be part of her life, and right now, I don't care who her biological father is."

"But I do. I care very much, because if we know, then there would be no need for these hypothetical conversations. I'm going to be straight with you, Unai. I want the girl to be an Ortiz de Zárate, and I want her to wear the name with pride."

"You aren't even one yourself, and I don't see what the problem is with Alba's and my surnames."

"Don't mess with me, Unai, I could make life difficult for you. I haven't finished the screenplay yet." Once again, he was the hardened prisoner I'd met in Zaballa.

"Don't threaten me," I warned. "I let your hacker intrude into my life and spy on me. I haven't reported you or tried to stop you. And now you're turning it against me? Doesn't the word *loyalty* mean anything to you? You could learn a thing or two from MatuSalem."

"Blood is thicker than water."

"I hardly need to remind you of the way you treated your own flesh and blood when he came to you begging for help."

"That's exactly my point," he replied.

This was turning into a tit for tat, which is what always happens when tempers are frayed. I tried to take a deep breath, but that never worked when I was this emotionally drained.

I had to try again. I had to reason with him, not for myself, but because I had inadvertently given him the ability to destroy the lives of Alba and her daughter.

"Tasio, you know how it felt to be a pariah in a city like Vitoria—"

"I did and I still do. Why the hell else would I be baking in California when it should be the middle of winter?"

"You want your niece to go through the same thing? Wouldn't it be better for her if people think she's the daughter of a hero?"

"Very clever, Kraken. Very clever. But you can't trick me. I'm going ahead with this. I want to be a part of her life, and you can't stop us."

"Damn you!" I yelled at him, finally losing my temper. "I wanted a family and you took it away from me!"

Hearing myself say the words out loud made me realize that the breakup with Alba was permanent and that, through my stupidity, I had destroyed any possibility that the three of us would one day be a family.

56

SANTILLANA DEL MAR

SATURDAY, JANUARY 14, 2017

I couldn't sleep, and when I can't sleep, I brood. I didn't want to agonize over losing Alba. It would be too painful, and I know my limits. So I traded one obsession for another—in this case, Rebeca Tovar.

Who are you, Rebeca?

Who are you . . . ? I returned to the source, where everything began: Santillana del Mar, home of the Tovar family.

I switched on my new, secure phone. I called her early on Saturday. I knew she was up with the birds, like me.

"Inspector Ayala, any news?" she asked with a mixture of trepidation and surprise.

"Don't worry, Milán. I know you were telling us the truth. And I need you to work a little of your magic for me."

"You name it, boss," she said, sounding relieved.

I told her what I needed: a list of all known addresses for a certain student at the University of Cantabria. It was a walk in the park for her.

I decided not to ruin Estíbaliz's day off. I wanted to get going, and maybe Alba was right, maybe I preferred to work on my own. I needed to be alone. It was better that way, because at least I didn't wreck the lives of the people I cared about the most.

I arrived in Santillana del Mar two and a half hours after I'd called Milán.

I found the boy with the different-colored eyes at the address she had given me: a tiny store set in the yard of an old house. Inside you could buy a glass of milk, a piece of pound cake, and nothing else.

I lay in wait, patient as a hunter, while he served a group of tourists.

When he raised his eyes and saw me, he gave a start and tried to bolt up the stairs at the back of the store.

"Don't even try it," I said, seizing his skinny arm in my fist.

"I don't want the neighbors to see me with you."

"Well, smart-ass, you should've thought of that before you ran a marathon the other day. Did you really think that would stop us from questioning you?"

"I guess not . . . What do you want?" he asked. He didn't seem as tense now that the store was empty, but he was still peering outside nervously.

"What you said about Bluebeard is robbing me of sleep."

"And me of a father."

"You need to explain that."

"I guess it serves him right," he muttered.

"What serves who right?"

"It serves my father right if somebody in this town sells him down the river and tells the truth for once."

"I'm all ears. What's the connection between your father and Saúl Tovar?"

"They both slept with the same woman."

"Saúl's wife?"

"His wife? Poor thing, how could anyone say that after the way she ended up? I'm not the first to call him Bluebeard, you know. When Asunción Pereda died, people weren't afraid to talk anymore, and word was that once she'd given him a daughter, he got rid of her. They said he had strange tastes, that he didn't like real women. He had tons of them here in Santillana, but nothing ever lasted.

"No, I'm referring to his bitch of a sister, Sarah Tovar. That stuck-up hypocrite destroyed my mom's life. Look, if you don't mind, I'd rather you come upstairs in case someone recognizes you. You are *the* Kraken from Vitoria, right?"

I grunted in reply. I was so tired of the whole Kraken thing.

Just then, an old lady emerged from the back of the store and came over to the boy. "Is everything all right, son? I thought I heard voices."

"Everything's fine, Grandma. This is a professor from the university, we were just excited to see each other. Actually he and I need to talk, can you watch the store for a while?"

A couple of Americans came in with tourist guides tucked under their arms, and the old woman picked up a tray of cakes, ready to serve them.

I took the opportunity to duck under the counter, and we climbed a wooden staircase into a back room. The furniture was dated and the smell of milk permeated everything. The aroma took me back to my early childhood, eating snacks while watching clowns on a black-and-white TV. My parents' benign, protective presence.

The boy invited me to sit down on a rickety aluminum chair and took a seat next to me. He was still nervous.

"So tell me what you know."

"My father was always in love with Sarah Tovar. He was older, but they must have known each other here in Santillana, and they both studied medicine. The two have worked at Valdecilla together since the nineties. But I can only tell you what I heard my mom say: the Tovar family was always odd. Sarah and Saúl's mother was bedridden for the last years of her life, and their father was very strict and very religious. As for the siblings . . . they were close, *too* close, if you get me."

"I'd rather you spell it out for me."

"Here in Santillana, it was rumored that Sarah and her little brother were a couple. Everybody caught them holding hands or kissing at one time or another."

"All towns have their local gossips," I said.

"You don't understand. I mean everybody, not just the town gossips. Neighbors, friends . . . These were more than idle rumors. My mother said the stories made my father furious. Eventually, I discovered that my father had only married my mother, who wasn't considered good enough for him, because Sarah Tovar had rejected him so often. My mother was consumed with jealousy when she discovered that they were working at the same hospital."

"Your father treated Saúl's daughter."

"And just after that my parents split up."

"Why was that?"

"Because Sarah, who already had a lot of influence at the hospital, and my father started having an affair. One night my father didn't come home, and Mom was so sick of it she packed his bags for him. She was pregnant with me at the time, and she had to struggle to bring me up on her own. He's been paying her alimony since I was born, but he was never around, not at my First Communion, not at Christmas . . . It was as if I didn't exist. So, as you can imagine, the Tovars aren't my favorite people, and having to see Saúl every day at the university pisses me off."

An estranged father.

The boy continued to talk, and I looked at him with a guilty conscience, wondering whether someday my daughter would be telling a stranger about her absent father.

57

LA FUENTE DE LOS PATOS

FRIDAY, JULY 24, 1992

U nai tried to push his way through the crowd that was dancing and jumping around in La Kutxi club. He was feeling
overwhelmed.

He had spent the week in Villaverde, helping his grandfather
with the harvest and trying to recover from the events in Cantabria.

His eleven-year-old brother, Germán, was shocked when he
saw Unai's bandaged arms. Grandfather made less of a fuss. He
just quietly said, "Tell me about it later. We don't want to upset
the young'un." After Germán had gone to bed, Grandad rubbed
some herbal liniment on Unai's wounds; it was greasy but helped
them to heal.

Within a few days, Unai was able to remove the bandages.
From that point, everything returned to normal much more quickly
than he had expected.

Jota's tentative call came first, then Lutxo and Asier checked
in. No one talked about the last day of camp. It was an unspoken
pact of silence. Friday was the eve of El Día de Santiago, also known
as El Día de la Blusa, and they were going to burn up Vitoria and
the Old Quarter and all the bad vibes and the memories and . . .

They wanted to burn it all.

All week, Unai had been skipping over one page in his little address book. On the first page, the one with the A's, Annabel Lee had written her number in Gothic script, and scribbled *call me* next to it. It was an instruction Unai didn't know whether to obey or ignore.

He was annoyed at her, particularly because of her indifference to Marian's death. Unai had the impression that nothing was ever going to be clear-cut with Annabel.

Then, at noon on Friday, while Unai was unloading wheat into the barn, his grandfather came to tell him there was a call for him, a girl.

The boy bounded up the stairs and pounced on the receiver.

"Yes," he panted.

"You haven't called me."

"No, I haven't called you."

"Tomorrow, Saturday. Look for me in El Rojo, at midnight." And she hung up.

That Friday evening, he was meeting the *cuadrilla* at eight. They had picked up where they'd left off before summer camp, as if nothing had ever happened. They seemed relieved that life was back to normal, although it could have been feigned indifference.

On Saturday, they spent the day wandering the streets in their smocks. They ate a tortilla sandwich at the Deportivo Álaves and had a few *pintxos* in Calle Dato.

When night fell, they headed for Cuesta de San Vicente and kept partying, moving between the bars La Kutxi and El Pinto.

The four had a hard time staying together. Unai met up with friends from Villaverde, Jota with colleagues from his choir, Asier with his basketball team . . . that night, all Vitoria had congregated in the Old Quarter.

At midnight, Unai was still in La Kutxi. He said good-bye

to Jota, telling him that he'd meet him in a couple of hours at El Okendo. Unai left the crowded bar intending to go back up the hill, in the opposite direction of the stream of *blusas* and *neskas* coming down.

On the way, he lost his beret. It was an Elosegui that his grandfather had lent him for the day because he no longer wore it. Unai stopped to look for it and finally found it on the ground next to the entrance to Casa del Cordón.

He pulled it on tightly and finally entered El Rojo, which was packed to the gills.

He was fifteen minutes late for his rendezvous with Annabel. He searched for her in the crowd at the bar. He tried to find her among the people dancing and chanting the chorus to "La negra flor" by Radio Futura—*"Al final de la Rambla . . ."*—on top of metal beer kegs. He looked for her next to the red-framed window at the front of the club, but there was no sign of his . . . girlfriend?

Frustrated, Unai resigned himself to giving up on their date. He thought about going back to El Okendo to meet up with his *cuadrilla*.

Tomorrow I'll call and apologize, and arrange to meet her for a real date, he thought.

But just then, he thought he glimpsed her long hair entering the bathroom, and he followed her.

It took him a while to push his way across the crowded bar, and by the time he reached the door to the bathrooms and went inside, he realized there were two people in there. And he knew them both.

Annabel, in her traditional *neska* costume, was perched on the edge of the sinks. Her skirt was hitched up and her white stockings were rolled down. A guy in a smock, his striped pants pulled down to his ankles, had his back to Unai and was thrusting away.

Unai recognized the hair poking out from beneath the beret. It was Lutxo.

This was the third time Unai had surprised Annabel with one

of his friends, and this time he didn't bother to mutter an apology the way he had before. He just looked straight at Ana Belén Liaño and pronounced his last words to her:

"You and I will never speak to each other again. That's a fact," he said.

Before he wheeled around, he saw Lutxo stop gyrating and turn around to doff his beret at him. Unai couldn't tell if Lutxo was surprised or not.

But with that, the boy resumed his labors.

Unai let it go; he let it all go. And after the fiesta, he fled to Villaverde and hid there.

He had his lifeguard job at the Bernedo pools as an excuse, and then he spent the first weekend in August helping his grandfather bale straw, and he taught Germán to drive the John Deere tractor by having the boy sit on his knees. His little brother was more clingy than usual after three weeks without his big brother—his hero. He had been afraid that Unai, like their parents, might never return.

Unai wanted to avoid going back to Vitoria for the rest of the summer, but Asier and Jota persuaded him to attend las Fiestas de la Virgen Blanca on August 9. He had one stipulation: Ana Belén would not decide what they did as a *cuadrilla*.

He even tore the *A* page out of his address book. Until he transferred all his contacts to his cell phone, the Antonios and Aguirres were all consigned to other letters.

But despite Unai's best effort, it still happened. August 9, after saying good-bye to the Celedón in the Plaza de la Virgen Blanca and before going back to their respective homes, while they were waiting for Lutxo at the Fuente de los Patos fountain at the end of Calle de la Herrería.

Lutxo arrived a little late, and he was agitated.

Unai didn't see him, or rather he didn't see the punch Lutxo threw, which landed on his right cheek.

"She's back with you!" Lutxo yelled. "She told me she's seeing somebody else, someone I know. It's you, isn't it?"

Stunned by the unexpected blow, Unai lost his balance and toppled over.

"You're out of your mind. Do you really think I'd get back together with her?" he managed to say.

"You didn't answer my question."

"Yes, I did."

Unai was on the ground, quivering with rage, but he didn't get up. Lutxo was overweight but muscular, and he was too drunk to be in control of himself. Unai let Lutxo level a few weak kicks to his stomach, which hurt more than he'd expected. Then, fists clenched, Unai rose slowly to his feet.

"Get out of here, Lutxo," he said. "You need to leave now."

At that, Lutxo burst into tears, much to the astonishment of his friends.

"You don't understand, she called herself Annabel Lee because of me! She and I were inseparable in preschool!" he cried.

"But you went to the one in San Mateo," replied Unai, puzzled. "She was at La Senda, with me."

Then a bemused Jota spoke up. "Annabel was at your preschool?"

"Yes . . . well, that's what I remember," Lutxo said with a hiccup, still a little out of it.

"I didn't want to hurt you guys," Jota started to say, "but the feelings Annabel and I had for each other were stronger than—"

"Don't make a fool of yourself," Unai broke in. "She told me the same story."

"Shit," interjected Lutxo, fists still clenched, "she gave me this whole spiel about how we were boyfriend and girlfriend in preschool, and that I was the first, the only one—"

"*Fucking shit*, she told me the same thing," Jota admitted, crestfallen, "about how we were at the Desamaparadas preschool together. She said she'd changed her name because of me, because of a drawing she gave me on our last day, the day the Fates and our parents separated us when they saw what we had—"

"Shit," Asier said simply, confirming a fourth version of the story.

This proved too much for Lutxo. He still needed somebody to blame.

So he punched Unai again, in the same place. This time Unai's cheek split and started to bleed.

"It was you, it's always been you!" he yelled at Unai. "You were her favorite, weren't you? She was just playing with the rest of us!"

"Asier, get him out of here," Unai implored, trembling from head to foot. "Right now."

Asier didn't need to be told twice. He dragged his friend back toward Calle de la Herrería.

"Come on, the last drink is on me," he said.

And maybe because it was such a rare offer, Lutxo let himself be persuaded, and they moved away from Unai and the danger he posed.

Jota stood there for a moment. He clearly also wanted a last beer. But this time his friend's pitiable state was stronger than his desire to forget.

So Jota walked over to him, draped Unai's enormous arm around his shoulder, and led him to the fountain.

"Why did you do that, Unai? Why didn't you hit him back?" asked Jota.

Unai plunged his head into the Fuente de los Patos to wash off the blood and slow down the bruising. One side of his face was already swelling.

Because I could have killed him, Unai thought, *and it wouldn't have been the first time somebody died because of me.*

POISON IVY

SUNDAY, JANUARY 15, 2017

It took me years to understand why Annabel Lee wanted to be caught having sex with each of us. She had once told me her nickname was Poison.

That's what she was for the four of us. The poison ivy we allowed to spread and to destroy our carefree trust in one another. She was the end of our innocence. Our time with her marked the last vestige of our childhood.

Annabel wasn't really a person. She was like one of the characters in her graphic novels: the maiden who is really the crone Death in disguise; the bearded old man who is, in fact, the Mentor; the messenger who acts as a Herald; the young recruit who obeys orders without question and so personifies the Soldier.

Twenty-four years later, after we had all licked our wounds, after we thought we were cured, she had come back to show us that we hadn't healed. Like an ancient spell, the mere mention of her name wreaked devastation in our lives once again, striking at the heart of our *cuadrilla*, which we thought had survived.

THE HOSPITAL CHAPEL

MONDAY, JANUARY 16, 2017

I spent the entire weekend in Cantabria. I had no desire to go back to frozen Vitoria, my frozen apartment, or my frozen love life. I was reaping the benefits of the sea air at the place I had rented on the Costa Quebrada in Somocuevas.

My bedroom opened onto the back lawn, and across the way stood the cliffs I had hated for so many years. I forced myself to look at them, to contemplate the pounding waves for hours at a time, until I grew accustomed to their ebb and flow. For the first time in decades, I didn't feel oppressed by my guilty conscience. I no longer had a knot in my stomach. I wasn't at the mercy of the sea anymore. I was a grown man, watching a glorious winter sunrise from my bed.

I walked along the cliffs. I went back to Portío beach, across from the sea stacks where Marian Martínez had met her death. I tried to forgive myself for not being able to save her during a terrible storm when I was seventeen. I finally made peace with the Cantabrian Sea.

And, after hearing Doctor Osorio's son's story, an alternative to the report Saúl Tovar had shown us was forming in my mind.

What if Rebeca . . . ?

Grandfather always said that every good question begins with a what-if. And after rigorously employing his sensible Socratic method, I didn't like where the answers were leading.

And that was because of what they implied. Because of their ramifications.

Still, my weekend in Cantabria wasn't spent in vain. I developed a somewhat underhanded strategy to ensure that I wouldn't return to Vitoria empty-handed.

Early on Monday morning, I walked into the Valdecilla hospital. I gave the receptionist my most dazzling smile and asked, in a jovial voice, if she would page Doctor Osorio and ask him to go to the chapel. "Please tell him it's urgent."

"Of course, I'll do it right now," she said, all smiles.

Then I headed for the Department of Endocrinology and approached the nursing station where a young man somewhat perfunctorily offered to help me.

"Could you please ask Doctor Tovar to go to the chapel? It's urgent."

I adopted the mournful expression of a grieving relative, the kind that nobody can refuse.

"I'll tell her right away."

"Thank you, I really appreciate it," I replied. I vanished down the hallway, head bowed shamelessly.

As soon as I was out of sight, I dashed through the emergency exit and ran down the stairs as if the building were on fire.

Minutes later, Sarah Tovar appeared at the entrance to the isolated chapel. She gave a start when she saw Doctor Osorio.

Neither of them said a word for a few seconds.

"It's been a long time," a hoarse male voice finally said.

"It's been a long time," the sharp female voice responded.

"You have nothing to say to me after all these years? I'll be retiring in a few days. You won't have to see me anymore and—"

"Apparently Rebeca isn't dead," Sarah interrupted him.

Another brief silence followed.

"What do you mean?" The man spoke first.

"The police have been to see my brother, Saúl, and they assure him my niece wasn't murdered after all. They have a witness who claims Rebeca ran away from home, and that the photographs were taken to fake her death and prevent us from looking for her. Do you know anything about that?"

"Do I know anything about that?" the psychiatrist yelled, agitated. "Do I have to remind you of the terrible accusations you made against me? How dare you involve me in your sordid affairs? I want nothing more to do with this. And if it turns out that Rebeca is alive, then you owe me an apology."

"I don't owe you anything. And lower your voice, we're in God's house."

"Damn your pride, woman! You used me, slept with me, jeopardized my career, and wrecked my marriage, all for your brother's sake. I've never forgiven myself for what I did to that wretched girl."

Sarah Tovar took her time replying.

"I'm so glad this is good-bye, Doctor Osorio. I hope you burn in hell for your sins," she said at last, her voice as dry as dust. And with that she left the chapel without another word.

The psychiatrist remained in the pew, staring into space.

I took the opportunity to come out of my hiding place in the confessional. "What did you do to her?" I asked. "What the hell did you do to Rebeca Tovar?"

60

THE REAL HOTEL

Monday, January 16, 2017

Doctor Osorio was astonished to see me coming toward him, brandishing my cell phone.

"Don't bother denying it. I recorded your entire conversation."

He leaped to his feet, smoothed his white coat, and confronted me with a dignified air.

"That's against the law. No court will admit evidence that was obtained without my consent."

"But it would . . . be enough to have you hauled up in front of a disciplinary committee at the hospital."

I faltered before continuing, but luckily it came across like a dramatic pause.

"Believe me . . . I will make sure they get this recording. And I haven't even told you how I plan to involve the press."

Doctor Osorio realized I was being serious. And I was. I was prepared to resort to desperate measures.

"Look, I'm retiring in a few days," he said at last. "You can't do this to me."

I sat down on the pew beside him. One of the Virgins gazed at us solemnly.

"It's very simple," I explained. "I won't do anything to you if you tell me exactly what happened twenty-four years ago."

"You shouldn't issue empty threats," he said, backtracking. "This is all bravado."

You asked for it, I thought.

I searched online for the hospital switchboard's number.

"Hospital de Valdecilla? I'd like to speak to the director. I'm calling from police headquarters in Vitoria," I said. The doctor looked at me aghast.

"Stop, please! Hang up!"

"I certainly will not," I told him, the cell phone pressed to my ear.

Vivaldi's "Four Seasons" came on while I waited patiently.

"For God's sake, hang up!" he implored, growing increasingly flustered. "I'll answer your questions, but please hang up the phone."

I did as he asked. Now he understood that I meant business.

He capitulated with a sigh.

"I suppose one day I'll have to atone for what I did to that little girl."

"You can start by telling me the truth, if you'd like."

"Fine, let's do it. It's time."

He spent a few minutes wringing his hands. I imagined he was trying to make sense of it all in his mind.

"The girl showed no signs of psychosis at all. Yes, she had an exaggerated love for her father, an Electra complex of sorts, but she was also immature for her age, so that kind of behavior was within the bounds of what was considered normal. It certainly wasn't enough of a justification to have her committed. Her unresolved grief over her mother's death was Sarah's invention. The girl was sad sometimes, but in my opinion, her attachment to her father more than compensated for her loss. But then the girl went to Sarah in a state of agitation. She told Sarah that Saúl was sexually abusing her. Sarah told Saúl, and they decided they couldn't risk a scandal.

They wanted to teach her a lesson, something that would ensure that she wouldn't tell anyone else about what her father was doing. That is why Sarah approached me. She knew I had been madly in love with her since we were teenagers."

I was still listening, but I was stuck on what he had said about Rebeca showing no signs of psychosis.

"So . . . Rebeca was telling the truth?"

"I believe she was. I heard her side of the story. She referred to inappropriate touching, nothing more. Her account was consistent, and in my professional opinion, she was telling the truth. Her account also seemed plausible given her father's narcissistic personality and his age preference."

"Age preference?"

"Pedophiles have a victim age preference. I suspect Saúl has a predilection for prepubescent or preadolescent girls. Or women who aren't sexually developed, who look a lot younger than their age. His wife is a case in point. It's likely that . . . his first sexual encounters were with a prepubescent girl. When he and Sarah were young, there were lots of rumors in Santillana about what went on in that family. I had always refused to believe the gossip, but when I heard it from Rebeca firsthand I realized it had been staring me in the face the entire time."

"What did you do then?" I asked. I felt sick to my stomach.

"When Sarah asked me to give Rebeca a false diagnosis, I pointed out the seriousness of what she was asking me to do, but I also took advantage of the situation. In exchange, I demanded that she sleep with me, even if it was only once. I'm not proud of what I did. I beg you not to condemn me; I'm my harshest judge. Anyway, she agreed, despite being deeply religious, as I'm sure you've noticed. Sarah prostituted herself to protect her brother—and then I knew the rumors in Santillana were true. They had been intimate from the beginning."

"What happened then?"

"We both kept our part of the bargain. I spent one night with her, and, fool that I was, I thought that would be the start of a relationship. Here I was, forty years old, behaving like a lovelorn teenager. I didn't go home that night. We checked into the Real Hotel because I wanted the night to be wonderful. It wasn't. It was a simple transaction for her, and afterward she never spoke to me again outside work. She and I have spent the last twenty-four years avoiding each other in the hospital hallways. I've scarcely set foot in the village, either. I feel unclean. I know I'm a bad husband, and I'm incapable of facing up to the gossip and the fact that I am the villain in the story of my life."

"Yet you have a son."

"A son who detests me."

"A son you haven't tried to have a relationship with," I blurted out. "Forgive me for meddling . . . but the kid is twenty-five years old now. And you're both punishing yourselves for something that took place on a night before he was even born."

"I don't know if I have the courage to go through with it . . . What happens now? Are you going to report me?"

"I'll have to write a report mentioning your testimony and speak with the Santander police department. Then it's up to the investigating judge to decide. My job is to present the evidence and the facts relevant to the investigation," I said. I had adopted a formal tone, the one I used when a case was too personal and I risked getting emotionally involved.

Doctor Osorio sat gazing at the statue of the Virgin, as if that diminutive figure might hold all the answers. "It's up to the judge to decide. If I have to pay for what I did, then so be it. Anything is better than this cloud that's been hanging over me for twenty-four years."

I could tell the man had made up his mind over the course

of our conversation, and that this was a huge relief for him. And yet all I could think about was Rebeca, who had repeated eighth grade, who had been drugged with antipsychotics she didn't need, and who had been forced to flee her own home after giving birth to a stillborn child . . .

"Yes, you will have to pay," I told him, my rage finally boiling over. "What you did to that girl is unforgivable, whether the abuse was real or not. It's quite possible that your actions drove Rebeca to madness, and that two people have lost their lives because of it. You should also carry those deaths on your conscience."

Then I left that accursed chapel, a place that had kept a secret that destroyed several lives for more than twenty years.

61

SOMOCUEVAS

Monday, January 16, 2017

I returned to the mansion in Somocuevas where I'd spent the previous two nights, lost in thought about Doctor Osorio's revelations. I sat on the grass at the cliff's edge like a mechanical doll, staring out at the rough sea and the spray pounding against the sea stacks.

So you were telling the truth, Rebeca. You wanted to warn us all, and we all let you down.

The fact that Rebeca wasn't psychotic, that she had been telling the truth about her father's abuse, made me consider a new theory, one that was even more disturbing. But I needed solid evidence to back it up. Simple accusations wouldn't cut it. Saúl could deny or refute them, and I was determined to use my stay in Cantabria to make a breakthrough.

I called Estíbaliz on my new cell phone and told her about the latest contribution to the investigation.

"Are you sure? Up until now you saw Saúl as a kind of holy father."

"Estí, just get in touch with Alba, please, and ask her if she'll do what I just told you. It's urgent. Call me back as soon as you have an answer."

Estíbaliz took a while to return my call, and I was just about to go inside the house and return to the warm nest of the bedroom when my phone rang.

"Judge Olano agreed to sign the warrant. He was reluctant, but given the lack of progress on the case, he gave in. Do you have a printer handy?"

"Yes, there's a computer in the reception area. E-mail me the document right now," I said.

I didn't want the whole sordid business to go on a day longer than necessary.

I called Paulaner and brought him up to speed. He said he would get in touch with the judge in Santander and pass on Doctor Osorio's confession. In the meantime, we got busy. In less than two hours, we were outside Saúl Tovar's villa with a search warrant in hand and the court clerk at our side.

Saúl looked a little rough when he opened the door. His gray-streaked beard needed to be trimmed, and he had dark circles under his eyes.

"What the hell is this, Unai?" he demanded sternly, after reading the warrant. "What exactly is it you're looking for?"

"You'd better stay outside, Saúl, and let me do my job."

He looked straight at me with dread and determination. We squared up to each other for a few seconds, but then he backed down, stepping aside to let me through.

Inspector Lanero remained in the doorway with him, making sure he didn't try anything stupid. I went upstairs to the main floor, where the bedrooms would normally be located, and pulled on the pair of latex gloves I always carried in my car.

I needed something of Gimena's.

I found her bedroom right next to Saúl's.

The decor was infantile, complete with teddy-bear motif. The bed was made, and the desk had been cleared, but several photographs smiled at me from the walls. One was of Gimena on her graduation day. She wore a gown and mortar, and Saúl was embracing her from behind. They looked happy.

I opened the closets. They were practically empty. Saúl had gotten rid of his daughter's clothes.

I searched frantically for something I could use.

Come on, this can't be the end. Gimena, you must have left some mark on this world. I begged the universe, just in case somebody up there was listening.

And they were.

I was on the verge of turning around and leaving when I noticed an item at the very back of the top shelf in the closet that had escaped Saúl's purge. It was Gimena's beret, wrapped in see-through plastic.

I picked it up with the reverence you would give to a votive offering and gently slipped the beret out of its plastic covering. I found two hairs trapped under the inside band, one with the follicle bulb intact. And that little hair gave me the hope I needed to pursue my new theory.

I labeled the bag to preserve the evidence chain and went downstairs. I brought the beret, now back inside its plastic bag, with me.

When Saúl saw me walk past, trophy in hand, he seemed to lose his balance for a second. He had to steady himself against one of the porch columns, although he quickly recovered his composure and feigned his habitual serenity.

"Leaving already?" he asked, or perhaps begged.

"This is for you, Saúl." I handed him a folded piece of paper. "Can I trust you to come in and have a DNA swab taken?"

Saúl read the document, his big hands shaking slightly.

You are hereby required to report to the University Hospital of Marques de Valdecilla, where three buccal swab

samples will be collected from you and subsequently
conveyed to the Santander Judicial Police.

I saw Saúl's Adam's apple bob up and down several times before
he nodded silently.

"Please leave," he murmured, and I thought I detected an air
of defeat.

We were all preoccupied as we left the villa.

"What do you think, Inspector Lanero?"

"He's a flight risk. We'll ask the judge's permission to watch
the house. I don't trust him."

"I agree. Get a surveillance team together. I'll take this sample
back to Vitoria to see what forensics has to say."

And now I just needed to convince Golden.

62

THE ZADORRA RIVER

Monday, January 16, 2017

I arrived in Vitoria in the afternoon. I had arranged to meet Doctor Guevara and hand over the hair sample, but I still needed more evidence, and Golden was the only one who could give it to me. The only problem was that I didn't even know if I could get in touch with her.

I went back to my apartment and made a cross on the glass balcony door using a couple strips of black electrical tape.

I had no other choice but to wait.

I waited . . .

And waited.

Every couple of hours, I checked my mailbox. Empty. I knew it was too soon. Several days might go by before her contact passed through the Plaza de la Virgen Blanca and told her about my call for help.

I couldn't sleep that night. I practiced my voice exercises and read paragraphs out loud. Anything to stop thinking about Alba or Rebeca.

The next morning, Estí called. I told her I was still waiting, and since she didn't need me at headquarters, I stayed home all day.

My warm nest helped ease the tension. I also realized that I needed some time alone to mull over the breakup with Alba and to assimilate the fact that we weren't going to be together.

The hours went by and Golden showed no signs of life.

It was the same story on Wednesday morning.

And in the afternoon.

Maybe she had fled the country after all. Maybe she had decided to bail on everything that had happened in Vitoria.

Maybe she was already forging a new identity and wanted to leave the past behind: hers, Rebeca's, mine.

That same day, I received a call from Paulaner. He confirmed that Saúl had been to the hospital on Tuesday to have a swab taken. They were still following him in case he tried to run.

Finally, on Thursday morning, there was an envelope, no return address.

I tore it open right there in the narrow entrance to the building. There was no risk of anyone else seeing the message. It was Golden, summoning me back to Atxa Park. This time she wanted me there at five o'clock that afternoon. No phones, no devices, no colleagues. I obeyed. We'd been through this before.

The giant courier on the tiny scooter arrived on the hour. We were both more relaxed this time, and he greeted me as if we were old friends. He put the package down at the base of the ruins, and this time he didn't wet himself.

"Sign here, please," he said, pointing.

I made a squiggle and pulled out the high-tech tablet Golden had sent me. Her chat box was still blinking on the screen.

I sat on the dry grass, gazing at the River Zadorra and the fields of wheat stretching before me. A lone crow flew by. It felt like an omen, and I hoped Golden wouldn't do something similar when I told her what I wanted.

I'm all ears.

Now she was waiting for me.

You won't like what I'm going to ask you to
do. But just let me update you before you
refuse.

I told her everything that had happened during my recent trip
to Cantabria.

So you want me to . . .

I ramped up the pressure.

Yes. You're the only person left who can do
this. There's no one else.

Have you located the baby's grave?

Her question puzzled me. *Was he buried?*

What grave are you talking about?

When they told Beca that her baby was
stillborn, they said he would receive a
Christian burial but that it was better if she
didn't know where the grave was.

I explained.

Saúl told me recently the baby was
cremated. No, Golden, I have a different
suspicion.

She took a few seconds before replying. At last she wrote:

I've been toying with the idea myself over
the past few months, but I didn't want to
believe it was possible.

And yet you had your suspicions, didn't you?
Tell me that at some point you suspected this
as well.

Only after I saw the news about the young
people's suicides. Then I decided to look into
it. Yes, I had my suspicions, but I didn't say
anything to you.

And yet we reached the same conclusion.
That's why I need you now.

Do you realize what you're asking me to do?

Yes, but this is for Rebeca. We need to know
what happened. This is the only way.

She was wary, and I understood why.

Can you promise me this isn't a setup?

No one is going to arrest you. Your
cybercrimes don't interest me. I want to catch
a killer, and you aren't a suspect.

What about assaulting a police officer?

If you help us, the judge will cut you a deal.
You know I won't file a complaint, even if the
prosecutor does.

And kidnapping a minor?

That's exactly why we have to go after Saúl.

I waited for her to reply. As my words hung in the air, I began to worry that my proposal might have scared her off, and that this would be my last communication with her.

I was relieved when letters finally began appearing on the screen again.

I don't want to reveal myself. I can't risk it.

I tried to calm her down before she let her fears get the better of her.

I only need a tiny part of you.

Again, Golden didn't reply immediately.

All right, but I want you to know I'm doing
this for BK.

I wasn't sure what she meant.

BK?

BK, Beka. When we got our new identities,
Rebeca kept her name coded: BK for Beca,

which was what we called her when she
was a kid. That's how she signed her e-mails.

Good, do it for BK. I'll explain the procedure.

I told her where to get a DNA testing kit. I knew that a defense
lawyer would reject the sample because there were significant
chain-of-evidence issues, but all I needed was to prove my theory.
If I was right, I could persuade Golden to provide another sample,
one we could use in court, once Saúl was in custody.

Just one other thing: Do you know what
subject Rebeca wanted to study?

She could have chosen a range of
subjects . . . maybe computer science. She
loved history, but was reluctant to work in the
same field as her father, and whenever she
looked like she might reconsider, I dissuaded
her. I wanted to minimize the risk of her
meeting him in a professional capacity. She
showed an interest in working with children
and sometimes talked about becoming a
teacher or a child psychologist. As you can
see, she was very capable, but she was a
typical teenager. She didn't know what to do
with her life. Does that help at all?

I don't know yet. Maybe. I'm going to need
that sample from you as soon as possible.

I'll do it right now, before I have time to
change my mind.

———

And so on Friday morning I was able to bring her sample to Doctor Guevara.

"Four or five hours," she told me. "I'll call you this afternoon, the second I have the results."

I went back home and watched the clock. In the evening I attended my session with my speech therapist, and then, just to punish myself a little while I was waiting, I put on my sneakers and went for a short run toward Olárizu.

63

THE LAW COURTS

FRIDAY, JANUARY 20, 2017

I was running back through Prado Park when my new cell phone rang in my sleeve pocket. It was Estí, and she was as hurried as ever.

"Meet me at the law courts. The test results are in."

I showed up at the triangular building in my running gear.

I entered Doctor Guevara's office to find Alba and Estíbaliz already there.

"Deputy Superintendent Salvatierra, Doctor Guevara, Inspector Gauna . . . ," I greeted all three, still breathless after my final sprint.

"You'd better sit down, Inspector Ayala," Alba said solemnly. The shadows under her eyes suggested she hadn't been sleeping well.

I felt like an ass for giving her such a complicated pregnancy.

"You were right," she went on. "We're all in shock after hearing the test results. You explain, Doctor Guevara."

"I submitted all three samples for a PCR test, and I can give you my interpretation of the lab results. As I explained when we performed DNA testing on Ana Belén Liaño's unborn child, for a paternity test to be positive, probability must exceed 99.73 percent. In this case, the results are conclusive: Gimena Tovar is Saúl's daughter, and she is also his granddaughter. On the maternal side, the sample taken from Lourdes Pereda shows a degree of kinship that suggests she is almost certainly Gimena's great-aunt."

"So your theory is correct, Unai," said Estíbaliz. "Rebeca gave birth to Gimena, who was the result of an incestuous relationship—"

"A rape," Alba cut in sharply. "At thirteen years old, Rebeca was not legally considered to have an independent sexual identity. Even if the act was consensual, it is still sexual assault. The fact that the perpetrator was also an authority figure, in this case her father, will add several more years to an already hefty sentence."

I was also in shock. It was one thing to speculate about what might have gone on in that family; it was quite another for the genes to present us with the awful, irrefutable truth.

"Saúl and his sister lied to Rebeca. They told her that her son was stillborn and that they buried him." I was thinking aloud. "Saúl told me Sarah Tovar had incinerated the child's body. But it was all a web of lies."

"In fact, they kept the child, a girl," added Estíbaliz. "Now we need to find out how they concealed her from Rebeca, and what they planned to do with her. Rebeca ran away days after she gave birth, but Saúl couldn't have known she was going to do that."

"I think Sarah Tovar was behind this," said Alba. "She was her brother's accomplice. Maybe she planned to bring up the girl herself; maybe it was easier for her to fake an adoption. In any case, we'll need to question them both, and we'll also need a statement from Rebeca Tovar's psychiatrist."

"Doctor Osorio has agreed to cooperate," I said. "Inspector Lanero already knows about his part in this."

"I'll update Judge Olano about this new development and have him sign the appropriate warrants. We need to call the Santander police to set up a joint operation for Saúl's arrest," Alba told us. She was still as solemn as she had been before.

"Great," replied Estí, who was as eager as I was to have some closure on the Saúl Tovar affair.

"Let me remind you that the murders of Ana Belén Liaño and José Javier Hueto remain unsolved. Based on her aunt's witness statement, we're acting on the assumption that Rebeca Tovar is alive and that her motive is revenge. If these suspicions are correct and she is the perpetrator, you're still no closer to discovering her current identity, not to mention the embarrassing blunder you made regarding one of our finest officers, Milán Martinez," Alba pointed out.

"If I may, I'd like to say something at this point," Doctor Guevara interjected.

"Be my guest."

"You remember how frustrated I was about the fact that during the inspection of Ana Belén Liaño, we were unable to retrieve any of the killer's DNA from the crime scene. In the weeks following Andoni Cuesta's death . . . Inspector Muguruza and I spent many long hours working on the few items we did manage to salvage. I don't like anybody's death to be in vain. And eventually we got lucky. We found several long black hairs on Ana Belén's hoodie. I assumed they were all hers, but since seven of them still had the follicle attached, I sent them all off to be tested anyway. And one of them has a different genetic profile. It belongs to somebody else."

"Excellent work, Doctor Guevara," Alba congratulated her. She sat back down.

I was worried; she was looking tired.

"So we might finally have some of the killer's DNA. But, correct me if I'm wrong, doesn't this just prove that somebody was with her at some point before she died? It doesn't necessarily place them at San Adrián," said my boss.

"Correct, but here's the good news: we also found hairs on José Javier Hueto's jacket, one of which was long and black. Although fifty-seven percent of people in this country have dark hair, only twenty-six percent have black hair, which narrows down the search considerably. And it isn't dyed."

"Rebeca had dark hair. Verging on blue-black, like her father and her aunt," I said. "Go on."

"I sent the two hairs to be tested, and they are from the same person. This means that, coincidentally, somebody with long, straight black hair was in close contact with both victims either before or when they died. That's all the judge will be able to establish. And we still don't have that person's identity. We can cross-check the national DNA database, but judging from what you've told me about the killer's profile, we're unlikely to find a match, because this person probably doesn't have a criminal record."

"I appreciate your perseverance. This discovery could still help us arrest the killer. If we find Rebeca Tovar under some other identity, a simple DNA sample would tell us if she was with both victims," Alba said, nodding.

And with that she ended the meeting. The three of us left the Law Courts with a glimmer of hope, despite the fact that the outlook for the weekend's weather was bleak.

"By the way, Unai, say thank you to your grandfather for me, would you? He stopped by my mother's place in Laguardia and gave her several jars of honey and packets of sugared almonds for me," said Alba, holding up a plastic bag she had just pulled out of her coat pocket. "The way he fusses is touching."

"I'll tell him," I managed to say, overwhelmed by tenderness and guilt.

And just at that moment, I received a very badly timed call from my brother. Alba used the opportunity to walk away. She waved her hand and left, and Estíbaliz and I were left standing alone on the avenue.

"Unai, how are you?" Germán asked tentatively.

"Busy, to be honest. What's up?"

"I need to talk to you, preferably somewhere quiet. Are you going to Villaverde this weekend?"

"Yes, let's meet there tomorrow. Can it wait until then?"

"I guess so. We'll talk tomorrow, then?" he said, although he didn't sound reassured.

"Tomorrow I'm all yours, Germán," I promised.

In less than two and a half hours, we pulled up at Saúl's villa. Alba had been in touch with the local police, and by the time Estí, Milán, Peña, and I showed up, Paulaner's squad from the Santander police force had already surrounded the property.

The coastline was poorly lit by a few distant streetlights, and the wind that greeted us seemed more blustery than usual.

I knew something had gone very, very wrong when I saw Paulaner's morose expression as he walked toward us.

"What happened?" Estíbaliz yelled at him, her hand going for her gun automatically.

"You won't be needing that. Saúl Tovar is no longer a threat to anyone."

"No!" I cried, and ran into his house, leaping over the police tape that was already in place.

I found his body on the living-room floor.

Saúl was naked from the waist up, and he had on the same pair of tattered jeans he wore on the Monday we searched his house. His face held no trace of the handsome man with green eyes.

One of the replica Cantabrian daggers had pierced his heart.

64

THE HOVEL IN SANTILLANA

Saturday, May 25, 1968

Her mother called Sarah again. She had woken up in a good mood. It was the girl's birthday, and at eleven she already felt grown-up, but not grown-up enough.

"What do you want, Mother?"

From her bed, her mother ordered Sarah to come into the bedroom.

"Empty out my chamber pot and bring my breakfast. Isn't it a lovely day today?" her mother said, smiling as she looked out the window.

The views from the Tovars' house weren't very pretty. The window her mother was gazing out of overlooked a narrow street, and if you leaned out, all you could see was an old garden wall.

"Ah, and then your father wants you both down in the cellar for something."

The girl swallowed hard and hurried to fetch her mother a tray with a glass of milk and some biscuits on it.

"It's such a lovely day, Mother, wouldn't you like to get out of bed?"

"We've already been through this, child. I made a vow to Saint Juliana, and I have no intention of breaking it, not like some others."

"But it's my birthday. We could go outside and get some sun."

We have to go out. We can't stay in the house, because I know what Father's going to do, Sarah pleaded silently.

"No, child, I said no!"

"At least let Saúl go outside and play with his friends. They're waiting for him in the square."

"I don't know where you get this disobedient streak from. Go on, take your brother downstairs. I'm going to take a little nap."

"Yes, Mother."

So, clasping her brother's hand in hers, Sarah went down to the cellar where their father was waiting for them. The amateur pornographer picked up his video camera, just as his father had picked up the Kodak 16mm imported from France back in the thirties.

He gave the children instructions.

Sarah stared straight at her little brother. "Look into my eyes. Keep looking. I'll protect you, Saúl."

"No, I'll protect you," said the little boy.

"No, I will."

"No, I will."

"No, I will."

This was how the children distanced themselves from what was happening. They did it so that it would all pass quickly, so that their father's instructions would only exist in some dark corner of that dank cellar.

65

AN ALTAR IN THE SKY

FRIDAY, JANUARY 20, 2017

Peña and Milán followed me inside. I thought it might have been Milán's first corpse because she immediately ran out of the villa, with Peña close behind. I pictured her in the garden, gulping in the sea air to keep herself from vomiting.

A few minutes later, Peña came back inside, looking serious.

"Is Milán okay?"

"Not really. Could you go talk to her, please?" he whispered.

I found her in one of the big armchairs where Estíbaliz and I had sat during our interview with Saúl. She didn't appear to be crying, but her head was buried between her knees and her tousled hair hid her face.

"How are things, Milán?"

"Now I'm never going to know, am I? There's no way I'll ever know," she said in her raspy voice.

I sat down beside her. I was as shocked as she was by Saúl Tovar's death.

"I've been dreaming about coming here to confront him for twenty-four years," she said. "I thought that if I looked him in the eye, I'd know whether he pushed my sister over that cliff. But I never found the courage. I was shaking like a leaf when we came here to arrest him, scared to death. And now I'll never know."

"You might never have known anyway. Saúl is, he was," I corrected myself, inwardly cursing the Grim Reaper, "very persuasive. He . . . he looked straight at me and told me his daughter suffered from psychosis. I'm a profiler . . . and yet I believed him. I gave him a hug. I took pity on him. He would have taken you in. He took us all in."

"You're not very good at consoling people."

"Alas, no," I had to admit. "I need to go in, Milán."

"I understand. I'm okay, really. I'll be okay."

So I went back inside Bluebeard's cave.

Inspector Lanero had called the investigating judge, who had called the pathologist. He hazarded an informed guess: suicide, which he would confirm after the autopsy.

"This is a very unusual and difficult way of doing it. You need to know exactly what you're doing to make the blade penetrate your heart. It is common for people to remove clothing from the area they plan to self-harm, though," commented the doctor after studying the body.

Judging from the state in which we found the body, Saúl had taken his own life on Tuesday, shortly after his return after taking the DNA test at Valdecilla hospital.

He knew we would find a match and discover that Gimena was his daughter as well as his granddaughter. He couldn't face being arrested. Or maybe he cared more about the scandal than the prospect of arrest. At least he had left us in no doubt.

And, curiously, he came out of it relatively unscathed.

A brief news item appeared in the online version of a local newspaper the next day:

> The academic community has responded with shock to
> the news that a 55-year-old professor at the University
> of Cantabria, S. T., was found dead at his home yester-

day. The rector and dean of the Humanities Department
plan to hold a ceremony this coming Monday to honor
his tireless efforts at disseminating the local Celtic-
Iberian culture.

Saúl would have been extremely grateful to the editors at *El
Periódico Cántabro* for refraining from linking his name to any ongoing investigation and confining themselves to a short report on
his death.

In the meantime, I couldn't stop thinking about the long black
hair that forensics had discovered on the victims' jackets. Could
Saúl's sister, Sarah, be behind those deaths? Maybe I should ask
Doctor Guevara to compare the two hairs with Sarah Tovar's DNA,
but wasn't there a risk that she might also take her own life, or run,
if we turned up at her house demanding a sample? There was an
easier option, of course, which was to compare it to Saúl's DNA. If
the hairs did belong to Sarah Tovar, there would be a genetic match.

But that theory didn't convince me.

Our team returned to Vitoria silent and circumspect. Maybe I
was the most affected because I knew him. Or Milán, who was still
punishing herself for not acting sooner.

The next day I drove to Villaverde for lunch, while we waited for
the autopsy results. I needed a break from the investigation. I found
Grandfather uprooting weeds that had grown around the hazelnut
trees. My brother was nowhere to be seen.

"Isn't Germán here yet?" I asked, as I helped him with the
weeding.

"No, and I don't know what's keeping him. He told me he was
coming first thing this morning."

"He probably had some work to do at the office."

"Probably," he said. We continued with the task at hand.

But when Germán still hadn't shown up at around three thirty, I gave him a call. It wasn't like him not to let us know he would be late. He wasn't answering his cell phone, and I got his office voice mail, which invited me to make an appointment.

We ate the meal of beans with chorizo and chili that Grandfather had cooked in the little downstairs kitchen in silence.

Then Grandfather went to go take a nap and I spent the afternoon gazing into the fire and daydreaming. Relaxing. Recuperating.

We started to get seriously worried about my brother's unexplained absence when it got dark.

"Grandad, did Germán say anything else to you, other than that he was coming here this morning?" I wondered. I had just brought in some logs to keep the house warm overnight.

"Yes, son, he told me something and said he wanted to talk to you about it today."

Germán and I were both in the habit of telling Grandfather about confidential work issues. We knew our secrets were as safe with him as they would be with a statue, and since he was almost one hundred, there was the additional advantage of getting his insight into our problems.

"Is it something you should tell me about?"

"I don't know. He was a little worried, you see, about something that he discovered about his girlfriend."

"By his girlfriend you mean Beatriz, my speech therapist?"

"Yes, something to do with her building—you remember, the one I told you about in Calle San Antonio where they removed the dome in order to put up a machine-gun post during the Civil War?"

"Yes, Grandad. The Pando-Argüelles building."

"Well, Germán told me there aren't any offices available to rent in that building. He said a property developer bought it but never finished the refurbishments. And when a client came to consult him about something to do with the auction for the space, he couldn't understand how his girlfriend could be working there, so he did some digging and found no record of a Beatriz . . . Korres, is it?"

"Yes, Korres."

"He says the property developer isn't legally allowed to rent the place, so she can't have a space there. I don't know, I think he wanted to see what you thought before he asked her about it."

"They must have rented it out illegally."

"Yes, that's probably it. But it isn't like the young'un not to show up. Should we give him another call?"

"Yes, let's do that."

I also called my *cuadrilla*. At eleven o'clock that night nobody had seen him in Vitoria, either. They all assumed he was with Beatriz. I called her cell phone. It was switched off.

Grandfather and I sat in front of the open kitchen fire waiting, but when the clock struck midnight, I persuaded him to go to bed. I assured him that I'd drive to Germán's apartment in Vitoria the next morning and see where he was.

"He's a grown man, Grandad. He's probably at the movies with Beatriz, or maybe they just wanted some time alone. We can't get upset, just because for once in his life, he's forgotten to act responsibly and let us know his plans."

"You're right," Grandfather replied, but he didn't sound reassured. "Well, when you talk to him tomorrow, tell him I bumped into one of your pals from the *cuadrilla* this morning: Asier's wife. She was wandering around the village. She said she wanted to talk to one of you, but I don't know which one."

"Asier's wife, Araceli?"

"That's her. I didn't really understand what she wanted. She was agitated, that's for sure. 'I'm looking for your grandson,' she said, or something like that, and then she hurried off. Tomorrow you can tell Germán about it."

Why on earth did Araceli come to Villaverde looking for Germán? I thought. *Or did she want to speak to me?*

I went to bed feeling wide-awake. I was worried and annoyed with my brother for not showing up and not calling to let us know.

Araceli's visit also made me suspicious. She and I weren't particularly close, but even I could tell she had been acting strangely lately: on edge, nervous, stressed.

As I whiled away the dark hours in my bedroom, I kept returning to the question of names. The three bogus account holders who had contacted Annabel: Geneva, Linett, Begoña Kortajarena. Perhaps one of them held the key. A name that held a special meaning for Rebeca, possibly linked to the Celtic Threefold Death ritual. Hanging, rope, altars, water . . . Vaguely curious, I reached for my phone, which was still on in case Germán called, and searched for the meaning of the name *Rebeca*.

What I found was, at the very least, intriguing. *Rebeca* was a biblical name, Hebrew in fact. One possible translation was "rope" or "noose." In Greek it referred to fertility. In Aramaic, Rebeca was an earth goddess. The wife of Isaac, son of Abraham, who married his own sister, Sarah. It was interesting to find such a clear allusion to incest in a family like the Tovars.

I looked up other names, like *Saúl*. Also biblical, also Hebrew. It meant "the desired one," appropriate for a man who was seduction personified. My search for ancient names brought me to *Araceli*. *Ara* was Latin for "altar" and referred to the stone where offerings were left; *caeli*, from the Latin *caelum*, signified "sky." For the Romans, the Ara Caeli was a stone that permitted them to communicate with the supernatural world.

I remembered the altar of las Matres at the Barbacana pool, and that of the Araia nymphs near San Adrián.

And then early in the morning, just as the dawn light was beginning to seep through the gaps in the shutters, there was a moment when I saw clearly what I hadn't wanted to see before.

A clone of Annabel Lee, who had married Asier and was close to my *cuadrilla*, a computer expert who could easily hack into my cell phone, somebody who had plenty of reasons to want to murder Annabel when she found out she was pregnant, if she believed Asier to be the father. And her long black hair matched the description of the one found on Jota's and Ana Belén's jackets. I was convinced she had been with both victims shortly before they died, and I knew a DNA test would prove it.

I remembered something MatuSalem had said in the crypt at the New Cathedral, when he told me how Cisco Systems got its name: "Sometimes we don't see the whole word, but part of it is enough to create a meaning of its own."

How many times had I called her Ara without making the connection to the altars of las Matres?

Could our elusive Rebeca be hiding behind Araceli's identity?

66

THE ESCORIAZA-ESQUIVEL PALACE

SUNDAY, JANUARY 22, 2017

I waited until what I considered a reasonable time, around nine in the morning, and then sent a WhatsApp to Araceli. She was clearly awake, because she replied instantly.

> **Can we have breakfast together, Ara?**

> **Alone or with Asier?**

> **Alone.**

> **I've already eaten, but let's meet by the medieval wall, the same place we met on the Night of Candles.**

It seemed like a good place for me to speak to her in private without making myself vulnerable. It wasn't too secluded, but there wouldn't be too many people around that early on a Sunday morning.

We arranged to meet in an hour, so I said good-bye to my grandfather's worried face—he was constantly calling Germán's cell phone, which was still going to voice mail—and set out for Vitoria.

Araceli was waiting for me in the courtyard of the Escoriaza-Esquivel Palace, in the top section of the medieval quarter. She looked more like Annabel Lee than ever. It was freezing and rain was threatening, but we installed ourselves on a bench by the wall.

I decided to come straight to the point. "Ara, do you know where Germán is?"

She looked at me, furrowing her brow. "Hasn't he been in touch yet?"

I shook my head, frustrated. "I haven't heard anything since yesterday, either."

"I know you went to Villaverde yesterday morning. Were you looking for me?"

She was a little taken aback by my bluntness, and I prayed to whatever god there was that she wouldn't lie to me.

"No, actually, I wanted to speak to your brother."

"About what?"

"It's a professional matter. Well, a personal one, too."

I backpedaled, and then I got it.

"Oh, God! I get it. You're going to separate, and you wanted to consult him, am I right?"

She looked at me rather sheepishly.

"How . . . how did you know?"

"I'm the brother of a lawyer. You wouldn't believe how many people we know who go to him for that kind of advice."

"Well, am I that obvious?"

I refrained from mentioning everything Asier had told me about their marriage; this wasn't the right time.

"Why did you call me, Unai?"

"I need you to be honest with me about the woman who died at San Adrián."

Araceli ran her fingers through a lock of long black hair.

"I told you, I never met her."

"And yet we found a long black hair on the jacket she was wearing when she died. If I told you I was going to request a warrant to take a DNA sample from you to compare the two, would you still stick to your story?"

She swallowed hard, visibly upset.

"And you'd do that to me?"

"Yes. Because I want to find out who killed Jota."

She gritted her teeth and stared at the ground. She seemed shrouded in helpless silence.

"Jota told me about it," she said finally.

"About what?"

"About Ana Belén and Asier's affair. Jota was devastated. He was in a terrible state. I was worried about him. He didn't deserve that—"

"So you did meet her?" I interrupted.

"Yes, in mid-November, maybe a day or two before she died, I honestly don't remember. I used Asier's phone to send her a text. I wanted to be sure she'd show up."

"And what happened? Did you two fight?"

"Are you joking? She was impossible to pick a fight with. She didn't give a damn about anything, including Asier and Jota . . . actually, it was incredibly frustrating."

I nearly smiled, although I didn't find it funny.

"Yes, that sounds like her. So you lied to me, Ara, and not just about that. Were you with Jota the night he died?"

"We all went out drinking together. Did you find my hair on his jacket, too?"

"You tell me."

I saw a look of pain on her face that I hadn't seen before.

"It's not what you think."

"You don't know what I think, but I'm going to tell you. I believe you could have killed them both in the early morning while

Asier was fast asleep." I paused for breath before continuing. "I believe you could have killed Jota, dumped him at the Barbacana pool, and then gone back to bed with your husband."

I looked her in the eye as the anger spilled out of me, and then she stood up, her cheeks burning, and I followed suit; I didn't want her to escape. What I hadn't anticipated were her next words for me:

"We were together! Jota and I were very much in love. He was the best one out of all of you. He was a good person . . ."

"You and Jota?"

I found it hard to imagine them together. The depressive train wreck that was Jota and the cool, calm, and collected Araceli. What kind of chemistry or need could bring two such different people together? And even more confusing: Did Araceli know Annabel was expecting Jota's child?

"Jota was a good person, Unai!" She was almost yelling now, beside herself.

"I know he was. We'd been best friends since we were six. Come and sit down," I pleaded.

She obeyed. It was as if her confession had drained the strength out of her.

"What happened between you two?" she asked, a little calmer.

"Annabel. Annabel happened to us."

Araceli nodded. Maybe those five words were all I needed to convey a story I had thought was a lot more complicated, I don't know. I wasn't in the mood to bare my soul right there and then.

At that moment, I heard the "Lau teilatu" ringtone on my old cell phone. It was my speech therapist, Beatriz Korres.

Feeling relieved, I motioned for Araceli to stay seated, while I moved a few feet away to take the call.

"Beatriz, thank goodness. Do you know where Germán is?"

Her voice was different: angry, jittery.

"Of course I know where he is, I've got him," she said.

"What do you mean, you've got him. Is something wrong? You sound . . . upset."

I didn't understand. I didn't understand a thing.

"Upset? You noticed? You, who never sees anything?"

The compassionate, cautious Beatriz Korres who had been training me to talk again for months was gone. This person's words oozed bitterness.

"I don't know what you're talking about, Beatriz . . ."

"Of course not, how could you? All this time, it's been right in front of you, and you couldn't prevent a single death. My father's dead and it's your fault!"

"Your father? What are you talking about?"

"Yes, my father, Saúl Tovar. It's your fault he's dead, Kraken!"

And then a stranger I thought I knew was sobbing at the other end of the phone. She was furious, hysterical, heartbroken.

It dawned on me.

The names: I was wrong.

The initials. *BK.*

Beatriz Korres was Beca, and so was Begoña Kortajarena when she contacted Annabel Lee.

It was like a spark lit up my brain. A flash of lucidity, long overdue.

Too late for my brother.

67

OKON

SUNDAY, JANUARY 22, 2017

Imagining my brother hanging from a tree with his head in a cauldron after having been stunned with a Taser was too much, but I was equally shocked to discover that Rebeca was disguised as the person to whom I had entrusted my new life. I owed her for so much—for the hours and hours of patient repetition, the encouraging pats on the back, the Chupa Chups lollipops for each new word I tacked on to the end of a sentence.

"Rebeca, is that you?" I asked incredulously.

"He wasn't supposed to die!" she screamed in my ear, frenzied. "I always loved him. I missed him. You're to blame for his death!"

"Saúl isn't dead because of me. He's dead because he was afraid everybody would know what he did to you."

"That was my fault, I started the whole thing. I wanted him to want me. I wanted what happened to happen."

"No, Rebeca. You were thirteen years old . . . he manipulated you into believing that. He seduced you. Many victims of sexual abuse suffer from feelings of guilt. You did not seduce your father, and you're not responsible for his actions."

"Yes, I am. I started the game," she said, her voice quaking.

That was her truth.

And she sobbed. I don't know whether it was over the loss of her father, or if it was the emotional release of finally talking about what had happened with somebody who had been there.

Twenty-five years earlier we had begun a conversation. I never imagined we would finish it like this.

"Rebeca, this is about guilt. Your guilt turned morbid and irrational, and now you've killed several people."

"People who didn't deserve to have children."

"I don't deserve to be a father, either. You want to . . . You want to . . ." My brain seized up. The pressure was too intense.

"Take a deep breath, Unai, the way I taught you," she repeated.

And for a split second, I was talking to my speech therapist.

I did as she said, inhaled, held my breath, exhaled for a count of three.

"You want to punish me for not seeing what was happening at the settlement . . . do it! I didn't listen to you, I didn't help you. I practically let your father rape you right in front of my eyes, and yet I saw nothing. Tell me I don't deserve to die."

"No, you don't deserve to be a father. You wouldn't know how to protect your daughter. And Alba didn't deserve to be a mother, either."

When she mentioned Alba, my mind was made up.

"Don't drag her into it," I snapped. "This is about what happened at the settlement. It's between you and me. Let's set up a trade, me in exchange for Germán."

"Don't play games with me, Unai. If you think you can trick me by—"

"No, no tricks. Tell me where to meet you . . . I won't hang up until I get there, and I won't tell a soul. Sacrifice me, then it'll all be over. Isn't that what I deserve for not preventing your father from doing what he did?"

Rebeca thought about it for a few long seconds.

"All right. At the chapel at Okon. There's a small pond with a carving of a *lauburu* and a cluster of oak leaves—"

"I know it," I interrupted. *Germán probably took you to see it,* I thought angrily.

"If you call your colleague, I'll kill your brother."

"You know I'm not going to do that. Don't you dare touch a hair on Germán's head, damn it," I said. At this point I was walking around in circles by the wall.

Just then Araceli approached, alarmed by my pacing, yelling, and gesticulations.

"Unai, is some—"

Terrified, I pressed my hand to her mouth.

If Rebeca discovered that someone could hear us, it would spell the end for Germán. *And Germán can't, he mustn't, he—*

I thrust the thought aside.

Araceli fell silent when she saw the panic on my face. I needed to keep Rebeca engaged, I couldn't let her realize what was going on.

"You've changed a lot . . . I would never have recognized you."

"I did everything I could to be the opposite of the type of woman my father found attractive. I thought if I did that I'd be—"

"Safe. In case your paths ever crossed again . . . or if he somehow found out you were alive and tried to draw you in again."

There was no response on the other end of the line, but I could hear her shallow breaths, and I thought she was crying. I forced myself to keep the dialogue open.

"You've never stopped loving your father, he always . . . attracted and terrified you. You transformed yourself into this voluptuous woman to protect yourself from him, and from yourself as well, because you doubted your ability to resist his charms."

Rebeca said nothing, which was tantamount to yes.

I took the opportunity to pull out my notebook and write a note to Araceli. *Don't tell anyone anything. I need you to go to my place and do something for me. Now hurry!*

She read my instructions, and I tossed her my keys. My grandfather's carved wooden mountain range flew through the air in a graceful arc.

Don't get hurt this time, she wrote, before running out of the square.

No promises would have been my reply.

But by then I too was running down Cantón de las Carnicerías at full speed. I needed to get to my car, so that I could get to Germán.

Just over an hour later, I arrived at the Church of Our Lady of Okon. On the way there, Rebeca and I had been in frequent communication. I asked her permission to refuel at the gas station at Ventas de Armentia. She didn't want me to take any longer than necessary, but in the end she agreed.

The chapel stood in the middle of my beloved hills, only a hundred yards or so from the town of Bernedo. I drove slowly along the track that led to it. Two other cars were parked in front of the building.

I stopped next to the clock tower and, cell phone in hand, made my way toward the pond. It was hidden beyond a grove of trees where tables and benches had been installed for picnickers. Not many people knew about the fountain and the old washing place, a tiny basin dug out of the rock in a remote part of the copse.

My heart practically stopped when I saw my brother's diminutive figure dangling above the water. His stylish blue suit looked incongruous amid the brown and gold leaves. His feet were bound, and he was hanging upside down from the bough of an old oak. His arms hung limp, and his dark hair brushed the surface of the basin.

"Stay where you are, Unai!" Rebeca shouted, pointing a Taser at me. "Take that coat off!"

I realized that she was planning to use the Taser on me after making sure I wasn't wearing a bulletproof vest or carrying a weapon.

"I'm not armed!" I cried. "What did you expect?"

She's going to tase me, I thought. *She's going to sacrifice me right here in this basin.*

Under any other circumstances, my survival instinct would have been running through a host of plans to thwart her, yet the sight of Germán, so defenseless . . .

I let my coat fall to my feet. I raised my arms. I surrendered.

"Now walk toward me!" she shouted.

Rebeca wanted me close enough to stun, and the Taser wires were only twenty feet long.

"Hurry up, I don't have all day. I have to make sure las Matres are happy with your daughter," I thought I heard her say.

"What was that?" I asked in disbelief, even as I walked toward her, hands behind my head.

But Rebeca had no intention of responding, nor did she plan to exchange me for Germán. I suddenly realized that she couldn't let him live, of course she couldn't. He knew who she was, her fake identity. This was a trap, and Rebeca was going to kill both of us.

That's why, when I saw a white hood appear behind her and MatuSalem and his blue hair aim a yellow Taser at her back and fire, I did nothing to stop him.

The pulse cycled for five seconds. Rebeca fell onto the muddy leaf-strewn ground, her muscles twitching uncontrollably.

Matu wasn't alone. Golden Girl was with him. The old hacker cried out and limped to her beloved niece.

"Beca, my darling girl! It's me, your aunt. Rebeca!"

I hurried over to untie my brother's feet. His face was purple. I had to wade waist-deep into the freezing basin to get his body down on my own.

"It's over, Germán. It's all over," I whispered, but he was barely conscious. Rebeca must have tased him before she hung him from the tree.

I carried Germán out of the pond, holding him in my arms on the ground, like the Pietà, the sculpture of the Virgin Mary weeping over her dead son. Overwhelmed with joy that my brother was still alive, I broke down and began to tremble like a leaf.

"Very clever of you, Kraken, to put a white *and* a black cross in your window," said MatuSalem, coming up behind me. "Golden was watching me, I was watching her, and we were both watching you . . . We figured you might need the Taser she got on the deep web."

In fact, my intention had been for Golden, or rather Rebeca's aunt Lourdes Pereda, to come to Okon. I wanted her and Rebeca to meet face-to-face, to force Rebeca to relive the positive part of her past. But I knew she might not get the message quickly enough, so I asked Araceli to put another white cross there for MatuSalem.

Genius that he was, he would immediately understand the ploy, and I knew he would act.

Which he did.

They saved my life.

I knew what Estí would have said if I'd called her: "Wait, we'll set up an operation. Don't go alone." After this one-man disaster, I'd have a lot of explaining to do back at police headquarters . . . and yet.

"You two need to get out of here. Use some branches to erase your footprints in the mud. You weren't here. I tased her; my brother won't say anything. Rebeca didn't see you."

I took the Taser from Matu's gloved hands—the kid had thought of everything. I made sure my fingerprints were all over it and positioned myself where he was when he fired it. My boots sank into the mud.

But Golden was still holding Rebeca, who lay sprawled on the ground. I was getting worried. She should have started to regain consciousness. I was ready to restrain and arrest her.

"What's the matter, Golden?"

"She's not coming around, Kraken. She's not coming around," she murmured, cradling Rebeca like a little girl.

I hurried over to them. So did Germán, moving as best he could. And I couldn't help noticing his concerned expression.

I found a pulse on her neck, but Rebeca remained unconscious.

"We need to call an ambulance. Rebeca has slipped into a coma."

68

PUENTE VIESGO

SATURDAY, MAY 15, 1993

S arah sat in the rocking chair, cradling the slumbering infant. Outside, the sun beckoned her. She would have loved to take a stroll in the nearby woods, but she knew what she was risking if a neighbor should happen to see her.

The tinkling of the telephone made her anxious. Only her brother called this number.

"Sarah, I need you to bring the girl here," he said brusquely.

"You want me to bring the baby? Aren't you worried somebody might see me with her?"

"Just bring her, I'll explain when you get here," Saúl said, and hung up.

Sarah did as she was told. In truth, she was intrigued. Her brother hadn't been himself since Rebeca disappeared . . . She preferred to keep quiet about her suspicions. She was ashamed to have given herself to Eulalio Osorio. She knew he could have betrayed them—the man was a coward. She could teach him a thing or two about living with shame . . .

And, if that had happened . . . well, ever since she had seen the photographs somebody had sent to the press, she was haunted by the idea that her brother might have killed the girl to stop her from talking.

Sarah lived alone in an isolated villa near Puente Viesgo. She had taken Gimena straight there after she was born. Sarah was planning to start a new life in London, but the girl was still too weak to travel. She liked to imagine that Saúl might join them and they would be a family. Perhaps, through her contacts at the British Museum, she could secure an attractive post for him now that Rebeca wasn't there to create tension.

The next evening Sarah pulled up outside the entrance to her brother's villa. It was after dark, and the neighbors couldn't possibly have seen that she had a baby in her arms.

"Give her to me. I want to look at her. I can't stop thinking about her."

"She's such a good baby. If she keeps gaining weight at this rate, I'll be able to take her away soon. I just need to ask the hospital to grant me a voluntary leave of absence. The paperwork in London is ready for my signature. The adoption will be a little trickier."

"That's exactly what I wanted to talk to you about. I've changed my mind," said Saúl, cradling the child. "Come upstairs. I have something to show you."

"Give her to me, you're going to wake her up," Sarah said to him, a little suspiciously.

"Don't worry, she likes me. Look at the way she's nestled in my arms. I'll carry her. You follow."

The two siblings climbed the stairs and stood outside Rebeca's old bedroom, which was next door to her father's.

Sarah recoiled as they entered the room.

Everything had changed. The bed Rebeca had given birth in a few weeks ago was gone, and so were her history books and posters of Celtic goddesses.

"What have you done, Saúl?"

"I've turned the room into a nursery for Gimena. I made her a crib and repainted the walls. I bought clothes, diapers, formula . . .

I've already brought up one daughter, I know what I'm doing. As of tonight, Gimena will be sleeping in her new home."

"No! You can't do this. You told me I was going to keep her. You know I can't have children of my own. I wanted this little girl. She is special, she is—" She broke off. Sometimes she was scared of Saúl, when he looked at her exactly the way their father had, and he was doing that now, gazing at her with those piercing eyes.

"I'm going to ask for one last favor from you. I plan to register her as my daughter, and I need you to falsify the adoption papers. It's a simple court order that grants me custody. You have access to other adoption files, so it shouldn't be hard to do. Just get it done, or we'll both be ruined."

"For pity's sake, Saúl, don't take her away from me. Let me be her mother!"

But Sarah's plea fell on deaf ears.

Saúl placed his daughter in her new crib and covered her with a baby blanket.

"We will be Gimena's father and mother, Sarah, family comes first. This time all will be well, I promise," he told his sister, embracing her.

He held her tight, and although Sarah wanted to resist, this was all she had ever wanted. She grew calm. She looked down at the girl, who smiled back at her. Gimena was the sweetest baby, nothing like troublesome Rebeca, who had cried incessantly.

For months, brother and sister had barely spoken to each other. Sarah couldn't forgive Saúl for making her give herself to another man, but sweet Gimena smoothed the friction between them, and they became the family of three that Sarah had always dreamed of.

Their own flesh and blood, the way Father had taught them.

And things *were* good, until Gimena, unable to accept that her father had lost interest in her as soon as she became an adult, took her own life.

69

GRANDFATHER'S HOUSE

After MatuSalem and Golden had vanished in Matu's old car, an ambulance arrived to take Rebeca to Txagorritxu hospital. They also kept my brother under observation there for a few hours. Blood tests revealed that she had given him enough sedatives to kill a horse. Germán couldn't remember anything that had happened since Saturday morning, when he went to my speech therapist's consulting room on Calle San Antonio for coffee.

Grandfather, Germán, and I spent that night at Villaverde sitting on the sofa in front of the hearth. Alba wasn't answering my calls. I'd asked Estí to bring her up to date. I didn't want any contact with the outside world anyway. I just wanted to be with my family. I wanted to help lift our spirits; I wanted Germán to recover.

"I need to be at the hospital. Someone has to watch over her," Germán murmured, trying to get warm beneath Grandfather's thick wool blanket.

"They won't let you see her tonight. Get some rest and see how you feel tomorrow," I said. I kept telling him the same thing, hoping he would eventually listen.

"I need to know if I was just a patsy, or if these past few months were real," he said. There was such sorrow in his face, it made me want to curl up and die.

"I very much doubt you were part of her plan," I told him. "She had already hacked into my e-mail and intercepted the message I sent to my neurologist—I reread her reply passing herself off as a speech therapist, and she signed it BK. Can you believe it? There it was, right in front of me, and I didn't see it. I guess it was all the media exposure after the double murders last summer that put her on my trail. She knew about the brain injury, and she built an identity around that."

"I want to believe you, Unai, but I need to be sure, don't you understand?"

"I've failed . . . to keep you out of my disasters, Germán. I can't even look you in the eye right now. I know you're going to ask me to resign again, to do something else with my life."

Germán rose to his feet, clearly wondering why we would prolong an already endless day.

"Let's talk about this tomorrow. I've had enough. But . . . thank you for saving my life," he said, leaving the kitchen on his way to bed.

"A thousand and one times, Germán. A thousand and one times."

I arrived at my office in the Lakua police headquarters early. The moment I opened the door, I was greeted by cheers and a chorus of applause. Everyone was there: all the officers from the other units, Superintendent Medina, Estí, Milán, Peña . . .

We drank a toast with cider, and there were pats on the back, smiles, and relief all around. We had caught the killer, the Hangman Game was over. The Water Rituals case had been solved.

The superintendent came up to me, beaming. He seemed genuinely pleased for once. He drew me away from the hubbub in the office to have a word privately.

"Well done, Inspector. I'm confident that you'll soon be fully reintegrated into this department. You've shown you're more than fit for work. The unit is extremely grateful to you."

"It's kind of you to say so, sir. What's the news from the hospital?"

"I still hope that Rebeca Tovar recovers, but her medical team isn't very optimistic."

"What do they say happened to her?"

"It seems she had a congenital heart defect that had probably never been detected. The charge from the Taser triggered a heart attack. She's still in a coma, and they don't know if she'll ever wake up."

I nodded silently. The idea gave me no pleasure.

The superintendent looked straight at me, trying to anticipate my response. "You know I have to ask you this. What on earth were you doing with an unauthorized weapon?"

"It was part of my investigation into the deep web. I was trying to track the purchase of the Taser Rebeca Tovar used on her victims," I lied.

"Then you realize that you'll need to write a report."

"I know. Will you report me to Internal Affairs?"

"First write the report and then we'll see. But today is a day for celebration. Where is your partner?"

"Sorry, who?"

"DSU Salvatierra. Inspector Gauna was the one who called me yesterday to inform me that the case had been resolved, which struck me as odd. So I called DSU Salvatierra, but her phone was switched off. Hasn't she come in yet?"

"Don't worry, I'm sure she'll arrive any minute now," I replied.

But when I left him, I went in search of Estíbaliz.

"Where is Alba?"

"I guess she decided to disconnect this weekend, because she isn't picking up her phone. Shouldn't she be here?" she said, plastic cup in her hand.

I pulled out my cell phone and called her mother. Nieves picked up straight away.

"Nieves, when did you last see or hear from Alba?"

"On Friday after lunch. She came to pick up the sugared almonds your grandfather left for her. She's craving sweets at the moment, I hope it won't play havoc with her blood sugar. Germán's girlfriend called, and they went off somewhere. Why do you ask? Isn't she at work?"

My head started to spin, and I leaned on my desk to steady myself.

Then it dawned on me: Germán had been a trap, a diversion, a diabolical ruse to buy time.

Rebeca's real victims were Alba and my daughter.

ALBA'S APARTMENT

MONDAY, JANUARY 23, 2017

Estíbaliz and I raced down the stairs and drove to Alba's apartment on Calle Prado. We rang the buzzer at the main entrance, but there was no reply. Finally, a neighbor on her way back from the shops let us in. We ran up to Alba's apartment, but there was still no reply when we rang the doorbell, and no sounds were coming from inside.

I pounded on the door with my fists in despair. Nothing. Alba's silence was eating away at me, and it was eating into Estí's scant reserves of patience as well.

We looked at each other, more like lost kids than police officers used to life-and-death situations.

"I'll talk to Milán and see if she can triangulate Alba's cell phone."

I collapsed onto the third-floor landing and sat leaning against the wall. I barely noticed when the lights went out, plunging us into darkness. The fear that had me by the balls was far blacker than that hallway.

I kept thinking about what I thought I'd heard Rebeca say.

"She said something about needing to make sure las Matres were satisfied with my daughter. I wasn't sure what she meant. It sounded cryptic to me."

"Don't worry about that now, Unai," replied my colleague, pressing the time switch to turn the lights back on. "As soon as we find her phone signal, we'll set up a search operation. Now come on, you're the profiler and you caught the killer, so give me a list of places where she might have taken Alba. If she didn't kill Alba before abducting your brother on Saturday, we could still find her alive."

"I meant to do that. I'll do it now."

"Nieves said Beatriz, or Rebeca, picked up her daughter at five o'clock on Friday afternoon, before it got dark. So if she'd arranged to meet your brother the next day at one o'clock in Vitoria, she had twenty hours in which to abduct Alba . . . A ten-hour round trip, max, from wherever she took her. That covers an impossibly vast area."

"Let's see what happens with her cell phone. In the meantime, we should probably call Paulaner and ask him to coordinate a search in Cantabria," I said. I was already writing down all the possible crime scenes on my notepad. "Lots of the places on my list are there."

"I'll get on to Paulaner. Are you done with that list?"

I tore out the page and gave it to her. I had begun with places in Cantabria I thought might be significant to Rebeca: the settlement at Cabezón de la Sal, the Conde de San Diego palace, Monte Dobra, Fontibre, Saúl's villa, the cliffs on the Costa Quebrada between the Arnía and Portío beaches. The list was endless. In Vitoria itself, we needed to search her office in the Pando-Argüelles building. Germán never discovered his girlfriend's home address. In Álava, the only places I could think of were the San Adrián Tunnel and the Barbacana pool.

I called Héctor del Castillo, filled him in, and asked if he could send me a list of all the Celtic-Iberian ruins in the province of Álava that were close to a river, pool, or well—though there weren't many—and anything with a strong Celtic-Iberian connection. He sent it very quickly. It looked like we needed to search the Lastra and Olárizu hill forts, the La Hoya ruins . . .

"Tell me I've got this all wrong, Estí. Tell me this isn't happening."

"Alba is alive, Unai. She's a survivor . . . she can't be dead. She wouldn't abandon us. She's the toughest of the three of us," she said, as though reciting a prayer.

As we made our way down the street, the cold wind drove stinging rain into our faces.

"Call Nieves in Laguardia and ask her to bring us the keys to Alba's apartment. We need to make sure she hasn't passed out again," I instructed Estí.

But there was no sign of Alba. Her apartment was empty.

We organized search parties in Álava and Cantabria.

By midafternoon, we'd received some good news.

Some hikers found her cell phone in a ditch just outside Laguardia.

Our colleagues there located CCTV footage of Rebeca's, or rather Beatriz Korres's, car. We knew they had headed north, but we lost them as soon as they turned onto the country roads.

I had a slight disagreement with the superintendent after the emergency meeting that was convened at the Lakua headquarters. Everybody was looking at the ominously dark skies with alarm. Andoni Cuesta's death was still on their minds. It would soon be dark, and the forecast was for heavy rain and plummeting temperatures. People were nervous.

"You're staying here," Medina ordered when he saw me getting ready to leave.

"No, I'm not," I said, simply.

"It's an order. If you disobey it, there will be consequences. We have no idea what state DSU Salvatierra will be in when we find her, assuming she's even alive. Don't put yourself through this."

"I'm fully aware of that, sir. As I told you once, this is my daughter."

And I went off to search for them.

It rained all Monday night.

No trace of Alba.

On Tuesday, a group of volunteers joined in the hunt. The search area was vast, and we really didn't have enough time or personnel to find a pregnant woman and her child.

Paulaner led the fruitless search in Cantabria. Estíbaliz headed the one in the north of Álava. I focused my energies on the south and set up my base at Villaverde. Grandfather, Germán, Nieves, Asier, Lutxo, Araceli, Nerea, Xabier . . . all of them left their offices and their homes and searched for her. Alba restored what Annabel had sought to destroy, a friendship that was stronger than any rivalry. Everyone wanted to stick together.

The only stain on that sea of solidarity was my brother.

Inexplicably, he made daily visits to Txagorritxu to sit with Rebeca. I found his Stockholm syndrome unbearable.

He went off again on Tuesday afternoon after saying good-bye to me in the kitchen. I kept my back turned and focused on making dinner for two.

"Unai, my lad, Germán has been through a lot. You can't not speak to each other. It's gone on long enough," Grandfather told me.

I didn't feel like responding to him, either.

After another exhausting and unsuccessful day's search, I went to sleep at home in Vitoria. I wanted to be alone.

The weather was rainy and cold, drizzle interspersed with occasional downpours. The streets were full of black umbrellas. The weather was mad at God knows who, and I was furious at the weather gods.

"Stop raining, will you? Damn it, just stop fucking raining. This isn't helping them," I repeated aloud. It became my mantra.

In the meantime, I climbed up onto the roof, fool that I am, the same roof that had welcomed Alba and me during las Fiestas de la Virgen Blanca, the same roof where we had listened to "Lau teilatu"—the tune that no longer rang on her cell phone.

Temperatures dropped below freezing that night. Supposedly nobody knows what it's like to sleep outside in Siberia-Gasteiz in January, but I do. It felt so good not to have anybody telling me what I should do, or giving me pitying looks . . .

"There's a remote chance," Estíbaliz had said to me, "that Rebeca might wake up from her coma. Then we may be able to find out where she took Alba. But the doctors think it's unlikely, her heart is too damaged."

I returned to Villaverde on Wednesday morning, only to find a car from our unit parked under the balcony outside Grandfather's house. I raced up the stairs, expectant. Some news at last.

But when I entered the kitchen, I found Estíbaliz staring out the window. She turned to face me.

Estí is crying because of something else, something unrelated. She started crying here because of something that just happened. That tear-stained face and those trembling lips aren't for Alba and Deba.

"What are you doing here?" I demanded. I was almost shouting.

She remained silent. Maybe she was plucking up her courage.

I wouldn't let it go: "Did you come here to give me the bad news? Do they think you're the right person to do that?"

"I'd rather you hear it from me."

"You're so brave, Estíbaliz. You could have asked Milán, Peña, the superintendent . . . but no, you're the one who is going to look me in the eye and tell me . . ."

"I'm sorry, Unai."

"Sorry for what?"

"They've called off all the searches. Rebeca abducted her five days ago. I doubt we'll ever find her body. We're hoping the weather will improve and some hiker will find her, wherever she is."

"Say it. Go ahead, say it out loud. No one is saying it, but everyone is thinking it."

"I think you need to accept that Alba's dead."

"Okay, there it is. Now it's out there."

I used the fire to keep me anchored. Time stopped. I stood still for a while. Alba was dead, and all I could do was stand motionless, like a statue in a graveyard.

I was completely drained.

Thankfully, someone was there to rescue me from that purgatory, to bring me back to Earth.

Grandfather made me sit on the sofa.

His hundred-year-old hands, with their rough skin and bulging veins, clasped mine. I think he was trying to tell me, *Don't worry, son. I'm here by your side.*

What's the first piece of advice a mentor gives? *Keep breathing.*

The flames' movement kept the pain at bay for the next few hours.

I was stunned and distraught. I was moving in a different dimension, where the floor beneath me was less hard, the air I breathed less cold. I was floating in oblivion.

I abandoned myself to nothingness.

Calls to my old cell phone were accumulating—apparently the entire planet wanted to offer me their condolences. I had no choice but to pick up for Superintendent Medina.

"I know you've been told that the search has been abandoned.

There is little chance that DSU Salvatierra is still alive, and with the weather these past few days . . . Well, I can't risk another casualty, not after what happened at San Adrián."

"I understand, sir," I said.

"My most sincere condolences for the loss of your partner and your child."

"Daughter. She was my daughter, and her name was Deba."

Deba, my little goddess, who never got to be born and who never got to protect her mother. I had given her the name a while back and never had a second thought about it. I knew immediately that it was hers.

Alba wasn't leaving this world alone. Saúl once said that the guardian god Tulonio waited at the port for spirits to come to him on the river of life. I hoped he would take both my girls.

Just wait for me. One day the three of us will be reunited, and we'll be the family we were destined to be.

Today, then, is the day of acceptance. I must behave like a grown-up and face reality.

I need to accept that they have called off the search for her body, that Rebeca probably changed her modus operandi, that Saúl and Rebeca are responsible for the loss of all these lives: Annabel Lee, Jota, their unborn child, Gimena, Marian Martínez, Andoni Cuesta, Asunción Pereda, Saúl himself, and, very soon, Rebeca . . . and Alba and Deba.

I need to start accepting that the woman I love is dead and that it won't be easy to find her remains.

And I don't know why—is it the emotional maturity that comes with distance?—but today, suddenly, I have a clear understanding of what happened at that settlement in Cantabria.

Four of us were the hunted and three were the hunters: Annabel Lee, Rebeca, and Saúl were stalking Jota, Lutxo, Asier, and me. They monitored us, cataloged us, and then used us to achieve whatever had brought them to that camp.

Annabel Lee took away our innocence, not just our sexual innocence, but the naive belief that our *cuadrilla* and our friendships were indestructible. She showed us how easily and how quickly an outsider could destroy it all.

Maybe that was the most humiliating part of our defeat.

As for Rebeca, we were her last line of defense against her father. She was looking for a faceless hero who would protect her and do the right thing: denounce the adult.

None of us was that hero.

Saúl moved us like pawns in a game. He studied our emotional needs and filled them with a tailor-made father-son relationship.

I don't forgive Rebeca; she had a choice and she didn't take it. Golden offered her a new life far from the abuses of a dangerous father. Instead Rebeca chose to perpetuate the cycle. My strength is that I won't be like her. Alba wouldn't have wanted that.

I know that Nieves and I must begin organizing a memorial service for Alba Díaz de Salvatierra and Deba López de Ayala. They aren't coming back, but we have to go on living.

We must accept their loss, cross the line from hope to acceptance.

As soon as this is over, I want to climb up San Tirso, where I once saved a life.

That is what Saúl and Annabel bequeathed to me: my essence, who I am. I won't look the other way. I'll jump off the cliff. I refuse to be brokenhearted again, and since there's no way of knowing how long I'll live, I've decided to skip the grieving part.

Alba never complained. That was her legacy.

I won't, either.

EPILOGUE

DEBA
WEDNESDAY, JANUARY 25, 2017

German started to call around noon, and he kept calling. I didn't pick up. I didn't have the strength. He insisted on calling until I switched off my phone.

Even then I knew he hadn't stopped, because I could hear the antiquated tinkle of the old telephone in the kitchen. I assumed Grandfather would pick up.

A couple of minutes later, he came to give me the news: "Your brother called. Rebeca is dead."

I started to sob uncontrollably. I couldn't take anymore.

"Get ahold of yourself! Listen to me, your brother has something to tell you."

"I don't want to know!" I yelled.

"Don't you understand? He's been going to the hospital every day to ask her about Alba. He was determined she would tell him before she died. Rebeca regained consciousness for a moment and confessed everything: Alba is at the ruins of the Toloño monastery."

Santa María de Toloño sits high up in the Sierra de Toloño. Maybe Alba passed the story I told her about the Celtic-Iberian origin of the name on to Rebeca, or it could've been Germán, trying to impress her.

I switched on my cell phone and spoke to Estíbaliz. Within minutes, we'd organized a helicopter for a rescue operation.

I flew down the stairs, forgetting to even put my jacket on.

I was about to drive off when Grandfather opened the car door and climbed in beside me.

"Where do you think you're going?"

"With you, son. We used to go past those ruins on the way from Peñacerrada to Labastida to sell food on the black market, so I know the terrain. If I slow you down, just go on ahead."

I was on the verge of saying no, but then I saw that he had brought a blanket, a flask of water, and some crackers, and I realized he knew exactly what he was doing. And that if I got there before the rescue team, I would need somebody with his common sense to restrain me.

In less than fifteen minutes, we arrived at Peñacerrada. Grandfather guided me along ever-narrowing forestry tracks as we sped through the beechwoods. I got us as close as possible to the top of the mountain.

When it became clear we would have to continue on foot, I pulled over, stopped the car, and leaped out. Grandfather followed me at a brisk pace. Soon after, we heard the whirr of helicopter blades above our heads. It would be dark in an hour. If we didn't find her now, they would halt the mission and we would return home empty-handed.

I quickened my pace for the last hundred yards, leaving Grandfather behind. He had already shown me a shortcut to the ruins.

I arrived just as the helicopter was landing in a small clearing.

Estíbaliz jumped out, and for a moment I thought the wind might blow her away, but she remained on her feet.

We searched inside the three remaining walls of what had once been a Gothic monastery. All that was left were stones, weeds, tree shoots, and then . . .

I saw something move, something white.

I don't believe it, that's her coat.

"Over here!" I cried.

And I found Alba, or the muddy, gaunt person who once was Alba, wrapped in her long white coat, hands and feet bound with plastic ties. She was curled in a ball, trying to preserve her body heat, I imagine, to protect our daughter. Her wrists were rubbed raw and red. And next to her head was a tiny improvised survival kit. Rainwater collected in the hollow of an old crushed Coke can.

"She's in a bad way. We'll stabilize her, then take her to the hospital!" somebody yelled.

"Will she make it?" I remember asking.

"It's hard to say. Her vitals are very low. She's in critical condition."

"She's twenty-five weeks pregnant and has preeclampsia," the mechanical part of me—the part of me that wasn't petrified with fear—told them.

"We'll do our best, but I can't promise anything."

There was a lot of talk about a human being's capacity for survival when, after hovering between life and death for three weeks, Alba was finally out of danger. Another near miracle was that Deba had also survived, and her little hummingbird heart was beating fast and strong each time they showed her to us on the ultrasound.

Grandfather's sugared almonds, which Nieves had given her on the Friday she was abducted, had kept Alba's blood sugar levels up.

Even with her hands and feet bound, Alba had managed to survive by rationing her reserves and drinking rainwater. She'd dragged herself over to the most sheltered part of the ruins and put herself in the hands of the gods of that sacred place. I like to believe that Toloño, or the god Tulonio, watched over her and Deba. Alba says she was in an altered state of consciousness.

I think that, deprived of the nutrients it needed, her brain slowed her metabolism, allowing her to survive.

In his usual incisive way, Grandfather explained his theory to me: Alba had hibernated. She went into a state of torpor, like a polar bear protecting its cub.

As a profiler, I gave a lot of thought to Rebeca's change of modus operandi. My conclusion was that she had wanted to close the circle of Gimena's death by killing my daughter in the same way that her daughter had departed this world: leaving Alba and Deba to die of exposure on top of a sacred mountain named after a Celtic deity.

But Rebeca didn't know Alba and Deba the way I did, so how could she have known how strong they were?

I didn't go back to work until after Deba was born, on April 28, San Prudencio's day. And I didn't leave Alba's side for a single moment while she was in the hospital. Our brush with death finally set us straight. We resolved to try again. I have learned to appreciate the nuances of our relationship, and I've grown accustomed to them.

I was there when she gave birth. I've never felt more terrified, but when they handed me tiny Deba, small and cocooned in blankets, and she gripped the finger I offered her ever so tightly, all my doubts vanished. I knew she had her mother's tenacity, and that she was choosing me, and I thought I understood what she wanted to convey: *You are my father. I know about my past. I know about everything that has brought me here. But I've decided that you are going to be my father. Period.* And that *period* defined her personality. My daughter was born in the midst of rainstorms, and yet none of us seemed to

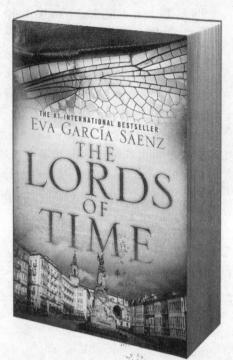

care. I cradled her and danced in circles, her head nestling in the crook of my shoulder. Deba was searching for her place, but she knew she was home.

She was blond-haired and blue-eyed, like her grandmother Nieves, but nobody could describe her as a beautiful baby. She looked too much like Grandfather.

And I know that people gossip behind my back and say she's the spitting image of Tasio and Ignacio. I honestly don't care.

Even if that was true, no matter what genes she may or may not have, I am determined to break the cycle of violence that stretches back to Paleolithic times.

Deba is going to have an indestructible mother, a father who would walk through the fires of hell for her, an uncle and an aunt, Germán and Estíbaliz, a grandmother . . .

. . . and a great-grandfather who will outlive us all.